Salty

Iris Kain

The following book is a work of fiction. All characters, incidents, and dialogue spring solely from the author's imagination and should not be mistaken for real. Any resemblance to actual events or persons, living or deceased, is purely coincidental.

A quote from Fyodor Dostoevsky's *The Brothers Karamazov* appears in this work. The original text is in the public domain.

ISBN: 978-1-957244-30-3

Also by Iris Kain:

Shadow Hunter

Eternal Spring

Offshoot

The Murphy Blackwell Chronicles
Sour (Book 1)
Sweet (Book 2)

The Blood Tribe Trilogy:
Blood Tribe (Book 1)
Blood Trials (Book 2)
Blood Treason (Book 3)

To the brave. The loud. The voices that won't be rewritten. For the souls who hold the line when the world storms around them.

Stay salty.

Salty

Chapter 1

Thursday, the third of July, was going to be a dead day in the shop, especially once the lunch rush ended. No amount of sales or red banners in the window of Witch's Brew would draw small-town Alabama folks into a shop selling coffee and metaphysical supplies when fireworks were sold at half a dozen local roadside stands. And there was plenty of nearby countryside to blow them up in.

I figured it was as good a day as any to practice my spell-work.

The heat of the afternoon in Gryphon, Alabama, during the summer was no joke. Forecasters that morning (meteorological—not the sort of predictive folks like my foster father, who is an orange witch able to see the future) had estimated the day's high to hit nearly a hundred degrees with a heat index of a hundred and ten. I love small-town Alabama, but there are some things I could do without. Sweltering heat is one. Being one of the few for-real-no-kidding witches within a hundred miles and having to hide that fact to keep safe was another thing I wasn't crazy about.

At least I didn't have to deal with snow often.

The only sounds I'd heard for the last hour were the constant drone of the ancient air conditioner rattling in its frame and the steady rhythm of my cat Rex's purring from his perch on the counter. The aroma of freshly ground coffee beans still lingered in the air from the morning rush, but the shop had fallen eerily quiet. The mismatched chairs and small tables, tucked into the cozy space of Black-well Manor's parlor-turned-café, sat empty. I hadn't had to brew a single cup of coffee for going on ninety minutes now, and the silence was starting to bug me.

"What do you think, Rex? Should I lock the door? Try a new spell?" I quickly glanced at the front of the shop and its empty tables. Then, I poked my head around the corner and looked into the other rooms—what were once the sitting room and parlor—and verified no one was there.

At the counter, Rex stood and stretched, arching his silky black back, which shone in the summer sun coming in the front window. I stroked his back absently. "Not much point putting it off, is there?" I asked my feisty feline. "It's just a little glamor spell, anyway. Hanna says it should be a piece of cake."

Rex regarded me with unblinking, wide, green eyes, the pupils narrowed to slits under the shop's bright display lights. I didn't usually let him sit on the counter, but my best friend Hanna, who usually kept the shop's baked goods in stock, hadn't been by in a couple of days, so the counter was clear of food. I'm sure the Alabama Department of Health would say something about it if they came in, but they tended to steer clear of my shop. Probably due to all the protection spells. I kept my shop hygienic almost all the time. If I let my cat hang out on the counter on a slow day, it wouldn't hurt anything.

"Come on," I said to Rex with a tilt of my head. "Let's see what this spell Hanna gave me is about."

I knew what she'd designed it for. My bestie's an unusual

witch—double-gifted with both brown and red witch powers. Brown witches work through food and hearth magic—what they cook carries intention, sometimes even healing. That's why her baked goods sell out faster than rumors in a small town. Red witches deal in love and glamor, both the tender and the dangerous kind. She's got both. I already had the love part covered—my fiancé, Conall, had proposed just before Valentine's Day. (He's an orange witch—one of the prognosticators. They're always watching for patterns, reading signs, dreaming things before they happen. Comes in handy. Makes arguments a little lopsided.)

Anyway, Hanna's spell was a favor to me. I have a big freckle on my temple—blame my Scottish ancestors for the light copper tint to my brown hair and the damned freckles on my nose and cheeks. Anyway, I'd asked Hanna to help me with a spell to get rid of the large freckle for me in time for the wedding. Sure, I could have it removed by a doctor, but why spend money when my best friend had a spell that served the same purpose and didn't require a trip to the doctor's office?

Eyeing the shop door once more to ensure no one was coming, I stepped just beyond the swinging saloon doors into my tiny stock area that spanned the narrow stretch between my shop and the kitchen. Rex hopped off the counter to the floor and wound between my legs as I retrieved the small brown glass jar with Hanna's magical freckle removing... stuff and a small mirror pulled from the depths of my purse.

Returning to the checkout counter, I retrieved the inventory record notebook from its place next to the register. I flipped to the back, where Hanna had jotted down the words to help increase the efficacy of the concoction in the brown jar. I don't speak Hebrew, Hanna's spelling language, so she wrote everything down in a transliterated version:

Hanekudah mi'panai timash,
Lo yishar mimena reshima ba'olam.
Tikach oti ha'ruach ha'ktana,
V'tashlik otah b'chalon shama.

Meandering back to the shelf in the stockroom with the notebook in hand, I mouthed the words a few times to rehearse the stanza, trying to remember the exact meaning so I could add the proper emphasis at the right points. Spells are all about intention, so it was important that I at least had an idea of what the words meant. Hanna suggested I cast the spell in my own spelling language (English—I'm boring), but I insisted that my spirit would have greater faith in the power of the words I used to cast if they felt as if they came straight from the red witch herself. I remember the spell said something about the spot upon my face vanishing from the world, being cast through the window or something. I didn't care where the bugger went, as long as it wasn't on my face for the wedding pictures.

"OK, buddy," I said to Rex. "Let's hope this glamor—glams. Or whatever."

Uncorking the brown jar, I made an amateur's mistake, leaned forward to smell the concoction, and grimaced. It smelled like a mix of lemon juice, licorice, and old pennies.

"Yuck," I said. Rex, back at his counter perch, merely blinked sedately. Apparently, his sense of smell wasn't as offended as mine.

I positioned my tiny folding mirror so I had a decent angle on my face and heaved a sigh.

"Welp, here goes, Rexicus." One of my many nicknames for him. Other names include Rexall, BooBoy, and Tyrannosaurus Rex. His whiskers twitched, but other than that, he showed no sign of acknowledgment.

I stuck a finger in the goo, set the bottle back on the shelf

with my un-gooey hand, and applied the concoction on my
temple over the freckle as I chanted.

"Hanekudah mi'panai timash,
Lo yishar mimena reshima ba'olam.
Tikach oti ha'ruach ha'ktana,
V'tashlik otah b'chalon shama."

Or at least, that's what I was trying to say. My Hebrew is
not great, to put it mildly. Definitely not as good as Hanna,
who (on top of being a witch) had celebrated her bat mitzvah
at thirteen. Her family wanted to make sure she had the best
of both of her parents' religions, and while she'd opted to be
a part of the coven, she still observed High Holy Days at the
temple with her stepmother. Have I mentioned yet that
Hanna's dad and stepmom are awesome?

I felt a tingling at my temple, which was now dripping
with what I was guessing was mostly lemon juice. I went behind the counter to grab a paper towel, chanting as I went and
praying I was pronouncing everything correctly, even though
I knew what mattered was the energy I put into the spell. I
imagined this stupid freckle gone, thrown out the window, or
whatever. Didn't some of the words mean something about
being on the wind? Sure. That sounded good. As long as it
was gone, it could blow to the Bermuda Triangle for all I
cared. I'd hated that thing since it cropped up on my face the
summer between fifth and sixth grade. It wasn't just a freckle;
it was a *freckle*, a discoloration the size of the end of the wee
tip of my pinkie finger, and it drew my attention every time I
looked at my face in the mirror. Vanity, thy name is Murphy
Blackwell.

That's my name, by the way. Murphy Blackwell.

I caught the worst of the juicy goo before it dripped down
my elbow onto the floor and threw the paper towel into the
trash bin under the counter. Oddly tired, I plopped down on

the tall chair behind the counter.

Wait. Better go get the stuff and the mirror in case it takes a second dose.

Chances were slim it'd need a second try. This might be a good time to mention that my witch powers are unusual. I'm what my coven, the Lughaidh, calls a Summate—a rare type of witch that only crops up on earth about every three hundred years.

While most witches are limited to one variety of power, expressed in our world as a color, I don't have a single color's ability—I have all of them. The full spectrum. Not only can I do pretty much any spell, hex, or display of power, but sometimes the spells wind up a bit... supercharged. Excessively. Which has been known to be kind of fun on occasion. Not so much when I didn't plan it. Clearly. I'm a work in progress.

Back in my tiny stockroom, I scooped up the mirror, made my way back to the tall chair behind the register, and— *Wait a minute.*

Why was the mirror floating? Where were my arms?

Rex, amused by the mirror suspended before him, sat up on his haunches and swatted at it like a bug.

"Rex, don't," I said, my voice tense. I was holding the mirror. I could feel the solid weight of it between my fingers. So, why wasn't it in my hand?

Where *was* my hand?

I looked down. For that matter, where was the rest of me?

I set the mirror on the counter and patted myself down. I was there, physically. My clothes were there; my fingers touched the texture of the cotton shirt and denim jeans. I wiggled my toes and felt the Converse shoes on my feet. But everything about me had grown transparent. Apparently, I'd vanished a bit more than the freckle.

Remember what I said about sometimes spelling a little

too powerfully? Yeah. This was the sort of thing that happened from time to time.

The bell over the door tinkled, and I gasped, then covered my mouth. *Oh, shit! How'm I going to explain this?* I stood, my mind racing to come up with ideas for how to deal with a customer who couldn't see me. *Dammit, I should have locked the door. I know better. New spells are always risky!*

Witches with real power haven't exactly come out of the broom closet, so to speak. Sure, there are whispers of us. And yes, last year my coven had to battle a dark coven who wanted to expose witch kind and, you know, take over the world. But most of us were just fine hiding our power and not getting hanged or burned at the stake. Or being confused with Wicca, which was more of a nature religion.

Thankfully, it was Hanna, entering the shop with a wide silver tray laden with muffins. The tips of her red, white, and blue manicure were chrome, and part of me wondered if she'd done so to match the tray. Coordinating outfits are her thing.

"Murph? You here?" Her long hair swayed behind her in warm hues of honey and polished bronze as she scanned the store for me.

"Closer than you think," I said.

Hanna jumped, squealed, and nearly dropped the muffins on the floor.

"Holy bananas, Murphy! Where are you? Is that your phone?" Her eyes traveled to the far corners of the room in search of the source of my voice.

I snorted at my bestie's reverent reference to tropical fruit and said, "No, it's me. You're seeing as much of me as I can. I can't see me, either."

She gave the countertop a dubious look, brushed Rex off with her free hand, and set the tray down. "What happened? Are you practicing some witchy spy skills?"

"Not exactly." I plopped back down into the tall chair and watched with amusement as Hanna's wide, brown eyes grew even wider at the sight of the indent in the fabric. "I tried that glamor spell you gave me to get rid of the freckle. Guess I gave it a bit too much oomph."

"Oh my goodness, Murph. I guess you really wanted that bugger gone, huh?"

"Yeah," I said. "Now, I guess I'm going to have to figure out how to conjure myself back."

Hanna brushed through the swinging doors into the kitchen and returned with a large glass cake stand, the heavy glass making the toned muscles in her slim arms bulge. She began setting the muffins in place with practiced ease. I guess I should have been flattered by her faith in my ability to solve the problem on my own, but I was still a little too weirded out by my invisibility to contemplate a way to undo the spell.

From the wide front window, I saw another familiar face heading into the shop. Betony Yarborough, one of my regulars who was about to enter her senior year of high school, crossed the wide wooden veranda. She pulled open the shop door with the hand not holding her cell phone and brushed a lock of platinum-blond hair behind her ear. It was the closest thing to a natural color I'd ever seen her in.

Leave it to the chaos witch to arrive now. She'll love this.

Chaos witch didn't mean Betony was out here with a smoke bomb in one hand and a middle finger in the other. It meant she was born wired to the world's entropy, like she had a backstage pass to the mess everyone else pretends doesn't exist. Where most witches avoided volatile energy like it was a drunk uncle at a family reunion, Betony walked straight into it, smiled, and asked if it needed a snack. She didn't just *manage* chaos—she metabolized it. Could pull it off and wring it into something useful. Most witches would've gone mad trying to balance that kind of magic (the way I did for years when I reflected it). Betony? She made it look like a spiritual spa day.

"Hey, Hanna," she said, her curvy face and broad smile as friendly as ever. "Where's Mama Murph?"

Mama Murph was a nickname bestowed upon me by the handful of high school kids who knew I was a real practitioner of the Craft—and all that entailed. Although Betony was eighteen to my twenty-seven, she'd given the moniker to me a couple of years ago, and the name stuck. Even more, now that I'd become the guardian of one of their peers, who had defected from the dark coven I mentioned.

"Right here," I said. Betony jumped about a mile.

"Holy guacamole!" she squealed.

"What is it with you two deifying fruit?" I laughed. "First bananas, now avocados."

"What happened?" Betony asked, eyeing the muffins hungrily. Hanna handed her one, and Betony carefully peeled the paper lining from the bottom. I didn't mind. With the shop closed tomorrow, it was likely that Hanna had brought the muffins over for us to eat anyway.

"Overzealous glamor spell," Hanna explained.

"That's a RIP, man," Betony replied, pulling a cranberry from the soft bread of the muffin and popping it into her mouth. "What are you going to do?"

"Reckon I'm going to have to make myself visible again unless I plan on living life like an H.G. Wells character."

Hanna turned to Betony. "Invisible Man reference," she explained.

"Ah."

"I could use both of your help, if you don't mind," I said. "Betony, do you think you could siphon some of the chaos from this situation? And Hanna, if you could come up with a... I don't know... reverse invisible spell?"

Hannah placed the glass cake stand cover on top of the muffins and licked the sticky remains off a finger. "Um... yeah. I can do that. Do you have—?"

I handed the notebook over the counter to her, and two sets of eyes bugged out. In their defense, it *did* look like it was flying at them rather aggressively.

"*So* weird," Betony said.

"Yeah," Hanna agreed, reaching for the book tentatively.

"It's just me, Hanna," I said, waggling the book at her. "You've known me since we were in diapers."

"I know, I know," she said, taking hold of it with her fingertips. "It's just... *weird.*"

I scoffed. "So you've both said. But I doubt it's contagious."

Betony walked to my side of the counter, and I had to back up a step to keep her from colliding with me.

"What were you thinking I could do to help?" she asked. "Do you want me to pull off some of your anxiety?"

"Yes, please," I sighed. "Anything that's keeping me off-balance right now, I can do without. I need to be steadier if I want to get myself back in full color again."

"You got it." She extended her arms until her forearms were level with the floor.

"Reaching now," I said, and gripped her arms at the elbows from underneath. She wrapped her hands around my arms as well. I loved the way it felt whenever I could touch Betony. She wasn't much for physical contact, having come from an abusive home, but when she did, it was literally magical. Like touching a gentle, steady hum of power.

"Is it weird that this is kinda cool?" she asked as she squeezed my invisible limbs. "You being invisible, I mean."

"No, but... let's not waste time. I know the shop's not

busy, but…"

"You got it."

Betony had chosen French as her spelling language. She lived with my former foster parents, and Luke—my foster father, who also spoke French—was teaching her.

Tipping her head forward and casting her eyes to the floor as she focused, Betony pulled in a deep breath. A hint of my body's tense energy was gently extracted from my essence and flowed into her lungs as she inhaled. It felt as though an invisible thread was pulled from deep inside me, unraveling the tight knots that had settled in my chest and shoulders. A prickling warmth radiated from the center of my chest outward, almost like the pins and needles of a limb waking up after being asleep—but softer, more soothing.

I wondered, not for the first time, at the incredible power that this beautiful young woman embodied. The words flowed from her like a song.

"*Comme l'arbre s'enracine dans la terre,*
Trouve ta force, calme et lumière.
J'attire le trouble, je le fais partir,
Et laisse en toi la sérénité surgir."

As she repeated the incantation, the sense of relaxation deepened. My heartbeat slowed to a steady rhythm. A faint, sweet scent of earth and flowers tickled my nose as a cool, airy lightness spread through my limbs. She repeated it only once; that was all it took. We let go, and I sighed in relief. By the time she was done, the tension was utterly gone.

"That was beautiful, Bet," Hanna said. "What does it mean?"

The gray ring around the center of Betony's hazel pupils had grown noticeably, making her eyes like a stormy forest.

"It's one Luke and LaDonna came up with together. The words mean, 'As the tree roots itself in the earth, find your strength, calm, and light. I draw in the trouble, I make it leave, and let serenity rise within you.'"

"That's very Luke and LaDonna," I agreed. LaDonna, my foster mother and our coven's high priestess, was a green witch with power over flora and fauna—anything living that grows or breathes. Thanks to her, my shop had fresh herbs year-round—her garden tended to green-thumb its nose at the calendar. LaDonna was also why I hadn't gone completely feral when I unknowingly reflected Betony's chaotic energy. For years. Hell, I'd thought *I* was the gray until fairly recently.

That's a whole other story. Moving on.

Hanna pulled herself away from where she'd been studying her newly written spell to bring me back to the land of the seeable.

"OK," she said, the pen still at her lips. "I think I've got something here. Do you want me to teach it to you or—?"

"No, just let it rip, and I'll give it a little extra oomph so I can get this over with."

Hanna raised her eyebrows. "Not too much oomph. I'm not trying to pop like a Fourth of July spectacular."

"I'm rolling my eyes at you," I said drolly. Betony giggled.

"Alright, come on," Hanna said. She held out her hands. Betony took one side, and I stepped between them, completing the circle.

It was then that I noticed that Hanna's breath was a little shaky. Did she feel bad that her spell had been the source of the words I used to make myself disappear? I hoped not. It wasn't her fault I was still learning how to wrangle my power.

Her words poured forth, her Hebrew flowing like an expressive, hypnotic chant.

"*Ani koreh l'shuvcha el ha'or, Uv'kach asheev lecha*

tzuratcha v'tifartecha. Ani koreh l'shuvcha el ha'or, Uv'kach asheev lecha tzuratcha v'tifartecha."

Imagining a wire-thin strand of power flowing from my hand into Hanna, I pushed a bit of extra strength into her words. Within seconds, not only my temple but my whole body tingled and grew warm. I closed my eyes and pulled in a monstrous breath, imagining as I did that the air filled every cell in my form and that I was pulling the color back into my body and clothing. All of it, that is, except for the part where that stupid freckle had been.

"Holy shit!" Betony exclaimed. Her grip on my hand tightened excitedly. "It worked!"

"Thank the stars above," Hanna said. Her shoulders slumped in clear relief. I took her by the arm and pivoted her to face me. She towered over my five-foot-six frame by a good couple of inches, her height enhanced even more by her high-heeled sandals.

"Please tell me you're not blaming yourself for the fact that I still need training wheels to spell sometimes," I said. Hanna bit her lip, and I noticed her eyes were glassy. Her response was cut off by Betony's panicked exclamation.

"Oh my god. Oh my god!" Betony's stubby fingers clutched her phone in a white-knuckled grip.

"What is it?" I asked. Knowing Betony, it could be anything, but the last time I'd seen her this freaked out was when she'd received a notification that her mother had escaped from prison.

She held up a finger and read the notice that had popped up on her phone. "Governor Terry Waite, long-time Alabama governor who was once considered a potential candidate for the U.S. Senate, was shot and killed today on the steps of the Leland County Courthouse. *A group calling themselves the Stygian* has taken the credit for the assassination, but no one has been taken into custody at this time."

Hanna's slender hand covered her mouth. My thoughts stuttered as the meaning of the words sank in.

Governor Waite… Dead… Shot…The Stygian.

The Stygian. The dark coven that had tried to pull a horrible, dark power into the world and embody it in Rene, the young man who was now under my care. Who had planned to cause global chaos and allow corruption and malevolence to be the universal norm. Who had set fire to my house. Whose leader, Ericka Moore, had attempted to worm her way into our coven to get close to Betony, the chaos witch—and to kill me.

Lovely.

"Can you find anything else about it?" Hanna asked.

I leaned in to read over Betony's shoulder as she scrolled. "Another site might have more information," I added.

"I'm looking, I'm looking," Betony said, her fingers caressing her phone screen dexterously. She found a breaking news story on a major cable network where a reporter with severely styled hair and a very professional demeanor delivered the story in the detached tone so many talking heads use.

"Good evening. Tragedy struck this afternoon on the steps of the Leland County Courthouse, where Alabama Governor Terry Waite was assassinated in broad daylight. Witnesses describe a chilling scene as shots rang out during what was supposed to be a routine press conference. The killers eluded police, but an active investigation is underway.

"Governor Waite, widely regarded as a rising star in conservative politics, was known for his outspoken Christian views and was considered by many to be a strong contender for a future presidential run. His blunt criticisms of atheists and individuals outside of the Christian faith sparked both admiration and controversy, elevating his profile on the national stage.

"Tonight, a group calling itself 'The Stygian'—a self-described coven of witches—has claimed responsibility for the killing. In a chilling statement, the group cited the governor's pro-Christian rhetoric as the reason for their actions, condemning what they called his 'campaign of intolerance.'

"As law enforcement works to secure the area and investigate this shocking act, tensions are already rising, with protests and vigils quickly forming in cities across the state. The nation mourns the loss of a polarizing figure whose legacy is sure to be as complex as the circumstances surrounding his death."

Betony hit mute, and the three of us looked at each other with wide, disbelieving eyes.

I cleared my throat. "Well, that's bad, but nobody's going to think anything about a bunch of kooks who call themselves witches. A lot of people call themselves witches who don't... you know... have the sort of power we do."

"Here's another one," Betony said, and started another video.

"...and in a chilling development, the group identifying themselves as 'The Stygian' has issued a statement, declaring Governor Waite's assassination to be only the beginning of what will be a series of global strikes conducted by 'true witches.' The statement, released through encrypted channels and verified by authorities, promises what they describe as 'a reckoning' and warns of future attacks.

"In their words, quote, 'The world will no longer dismiss or silence the power we hold. This is the dawn of a new era where true witches will no longer hide in the shadows.'

"The message, while vague, has sent shockwaves through both political and religious communities, already reeling from today's tragedy. Security measures are being ramped up across the country as authorities race to determine the group's next move and the scope of the threat.

"Governor Waite's assassination has ignited fierce debate, with supporters calling for swift justice and others questioning whether his divisive rhetoric played a role in escalating tensions. One thing is clear: the events unfolding today are unlike anything we've seen before, and the implications for the nation—and the world—are profound.

"We will continue to bring you updates as this story develops."

The silence in the store when Betony muted the phone was so complete I could hear myself breathing.

"They're back," Betony said, her eyes glassy with tears. She and Rene shared a special bond that had continued even though they had decided shortly after they started dating that they were not meant to be a couple.

"They're back," I agreed. "And this time, they plan to kill people."

"And expose witches to the world," Hanna added. "All of us."

Chapter 2

I fished my charger out of the bottom of my purse—think bottomless pit meets black hole—and plugged my phone into the outlet behind the counter. From that moment on, whenever we didn't have a customer to ring up, I was uncharacteristically huddled around that tiny screen with Betony and Hanna, our eyes glued on the news. The Stygian had finally crawled out of the shadows, and their grand debut was to assassinate a big-name politician.

The stories grew redundant as the day passed with no recent developments. We couldn't shake the feeling that if we blinked, we'd miss the next horrifying move in the Stygian's playbook. But we were wrong. Their next ploy remained a mystery.

A few months back, my coven—the Lughaidh—had put the hurt on their dark coven. We broke up their ritual in the woods and saved Rene, their golden boy (the high priestess's own son, no less), from something called the "Sovereign Darkness," and sent them packing. No doubt Rene's body would've folded under the weight of all that supernatural power. If Erika—the high priestess—didn't see a problem sacrificing her son, well, that says a lot about her parenting skills, doesn't it?

After that, we didn't hear a peep from them. But now, the Stygian had strutted back into the spotlight with a high-profile assassination that put witches everywhere on edge. If that was their opening act, I didn't even want to imagine what they had planned for an encore—and whether we'd be ready to face it.

Not all witches are evil—no more than any other group of humans. Most of us lead everyday lives. Run coffee shops. Bake muffins. My foster mother runs a greenhouse, and my foster father is a jeweler with unparalleled skills in metalsmithing. I mean, yeah, the bulk of my shop was devoted to metaphysical supplies like herbs, wands, tarot decks, and crystals, but the Craft is a practice—a way to harness energy. It doesn't make us evil.

Conall didn't bother to shower after he finished a briefer-than-usual shift working for his dad's construction company. He headed straight to Witch's Brew after work, his tanned face a combination of concern and mild panic as he pulled me in for a fierce hug. He smelled like sweat and sawdust—a combination I'd come to love.

"I take it you heard?" I said, my voice muffled against his chest.

"My dad told me," he said. He gave me an extra squeeze and let me go so he could study my expression. "Are you doing alright?"

"So far," I said. "I think most folks are of the opinion the Stygian is an outlier. Like a crazy terrorist group or a cult or something. The pagan equivalent of the Eternal Spring or those Children of God folks."

"I hope so," he said. His troubled brown eyes noticed Hanna and Betony's presence, and he gave them a somber nod.

A buzz emitted from Conall's back pocket. He withdrew his phone and answered it. I couldn't hear the words, but his demeanor went from uneasy to troubled as the conversation went on. His part of the conversation was mostly "Uh-huh" and "I understand," and I grew increasingly frustrated the longer it dragged on.

By the time he hung up, I was incapable of waiting any longer. "What was that?" I asked.

He frowned and repocketed the phone. "That was Destiny Williams," he said. "She's canceling her reading for tonight."

Conall offered tarot readings to folks as a side hustle in what was once a generous first-floor closet of my house/shop. LaDonna always called the space a butler's pantry. Whatever the case, there was just enough room for a small table and a couple of chairs behind the colorful curtain. Conall never seemed to lack clients. Mostly women. I suspect his good looks drew them in as much as his orange witch gift for prognostication.

"Destiny canceled?" My eyebrows shot up. "Destiny never cancels. Is she sick?"

He turned away slightly, avoiding eye contact with me. "She said it felt risky coming here after what happened today."

I fidgeted with the bottom hem of my T-shirt. "Does she really think something that happened all the way down in Montgomery will affect us here?" Though the question was about Destiny's concern over Governor Waite, everyone knew what I was really asking: did we witches in Gryphon need to worry about the Stygian striking here already?

Conall licked his lips slowly before responding. "Destiny was my second cancellation of the week."

"That's not good," Betony said. Her fingertips drummed softly on the table before her.

"No, it's not." Hanna agreed.

This shop was my livelihood, but it was also a source of supplemental income for Hanna and Conall. The cost of living was relatively low in rural Alabama, but the cost of living everywhere for Millennials was difficult. Conall had a small apartment, and I had inherited my mother's house, but Hanna lived with her father and was scraping every penny together to buy a small place. If sales took a downturn here, it would hit all of us in the pocketbook hard.

"We need to get the Lughaidh together soon," I said. "Rita, too. Maybe her WorldWide Witch coven has information that might help point us in the right direction."

"I'll text LaDonna," Betony offered. "Luke, too."

"I'll get a hold of Rita," Hanna offered, her fingers flying across her phone's surface.

"Great, what'll I do?" I asked no one in particular.

Conall grabbed a hand and pulled me in close. "You'll come here and relax," he said, his breath hot on the top of my head. "It'll be OK. We beat them once."

"Yeah, and it was *hard*," I reminded him. "I almost lost my house. You lost your car—we almost *died*."

He kissed the top of my head. "But we didn't. And we know a lot more now than we did then."

"And you have me," Betony said. "And Rene, who the Stygian believed was strong enough to host a demonic, earth-shattering entity. Might be time to learn what all that's about."

I hadn't gone digging too deep into *why* the Stygian thought Rene could host some hell-level, world-cracking entity.

Not because I wasn't curious. I was. Deeply. Like, late-at-night-staring-at-the-ceiling curious. But every time I came close to poking that particular bear, I hit the same mental wall: what exactly was I gonna do with that information? If the answer turned out to be "yep, the kid was basically bred to be a magical doomsday device," what was I supposed to do—call tech support? Lock him in a magically reinforced shed and throw away the key? No thanks.

Besides, he'd defected. Chosen us. Trusted me. And trust's a two-way street—one I've never been great at navigating, but still. I figured if Rene was some kind of vessel for evil incarnate, we'd deal with it when the time came. Until then, I was letting him be a kid. A weird, powerful, possibly dangerous kid, but a kid all the same.

And sure, maybe that's reckless. Maybe it's parenting by magical denial. But I'd seen what the Stygian did to people they *thought* were useful, and I wasn't about to turn around and do the same thing under a different banner.

So yeah. I shelved the question. Marked it for "later." Right between "be a good business owner/Summate/bestie/fiancé/coven member," and "find time to sleep."

Footsteps descending the back kitchen stairs announced Rene's arrival. *Oh, crap. Now we'll have to tell him his mother is up to no good again.*

The swinging doors opened, and Rene padded into the room barefoot with Rex clutched to his chest. His jeans and T-shirt, emblazoned with the Shrewd Monkey band logo, were rumpled with sleep.

"Mornin' Sleeping Beauty," Betony drawled.

"I've been awake for hours," Rene shot back, rolling his eyes as he set Rex on the floor. "I was just chilling in my room." He ran a hand through his rumpled, dark curls. "Ooh, muffins." He helped himself to one and scribbled his "purchase" in the log. "My socials are blowing up."

None of us needed to ask why. At least he knew. I wasn't sure if I was more glad we didn't have to tell him, or sad that he hadn't heard it from us first.

"Damn, dude. That sucks," Betony said, her voice softening.

Rene scoffed. "She's crazy. No shock there. This was bound to happen sooner or later."

Although Rene had been under my care for the past few months, my role was that of a guardian, not a parent. Betony and her close-knit group had gone to great lengths to make Rene feel included at school and within the coven's circle. Known for her protective nature, Betony acted like a mama bear within her small clan of friends, which included Jake DePaulo, Lorina Maris, and Cadence Hemingford. This August, all of them—along with Rene and Betony—would begin their senior year at Gryphon High School.

Jake was a recent addition to the Lughaidh coven as a blue witch, one gifted with magical abilities tied to music. Lorina likely had a gift as well—her singing was absolutely otherworldly—but she'd never allowed herself to be tested. Whether it was the weight of her churchgoing parents' rigid expectations or her own uncertainty, something always held her back from fully embracing the Lughaidh.

Within minutes, arrangements were made for the coven to assemble at LaDonna's in a couple of hours. Though technically not yet part of the coven, Rene planned to join us to offer whatever insight he could into the Stygian. Rita, our dear friend and head of the WorldWide Witch cyber coven, planned to drive in from Huntsville and join us. Before the meeting, she'd send feelers into her global community to see if anyone had picked up any indicators of the Stygian's upcoming attack plans.

At this point, we knew it was only a matter of when and where.

Betony's trio of friends, Lorina, Jake, and Cadence—Jake's girlfriend—joined us after school. I was glad for their presence. Though their moods were justifiably somber, the energy of the young folks in the shop raised my spirit. Jake hailed me with a raised hand that loomed over his friends considerably. Jake was a good handful of inches over six feet and built like a truck. His girlfriend, Cadence, looked like a diminutive, frizzy, blond doll beside him. Lorina was nearly as tall as Jake and rail-thin with short, dark, wavy hair tucked behind her ears. They were all smiles and hugs, but the joy didn't reach their eyes.

"How you doing?" Jake asked, pulling out a chair for himself while Cadence slipped into the one beside him.

"It's fucked up," Rene replied somberly, stopping whatever video he'd been watching to give his friends his full attention.

"On today's episode of how fucked up is fucked up…" Lorina cued.

The rest of the group chimed in, perfectly in sync: "That's fucked up."

Laughter rippled through the table, but it wasn't their usual boisterous style, and it broke my heart.

I glanced around the room: the only folks there were two other customers, both regulars, and neither was the type to flinch at a little colorful language. No harm, no foul. Besides, this was how Betony's gang talked—half their conversations were stitched together with memes and video references. It was like their heads were plugged into a shared database of sarcasm and pop culture. Watching them communicate was half exhausting and half fascinating.

Jake and Cadence whipped out their phones, thumbs moving faster than most people could think. The soft chime of sent messages followed. Probably letting their parents know they were staying late and, yes, there were adults around to keep things aboveboard—or as aboveboard as a coven gathering could be.

Jake's parents had been surprisingly chill about him

joining the coven, all things considered. His mom, a practical woman with sharp eyes and a sharper mind, had insisted on meeting LaDonna and me first. It turned out that LaDonna's story about taking in Betony after her mom went to jail—and my little resume of homeownership and running a small business—had been enough to put her at ease. She seemed the type to appreciate a good track record of responsibility. I still didn't know if Cadence's folks knew about the coven. I figured she'd tell me when she was ready. Cadence was the group's sweet introvert.

Lorina frowned at her phone screen, thumbs hesitating over the keyboard before she sighed and hit Call instead. She held it to her ear, leaning her lanky body back in her chair as she waited.

"Hey, Mom. Yeah, it's me. No, I didn't forget to text. I just figured this was quicker."

A pause, and she glanced around the room, lowering her voice.

"No, I'm still at the coffeehouse. Yeah, Betony and Rene and Jake and Cadence are here, too." Another pause. "Adults? Uh-huh. Miss Murphy is here, and Miss Hanna just stepped out for a bit."

Miss Murphy? Miss Hanna? That was a new one. Usually, that was saved for older folks here in the South. Lorina probably dubbed me Miss Murphy when talking to her folks to make me sound more adult, I wagered.

Lorina winced at whatever her mother said next, then groaned.

"Mom, I'm not a kid. I can stay out late without it being a big deal. It's summer. Tomorrow's a holiday. And school doesn't start for *weeks*. It's not like I'm out partying or anything. We're just... hanging out." Her voice tightened on the last two words.

She tilted her head, watching Rene fiddling with his phone, and smirked. "No, nobody's drinking. Unless you count Rene chugging an iced caramel latte like his life depends on it."

Her expression shifted, the smirk fading as she sat up straighter.

"Look, I know it will probably be late before I get back. And I know what you said about... all that weird stuff lately. But it's not like I'm wandering around town alone, OK? We're sticking together. I did all my chores and already walked the dog and stuff." Her voice dropped almost to a whisper. "It's safer this way."

Another pause, longer this time, and she ran a hand through her short hair, and I noticed she'd gotten an undercut.

"Mom, I promise. I'll be careful. I just... I feel like I need to stay. Something's—" She hesitated, chewing her lip before shaking her head. "Never mind. It's nothing. I'll text you when I'm heading home, OK? Love you."

Lorina ended the call and let the phone drop onto the table. She stared at it momentarily as if expecting it to ring again, then let out a slow breath.

"Parents," she muttered, shaking her head. "Always worried about the wrong thing."

"At least they're letting you stay out," Betony said. "That's better than they used to."

"It's 'cause I have my own car, and I'm paying my own insurance," Lorina mumbled. "My dad says if I... you know... act up, he'll take the keys."

"Your dad's a dick," Rene observed, and heads around the small table bobbed in agreement.

Shortly after Lorina's call to her mom, Conall had commandeered my shower, leaving the kids to swarm my kitchen with Hanna while I closed the till and prepped the day's deposit. It wasn't exactly a windfall—barely worth the gas to drive it to the bank. I shrugged and stuffed it into the safe. Tomorrow's problem.

We all loaded into our vehicles—I sat shotgun in Conall's new-to-him Jeep Rubicon, a vehicle that looked itching for a mud fight even when it was clean. As we rolled down Desdemona Drive, the familiar spire of the First Baptist Church came into view, its marquee lit up against the growing twilight.

I glanced at the sign, expecting one of their usual cheerful platitudes. Something like "We Love Because He First Loved Us," or that awful pun about the "Best Vitamin for Believers is B1." Instead, my eyes snagged on today's offering:

Justice for the Innocent, Judgment for the Wicked.

I blinked. That was… different.

"Probably only the beginning," Conall said, his tone so matter-of-fact it sent a chill crawling up my spine.

I turned to look at him, but his focus stayed on the road, the expression in his brown eyes unreadable. The Jeep's engine rumbled on, a low, steady growl, but the weight of his words lingered, heavy as a summer storm.

Chapter 3

When I was a kid and went with my mother to coven meetings at LaDonna's house, in the years before she became my foster mother, I always thought of it as the Tree House. Large, gray, and set high in the woods of the Appalachian foothills, it, like LaDonna, somehow managed to be both earthy and regal. The interior consisted mostly of wood and stone, and the large rooms flowed seamlessly into one another in a comfortable, woodsy way that made folks feel immediately at home. It didn't hurt that she'd built a massive back deck to accommodate the trunks of four enormous walnut trees. It was a wonderful place for sipping lemonade on summer nights. As it butted up against the forest at the mountain's base, it also made a fine place to hold rituals.

Although the group had met at the summer solstice gathering only a few days ago, the coven greeted each other with heavy hearts and hugs that lingered a little longer than usual. Once everyone had arrived and the refreshments were served, we settled into the circle of chairs in Luke and LaDonna's living room.

"Well, they're back," Joey muttered, shifting his weight on the footstool he sat on so his heavy engineer boots were tucked under his bulk. "Any idea what we can do about it?"

LaDonna turned to Rita, and I noticed she had more white strands in her long, brown hair than I remembered seeing before. She pulled a lock over her shoulder, and metal bracelets tinkled down her forearm.

"Rita, have you heard anything from your coven?"

Rita shook her head, sending her pink and baby-blue-colored strands dancing. "No, nothing useful. A couple of folks offered to poke around the dark web this afternoon—after, you know... everything went down."

"I can't imagine that's a fun place to be," LaDonna said in a low, smoky tone that still carried across the circle.

"It's not," Rita confirmed. "It's like wading into a digital swamp. You never know what's watching you. I'm not going anywhere near it myself."

"Thank your friends for taking that risk for us, please." LaDonna turned to our other visitor. "Rene, what are your thoughts on what's happened?"

Rene let out a frustrated huff. "You already know my mother and her so-called coven are dead set on exposing 'real' witches to the world. Only she wants witches to be thought of as intimidating. Something to fear. Not... normal. Not like y'all."

"If they make a big spectacle of what we can do," I chimed in, "I don't want any of you coming out of the broom closet. The town already knows about me. Ya'll keep your lives business as usual. I can handle myself. I'm the Summate."

"Who is still learning the depths of her power," LaDonna reminded me. "And while you've come a long way—"

"My house is warded all the way to the street," I cut in. "The wards we put in place after the last Stygian attack on my house are stronger than anything we've built before."

"The ward is great for most attacks, but not everything," Conall reminded me. "Bullets can travel through a window without the gun ever leaving the street. And with tomorrow being the Fourth of July and this being Alabama, that sound wouldn't make most folks bat an eye." I shot daggers in his direction. Whose side was he on, anyway? And did he really think folks were going to take potshots at my house?

"We have to do something," Joey said. Leave it to the black witch—who had the power to protect but could also conjure powerful curses and hexes—to be eager to storm the gates. It was literally in his nature.

"Scrying," Conall suggested. "Looking into their future plans. It'll give us an idea of where to look next."

"Good idea," Luke said. "Conall, you and I can meet after the meeting and look forward and see what will likely be next on their agenda."

He hesitated. "Truth is, we've been catching glimpses for weeks, but nothing solid. The Stygian are always up to something, just not always here. It's hard to know which signs point to Gryphon and which are just more of their chaos elsewhere."

Conall nodded. "And they've got witches actively scrambling the signal. Trying to look ahead feels like tuning a radio with half the dial missing."

"I can help," I said. "I'll add some extra juice."

"Good," LaDonna said with a curt nod in my direction. "Rita, you're a tech witch. Have you added wards to protect those digging into the dark web from any psychic or technological repercussions?"

Rita swallowed, her eyes wide. "Yes, but probably not enough."

"We can add to that. And let's look into any other potential high-profile targets the Stygian might go after so Joey can put a protective ward around them. Murphy, he could probably use a boost with that, too, and this is a great time for you to practice your black witch skills. The Stygian are too large to bind completely, especially without having a focus, but we can try to protect folks." Joey nodded sagely in agreement.

"Yeah, they're global," Rene agreed. "My guess is they're looking for targets literally everywhere. That's a seriously big net to cast."

"WorldWide Witches is global too," Rita said, crossing her arms tightly and lifting her chin to stare Rene straight down. "I'll let the others know our plans. Chances are, other covens who have black witches are doing what they can, too."

"Yeah, but they don't have the Summate," Jake pointed out.

No pressure, though.

A hush fell over the room before Betony cleared her throat. "We gotta protect Murphy. And her business."

Everyone else chimed in like a squad of tenacious cheerleaders, and no matter how much I tried to shut them down, they just dug in their heels.

I raised my hands in surrender. "What exactly do y'all think you can do? My place is already warded six ways to Sunday. I barely leave the place. And—hello—Conall's there most of the time. Orange witch. Kinda sees trouble comin' a mile away. Most of the time, anyway."

"At the very least, you shouldn't be left alone," Miriam insisted, her pale green eyes never breaking contact with mine. "We can all take turns spending the day with you."

"Miriam, I—"

"I think that's an excellent idea," Luke said.

Miriam folded her hands in her lap and leaned forward. "At least then, even if she doesn't need our physical protection, she won't be alone. There are a lot of ways to attack someone."

I hesitated before firing back another rejection. What *could* the Stygian do if they set their minds to it? They could use a tech witch to send a virus to my ancient laptop. They could drive customers away from my store by using an influence spell. Hell, my luck, they could probably get an airplane to accidentally drop something heavy on my roof, like a grand piano. My wards weren't set up to thirty thousand feet, and I doubted any spell could stop a thousand-pound baby grand once it hit terminal velocity.

I glared at no one in particular and sighed. "Fine."

"That's settled, then," LaDonna said, sitting up. "Rita, if you wouldn't mind setting up in the dining room with your laptop and getting a hold of your coven? Betony and I will grab our computers as well, and Terry, you can use Luke's to help us while Luke and Conall work on scrying. That way, we can put our heads together on likely targets."

Terry, our indigo witch, was probably the most empathic person in the coven. Indigo witches specialize in spiritual cleansing and helping people tap into their intuition, so being helpful comes naturally to them. So, when I saw her throw her waist-long dark hair over the shoulder of her flannel shirt and march down the hall to Luke's office, I knew she was a woman with a mission.

God, this sucked. The Stygian once again had us playing defense. One big political hit, and they've undoubtedly got witches all over the world looking over their shoulders and jumping at shadows. If this was just their opening salvo, I wondered what they planned for an encore—and if the Lughaidh would be ready to stare them down again in another deadly confrontation.

Joey moseyed up to me, his expression grave. "Want to join me in the garden?"

"Time to raid LaDonna's herbs?" I ventured.

"Time to raid LaDonna's herbs," he agreed with a sly smile.

Together, Joey and I headed to the rear of the house, out

the French doors, and stepped into the huge herb-and-flower paradise LaDonna had cultivated. Thanks to her green witch gifts, she kept things blooming weeks earlier (or later) than nature intended. The plants she used the most never seemed to fade, regardless of the season.

"If you grab the lavender and sage," Joey said, nudging aside a long rosemary stem, "I'll get the basil and dill."

He and I found the herb clippers in LaDonna's storage area, which she'd adorably masked as a wooden outhouse with a crescent moon on the door and an iron horseshoe as a handle. Armed with fresh green bunches, we met back in La-Donna's kitchen. Joey headed to LaDonna's special cabinet, where she kept supplies for the coven. He rummaged around until he'd assembled iron shavings, moon water, frankin-cense, myrrh, graveyard dust, and a bag of black lava salt. Then he retrieved the athame, running his thumb along the hilt as if checking it for magical vibes.

"What are we going to do?" I asked.

"First, we meditate," Joey said, as matter-of-fact as if he were discussing the weather. "Then, once the rest of the gang in there," he tilted his head toward the dining room, "nails down the names of folks likely to be targeted, we'll cast a protection spell."

My eyebrows shot up. "How do you protect people you've never even seen?"

"We'll use their names and picture them in a mirror shield—like they're wrapped in reflective glass. Any hex or nasty mojo bounces right back to whoever sent it."

"What about the real-world stuff?" I asked, flashing on images of fists, bullets, or who-knows-what. "Mirror-shield's handy for hexes, but it won't stop a baseball bat."

Joey made a face like I'd just reminded him of overdue bills. "That's trickier. We can try confusion spells—muddle up the would-be attacker's thoughts so they can't carry out a plan. Maybe illusions to make them think they've got the wrong house, or wards that make them take a sudden detour."

I gave a slight shrug. "Guess that's where I come in."

He grinned and shrugged. "Exactly. We'll mix some protective runes into the circle, maybe slip in a misdirection charm or two. We might even add a 'repel' effect with enough focus and some of your Summate juice added to the mix. Force anybody with ill intent to get lost or give up."

"And if that doesn't work...?" I arched an eyebrow.

"Well, let's just say I've got a few more tricks up my sleeve," Joey replied, wiggling the athame playfully, then pretending to test the blade's sharpness.

A little grin tugged at my mouth. Joey once had a job that involved "extracting people from bad situations." He never said more than that, but I had no doubt he knew how to use an athame for more than just ritual work.

Joey set the athame down and cracked his neck. "Yup. Let's get these herbs set up before LaDonna chews me out for messing up her kitchen again."

Back outside, Joey drew a ten-foot circle with the black sea salt in a clockwise direction, followed by casting a circle with the point of the athame. We sat cross-legged in the center, where Joey produced a copper bowl. He added the herbs, resins, and oils to the mix, sprinkling in a dash of Florida water, then lit the mess with a wooden match, and we meditated.

By the time LaDonna and the crew returned with their list of names, I was so Zen it was like coming out of a coma. My body felt as if it were one with the planks beneath my seat, and when I opened my eyes, I became aware of the lingering scent of burned sage. Joey slid the list into my hands. It was massive. Names upon names, each one a potential Stygian target. Or at least a person who'd pissed off the wrong folks.

"I think we've narrowed down a list of likely targets." LaDonna's voice was simultaneously subdued and determined. She produced two black candles and candleholders. She looked from me to Joey, who nodded approvingly, then stepped back to give us room.

This is a lot of targets.

We set the list gently on the floor at the center of our makeshift altar. Joey lit the black taper candles, the flames dancing like they had minds of their own, reacting to the swirl of magic we'd stirred up.

"Time to channel some reflective energy." Joey's tone was all business, and he was a big guy with a grave face, but I caught the slightest tremor in his voice. The poor guy got stage fright about anything bigger than a single-protection ward—he'd never say it out loud, but I knew better.

Still half-floating in my Zen haze, I laid my palms over the list. "We call upon light, reflection, and…" I paused for a beat, collecting that last thread of calm I'd built up during meditation, "whatever benevolent force is listening to keep these folks safe from harm." It was not a good time to blank on the names of appropriate deities, but hopefully, they understood.

Joey had one hand on my shoulder and the other braced over the list, palm out. "Surround them with mirrors. Let all bad intentions bounce back."

I pulled in a breath of sultry summer air and drew from the depths of my Summate strength. I felt a tremor of power pass between us, like a ripple on the surface of a pond growing into a wave. The pages fluttered; the candle flames wobbled, then shot up tall. My pulse throbbed in my temples, and I could've sworn I heard someone—maybe LaDonna—suck in a breath.

"That's it," I whispered. "Keep it up, Joey."

Joey didn't respond. He was deep in the channeling zone. Instead, he took the tin of iron shavings and shook the filings around the list, forming a large, rough circle. Next came the graveyard dust, sprinkled across the iron like a fine gray mist. Somehow, that combination always made me think of railroad ties and the scent of petrichor. I imagined those borders growing like walls around the names. Massive, thick, impenetrable walls like those that protect people from radiation or infectious diseases. Like the Stygian.

Once he'd poured a thick enough boundary, I reached for a bundle of black lava salt, pausing to admire how it reflected the setting sun, like volcanic glass powdered down to a thousand needles. I traced a third ring atop the iron and dust and raised the mental walls even higher, completely encasing those within.

Joey's voice drifted from behind me. "Light it. Show these names to the flame, so they'll vanish in the minds of anyone who does them harm."

I nodded and, keeping the protective force in place, pulled out the long-neck lighter. *Flick.* The flame flared bright blue at the tip before settling into a steady yellow flicker. I set it in one corner of the list. Paper burned with a *whoosh*, the smoke rising in pale coils. It didn't smell like burning paper at all. More like incense, sweet and earthy, with a hint of frankincense meeting the tang of iron. The names curled into ash, the edges turning black as they succumbed to the slow, deliberate burn. I focused on the image of each person cloaked within my impervious walls, invisible to ill will. In my mind's eye, each threat or bullet or curse slid off them like water on a windshield.

I reached outside the spelling circle and dropped the pages into the Whelen's metal fire pit. The flames danced higher for a second, crackling like tiny fireworks. Then, just as quickly, they died down. What remained of the list was nothing but pale, flaking cinders. I almost felt the wards snap into place, humming with the afterglow of spent magic. A moment later, it was quiet again. Peaceful.

We glanced around, and I half expected something dramatic—a swirl of wind, a clap of thunder, maybe a triumphant choir. But the only sound was the faint wind in the trees. I let out a slow breath, feeling my heart rate climb back to normal.

Joey lowered his hands, cracking his neck with a wince. "Whew." He wiped sweat from his temple, a grin twitching at the corner of his mouth. "That should do it."

I couldn't suppress the satisfied little grin creeping across my face, even though my skin prickled a little with the residual energy from the spell. Adding a hint of my Summate power to spells always made me feel a little high after the fact. It was a helluva rush.

Joey let out a gentle laugh, weary but triumphant. "And that, my friend, is how you stage a vanishing act—coven style."

"Which is great," Conall said, breaking through the happy moment Joey and I were sharing, "except that Luke and I have seen another one of the things they're likely to do next."

I flinched. "What's that?"

His handsome face was the most somber I'd ever seen. "Magical bombs."

"Magical... bombs?" The word felt foreign on my tongue. I'd heard of potions, hexes, curses—but bombs? That was a whole new level of horrifying. What would anyone even stuff into one of those things? What was their purpose? How did they work? A control spell to hijack an entire city's free will? Elemental chaos—fire, hail, flood, tornado—unleashed at the wave of a wand? Or maybe they'd figured out how to fry electronics and power grids with an electromagnetic pulse. Worse yet, if they had a green witch who could manipulate tiny creatures like viruses or bacteria, what would stop them from brewing a magical plague and dropping it on a major city?

The truth was, they could strike anywhere, with anything. Our list of high-value targets had been guesswork—educated guesswork, but still guesswork. It was better than throwing darts at a map in the dark. At least it had given us a place to start—and a way to stay one step ahead while we figured out how to put the Stygian on the defensive.

Last time, they'd rolled into Gryphon looking for Betony and her rare gray power, planning to snuff me out so I couldn't balance her chaos energy. Years before that, when I'd been a child, they murdered my mother (and Conall's and Hanna's mothers) in a midnight Lughaidh coven meeting. Their big plan? Make Betony the Summate—never realizing they had the real gray witch right under their noses.

So, how the hell were we supposed to fight them now? Sure, I was the Summate—arguably the most powerful witch around—but I couldn't just fling my magic across the entire globe. I needed a target.

"We need to figure out where they're hiding," I said, forcing conviction into my voice. "And if Ericka Moore is still calling the shots, we find her. Then we take the fight straight to them."

Chapter 4

July Fourth was one of the few days of the year I bothered to close the shop. I slept in until the decadent hour of seven o'clock, still worn out from the spellwork Joey and I had pulled off the night before. Everyone in the Lughaidh coven had been wiped after the meeting, and we'd all gone our separate ways, understanding that we'd meet back up at lunch today and plan some more. Conall hadn't even stayed over, which was becoming rarer the closer we got to the wedding. We'd chosen Beltane next year for the ceremony—perfect timing for handfasting rituals, plus an extra excuse for the gang to party on Mayday.

Rex had fallen asleep on his favorite perch—my hip— where he lay in utter relaxation as only cats can.

"Come on, buddy," I said, sitting up. "Time for some coffee."

You'd think a decade of running a coffee shop would've cured me of the addiction to bean juice, but nope. Still hooked. I rarely went for the fancy stuff, though—I was more of a drip brew witch.

The sun was hidden behind the houses and trees across the street, its rays casting long shadows on Oberon. I scooped grounds into the filter, relishing the rich aroma, and poured water into the carafe. As I performed the familiar routine, my mind wandered to the Stygian coven. What were they doing this morning—gloating over the shockwave they'd set off across the country? Word had probably spread overseas by now. The Stygian were as global as Rita's WorldWide Witches, and odds were good they had people ready to broadcast their deeds as far as possible.

As the coffee bubbled and percolated, I sank into a chair at one of the small coffee shop tables. Rex hopped into my lap, and I stroked his soft black fur. Oberon Street was almost empty this early on a holiday, blissfully quiet. Hard to imagine a gaggle of treacherous witches were plotting world domination and chaos…again.

I'd never been a fan of killing, but I had to admit there were a few souls the world could do without. And while witches don't believe in karma or the rule of three the way many Wiccans or some other occult religions do, I knew killing the Stygian high priestess would likely trigger several new leaders in her place. Maybe ones worse than Ericka. If that's possible.

To keep myself busy—and sane—I did some housekeeping and started some laundry. I wrapped up the last bit of tidying the upstairs bathroom just as Rene staggered out of bed on sleepy teenage legs. On the plus side, my busy morning got my house much cleaner. On the downside, my brain replayed the same track on repeat: How Do We Take the Fight to the Stygian?

Hopefully, Rita and her dark web infiltrators would dig up something about their schemes. Or I could try a locator spell—I was decent at those. Conall, Luke, and I knew how to astral project, so if I pinned down a location, we could spy on the Stygian in person… so to speak.

Plans were good. I wondered why I hadn't come up with them last night. I suppose after the protection spell, I wasn't worth a pile of dust.

I was ready for more coffee and a late breakfast—or an early lunch by ten o'clock. Rene was sitting at the butcher-block table munching on some eggs he'd scrambled. I made another massive cup of brew instead of a mimosa and helped myself to one of Hannah's cranberry-orange muffins. Have I mentioned yet that I'm not one for cooking much? Maybe it wasn't much of a brunch, but the muffin was massive and filling. Plus, a sugary treat whipped up by my best friend, the kitchen witch, sounded amazing right then. Yeah, it might spoil lunch with the Lughaidh, but chances were good I'd be talking more than eating.

Sitting in the morning sun, I watched the street beyond the front window. Traffic had picked up, but was nowhere near its normal levels. I munched on my food while my mind mulled over my plan so far. Locator spell. Astral project. Learn their plans. Foil plans. Problem solved. Right?

Rene joined me in the coffee shop. "Smells good in here," he observed. "Super clean. You've been busy." I smiled, pleased that he'd noticed.

My phone pinged, and I grabbed it instinctively. It was Conall.

Conall:

I'm on my way over. Wait until I get there to check the news if you haven't already.

Oh, wonderful. Now I really want to check the news. Had they used one of those magic bombs Luke and Conall had learned about? And what the hell *was* a magic bomb?

"What is it?" Rene asked, his eyes flicking to my face.

My face must have given away my frustration. "Conall. He's on his way over."

"Y'all going to LaDonna's early or something?"

I let out a long sigh, propping my elbow on the table and resting my chin on my palm. "He said there's something on the news he doesn't want me to see until he gets here."

Rene started to say something, then paused. "Shit."

A bitter laugh escaped me before I could stop it. "Yeah. Shit."

To his credit, he didn't whip out his phone to look up the headlines. Probably didn't want me hounding him until he spilled whatever terrible thing had happened. My fingers drummed out a restless rhythm on the Formica tabletop. A part of me—maybe the stubborn part—wanted to grab my phone and see for myself. But I held off. Conall knew me better than I knew myself some days. If he said I needed to wait, I'd trust him. Even if it left me edgy as hell.

Biting my lip, I picked at the muffin. Up until my last bite, it had tasted delicious. Now, it looked heavy, overly sweet, and horribly oversized. Whatever Conall didn't want me to see had to be nasty. There was no question it involved the Stygian: they'd struck again, and Conall knew the story would shake me to my core this time.

Within minutes, Conall's Jeep rushed up to the curb. He threw it into Park and leaped from the driver's seat, only locking it as he crossed the veranda as an afterthought. He'd dressed for the day, but his dark hair was still rumpled from sleep, and his face bore a five o'clock shadow. He'd look adorably sexy if not for the concern painted on his lean face.

I met him at the door, and the minute he was through, he pulled me into his arms as if to shield me from a storm.

"What?" I demanded. "What's wrong? You've got me so worried."

"They've—" He couldn't finish the sentence, but there was no need to ask who he meant by "they."

"Tell me. Or show me. Please. Get it out."

He nodded and led me by the hand to the table, where my uneaten muffin lay next to my steadily cooling coffee. Once we sat down, he pulled out his phone and looked up a video for a news article. Rene moved to better read over Conall's shoulder. My stomach turned at the chyron at the bottom of the screen: DEADLY CHURCH BOMBING IN HOOVER: STYGIAN COVEN CLAIMS RESPONSIBILITY.

"Holy shit," I breathed. Connor hit Play, and a blond woman told the horrific story with a dispassionate newscaster delivery.

"A bombing during a Fourth of July church festival at Hope Harvest Baptist Church in Hoover early this morning has left the community reeling in the aftermath of what local authorities are calling one of the deadliest local tragedies in recent memory. According to first responders on the scene, the explosion occurred just after the children's choir finished performing the national anthem, causing significant structural damage throughout the church and claiming the lives of several parishioners, including seven children.

"Investigators with the Hoover Police Department and the FBI have confirmed that a group calling itself the Stygian Coven has claimed responsibility for the attack. Authorities also note that the same group took credit for the assassination of Governor Waite that shocked the region only yesterday. In a chilling statement disseminated through social media, the group declared they targeted Hope Harvest Baptist Church because of its outspoken stance against witchcraft. The statement also warned of further attacks in communities across the globe, indicating that the bombing in Hoover was 'only the beginning.'

"Authorities have encouraged people across the state to remain vigilant, while faith leaders from various denominations have gathered to offer support and condemn the violence. Mayor Paul Durham called the bombing 'a heart-breaking tragedy' and promised that law enforcement would 'pursue every lead to bring justice to the victims and their families.'

"Meanwhile, the nation watches closely as investigators scour the scene for evidence, attempting to piece together how the perpetrators orchestrated such a devastating attack. Faced with this tragedy, locals are uniting to support one another with prayer vigils and community drives for the families affected by the bombing, determined not to let the Stygian Coven's threats fracture their faith or resolve."

Seven children. They killed seven children.

I don't know why it surprised me. Their high priestess had been willing to heave her own flesh-and-blood on the chopping block to satisfy her greed. What was a little collateral damage that involved kids she didn't even know?

The newscaster had said for people across the state to "remain vigilant." Clearly, they knew little about the Stygian's reach. Didn't reporters do any research before reporting news anymore?

A teardrop hit the side of my hand. Then another. I wasn't full-on bawling, but this hit me like a punch to the gut. Those kids... The Stygian had zero respect for human life. None. Not even children were spared from their evil.

Images of that terrible night when Conall, Hanna, and I lost our mothers filled my head. The Stygian had butchered them and fled like the cowards they were—almost got away with it, too. Now, a group of parents had lost their children.

Had they suffered? Had a parent held their child in their arms as they took their last breath? The report hadn't said how many adults had died. How many children would go to bed tonight without a mother or a father, Independence Day forever horribly ruined by this nightmare for the rest of their lives?

A sob rattled out of me, one so forceful that pain stabbed me in the chest. Conall wrapped his powerful arms around me, and that was all it took. The ugly crying came on hard, and I didn't care if Conall or Rene heard every choked, snotty gasp.

They'd killed seven children.

Chapter 5

I'm pretty sure the entire coven felt the same way I did—the time for waiting and guesswork was over. It was time to take the battle to the Stygian. We'd taken some steps to protect some of those at risk last night. Hopefully, our spells were hard at work protecting those potential political and religious targets. I don't think anyone expected they'd strike again so soon, or so hard, including people *looking* for the latest disaster—newscasters.

Conall fiddled with the dial on his Jeep stereo until the smooth cadence of Maria Jensen, national newscaster, flowed from his speakers. I listened disbelievingly to the banter between the newscasters.

"And now for more on today's top story," Maria began, her tone a perfect mix of gravitas and curiosity, "Governor Terry Waite's assassination in Birmingham, Alabama, followed by today's tragic bombing at Hope Harvest Baptist Church in Hoover just outside of Birmingham. The question everyone's asking is: Are the Stygian behind both attacks? With me, as always, is our resident skeptic, Jack Delaney."

"Skeptic, realist—you say tomato, I say common sense," Jack shot back. "Come on, Maria. Two wildly different crimes, back-to-back, in the same state? Practically the same *town*? This doesn't scream 'global witch coven' to me. It screams…I don't know…coincidence?"

My gaze was fixed on the radio, jaw tightening with every word.

Maria wasn't giving up so easily. "Coincidence?" she repeated. "Jack, the Stygian has been linked to crimes across Europe and South America for years. Just last month, Interpol reported a similar pattern in Madrid—a high-profile assassination followed by an attack on a faith-based community."

I turned to Rene, my voice low. "Did you know about that?"

He shook his head, wide-eyed. Of course he didn't. Why would his mother let him know her group was killing people? Rene was kind-hearted despite his mother's corrupt nature. If he knew that she was slaughtering folks, it might make him less willing to become their Sovereign Darkness.

Jack's voice cut through my thoughts. "Oh, right, because witches with magic powers—or whatever they're supposed to have—definitely care about geopolitics and church calendars. Maria, think about it. If they're so global and so organized, why are they suddenly focused on Alabama? Did someone forget to book the flight to Salem? Isn't that where women were falsely accused of being witches?"

Maria was quick on the draw. "You're oversimplifying," she countered. "Governor Waite was outspoken against what he called occult activity, and Hope Harvest has been involved in what some locals describe as widespread spiritual 'counter-witchcraft' efforts. Both could've made them targets."

Jack laughed, the sound razor-sharp and dismissive. "Fine, but if these Stygian witches are this all-powerful force, why didn't they hit New York? Or D.C.? Why are they blowing up comparatively small-town churches and assassinating governors? Sounds less like a calculated coven and more like two random crimes—probably conducted by two separate gangs and slapped with a spooky name to sell papers."

"Or maybe the Stygian are shifting their focus. Maybe this is about controlling the narrative, inciting fear in areas more likely to panic. You've seen the protests cropping up—people are terrified."

Protests? My stomach knotted. *Are they protesting the governor's murder, or witches?*

Jack's voice dripped with sarcasm. "Exactly. People love a good villain, especially one that checks all the scary boxes—witches, global conspiracies, dark magic. It's straight out of a bad thriller. How do we even know the Stygian are real?"

"You sound like the conspiracy theorists you mock," Maria shot back. "Are you saying the Stygian doesn't exist? What about the international reports? For all we know, they could be the new Al Qaeda."

I felt myself slumping into the seat. *Oh, great. Witches as the new religious extremists. That'll help.*

Newscaster Jack scoffed. "Sure, maybe the Stygian exist, but as what? An underground group with a grudge against the world? Or a convenient boogeyman? And why Alabama, Maria? If they're this big, scary, global group, why are they so focused on the Deep South? They're witches, not Walmart."

"The same argument could be made about Birmingham and Hoover being perfect testing grounds. If they're trying to test their tactics, smaller cities draw less federal attention—"

"Less attention?" Jack interrupted. "The FBI's crawling all over Birmingham like ants at a picnic. Which brings me to another point—how does an 'all-powerful coven' manage to leave enough breadcrumbs for every government agency to follow?"

Because they want everyone to know they're real. They aren't afraid of being caught.

Maria sighed audibly. "We'll have to wait for law enforcement to release more details, but let's not dismiss this as hysteria. Whether or not the Stygian is behind this, people are scared. And fear doesn't wait for facts."

"Neither does a good conspiracy theory. But hey, maybe Bigfoot will make a cameo next week to spice things up."

"Always the comedian, Jack. Listeners, what do you think? Are the Stygian behind these attacks, or is there another explanation? Text us your thoughts, and stay tuned. We'll be right back after this break."

The jingle for a local auto parts store replaced their voices, and Conall shut off the radio. Silence filled the Jeep, broken only by the tires' steady thrumming.

"They think it's all fake," I murmured.

"Could be a good thing," Conall replied. "If we can cut off the Stygian before they do too much damage, it means the world can go back to normal as we know it."

I paused before turning to where Rene sat in the back seat. "Your mom has really stirred the shit pot this time, kid," I said, aiming for lighthearted but landing somewhere closer to grim. My voice sounded flat and unconvinced.

Rene scowled. "I know what you're thinking. And I agree. She's going to have to die." His dark eyes were flinty, cold.

"Maybe," I agreed. "But if we take her out and leave the rest of the Stygian, someone will take her place, and they might be just as bad. Or worse."

The corner of his lip turned up in disgust, and he laughed humorlessly. "I doubt there's anyone worse on this planet, Murphy. I'm serious. My mom—Ericka. Ericka is a horrible, calculating woman. And I kind of hope she dies."

Chapter 6

Everyone in the Lughaidh turned up at LaDonna's house well before lunchtime because, of course they did. Rita, our honorary guest, was sitting at the dining room table, tapping furiously on her laptop, her expression grim. When Conall, Rene, and I stepped inside the Whelen living room, the television was on—a rare sight in that house—and everyone was glued to the local news. Luke had his arms crossed like he'd rather be anywhere else, but even he couldn't peel his eyes away from the screen.

Paul Berry, Conall's father, stood unmoving in front of the TV. Paul looked like an older, more seasoned model of Conall—distinguished but rugged, with matching deep brown eyes. Today, though, the usual calm was swapped for a grim frown. His typical casual posture was replaced with a tense stance that screamed something was off.

"What is it, Pop?" Conall asked, slapping his dad more softly on the shoulder than was typical.

Paul shook his head in disbelief, glued to the screen as if afraid to miss a second. "The local newscasters are suggesting that people be cautious of others they suspect are interested in witchcraft because people don't know who may or may not be part of the Stygian."

I was flabbergasted that he'd uttered that many words at

once. Paul Berry is typically as quiet and stoic as a guy gets.

Terry chimed in from the couch, where her waist-length hair was getting its usual nervous fiddling treatment. "They added that it wasn't a reason to persecute anyone for their religion. But the way they said it…" She bit her lip.

"The implication that witches are bad was there?" Conall ventured.

Paul finally turned to him, eyes dark. "It was there." His voice dropped a notch as his hands went to his waist. "At least, I thought so. Maybe I'm overreacting."

"Nope," Terry said, her voice thin but firm. "I felt it, too."

I glanced at the screen and resisted the urge to roll my eyes at the somber expressions on our local newscasters. This was bad, but not unexpected. It seemed that the Stygian had been ruining lives and reputations without even trying lately.

Before I could comment, Jake, Rene, and Betony shuffled in, their expressions collectively screaming *bad news incoming*.

"Lorina spending the Fourth with her family?" I asked. Although Jake's girlfriend, Cadence, was often recruited to help wrangle the smaller children at her family functions, it was unusual for Lorina to not be a part of the gang—unless she was grounded, which was pretty common.

"Lorina's not coming today," Jake said, sorrow in his downturned blue eyes. "Her family told her she's not allowed to hang out with the three of us anymore because we go to your coffee shop. She can't go to Witch's Brew anymore."

Ah. My coffee shop, Witch's Brew. Where you can get a double-shot latte with a side of tarot cards or crystals. Charming, apparently, until the neighbors decide you're summoning the devil. Or killing people who are anti-witch.

Rene jumped in with an optimistic spin. "She's gonna sneak out later, though. Said she'd grab her car and tell her parents she's meeting Cadence to watch fireworks."

"That'll go well," I said dryly. "Hopefully, she'll remember to turn off the GPS on her phone this time."

Betony smirked, but it didn't quite reach her eyes. "You know Lorina."

Indeed, I did. What I didn't know, other than from secondhand information gleaned from the kids' conversation, was Lorina's parents. I hoped this wasn't the end of Lorina and Jake's band. I loved the kids' friendship, and their unplugged performances were the highlight of my Friday nights at Witch's Brew.

LaDonna glided to the center of the room. Today, her usual skirt was replaced by well-worn, faded Levis. *She must have spent the morning in the garden.* I felt a pang of guilt. What had I done that morning to focus my power? I didn't think scrubbing the grout on my bathroom floor counted as a banishing spell.

"Everyone, gather around," she called, her smoky voice especially urgent. "We need to discuss our next steps. I'm assuming we've all heard about this morning and the events at Hope Harvest Church?"

We all had. Every face in the room looked ready to go to war.

"We've had a few hours to think about our next steps, and I don't think what happened there has affected our resolve to take action against them."

Heads around the circle bobbed in agreement.

"Rita, do you want to tell us what you've found?"

Rita, visibly uncomfortable without a laptop or a tablet to fidget with, took a deep breath. "They're bigger than we thought," she admitted, her voice tight. "Global, sure, but I'm talking everywhere. London. Rome. Buenos Aires. São Paulo. Mumbai. Melbourne. Cape Town. Cairo. Even smaller cities. They've got their hooks in *everywhere*."

"Where's Ericka?" Rene interjected. The shift in the room was immediate, all eyes snapping to him. I don't think anyone missed that he'd called his mother by her government name.

Rita's eyes fell to the ceramic tile floor. "She's back in Atlanta. Or will be tonight if the information I was given is correct."

Luke rubbed his hands together. "That's a start."

"Astral projection," I blurted. "I mean... I think you, Conall, and I should astral project and look in on Ericka and maybe her lieutenant. Rene, do you know—"

"Valeria Andersen," Rene said. "If she's not in Atlanta with my mother, I'm guessing she's in Savannah or St. Augustine stirring up trouble. She tends to stick to the southeast."

"There's three of us," Conall said. "We can check all of those."

My phone buzzed in my back pocket. Normally, I would have ignored it, but I recognized the faint tune as that of my neighbor from across the street, Linnie Bass. I pulled the phone out and answered it, turning away from the group and steering myself to the kitchen so I didn't interrupt the planning.

"Murphy?" Linnie's voice crackled with age but somehow managed to be as spry as Linnie herself. "It's Linnie, honey."

"Hey, Miss Linnie. What's up?"

"Well, dear, I hope you don't mind, but I called Officer Hendricks because I saw something funny a little bit ago—some folks dressed as landscapers going into your backyard. At first, I didn't think anything of it, but then I realized it was strange, with it being the holiday and all. And I didn't see your car out front."

Heat rose to my cheeks, and my body started shaking. *They broke my wards. They broke through my wards!*

"So, I called that nice Officer Hendricks to check it out. I didn't think you'd mind. I've always thought he might be a little sweet on you. Anyway, they were gone by the time he got there, but he said they'd done some damage to your garden out back. I'm so sorry, honey. I should have called him sooner."

I thought about the circle we'd formed around my house the day the coven had come over after the Stygian's first attack. My wards had held then, but we hadn't extended the protections far beyond the house itself. The backyard was lightly warded—enough to deter casual intruders, but not enough for someone determined. Who breaks into a backyard, anyway?

"Murphy, are you alright?" Linnie's voice pulled me back.

"I'm here, Miss Linnie," I murmured. "Thank you for calling Kenny—er, Officer Hendricks. I'll be there as soon as I can."

I stepped back into the living room in a daze. My expression must've given everything away because the room fell silent.

"LaDonna," I said, my voice firm despite the tremor in my chest. "Someone's messed with my backyard."

Her green eyes locked onto mine, stormy with concern and anger on my behalf. "Was it the Stygian?"

"I don't—I don't know," I admitted, frustration bubbling in my chest. "But whoever it was, they wanted me to know they were there. I don't know how bad it is, but—"

The weight of my words settled over the room like a storm cloud. Conall leaned against the wall, his jaw tight. Rene stared at the floor, his arms crossed. Even Rita looked shaken, her fingers twitching as though itching for the safety of her keyboard.

LaDonna's voice cut through the thick tension. "After everything that's gone on, it could be someone else." Her tone was even, but the undercurrent of concern was impossible to miss. "Someone local."

The thought twisted in my gut. My neighbors. My town. People I passed in the grocery store or waved at on the street. Maybe even my customers. Someone among them had crossed the line.

"We need to figure out who," I said, my voice barely more than a whisper.

"And why," LaDonna added, her gaze piercing.

I didn't have an answer to either, but the sting of betrayal burned in my chest. This wasn't some faceless enemy from across the globe. This was home. And suddenly, it didn't feel like home at all.

☽○☾

Conall had barely brought the Jeep to a halt before I jumped out and tore around my house, through the back gate, and into my yard. What I saw there stopped me cold.

Someone had spray-painted "YOU'RE GOING TO HELL" across the compass design on my patio in glaring pink, the paint staining the once-pristine pattern. My wooden flowerpots were tipped over, their vibrant contents dumped haphazardly onto the decorative stones at the patio's edge. Flower stems lay snapped like discarded bones.

The garden I'd worked so hard to cultivate was unrecognizable. Uprooted plants sprawled across the concrete patio, their roots drying in the hot summer air. My pumpkins—tender vines with the promise of early blooms—had been doused in bleach, their leaves browned and curling like the edges of burned paper. The acrid stench of bleach mingled with the earthy fragrance of upturned soil and the chemical odor of spray paint. I gagged, swallowing back bile. I'll never forget that god-awful smell as long as I live.

More hateful words scrawled across the wooden privacy fence in angry strokes: HEATHEN. SINNER. EVIL. BLAS-PHEMER. DEVIL WORSHIPER. A crooked swastika glared at me from the middle of it all. *So much for "love thy neighbor."*

I hadn't even been gone that long. How many people had it taken to do all this damage in such a short time?

The combination of the smell and the shock churned my stomach. I bent double and vomited into the grass.

"Murphy! Murph—Oh, Mother Goddess," Conall breathed as he skidded into the yard. "What the hell? Who would do this?"

I wiped my mouth with the back of my hand, grimacing at the lingering taste. Rubbing the spit on my shorts, I pulled my hair back with my other hand. The smell was unbearable. "I don't know," I managed. "But this is too petty to be the Stygian, I think."

Behind us came the quick rap of knuckles on wood. My whole body tensed, ready to defend my yard against the next intruders.

"Knock, knock," called a familiar voice from the gate. My tension melted as my favorite cop in the world, Officer Kenny Hendricks, stepped into the yard and shut the gate behind him. He was tall, broad-shouldered, and dressed neatly in his uniform, which was probably why beads of sweat glistened on his dark brow. He wore his usual air of quiet authority, but his warm, brown eyes held a softness reserved for friends.

"I saw Conall's Jeep out front," Kenny said. "Figured I'd check in. Y'all okay?"

My vision blurred as tears threatened to spill. "Not really," I croaked. Conall pulled me in for a hug, which I accepted gladly.

Kenny shook his head as he scanned the wreckage. "This is a damn shame. I've been hearing tongues wagging about that weird witch group with the funny name—"

"Stygian," I muttered. "Means having to do with the River Styx."

"Yeah, them. Freaks. But dammit, Murphy, you're nothing like them. Folks around here should know better."

"Not everyone in town knows me like you do, Kenny," I said, stepping back from Conall's tight embrace. "You've always been there for me. Back when I was... accident-prone, you were always the one to help me pick up the pieces."

Kenny gave me a look that spoke volumes. I suspected he knew I was the real deal—an honest-to-Goddess witch—and I suspected he might have some hoodoo or Voodoo running through his veins. But we'd never talked about it. To him, I was just Murphy, the young woman with a trail of damage in her wake until the last year or so, not Murphy, who reflected Betony's chaos witch energy until I learned I was the Summate.

"You have any idea who might have done it?" Conall asked.

Kenny shook his head again. "Miss Linnie across the street has cameras outside her house. Her son's coming over to pull the footage, but the way they've got 'em angled, they mostly cover her front door and driveway. Not sure they'll catch much of who messed up your yard."

Conall's jaw clenched as he folded his arms across his chest. His lips were pressed so tightly together I wasn't sure if he was holding in more words or another scream. "This is bullshit," he muttered.

"Couldn't agree more," Kenny said, his voice low as he eyed the offensive words. I wondered if he, a Black man in Alabama, had ever endured prejudice this blatant.

Kenny eyed the pink spray paint scrawled over the compass and the hateful words on the fence. His jaw tightened, but his voice stayed calm. "I know some guys who can take care of this," he offered with a hand waving at the graffiti. "They'll get you fixed up in no time."

I heaved a heavy sigh. "I appreciate the offer, Kenny, I really do. But right now, I'm not feeling too comfortable letting strangers into my backyard, you know?"

His gaze softened, and the empathy in his dark eyes almost undid me. "I feel you," he said, his voice low and steady, the kind of voice that could talk someone off a ledge. He stepped closer and rested a warm, solid hand on my shoulder. "But if you change your mind, you let me know, alright? I know you got me on speed dial."

I choked out a short laugh. "I sure do." In addition to having a dozen or so of his Gryphon Sheriff's Department business cards tucked in various places around my house, I had his number saved under Favorites on my phone. I can only handle so many disasters alone.

His lips quirked into a faint smile. "Smart woman. With all the trouble you attract, I should probably start charging a retainer."

I was about to clap back with a snarky comment, but the lump in my throat swelled until it choked off my words. The dam finally broke. A sob escaped, raw and ugly, and I slapped a hand over my mouth to stifle the rest.

"Hey," Kenny murmured, stepping in and wrapping me in a hug. His calloused hand rubbed soothing circles on my back the way a parent might comfort a kid who'd scraped their knee. "Hey, Murphy, it's gonna be alright. It'll be OK. I promise."

In all the years I'd known Officer Hendricks, through all the car accidents, the broken bones, the smashed windows, and the endless stream of minor catastrophes that seemed to follow me around like a stray dog, he'd never hugged me. Not once. Then again, most of those incidents were self-inflicted—or, so I thought—fallout from chaos witch energy. I was terrified to let people touch me, even people I cared about.

And this? This wasn't some random mishap or accident. I wasn't tripping over my clumsy feet or reflecting chaos energy without realizing it. This was deliberate. This was personal. This... this had been an attack against me. Against who I was. Against *what* I was.

Kenny pulled back just enough to look me in the eye, his expression grave. "We're gonna find out who did this," he said. "And when we do, they're gonna learn what justice feels like."

His words struck a chord deep inside me. I nodded, wiping my face with the back of my hand. The tears hadn't fixed anything, but they'd eased the pressure enough to let me breathe again.

"Thanks, Kenny," I said.

"Always," he replied.

Chapter 7

Conall shut the gate behind Kenny with a soft *click* and turned to me. He scanned the uprooted, bleached remains of my garden and the obnoxious flamingo-pink paint on the patio and fence. He stretched, rolling his shoulders like a man trying to shed the weight of the world. I could relate. Goddess knew I was wound up tighter than an eight-day clock.

He cocked a hand on his hip and brushed the fingers of his free hand along my arm. "What's the plan?"

"You know that padlock in my junk drawer?" I asked.

"You want me to put that on the back gate for you?"

I nudged the paint defacing my concrete-embedded compass with the toe of my sneaker. It came away sticky, the tip smeared with a residue that looked like chewed bubble gum—and just as appetizing. Whoever broke in must've guessed the compass had a ritual purpose, and they were right. Plenty of rituals had been performed on that surface. If they thought a little paint was going to stop that, they had another think coming.

"Yes, please. And can you grab one of my Mason jars while you're in there, too? And a lid?"

He raised his eyebrows, curious where my train of thought had led me, but decided to let it play out and watch instead of asking.

While he was inside, I sat cross-legged on the grass near

my garden and cleared my head. Blades of grass tickled my crossed legs as I leaned forward, reaching down with my palms to ground myself on the earth. Once there, I closed my eyes, centered myself, and calmed my thoughts. Breathing deliberately, I inhaled for a slow four count, then out for eight until my heartbeat slowed. Then I imagined my fingers growing like roots into the soil, covering the distance between where I sat and where my garden began like a tunneling worm. My mind followed, burrowing through the dirt, threading between pebbles and the tangled roots of grass.

Then I hit the poisoned patches. The stench of bleach slammed into my senses like a wall, acrid and biting. The ground was burning—raw, aching, violated by chemicals that had no business being here. The stench of bleach grew overwhelming as I neared the upturned spots where only that morning, healthy, thriving plants had stretched toward the sun.

The poor ground was suffocating, smothered by unnatural substances that had no business there. *You need water*, I thought. And as if it could speak, I felt the earth responding with a gentle *yes* that caressed my mind like a breeze.

I pulled back gradually, retreating into my body, centering myself until it felt like waking from a dream. The sound of a shutting door let me know Conall was returning from his trip inside the house.

"Where do you want the jar?" he asked, wiggling the container in his hand.

"Just set it there on the patio."

He did, and as he headed to the gate to lock it from the inside, I retrieved a hose from the side of the house and set an oscillating sprinkler up to flush as much of the bleach residue from the area as possible. This year's garden was ruined, but if I rinsed down as much of the bleach as possible and diluted the damage, maybe aerated the soil, next year would have a fighting chance.

Tasks completed, we met at the center of the patio near the Adirondack chairs. Conall settled beside me, watching silently, knowing better than to interrupt but wanting to be close in case I wanted his help. I flashed back to the water blessing he and I had done before a tornado siren drove us to take shelter in a pocket of my home. Things had gotten... well, let's just say intense down there.

Yeah. Intense is one way to put it.

I shook off the memory and slid from the chair down to a patch of hot concrete just past the stained area to focus better on what I had planned.

I'd dealt with worse than this before—like the fire that took out a chunk of my upper story. A little paint? Child's play. Only instead of sending the problem stuff dispersing into the air as I had when restoring my charred home, I was trapping it.

What most people don't realize is that every thought and every action—especially those driven by raw emotions like love, hate, or fear—are charged with energy. And when those actions leave traces behind—like spray paint—that energy can be captured. In this case, in a mason jar.

Unlike the inquiry into the dirt, which had only used a bit of green witch energy, this one was going to use a little more of my Summate power. I wasn't just trying to remove the paint from the surface and disperse it into the atmosphere. I was pulling the droplets of paint from each area along with the emotional energy that had caused it to be there.

It didn't take much. A pluck of that harp string that was the constantly vibrating Source inside of me, and my mind zeroed in on each nasty word, then down to every molecule of pigment that had stained my property with those hateful words.

Within minutes, a thin layer of dirty pink gunk coated the bottom of the Mason jar. Some bits were dried flakes, others still a little gummy.

I popped the lid onto the top and whispered,

Ward within
Forever interred
Until released
Upon my word.

Conall eyed the jar's contents and grimaced. "What are you going to do with that?"

I shrugged, turning it in my hands. "Not sure yet. But I didn't see the sense in letting the energy go to waste. Might use it to track down whoever did this. I just haven't decided if it's worth it."

He rose and offered me a hand. "Probably best to cool off before you do anything."

I took his hand and got to my feet. "That's the plan."

Conall held the back door open for me as we headed inside, his hand brushing mine as I passed. "You sure you're OK?"

I glanced back at the garden, the fence, the jar on the patio glinting in midday light. "Not really. But I will be."

He gave me a lopsided smile, the kind that made my world feel a little less broken. "Good. Because I'd hate to see what happens when you're not OK."

I snorted, nudging him with my elbow as we stepped into the kitchen. "You've already seen it, Conall. And you're still here."

"Damn right I am." He flipped the lock on the door behind us and pulled me into his arms.

The air inside smelled faintly of coffee, cinnamon, and drying herbs. Safe. Home. I leaned into his arms, feeling the tension slowly drain from my shoulders. The jar and its contents were out there, sealed tight and waiting. But that was tomorrow's problem.

Right now, the world could burn, and I wouldn't care. I'd save it later.

$$)O($$

There was a part of me that didn't want to drive back to the Whelen's, that preferred the idea of curling up in my bed and ignoring the phone, ignoring my responsibilities, and turning my back on the world for the rest of the day. My backyard, once a place of peace, now felt tarnished, invaded, and defiled, leaving me feeling gross as well. Like my soul needed a shower.

Instead, I headed to the fridge, yanked it open, and stared at its contents like the answers to all my problems might hide behind the leftovers. My eyes landed on the half-empty bottle of chardonnay. For a second, I thought about it. Thought hard. But I grabbed a water bottle instead and snagged a second one for Conall.

"Thanks," he said as I handed it over. The seals cracking in unison the only sound between us.

The quiet stretched, but it wasn't an uncomfortable silence. I remained thoughtful and quiet, my mind too full of too many tumbling thoughts to say anything.

"Want to ward your backyard before we head back to La-Donna's?" Conall asked, breaking the silence.

I shook my head. "No point. The lock's on now, and I doubt they'll try anything again today. Plus, Kenny will probably get the sheriff's office to run a few extra patrols on Oberon Street to keep an extra eye on my place."

"You want to crash at my place tonight?" he offered.

I scoffed. "And give them the satisfaction of knowing they scared me? Not a chance. Anyway, if they come back, maybe I'll let them know witches aren't exactly helpless."

That earned me a laugh warm enough to chase away some of the strain. "They not only messed with a witch. They picked the Summate."

We sipped our water in tandem, the moment easing enough for me to take a deep breath that didn't feel so tight in my chest. I grabbed my phone, and Conall did the same, a signal that it was time to go.

"You OK with me staying over?" He asked.

"Am I ever *not* OK with you staying over?"

"Not so far," he said with a grin so sexy it made my knees weak, "But I like to make sure. Never hurts to ask."

His voice had that low rumble that always sent a thrill skittering down my spine, but I masked it with an exaggerated eye roll. "Let's go before you get any ideas."

He chuckled, stepping aside so I could pass. "Too late."

☽○☾

We made it to LaDonna's without taking a side trip to the bedroom, but it took some determination on both of our parts. When we arrived, I was glad we hadn't wasted time. Rita had pinpointed the Stygian lieutenant, Valeria Andersen, at her house in Savannah through some recent social media posts she'd made. While we were gone, Luke had astral projected to her location, but unfortunately, he hadn't picked up anything useful. He also hadn't been able to locate Ericka, which made it likely that Rene was right, and she was on the move.

Rita set up her lights and her phone to prepare to go live with a message from our coven. Once that was done, she paced the length of LaDonna's living room. The room smelled faintly of basil and peppermint—one for focus, the other for protection. Her fingers fluttered over the edge of her laptop as she took the last steps to start her broadcast.

"Relax," Conall said from the couch reassuringly. "You've got this."

She let out a huff. "I've got nothing unless they listen."

The WorldWide Witches weren't a formal coven in the traditional sense. No sacred circles or ceremonial robes. They were a collection of brilliant, independent minds scattered across the globe, connected by forums, live streams, and the occasional encrypted group chat. Some were healers, others scholars, and a few leaned toward chaos magic or blood rites. Getting them to work together was like herding cats, and Rita had popped open a can of tuna.

She took a deep breath and sat down at LaDonna's dining room table, adjusting the angle of her laptop camera. The live stream icon blinked, waiting for her to click it and broadcast to over three thousand witches. Most wouldn't catch it live— it was the middle of the night for half the network—but the message would spread soon enough.

"Here goes nothing," she muttered, clicking the button.

The screen filled with her reflection, and the chat window instantly populated with greetings. Handles like Shadow-Weaver79 and RuneMistress popped up in the sidebar, each accompanied by a short message.

Hey, Rita! What's this about?

Do we have any word on the Stygian?

Finally caught you live!

She leaned into the camera, her usual warm smile softening the tension in her jaw. "Hey, everyone. Thanks for showing up on short notice. I promise this isn't another webinar on keeping your familiars from wrecking your circles—though if that's still a problem, DM me."

A smattering of laughing emojis popped up in the chat. Good. Humor was a start.

"But seriously," she continued, her tone sobering, "this is urgent. Some of you may have heard about the bombing at the church in Hoover. If you haven't, here's the short version: the Stygian targeted the Fourth of July event, killing seven children and injuring dozens more. The assassination yesterday? It's connected. They're not just testing the waters—they're escalating."

The chat froze for a moment before erupting. Messages flooded the feed faster than we could read, but I caught a couple of the shorter comments.

What?!

Why wasn't this in the news here in Seattle?!

This can't be real.

Are they targeting other covens?!

Rita raised a hand, as if they could see the gesture through the screen. "I get it. It sounds insane, but this is real, and it's dangerous. Based on the statement they gave the press, the Stygian aren't just coming after Alabama. They're coming after all of us. We're not sure of their next move, but based on what we've uncovered so far, it's big. Catastrophic. Kind of like last time."

Her voice faltered for a second, and she glanced away from the screen, toward where the Lughaidh watched in silent support. She focused on the camera again. "That's where you all come in. We need your eyes, ears, and expertise. If you see or hear anything suspicious—strangers poking around magical hotspots, unexplained disturbances, anti-witch propaganda—you report it. Send it straight to my friends here in Gryphon, and we'll take it from there."

The chat slowed, the initial wave of shock giving way to questions.

How do we know the witches in Gryphon can handle this?
What's the Summate doing about it?
Do you really think we can stop them?

Rita bit her lip, leaning back slightly. I could see the tension in her shoulders. I was sure she wanted to scream that we didn't have a choice, but that wouldn't win anyone over.

"Look," she said, her tone firm but not unkind, "I know Gryphon doesn't have all the answers right now. But we have resources, and we have the Summate. If anyone can rally us, it's her. But we can't do this without you. This is bigger than any one coven, bigger than Gryphon. If we don't work together, the Stygian will win. I'm sure of that."

For a moment, the chat went silent. Then a single message popped up.

What do you need us to do?

Relief touched her eyes, but she kept her expression steady. "Stay vigilant. Share information. Keep an eye out for anything unusual, no matter how small it seems. And spread the word. The Stygian think they can pick us off one by one. Let's show them what happens when witches stand together."

More messages rolled in—agreements, questions about logistics, and offers of help. Rita let them flow, leaning back in her chair with a deep breath. Then she leaned in, fingers dancing across the keyboard as she fielded questions between her coven and the Lughaidh.

When the stream ended, she turned to us, her hands trembling slightly. "Well?" she asked, her voice tight with uncertainty.

I gave her a proud smile. "You're one hell of a witch, Rita."

Chapter 8

Despite my loud, borderline dramatic protests, the entire freaking coven followed Conall and me back to Blackwell Manor after the meeting at LaDonna and Luke's. Not all at once, of course—that would have been too simple. No, a quick conversation about protecting me from bullets fired from the unwarded street somehow snowballed into a full-blown Fourth of July-style shindig, complete with a potluck. Food and drink assignments were handed out, and the Lughaidh coven scattered to their various kitchens and Gryphon Grocery, which (thankfully) was still open until five, according to their website.

It was almost like they knew I can't cook.

The plan, ostensibly, was to extend the warding on my property to the fence line. That made sense. It also made sense that none of us really wanted to be alone right now. Strength in numbers and all that.

But what gnawed at me was the creeping suspicion that everyone else was arriving at the same unsettling conclusion I was: this time, the Stygian's reach might be too far, their scope too broad for us to push back effectively. How do you fight an enemy when you don't even know how many of them exist? There's no census for witches. Were there thousands of us? Hundreds of thousands? And out of those numbers, how many were happy to let the world burn? And how many of the so-called "good" witches even knew the Stygian existed, let alone what they were up to?

No answers. Just a lot of unsettling questions. So, we barbecued. We warded. We took control of what little we could.

While I waited for the others to show up, I sat at the butcherblock island in my kitchen with Rex sprawled next to me and a glass of homemade iced coffee sweating in my hand. Conall had been dispatched to grab his grill from his apartment, giving me a rare moment of quiet to think.

What exactly was the Stygian hoping to accomplish by revealing their existence? Their big plan to summon Sovereign Darkness had failed spectacularly. That plot had needed the stars to align just right and for the Stygian around the world to hold ceremonies at the same time. The Lughaidh had also put out a global coven call, with the help of Rita and the WorldWide Witches, and ultimately also called forth our ancestors. In the end, we'd foiled their plans and sent them scurrying.

It was also the night my father's spirit possessed Rene and helped him fight off the Stygian's Big Bad. Oh, and the night I'd found out I was half-fae. No big deal. Still didn't know what that meant. No one else in the coven had known that about Ryan Turner, my biological father. Not even my mother, apparently. I often wondered if that unusual genetic combination was what made me a Summate. Or was the world populated with thousands of people strolling around with fae blood who were absolutely clueless that they weren't entirely human?

What was the Stygian's play now? With eight billion people on the planet, what were the odds they could succeed in creating global chaos without their supernatural baddie? Did they have another Big Bad waiting in the wings? That didn't feel right. If they did, why waste time taking out politicians and planting bombs? And why send cryptic messages to the news claiming credit for their actions like some overdramatic anarchist PR team?

No, this didn't feel like a play for global domination. This felt like a tantrum. A way to stand up and scream, "Hey, we exist! Be afraid of us!" And if that was the case, maybe the best way to fight back was to prove that not all witches were assholes.

Sure, if the WorldWide Witch Coven—or whatever other network was out there—came across a Stygian plot that would actually hurt someone, they absolutely needed to tell me. I'd do everything in my Summate strength to shut it down. But this? This didn't feel like an attack. It felt like a cry for attention. It had Ericka's narcissistic thumbprint all over it.

I stirred my coffee with my long-handled spoon and watched the ice swirl in lazy clockwise circles. *Always deosil, never widdershins,* LaDonna always told me. The thought made me smile. My foster mother and I both knew the real power in the Craft wasn't in the motions themselves, but in the intent behind them. Still, we understood the value of ritual. There's something about the rhythm of it—the beauty of movement, the aroma of herbs and oils, the deliberate focus on each detail. It's not the ritual that works the magic; it's the way it shifts your mind, sharpens your focus, and sends your desires to be fulfilled by the power within the universe.

A tap came from the shop door, pulling me from my reverie. My brow furrowed. The Lughaidh always came to the kitchen door toward the back of my house when the shop was closed. So, who in the world was knocking in front on the Fourth of July?

Reminding myself that my property—the front part at least—was warded from intruders with bad intentions, I found myself tiptoeing to the coffee shop to take a peek at whoever was at the door. If it was a potential customer, I'd hope they'd have the sense to know I wasn't open during the holiday. They could come back and get their herbs or coffee another time.

The people at the door, however, were complete strangers—a woman and a man. And yet... there was something about them that drew me. They appeared to be about my age, late twenties to mid-thirties. The woman stood directly in front of the door, the man stood at her side, a backpack slung over his shoulder. He might as well have been shadowed by the sun, despite his companion's diminutive stature. I went from peeking around the swinging saloon doors to stepping through, studying the person behind it as though she was pulling me by an irresistible rope attached to my very soul.

Is she fae? Perhaps family? Could that be why I feel as though I can trust her?

Memories stirred in the back of my mind—snatches of old stories about fae traps, about Terry's endless offerings to the Seelie fairies—tumbled through my mind, setting off mental alarm bells and sirens that blared and shrieked. Still, I could no sooner have resisted the draw of this petite woman on the other side of the door than I could my next breath.

I met her at the door with my keys in my hands. She met my gaze with beautiful eyes the color of old pennies. Her smile was bright and straight. Dark brown ringlets tumbled past her shoulders. The man beside her was rangy, bald, with narrow, cunning eyes that reflected his intelligence.

Before I knew it, I was fumbling with my keys at the lock and feeling like a fool for my clumsiness. The click of the lock sounded loud in the stillness.

"Hello, Murphy," she said, her voice immediately

animated and likeable. "I'm Crystal."

"Are you... fae?" I asked, feeling stupid as the words crossed my lips, knowing somehow, now, that it wasn't the word I needed.

"No," she said, her tone brushing away my fears. "But you don't need to be afraid. Doyle and I are supernatural creatures, as you are. He's a vampire. I'm an aerocleaver. And we're here to help you."

$$\supset \bigcirc \subset$$

"I'm sorry, you're a *what*?"

Crystal squared her shoulders and met my eyes. "Aerocleaver. That's what my sister and I called it. I can cut a hole in space and connect any two places in the world. We didn't know the real name—if there even is one. I've never met anyone else who can do what I do."

My mouth flapped uselessly for a second. What exactly was the proper response to that? Eventually, I landed on, "I completely understand how that feels." Which was true.

The part of me raised on Southern hospitality screamed that I should've offered them sweet tea or at least a coffee by now. But a more pressing part of me—let's call it the survival instinct—was still processing the fact that *there was a vampire on my veranda*. Would he be stuck out there forever if I didn't invite him in? And what about the daylight? I thought vampires burst into flames or turned to ash or something, but here he was, standing in the early afternoon sun like it was no big deal other than to shrug the strap of his backpack from one shoulder to the other. He looked fine, aside from being pale as a peeled potato. There were a few red spots, like on the top of his head, but he wasn't dying.

My hand fussed with the door a little, but I clung to my

belief that bald-headed Doyle needed an invitation to come in while I evaluated what to do with these newcomers.

"You said you were here to help me?" I asked.

Crystal eyeballed the chairs behind me, but didn't make any other motions to indicate she wanted to get more comfortable before she explained. She heaved a sigh and fidgeted, her eyes rolling up into her head as if searching for the words she needed to explain.

"OK, I'm going to try to give you the shortest version I can, but there is a lot to this story. My—our—friend Jerusha has a kind of... ability. She just *knows* things sometimes."

Orange witch? I wondered, but kept my mouth shut for the time being.

"Yesterday, we were watching the news, and we saw these horrible things that were happening down in Alabama. Not in your town—"

"The church bombing in Hoover. And the shooting."

Crystal wrung her hands as she continued. "Yeah, exactly. And while Jerusha can't come right now—she's dealing with some other stuff—she said Doyle and I should come and talk to you. She said we could help."

I found myself mirroring Crystal's fidgeting as I glanced over her shoulder. Betony and Terry were pulling up, parking their cars at the curb. It struck me then: Crystal and Doyle hadn't arrived in a vehicle. Had she done her aerocleaving thing to get them to Gryphon?

"Did she say how you're supposed to help? Or how she knew to send you?"

Crystal shook her head. "No instructions, but she told me you were a witch, and we'd be going to meet other witches, too. She sensed some trouble was coming your way. Jerusha... she doesn't explain it much. It's like this wild power she has. Guides her. She calls it the Source."

It was as if she'd knocked the wind from my brain, if that makes any sense.

Almost short of breath, I swung the door open wider. "Let's talk."

☽○☾

I learned that the two of them lived in Savannah and that Jerusha was around two thousand years old, but our conversation hit the pause button as the Lughaidh coven trickled in. They arrived in ones and twos until the entire crew was under my roof, along with Rita, Lorina (who wasn't supposed to be there), and Jake's girlfriend, Cadence. As they took over my kitchen and backyard, everyone accepted the newcomers' presence as a matter of course. Meanwhile, I stuck with the one thing I knew how to do well as my contribution—making coffee.

Doyle and Crystal hovered awkwardly nearby, looking like kids at their first middle school dance until Luke drafted Doyle and Jake to haul tables and chairs from the coffee shop to the back porch. From the sound of clinking drawers, Hanna was busy giving Miriam and Terry directions in my kitchen. I swear that woman knows where things are in there better than I do.

Crystal stayed behind with me in the coffee shop, quickly getting swept up in a conversation with Betony, Lorina, and Cadence about music. The four of them took turns discussing songs saved on their phones, comparing bands and favorite tracks. When Lorina discovered that she and Crystal shared a favorite artist, Lorina started singing one of her most popular songs.

It started as something casual, but soon Crystal was gaping at Lorina's soaring mezzo-soprano. I wasn't surprised.

Lorina's voice is the kind of thing that could make angels weep—or at least leave mortals wondering how one person could sound so unearthly.

"That—that was *amazing*," Crystal gushed. "No, really. Your voice—it's almost otherworldly!"

"That's what I've been telling her," LaDonna said with her usual air of serene regalness. She grabbed a stack of napkins and a few cups, pausing to hold them up for my approval. I waved her off as I stirred chocolate into a colossal jug of iced coffee.

Jake sauntered over, his table-lifting chore complete. "She's beyond amazing—she's a freak of nature, according to the school choir director. She can sing every style of soprano there is."

"Seriously?" I asked, glancing over at Lorina, who was now trying to downplay her grin but failing miserably. "That's—that's unheard of. How is that even possible?"

"Tell me about it," Lorina said. She leaned a hand on the counter and struck a casual pose, but she beamed with the attention. She deserved it. From what I could tell, Lorina got little praise in her overly restrictive home, and seeing her soak up the spotlight made me want to hug her and tell her she was a star.

"Jake, can you help me with this?" I motioned to the heavy jug of iced coffee. "And everyone, let's take this outside. Crystal, I think it's time for you and Doyle to tell the coven why you're here."

Crystal swallowed nervously, her gaze darting toward the swinging doors leading to the kitchen and backyard where the Lughaidh coven waited. She gave a hesitant nod, then followed me and the others as we stepped outside into the golden glow of late afternoon.

Chapter 9

Standing under the last bit of shade on my porch just short of the glaring afternoon sun, I said, "Everyone, can y'all come closer so I don't have to holler?"

Conversations stopped, and the coven exchanged curious glances with one another as they drew near. Crystal stood by my right side, while Doyle—who'd been laughing at something Conall said near the grill—sauntered over to take his spot on Crystal's left.

Betony, who had been chatting with the gaggle of teens, moved slowly and cautiously away from them until she was almost within arm's reach, taking a seat at the nearby picnic table. It surprised me she didn't trip over her own feet, since her attention was locked on Doyle who, meanwhile, was either evading her scrutiny or oblivious of her intense focus on his every move.

Wonder what's up with that? I risked a quick peek at Doyle. Did she find him attractive? I wondered how old Doyle was, and if the legend about vampires not aging was true. For all I knew, the man could be centuries old. I hadn't had a chance to learn if two-thousand-year-old Jerusha was a vampire, too.

My backyard had gone silent, every eye fixed on me, waiting for introductions. The weight of expectation made my pulse skitter, but I inhaled deeply, letting a small trickle of the Source flow in and settle me. The nervousness melted away, replaced by a blissful serenity.

Crystal's head whipped toward me, her wide eyes boring into the side of my head.

Huh. Interesting. Most of the coven needed me to come into physical contact with them before they sensed the Source in me. What made Crystal so sensitive to the power? I didn't meet her gaze. No point starting a Q&A session before we got through this.

"I know some of you've already met our guests, but in case you haven't yet, this is Crystal and Doyle," I said, gesturing to them in turn. "They're not witches, but they do have supernatural gifts. They're—" I hesitated, then turned to Crystal. "Maybe it's better if you explain."

Crystal turned to Doyle. "You got the gloves?"

Doyle offered a curt nod and wordlessly pulled two pairs of silicone gloves from the knapsack he'd been carrying all this time. The coven regarded them curiously as the two donned the protective mittens. Crystal, I noticed, left one hand free.

"I'm an aerocleaver," she said. "And I know y'all don't know what that means, so I'm going to demonstrate real quick. Someone shout out a location anywhere in the world. Not a city, though. Somewhere quiet."

Brows furrowed as folks cast quick looks around, obviously wondering what this was all about. Miriam finally called out, "Arizona desert!"

Crystal nodded. "Nice. You know, I was just out there a few months ago. There's a—you know what? Never mind. OK, so what I'm going to do is... um... show you the desert. Hold on."

Turning to Doyle, she mouthed, *Ready?* He nodded, and I realized I hadn't heard the man speak this whole time.

Crystal extended a finger into the air. With her height—

which I gaged to be around five foot—the tip of her finger barely reached a point in space slightly higher than my head. The tip began to glow a bright white, and her eyes grew slightly unfocused. Her finger jabbed at nothing—but strangely, it wasn't nothing. My spirit, tapped into the Source, could tell that Crystal had touched some sort of universal fabric… and was rending a hole into it with the gentle whooshing sound that reminded me of a fire roaring to life. Her finger scored a glowing trail of light into the air. My heart hitched for a second before the part of my consciousness steeped in the Source assured me that everything was fine.

I watched, entranced, as Crystal quickly donned the second silicone mitt. Together, she and Doyle edged their fingers into the white-hot line and pulled in opposite directions, the air splitting open like a curtain being drawn back. Beyond lay an uninhabited stretch of what appeared to be an Arizona desert. Saguaro cacti clawed at a vast, cloudless sky, and purple mountains loomed on the horizon. In the forefront, desert brush peppered the landscape.

The coven watched in a mix of fascination and disbelief, each jockeying for position in order to peek through the hole, which was only about eighteen inches wide. I wasn't sure what to think myself, so I stepped closer to the fissure in space. When I was within an arm's reach of the rift, a breeze drifted through and hit my face. My eyes batted from the dry desert air, the sensation pure and weightless, unlike the humid Alabama air I was used to.

It was clearly an effort to maintain the hole; the muscles in their forearms both tensed with the exertion, though Doyle's effort was clearly much less than Crystal's. Once the coven had all had an opportunity to see for themselves what Crystal was capable of, our guests released the hold they had on the flaps of space. The glowing edges grew nearer and nearer, like a piece of paper burning itself in reverse, until nothing remained.

"That was amazing," Cadence said from her spot beside Betony, a long finger twined with a lock of her frizzy blond hair.

"It's come in handy," Crystal said with a modest smile and a raise of her dark eyebrows. "Sure saves on gas."

A titter of laughter broke out among the coven, and I sensed everyone relaxing a bit.

"What about you, Doyle?" Jake asked. "What's your superpower?"

Doyle's eyes were the color of ice, I noticed, and his effort to appear friendly seemed strained. If not for my finger on the Source coursing through me, I might have doubted his intentions.

"I'm a—a vampire," he said, his tone sounding almost like an apology. His voice reminded me a little of Jerry Seinfeld, but without the nasal quality of the famous comedian.

Silence fell over the group.

"Like, an energy vampire, or…?" Rene stood next to Jake, his hands on his hips, and although Jake stood a good head and shoulders over Rene, the young man looked ready to jump through the group and tackle Doyle if need be, vampire or no vampire.

Doyle rolled his eyes and frowned slightly. "Like, um…" He opened his mouth wide, pulling back a cheek with his index finger. As we watched, his canines grew from the normal human size to the elongated fangs of legend.

"Holy shit," Jake said.

Chapter 10

Have I mentioned that I have the most awesome coven family on earth? Not only did they keep their cool when Doyle revealed his fangs, but they let Crystal and Doyle lay their story out without so much as a raised eyebrow.

They shared a history of the vampire race and a centuries-old feud between dark vampires, who thrive on human blood, and those who refuse to feed from people. About how Doyle had helped the woman who was the world's oldest living vampire escape her sire, who then perished in battle. And about the fact that the world contains multiple thousands of beings not unlike ourselves—those who walk among humans, who live, and work, and commune with humankind, while hiding a part of their nature most of the world refuses to believe exists.

"How long have you been a vampire?" Jake asked.

Doyle offered a faint smile, his shoulders relaxing slightly. "Compared to most, I'm just a kid. Hundred and twenty-five years old. And for some reason, my vampire abilities haven't, you know, grown as fast as others' do."

"His growth was stunted," Crystal joked with a teasing wrinkle of her nose.

He shot her a sideways look, his piercing blue eyes sweeping her from head to toe. "Yeahyeahyeah. Look who's talking."

Crystal crossed her arms and rolled her eyes, but the corner of her mouth twitched in amusement as good-natured laughter ensued.

"What brings you to Gryphon?" LaDonna asked.

The good humor faded as Doyle's expression grew serious. He licked his lips, sharing a glance with Crystal before taking a breath and stepping back into his role of storyteller.

"That old vampire I mentioned—Jerusha—she had a hunch. Said you might need our help. That the witch… situation you've got going here is about to blow up."

"This friend of theirs can access the Source, too," I explained. "Crystal has said that's what she calls the power she wields. I don't think it's a coincidence."

Crystal's brows drew together, and she scanned my yard like she was expecting someone to hand her a map to the answers. "But why here? Why now? Gryphon's adorable, sure, but it's also tiny. Why would a coven trying to trigger a magical doomsday pick this place?"

I straightened, feeling the weight of their eyes on me. It was time to reveal our role in the story. "Because of me," I said. No point in sugarcoating it. "A Summate, which is what I am, only comes along once every three hundred years. I have the unusual blessing of being able to wield all varieties of witch powers. Add Betony to the mix—our chaos witch, who's just as rare—and we're basically a supernatural powder keg waiting for a spark."

"Not to mention that I'm the son of the Stygian coven's high priestess," Rene added. "And I sort of defected."

Crystal let out a low whistle. "Well, that explains the vibe here."

"The Stygian might very well come after us again," I said, my voice steady despite the weight of the words. I glanced at Doyle and Crystal, realizing they were still catching up. "Let me backtrack for you two."

I dove into a quick recap, keeping it to the highlights: what had happened last February, when the Stygian coven tried to raise the Sovereign Darkness to help them sow global chaos, and how we'd beaten them back.

Then I shifted gears, recounting the epiphany I'd had earlier today, back at the coffee shop with Rex—before the barbecue, before the commotion and the unexpected arrival of Doyle and Crystal with their shiny new powers.

"I think the Stygian are playing a different game now," I said, crossing my arms. "They're still aiming for chaos, but not the kind they need a giant shadow demon to pull off. They're trying to scare the world into fearing witches. All witches."

Crystal tilted her head, her eyebrows knitting together. "Why? What's the point?"

"Control," I said simply. "People are easier to manipulate when they're terrified."

Silence followed, thick with unspoken agreement. This wasn't just a theory—it fit too well. The kind of insidious logic the Stygian would gladly embrace.

I took a deep breath, the words tumbling from me before doubt could take hold. "I think our best bet is to come out of the broom closet. Or at least test the waters and see where it leads."

That got their attention. All eyes turned to me, some wide, others narrowed, all waiting for an explanation.

"We've talked about it before," I continued, the truth humming through me as the Source tuned me into the message I needed to relay. "And I believe this with everything I have: there are more good witches in the world than bad ones. I don't know how I know it—I just do. And if we step out into the light, if we show people who we really are, that we're not the monsters hiding under their beds…" My voice softened, but the conviction had folks listening intently. "We could stop them. The Stygian's fear-mongering only works if we let them dictate the narrative."

My heart pounded with a rhythm that wasn't just mine—something deeper, connected to that virtuous force within me. It wasn't just a hunch. It was true. I felt it like a current running through my veins.

"Well," Doyle said after a beat, his lips quirking in a faint smile. "If we're going for full disclosure, maybe someone should tell the world that vampires don't hang out in old castles or sparkle in the sun."

Crystal snorted, and the tension everyone had been displaying eased enough for the corners of my mouth to lift.

"Baby steps," I said, but the fire in my chest stayed lit. This was how we'd win.

Silence lingered for a moment as folks processed the idea of letting the world in on our secret. Then Conall broke in with, "Anyone still hungry?"

Before anyone could answer, Luke appeared, backing through my screen door and stepping into the moment like he owned it. He carried a tray of glasses, their contents fizzing and golden in the bright summer light. "I've got a better idea," he said.

Dang, he was good. His orange witch premonition skills had seen a need coming, and he'd filled it just in time. I hadn't even seen him sneaking into my house.

The glasses were passed around. Even the teens got one, though their faces scrunched in a mix of indignation and disappointment when they discovered their bubbly was ginger ale, not champagne. "Deal with it," I said with a smirk, lifting my flute. "You're not old enough for the real stuff yet."

Luke stepped back, a glint of mischief in his eye. All eyes

turned to him, waiting for the inevitable toast. He was famous for them in our little group.

He lifted his champagne flute high. "To us," he began, his voice deep and powerful. "To fighting the fights worth fighting, and to standing together when it counts. To the witches who stand in the light, the ones who walk in the shadows, and those who are still finding their way. And to every unexpected ally and uninvited guest who makes this unbelievable ride we call life just a little more survivable." He tipped his glass toward Doyle and Crystal with a wry smile before lifting it higher. "Here's to what comes next. May we be ready for it—whatever it is. *Sláinte mhòr.*"

"*Sláinte mhòr,*" the coven echoed. I turned to our visitors. "Great health," I explained.

"To your health," Doyle replied with a smile and a raised glass.

Glasses clinked, and the moment was sealed. Whatever came next, we'd face it together.

Chapter 11

"Goddess Hestia of the hearth, hear us. Goddess Brighid, protector of homes, hear our call…"

Once again, my coven was helping me ward my property—this time extending the protection to cover the entire backyard up to the fence. We'd waited until dusk to avoid attracting the attention of nosy neighbors who might think we were hosting a backyard séance. Not that they were entirely wrong—we were up to witchy stuff. And while I have a privacy fence surrounding my yard, I also have some tall coven members.

Fireworks popped, whizzed, and fizzled in the distance, the soundtrack of a small Southern town's Independence Day. The noise covered the sound of our ritual chants as we called to the north, south, east, and west, wielding the power of fire, earth, air, water, and finally, spirit. Our voices blended as we pleaded to the ancestors for guidance, and the air around my yard shimmered, catching the dim light like glitter on black velvet.

This time, the air around my yard glimmered as if dusted with multicolored glitter. It was easier to see in the twilight. I reckoned the neighbors would write it off as the aftereffects of fireworks. And as the circle of energy fell over my yard in a dome reminiscent of stardust, it was more breathtaking than any pyrotechnic display on earth. The mingling scents of ozone, earth, and freshly crushed pine drifted on the warm air, layered with the faint sulfur residue of firework explosions.

"Blessed be," we all murmured in unison, breaking the sacred circle. I took a slow walk along the perimeter, my third eye wide open, scanning the new barrier's strength. Thin as lightbulb glass and stronger than iron, it wasn't visible to the naked eye, but I could feel it. Besides the physical barrier, the new ward worked like a psychic shield, scrambling the brains of anyone looking to pick a fight until they forgot what they came for and wandered off.

When we were done, Doyle was full of questions about the craft, including what the various powers allowed us to do. When I told him Joey's specialty as a black witch was protection, he interrupted me.

"So let me get this straight," he said, pacing as he spoke. "You're saying Joey's a black protection witch?"

"Exactly," I replied, ready for the next volley.

"But your coven just did a protection spell on your yard. So, uh, how does that work if Joey's the only one with protection powers?"

"Good question," I said. "It's a kind of spiritual loophole. We can all protect what is ours, which extends to our homes and families. And the Lughaidh coven is my family. They're all I have left. My parents are both gone. LaDonna, the high priestess, is—was—my foster mother. She raised me after my mother was killed."

"She's my foster mother now," Betony interjected almost protectively.

"LaDonna helped raise both of you?" Crystal said. "And you're both so unusual?"

"So's LaDonna," Betony replied with a fond look at our high priestess, who was laughing heartily at something her husband had said.

"She didn't really raise me," Betony said. "I didn't move in with LaDonna until a few months ago. But my parents were pretty messed up. My dad's gone now, and my mom went to jail." I noted how Betony glossed over the fact that she'd been the one to take her father's life, and her mom was still on the run after breaking out of prison.

Seeing how Conall, Terry, and Miriam had begun cleaning up the remnants of the cookout, I excused myself from the conversation to help them, trusting that Betony would answer any questions that came up.

As my friends wrapped leftovers in aluminum foil and plastic containers, I hefted my mammoth glass beverage dispenser—emptied of its coffee but still sloshing with milky water from melted ice—into the kitchen and dumped it into the sink, watching the cloudy liquid swirl down the drain.

On the other side of the swinging double doors, Lorina and Jake were engaged in a heated discussion. Maybe I was quiet enough that they hadn't noticed me coming in. Maybe Lorina didn't care if I heard what she had to say. The two of them never argued, though, so I paused to see what had driven them to fight.

"You just jumped right in with them and didn't even ask questions," Lorina pressed. "You didn't think to ask how slim the odds are that you're a blue witch? You start hanging out with Betony and Murphy and them, and suddenly you're a music witch? Don't you think that's a little convenient?"

"Ever think maybe you are, too?" Jake countered. "Your voice is insane, Lorina. Your range isn't *normal*. What if your magic's in your voice?"

Lorina scoffed. "Like our shit-little town is the hub of a fuck-ton of magical power. I'm a freak of nature, not a witch."

"We're both freaks," Jake offered. "That's why we're friends."

I almost slipped out of the kitchen, convinced they didn't need me to mediate, when Lorina's voice softened.

"What if... what if my folks are right? What if witches are all bad?"

The chair Jake sat on creaked under his bulk as he moved. "That doesn't make sense. You've said it yourself. You'd rather be here than with them. And you've known me since middle school. You don't think I'm bad, do you? Doesn't that tell you something?"

There was a quiet scratching noise. I didn't need to see Lorina to know she was doing the thing where she ran a fingernail through a crack in the Formica tabletop.

"Maybe it's... you know... a spell or something."

Jake scoffed. "You don't honestly believe that."

"I don't know. I'm just... just be careful, OK? When I'm not around?"

Jake's laugh was soft, almost fond. "Yeah, like your scrawny ass could totally be my bodyguard."

The back door to the kitchen swung open, and Terry and Miriam entered with a clamor of laughter and rattling dishes, Conall trailing them, their hands laden with leftovers.

"Where would you like us to put this, Murphy?" Terry asked.

I plastered on a smile and gestured to the counter. "Right over here. Let's make some room."

Even as Terry and Miriam's cheerful chatter filled the kitchen, my mood didn't quite shift. My mind replayed the soft, almost broken tone in Lorina's voice when she said, *What if witches are all bad?*

The clatter of dishes plopped onto my zinc countertop brought me back to the moment, and I forced a grin for Terry and Miriam, who were already arguing about how best to organize the leftovers. Conall leaned casually against the doorframe, his intelligent eyes taking in the room and my mood. He motioned for me to approach him because he was whispering distance from the ladies attempting to Tetris boxes of food into my small refrigerator.

"Everything okay?" he asked, low enough that only I could hear.

Lorina was Jake's friend, not mine, but the thought of losing that gangly girl to her parents' backward nonsense hit harder than I liked. Jake would be wrecked if his band lost their singer—and honestly, I couldn't blame him.

As Marina turned to hand me a stack of plastic containers, I couldn't help but glance over the swinging doors to the table where Jake and Lorina sat. They weren't talking anymore, but Jake reached across the table, his broad hand steadying Lorina's jittering fingers. She didn't pull away.

Sometimes, the most potent spells aren't made of words or gestures. They are the kind you don't even know you're casting—minor acts of trust, threads of connection. And sometimes, if you weren't careful, those threads frayed faster than you could weave them back together. I hoped for Jake and Lorina that their friendship would weather the storms of life. Things change fast at that age. Sometimes too fast. But if anything deserved a shot at making it through, it was the way those two looked out for each other.

Chapter 12

There were too many mature trees on my street for it to have a decent fireworks show, but there was a neighbor (whose name I've never caught) who lived on Beatrice Bend—the crossroad to Oberon Street—who always put on a helluva show. Positioned as he was in a cul-de-sac between Gryphon High School's football field and Walker Hill Cemetery, and only two town blocks away from Blackwell Manor, he was in a perfect position to take advantage of an exception the town made for Gyphon High School to set off the occasional firework display. While this guy wasn't setting them off at the school, his adorable Craftsman bungalow was close enough to slide under the radar.

And boy, did he milk that loophole for all it was worth.

Heck, the folks at Walker Hill Cemetery liked the display so much, they'd started holding off on locking the gates until the last spark fizzled. People came from all over, dragging foldable chairs and blankets, kids toting glow sticks and sparklers like they were Olympic torches. Coolers clinked, wagon wheels creaked, and the hum of pre-show chatter filled the air with a low buzz of expectation. For a little town like Gryphon, where a trip to Huntsville was a pretty long trek, this was as good as it got.

This year was no exception. We unpacked a cooler of sodas and some contraband beverages, stuffing empty cans into a brown paper bag to keep things tidy. Crystal and Betony shared a quilt with Conall and me. When LaDonna and Luke weren't paying attention, I slipped Betony sips of the Prosecco that Conall and I had stashed in our wagon.

The first burst of fireworks lit the sky, scattering flecks of gold like celestial glitter, and the crowd let out a collective "Ooh." I leaned back against Conall's broad chest, his warm arms wrapping around me. Soon, the air smelled of spent gunpowder and summer grass, evoking a wonderful nostalgia.

Every explosion repainted the night sky. Crimson chrysanthemums bloomed, fading into shimmering blue willows that dripped like brilliant waterfalls. Spiraling golden comets shot upward, their white-hot tails snapping like the crack of a whip. The crowd gasped and murmured, each firework met with awe, as though this wasn't an annual event but some miracle unfolding above us.

We sat silently for a while, letting the show wash over us, until my thoughts wandered back to why we were there in the small community that allowed events like this to happen. Sure, Gryphon wasn't perfect. There were still vandals and bigots who couldn't mind their own business, but the good outweighed the bad. Most of the time.

"Conall?" I whispered.

"Hmm?"

"What do you think about using a town hall meeting to come out of the broom closet?"

Conall pondered my question for a moment. His chest rose and fell beneath me as he pondered the question.

"Why not contact the local media?"

I shook my head. "Too much chance the story will be picked up by other outlets. I don't want to address the whole world all at once. I'd rather start with Gryphon."

Conall was quiet, his thumb tracing slow circles against my skin. "How were you planning to address it, exactly?"

I fidgeted a little and brushed an ant from scurrying up my calf before settling back in his arms.

"I don't know. I was thinking I could bring up the way my yard was damaged as a talking point and take it from there."

He interlaced his fingers with mine. "That'd be a good way to get into the meeting. The vandalism. It'd open the door up to the topic. What were you thinking?"

"I thought that whoever in the coven feels ready to come forward should be there. I know LaDonna and Luke will support me. And you."

He kissed my temple. "Of course. And my father. Hanna. Her father, too."

"I'm not sure about the rest. I don't want anyone risking their livelihood. Poor Miriam just got back on her feet after losing her job."

He nodded, a motion I felt more than saw.

"Terry'll probably go, I imagine."

Crystal leaned in, her voice mischievous. "Doyle and I will come too. We'll tell everyone witches aren't the only weirdos in Gryphon."

Betony wrinkled her nose. "Are you sure Doyle should be there?"

I glanced at the next quilt over, where Doyle and Joey were deep in conversation, their faces glowing in the bursts of fireworks, and I wondered if he had superhuman hearing.

"Why wouldn't he be?" I asked.

Betony gave a shrug that struggled to appear cavalier. "I don't know. Maybe Gryphon isn't ready for vampires yet. It barely seems ready for witches. I mean, think about your yard…" She let the statement trail off, and I considered it.

She has a point. Vampires are known predators. Maybe baby steps are the way to go. Overall, I loved and trusted my neighbors, but clearly there were exceptions to the rule. If some of us came forward, it might give the town time to adjust, to see that we weren't a threat.

"I'll start small," I murmured. "We'll figure it out." Maybe this October, I could organize a canned food drive for Samhain. Something practical, something tangible. If we showed Gryphon we were here to help, not hurt, maybe we could chip away at their fears and show we weren't all unhinged like the Stygian.

Conall rested his chin on my shoulder. "They'll see, Murph. It'll just take time."

A deafening crackle-popper lit the sky in brilliant violet streaks, illuminating the smiles on the faces around me. My coven. Jake and Cadence. Lorina. Rene. Gryphon wasn't perfect, but it was worth fighting for.

Chapter 13

I took the weekend to contact each coven member individually. It was exhausting, but necessary to allow everyone to speak with me individually. I didn't want anyone to feel pressured to expose their beliefs just because everyone else in the coven did. Nearly everyone agreed to come forward. The only holdout was Miriam, but I couldn't blame her. It's hard to risk your neck when living paycheck to paycheck.

All told, our lineup included LaDonna, Luke, Terry, Joey, Rafael (Hanna's father), Paul (Conall's dad), Jake, Betony, Hanna, Conall, and me. Rene planned to join in, too, though he wasn't officially part of the coven. Yet.

Monday morning, after the morning coffee rush at Witch's Brew, I sat behind the counter where I could monitor the door and called the number listed for the Gryphon City Council office.

A woman answered, her voice conjuring the unmistakable image of a grandmother with a frothy perm and half-glasses dangling on a beaded chain.

"City Council Office, Pepper Shaw speaking. With whom do I have the pleasure of speaking?"

I cleared my throat. "Um... Ms. Shaw, this is Murphy Blackwell. I own Witch's Brew downtown—"

"Oh. Yes. I'm familiar with it." Her voice tightened with a note that might've been disdain—or maybe just the edge of a busy Monday morning. I couldn't tell. "What can I do for you?"

"My shop was vandalized, and I—"

"That's a police matter, hon. Not something the council can help with." This time, the edge in her voice left no doubt—her hostility was certain.

"No, I—I've already spoken to the police," I rushed. "This isn't about that specifically. I'd like to address the council about the recent attacks in our state. If you've been watching the news, you know there's a group causing trouble and blaming it on witches. I want to—"

There was a sniff, followed by a faint tsk. "You'll need to go online and request to be added to the agenda. Meetings are the first Tuesday of every month at six p.m. and the third Thursday at nine a.m."

"Do—do you think I'd be able to be added to tomorrow night's agenda?"

She left me dangling for an uncomfortably long pause. "I don't know, hon. You'll have to go online and see for yourself."

"Do you know if the city mayor goes to all of them?"

"I have no idea, honey. I just work the desk."

Maybe it was her tone, or perhaps it was her dismissive attitude and the way she kept calling me *honey*, but I got the impression she did, in fact, know, but didn't feel like telling me. Maybe I was being paranoid and reading too much into things. The attack on my backyard had me wondering just how many people in town had it in for me.

I forced a polite, "Thank you for your time."

"M-hm," was her only response. Since I was feeling a little pissy, and yes, a little petty, I sent a little charge through the phone to zap her in the ear before she hung up. Not much; she probably wrote it off as static electricity. Just enough to make me feel a little better about her rudeness. I smiled a bit when I heard a soft exclamation she made when it hit her.

Following the advice of the obnoxious Pepper Shaw, I used my phone to browse online for the municipal calendar. I found that easily enough, and it was clear what days had meetings planned. But it took some doing to uncover where to propose future agenda topics, and there was no information on when—or if—I'd find out if my topic would be addressed. Maybe that would pop up after I filled out the form, but it seemed like a lot of work for potentially nothing.

I bit my lip and stared in frustration at the tiny calendar squares on my screen. On the left, I noted the link to the page for the Mayor's Office.

Fuck it. Might as well give it a shot.

I clicked there and was greeted by a picture of the town mayor, Yamato Tanaka. I knew nothing about him other than being familiar with his name from the many election signs around town when I was in high school. It was a memorable name because he was from one of the few Asian families in town. I recalled how his charisma and obvious knowledge of the workings of Gryphon won the town over, and he won in a landslide.

He seems like a nice guy. Maybe I should go straight to the top.

A digital envelope on the screen indicated I could email him. There was also a phone number.

The store was still empty. I decided to go for it and dialed the number.

Here goes nothing.

A cheerful voice answered after two rings. "Mayor Tanaka's office, Taylor speaking."

"Hi, my name is Murphy Blackwell. I own Witch's Brew, the coffee shop at Oberon and Beatrice Bend—"

"Oh, I *love* your shop!" Taylor gushed. "Your French roast is a*mazing*."

The unexpected compliment threw me off. "Oh—uh, thank you. That's kind of you to say. I was wondering if Mayor Tanaka might be available?"

"You're in luck! He had a cancellation this morning. Let me transfer you."

Well damn. That was easy.

Mayor Tanaka answered right away, his voice balancing the narrow line between authoritative and charming with ease. "Ms. Blackwell, nice to speak with you. Taylor said you had a concern?"

"Mayor Tanaka, thank you for taking my call. I was hoping to address the city council—and you—at tomorrow's meeting."

"Regarding the recent attacks?" His tone was calm but edged with justifiable concern.

"Yes, sir. My home—my yard, actually—was vandalized, and clearly by people who are anti-witch if the graffiti they left behind is any sign. I've spoken with Officer Hendricks, but I'd like to speak publicly. People need to understand that witches aren't the threat that the Stygian group claims they are."

A heavy silence fell on the line, and my pulse quickened.

"Ms. Blackwell," he said carefully, "are you saying that you're a witch?"

I hesitated, then took the plunge. "Yes, sir. I am."

"I see." Another lengthy pause, during which a million and one scenarios played out in my head. He'd turn me down, and I'd have to come up with another plan. He'd say no, and then I'd wind up finding my business suddenly shut down for some convoluted reason dreamed up by official bureaucrats. He'd say yes, but add a bunch of stipulations on what I could or could not say.

"Are you sure you want to do this?"

I paused. Blinked. This was one scenario I hadn't expected—him wanting to make sure I was ready to face the consequences. But more telling was what I heard in his voice with that last question: a hint of protectiveness. And then I knew.

He was one of us.

I didn't know *what* separated Mayor Tanaka from the average human, but in my spirit, I was positive he was trying to look out for me. To make sure I understood the potential ramifications of exposing what I was and what I could do.

"I'm... sure, sir."

There was a brief sound of the phone being moved around as Mayor Tanaka did something on his end. I heard the faint tapping of computer keys.

"Can you be ready by tomorrow evening's meeting? Six o'clock?"

I swallowed a hard lump of what turned out to be nothing in my throat. "Yes. I'll be ready."

The call ended, and I set my phone down, staring at it for a long moment, my thoughts racing. Yamato Tanaka, the charming, handsome mayor of Gryphon, was now aware of what I was—and he, too, was something not entirely human. And that potentially made him an ally who understood the weight of what I was about to do.

I really hoped he was on our side.

Chapter 14

I woke up on Tuesday with a sense of optimism, which should've been my first clue the day was going to hell. My coven and I had plans to stand before the town council that night, bare our magical souls, and convince the fine, upstanding people of Gryphon that we weren't like the Stygian—no ominous chanting or midnight sacrifices here. After all, we'd been active community members for years, and no one had suspected a thing about most of us. I was the only one who chose to stand out, and even that wasn't terribly risky—most folks just thought witches were powerless, harmless eccentrics with an affection for the esoteric and mystical.

Rene helped me handle the morning rush, slinging cappuccinos and scones like the pro he is, then parked himself across from me at a corner table once the rush was done. Sunlight streamed through the café windows as we worked on what I was planning to say to the council. It was hard not to feel like a kid practicing for a school debate. Rene, being a senior in high school and the resident Shakespeare of our group, added just the right amount of polish. Around noon, Jake and Cadence joined us, followed shortly by Betony, who brought word that LaDonna was on her way. Together, we cobbled together a speech that balanced sincerity and Southern charm. Jake's ability to write lyrics shone in his contribution. Still, I wanted to run it by LaDonna first to make sure it didn't sound too full of youthful idealism.

Then lunchtime hit, and my optimism turned into exhaustion. A few members of the town might've had their suspicions about me and my coven, but if so, they weren't above buying coffee and pastries from a woman with "Witch" hanging on a sign out front. Customers browsed the shop's shelves, chatting about how lavender was great for sleep or wondering aloud what dragon's blood incense even smelled like. It was business as usual, right up until the mood shifted, like the breath you hold just before a crash.

It started subtly—a twist in my mind that told me something was off. Then I noticed the wide eyes and slack jaws at every table. Nearly everyone was glued to their phones, which wasn't unusual, but the expressions sure were. People didn't scroll through cat videos or food reels with faces that looked like they'd been hit by a stunning spell. My stomach tightened.

I don't keep a television in the café. Never saw the point. I barely used the one upstairs in my living room. So I was flying blind as I hurried to finish with my last customer, trying not to let their fumbling with loose change make me lose my patience. Finally, I was free. I rushed to the table where Rene, Jake, Cadence, and Betony huddled, their faces locked on a tiny phone screen.

"What's going on?" I asked, leaning over the table.

Rene wordlessly tilted the phone so I could see, and my heart dropped into my shoes.

The screen showed downtown Washington D.C. under a cloudless blue sky—or it would've been cloudless, if not for the massive flock of birds. A writhing, screeching mass filled the air like a living storm made of feathers, claws, and beaks. Hawks, crows, sparrows, and pigeons swirled together in impossible patterns, swooping and diving in unison as if choreographed.

The camera panned shakily, revealing people running blindly away from the open plaza, or else frozen along the edges of the Reflecting Pool, their heads tilted back in disbelief. The still water mirrored the chaos above—rippling with each wingbeat, then settling with eerie calm as the birds formed shapes in the sky. Geometric patterns shifted into symbols too ancient to comprehend, yet primal enough to stir something uncomfortable deep in my chest.

If it weren't so terrifying, it would've been damned beautiful.

Then, as one, the birds froze midair. For a long second, the crowd held its breath. And then they fell.

Hundreds—maybe thousands—of birds plummeted like stones, their bodies thudding against sidewalks, slapping into the water, or, worst of all, crashing into people frozen in place. The reflecting pool rippled with impact as feathers and broken wings scattered across the marble and grass. Screams ripped through the gathering as panicked hands swatted away the dead birds. The camera jolted as the person filming turned to run, but not before catching one last wide shot: a landscape blanketed in blood, feathers, and broken wings, with the Reflecting Pool turning red beneath the plumed wreckage.

My blood ran cold. The Stygian had struck again.

)O(

Once again, I spent the quiet part of the afternoon glued to my phone as I researched what people around the country were saying about the event in D.C. What I saw shocked me.

Nobody could agree.

There was live footage from over thirty people of the event circulating the internet, and someone had even live-streamed it. And yet, the internet was a battlefield of opinions, each more bizarre than the last.

"That's my worst nightmare. I'm terrified of birds. NOPE NOPE NOPE."

"This has to be a deepfake. People will believe anything."

"Why won't the government admit chemtrails are real? It's not like we're not gonna notice when stuff like this happens in broad daylight!"

"Fake. Look at the shadows on the grass and the reflection in the water—totally superimposed. CGI, 100%."

"Y'all, my aunt was visiting when this happened. She said it was REAL. She's freaking out!"

"Yeah, okay, your 'aunt' saw it. Sure. Too bad people aren't waking up to the fact that the government is drugging the birds."

"It wasn't the government. There were people there controlling the birds. If you zoom in from :30-:35 you can see them in the background."

"Some people will do anything for hits."

"The Stygian aren't even real. Grow up."

"So let me get this straight: the same group that shot a dude and set off a bomb is now using birds? What is this, a bad movie?"

"You guys seriously believe this crap? It's probably a rogue military experiment or something."

"What kind of terrorist group does so many different things? That doesn't even make sense."

"A shooting, a bomb, and now BIRDS? LOL. This is just a bunch of unrelated stuff people are connecting for no reason."

"Unrelated? That's exactly what they want you to think. Look up the Stygian manifesto. They warned us this would happen."

"My cousin said the Stygian are just a cover for some shadow government operation. Like, they're not even real. They're the scapegoats."

"Y'all can keep doubting, but this has Stygian written all over it. Watch. Next week, it'll be something even crazier. Maybe sooner!"

"Meanwhile, the government's just sitting there like, 'It's fine. Let's wait until it's raining frogs.'"

The comments kept piling up—wild theories, sarcastic jokes, and the occasional alarmist rant—but one thing was clear: nobody knew what to believe.

When the time came to head to the town council meeting, I wondered which side the folks of Gryphon were on.

Miriam, thankfully, had volunteered to keep my shop open for the last couple of hours since she wasn't joining us there. I could've closed early, but the determined look in her eyes when she offered told me she needed this—something small she could do to feel like she was helping the coven. She arrived a few minutes after five, still wearing her work slacks and blouse. Tossing her blazer on the chair behind the counter, she grabbed the red-and-white-striped apron hanging in the storeroom, the one that said, "Coffee Is My Favorite Potion."

"It's the least I can do," she said, shooing me toward the door before I could argue.

Rene, fresh from the shower, met me in the kitchen, and together he and I piled into my Corolla and drove the short distance to city hall. He'd even shaved. I wondered if his attention to detail was for the benefit of the council members or if he was trying to impress someone. Then I wondered if Lorina was planning to join us.

Probably not. Her parents would never allow it.

By the time we pulled into the lot, Conall's Jeep was

already there, parked in the back. I slid into the space next to him and double-checked my purse. My notes were still there—a page full of scribbles and mostly finished thoughts with last-minute ideas added to the margins, barely legible, but hopefully enough to make our case tonight.

We were early. Half an hour early. But I wanted time to rally the troops and go over the speech the kids and I had planned.

Rene, predictably, sat in the car, still staring at his phone as I stood to join Conall. Teenagers.

I met Conall with an enormous hug. He smelled fresh out of the shower, too. In his case, he'd had to wash off a day of construction.

"Did you see about the birds?" I asked.

He nodded, wiping a hand through his still-damp hair, his expression grim. "Yeah. I saw it. Do you really think it was the Stygian this time?"

"Yes," I said without hesitation. "I don't know what footage you saw, but the one we watched showed the birds forming sigils. It wasn't random—it was a spell. They must've had a group of green witches working together to pull it off."

Rene got out of the car, his eyes still glued to the phone.

"Y'all, come here," he said, his voice tight.

I raised a brow at the "y'all"—he swore he'd never use Southern slang. The rest of me was too focused on the alarm written all over his face to tease him.

He held out his phone. Ericka Moore's face filled the screen, her pointed features as polished and unnerving as ever.

For a split second, I thought she'd called him and he'd foolishly answered. Then I realized she was live-streaming.

Behind her, a motley group of people stood in a loose semi-circle. I didn't need an introduction to know these were the green witches responsible for the chaos in D.C. The rag-tag assortment of people in mismatched clothes and hooded cloaks practically screamed "Stygian."

"So some of you think what happened earlier today wasn't real," she was saying, disdain oozing with every word. "Explain this."

She raised her chin at the group behind her, and as one, they turned their attention to an enormous group of rabbits trapped inside a large wire cage. A hooded figure raised the door and snapped it in place so the rabbits could escape. None of them did.

Half of the hooded group beckoned to the rabbits, who shuddered, their fur fluffing as they did so. This time, the creatures under their influence hopped over the stretch of ground in a slow, synchronized procession, forming a long, perfectly straight line through the dirt pasture. The synchronicity of their movements was so unnatural as to be unnerving.

The other half of the witches motioned to something off screen.

"What are they doing?" Rene asked, his voice a hushed whisper.

"Something bad," Conall muttered.

On the screen, the rabbits, huddled in a mass of fur, twitched their ears but didn't show any other signs of stress. Instead, their noses wiggled adorably. A few more astute rabbits' ears folded against their back. They looked ready to run, but they stayed put as if locked in place.

That was when I heard the horses' hooves growing louder. The camera panned to the right, where a herd was galloping into view.

Rene's phone was too small to do justice to what must have sounded like a stampede in the field where the Stygian held their demonstration. All the rabbits on the path trembled now, their bodies twitching as if they wanted to speed away but couldn't. The compulsion kept them rooted in place. To the point that they did absolutely nothing as the horses reached them. I flinched as the first horse trampled through the cluster of fur, and the rabbits let out a chorus of high, keening wails. It rose in sudden, jagged bursts as the first hooves met fragile bone, then multiplied, swelling into a chorus of shrieks that curdled the air. The colony was trampled, one by one, their bodies crushed under the stampede, leaving behind only a swirl of fur, blood, and dust.

"Oh, those poor creatures," I breathed.

"Jesus Christ," Rene sputtered.

Ericka's voice returned as the camera swung back around to her face, cold and smug. "Still think it's fake?"

The live stream ended abruptly, the screen cutting to black with an echoing silence that left the three of us standing in the parking lot like statues. My mind raced, trying to piece together what I'd just witnessed. Despite what Ericka thought she'd proved, she undoubtedly only gave folks more footage to argue about. And they hadn't even waited a day before pulling another stunt. It was like they were desperate to make a point.

"Murphy," Conall said softly, snapping me out of my spiraling thoughts.

The Whelens' old Mercedes rattled into the lot. LaDonna spotted us and swung her car toward our corner. I pulled my crumpled notes from my purse, the paper catching on a stray receipt, which I stuffed back inside. I wanted LaDonna and Luke to review them before we went in.

"It's never going to end," I muttered, the words slipping out before I could stop them.

"What's never going to end?" Conall asked.

"The Stygian," I said, louder now. "They'll keep doing this. Pushing. Trying to prove. Scaring people into seeing them, and all it's going to do is stir up more arguments. The louder they scream, the more the rest of the world will fight over what's real. And when that's not enough, they'll find something worse to do, just to make sure no one can ignore them. It's never going to end."

Conall's jaw tightened, and Rene gave me a look that was somewhere between worry and disbelief.

I shook my head. "You can line up a hundred rabbits, crush them under a stampede, and still not change a single mind. Like Dostoevsky said—*A hundred suspicions don't make a single proof, just as a hundred rabbits don't make a horse.* People will believe what they want, no matter what's right in front of them."

"You're sure you want to do this tonight?" Rene asked.

Before I could answer, LaDonna and Luke climbed out of their car. They didn't need to hear a word to know we weren't standing here to talk about the weather. LaDonna's gaze bounced between me and Conall like she was piecing together an unfinished puzzle.

I played with the edges of the pages in my hand, the fringes made where they were ripped from a spiral notebook. "It doesn't matter if I'm ready or not," I said, more to myself than anyone else. "We can't wait for the council to catch up. If we wait for them to figure out what's really happening out there, it'll be too late. We need to get ahead of this, make them see why it's important—why *we're* important."

The town council wouldn't get it. Not at first. How could they? To them, witches were just a legend, something to make Gryphon sound quaint. A spooky little story for bonfires and ghost tours. They didn't know we were real—or how much danger we were all in now that the Stygian had thrown down the gauntlet.

But they were about to find out.

I waved my notes at LaDonna, and she and Luke came over, their faces set with determination. Hopefully, together, we'd find the words to make the council listen. To make them understand that not all witches were dangerous. And that Gryphon was going to need every single one of us.

Chapter 15

The first part of the town council meeting touched on standard topics I imagined are found in every small city—road repairs, park improvements, and reviewing site plans for proposed developments. As they worked their way through the agenda, I found myself observing the people in the room more than the topics being discussed. Miss Linnie was sitting in the middle of the room, which didn't surprise me, her big, patchwork purse clutched in her lap. She seemed like the type of woman who wanted to do her civic duty—a fact I appreciated more since her call about the backyard break-in. I recognized Melody Martin, the curly-haired third-grade teacher who came in for a cup of flavored drip coffee—two sugars, no cream—every morning before school. Other faces looked familiar, but most of the names escaped me. My social circle had been pretty much limited to coven events and Blackwell Manor before last year, when I stopped reflecting Betony's chaos energy. I was still getting to know folks. My coven was there as well, dotting seats throughout the small chamber. There were twelve of us, and I'd wager we made up about a fifth of those present.

The table where the Gryphon town council members presided faced the small crowd like the table in Da Vinci's Last Supper, their names in bold letters on well-worn name plates before them. Handsome Mayor Tanaka was present, though he'd relinquished his usual seat of honor for the evening. That role belonged to Beau Fairchild, the acting council chair. The mayor sat at Fairchild's right, exuding quiet confidence even in his secondary role. Fairchild, on the other hand, had a staggering level of forced authority, as though he needed the position far more than the position needed him. He was the complete opposite of Mayor Tanaka. Fat and balding with heavy chins that extended walrus-like to the collar of his shirt, Fairchild carried himself with an air of smug self-importance, his booming voice ringing out as though he expected applause after every statement and grew offended when he didn't receive it. The term *petty tyrant* came to mind, and I took an immediate dislike to him.

The small council chamber felt cramped, and it didn't take me long to figure out why. At the back of the room, two local reporters now hovered, their camera equipment set up on tripods with red lights blinking steadily. A pretty, full-figured woman in a business suit and professional makeup with a notepad and an oversized camera slung over her shoulder whispered something to the casually dressed man beside her, who was adjusting a microphone. The town council clearly wasn't used to this level of attention—Fairchild, in particular, seemed hyper-aware of the cameras. His booming delivery and exaggerated gestures made it clear he was playing to the lens.

"The potholes on Hamlet Street near the diner are getting worse," Fairchild announced, his voice carrying more than the size of the room required, as if wanting to ensure the microphones didn't miss a word. He even leaned slightly toward the camera, his chubby hands splayed dramatically on the table. I fought down a scowl. "It's a safety concern and an embarrassment to the town." As much as I hated to give it to him, Fairchild had a point.

Sheriff Porter, seated off to the side, leaned forward. His broad shoulders and sun-lined face gave him the look of someone who had worked a lifetime outdoors. "Fairchild's right," he said, his deep voice carrying easily. "We've had people swerving into the other lane to avoid them. It's only a matter of time before someone gets hurt."

As he spoke, his watchful eyes swept the room and landed briefly on me. There was no mistaking the way his gaze lingered, sizing me up as though I didn't belong here. I straightened in my chair, refusing to flinch under the scrutiny. He didn't hold my gaze long, but the moment wasn't lost on me.

And from the corner of my eye, I noticed the camera swing slightly in my direction. The reporters were watching everything.

"Moving on," Fairchild said with a tone of exaggerated authority. "We need to review the site plans for the proposed development on Orsino Avenue. It's going to increase traffic, and we'll need to make sure the parallel roads are patched before construction begins."

Superintendent Eleanor Grace, sitting on the far-left side of the table, raised her shaky hand slightly before speaking. She was a petite woman with astute eyes and a warm smile, her silver-streaked hair pulled into a bun. "I'd also like to note that the new town development project could impact our school bus routes. If we're adding families to that area, we'll need to adjust schedules and maybe even bus stops."

Her voice was gentle but carried authority, and I couldn't help but like her. She seemed like the kind of person who genuinely cared about the town and its people, not just her own job. She also reminded me of what LaDonna might be like in a couple of decades.

Fairchild barely nodded, though he glanced toward the camera as he did, likely guaranteeing the gesture would be caught on film. "We'll take that under advisement, Superintendent," he said, his condescension thick enough to choke on. This time, I *did* scowl.

Before anyone else could speak, a screechy male voice cut through the room. "What about the park? You're all worried about roads and buses, but those raccoons are multiplying like rabbits!"

The interruption came from Earl "Cooter" Coombs, a wiry man in his late sixties who looked like he'd just rolled out of bed. I recognized him instantly—most folks in Gryphon could. He wasn't homeless, but he fit the stereotype. His mismatched socks peeked out from beneath too-short jeans, and his wild, wiry hair only added to the image of a man who lived in his own world. He was the town's resident oddball, known for his outlandish statements and conspiracy theories, as well as his unusual way of earning money—collecting cans from the side of the road and turning them in to a recycling center for cash. He was quirky, but most everyone loved him. Some even delivered their household recycling to his shack on Falstaff Road to help him in the only manner in which Cooter accepted charity.

Fairchild sighed heavily, the cameras forgotten for a moment. "Cooter, the park and its… wildlife are not on tonight's agenda."

"Well, they should be!" Cooter shot back. "Those raccoons are getting smart. I think they're stalking me, I'm telling you. One of them followed me home last week!"

A ripple of laughter moved through the room, though it was clear most people were laughing at Cooter rather than with him. Even Mayor Tanaka hid a smile behind his hand, and Eleanor Grace shook her head fondly. It was obvious this wasn't Cooter's first bizarre contribution to a council meeting.

Fairchild ignored him, moving the discussion along. "On to crime prevention," he said, adjusting the half-moon glasses at the edge of his nose. "Sheriff Porter, you had something to share?"

The sheriff cleared his throat. "We've had some issues with trespassing and minor vandalism in the new subdivision off Cressida Crescent. We're increasing patrols in that area to make sure it doesn't escalate."

His eyes flicked to me again as he spoke, his expression unreadable but intense. I could feel the weight of his attention, though I wasn't sure if it was because of the vandalism that had transpired at Blackwell Manor—which was several blocks away from Cressida Crescent—or the fact that I was the only known town witch. Did the folks at the table at the head of the room view me as another Cooter Coombs? Or maybe they thought I was a con artist, selling useless rocks and candles only suitable for lighting a room when the power went out.

I shifted in my seat, acutely aware of the cameras and reporters now. Their presence didn't just bother the council— it bothered me. Was this meeting going to turn into a soundbite about raccoons and potholes? Or worse, a convoluted scandal about the witch sitting quietly in the back of the room? Were they waiting for me to make a scene or start some trouble like the Stygian? The council chamber felt smaller by the second, and I wished the evening would wrap up sooner rather than later.

What also bothered me was that the council members didn't appear to be used to handling the news media. As far as I knew, my presence was the only one not on the agenda before yesterday. Were they there for me? If so, who had notified them? Mayor Tanaka?

Calm down. It's just a meeting so far. No sense borrowing

trouble. I closed my eyes and drew in a deep breath, until my heart rate slowed. I grew more attuned to the steady pulse of the Source, ever-present and always there to govern my spirit when I needed to feel more centered. When I opened them, Betony caught my attention and wordlessly offered to render her chaos-draining talent, but I motioned I was OK. For now.

The topics droned on. Concerns about the public water. Possible reuse of one of the old factories as a vocational arts school (which I thought was brilliant, but not everyone agreed). I watched the minutes tick by on the clock hung on the wall above the council members. Only fifteen minutes until the meeting was over. Were they going to ignore my request to speak?

"And now, we'll open the floor for topics," Fairchild said, clearly reluctant to give up his time in the spotlight. "If anyone has anything they'd like to address, please stand and approach the podium to your right with the microphone so everyone can hear you."

I almost laughed. The room was so small that even my voice, which barely carried across the coffee counter, could probably be heard with minimal effort.

Gripping the crumpled page with my letter to the council scribbled on it, I stood and set my purse on the floor beside Conall before crossing the room and approaching the microphone. The mouthpiece was low, and I took a second to adjust it so I didn't have to stoop. Standing tall as I addressed those present struck me as important. There were a few audible thumps as I set it in place. At least I knew the equipment was on.

Clearing my throat away from the microphone before drawing in closer, I wished I'd thought to bring a bottle of water. My mouth had quickly grown dry.

I made eye contact with everyone at the table before I

spoke, and maybe it was wishful thinking, but I believe Mayor Tanaka gave me the slightest head nod. I know for sure that the corner at one side of his mouth drew up as his warm brown eyes met mine.

"Good evening, members of the council, and thank you for the opportunity to speak. My name is Murphy Blackwell. I'm the owner of the coffee shop on Oberon Street called Witch's Brew, and I'm here tonight alongside my coven, not to alarm you, but to put you at ease."

At this moment, the coven—who had apparently coordinated this without including me—all stood, wordless, but supportive. My heart swelled. I swallowed a lump of pride and continued.

"I know the word 'witch' carries a lot of baggage because historically there have been stories about curses, dark rituals, and evil deeds. And lately, a group called the Stygian would have you believe that all witches are horrible. But I'm here to tell you that witches like us"—I motioned to my Lughaidh family— "are no different from anyone else in this community. We're community members, business owners, parents, and students. We live here, work here, and care deeply about the safety and well-being of this town, just like you do.

"For years, we've practiced our craft quietly and responsibly, blending our lives into the rhythms of Gryphon." I took a moment to smile at Jake when I used the line that he was most proud of adding to my speech. "Most of you probably didn't even know we were here—and that's because our presence has never been a threat.

"What sets us apart from the Stygian coven is simple: we believe in harmony, not chaos. We believe in using our abilities to protect and nurture the world around us, not to harm. It's easy to paint us all with the same brush, but I'm asking you to look beyond the fear and see the people standing before you.

"Our coven wants to be open and honest with this council because we value Gryphon and the people who make it the wonderful town it is. If you have questions, ask us. If you have fears, share them. We're here to listen and work with you, not against you.

"Thank you for your time."

☽○☾

As I stepped back from the podium, a low hum of murmurs rolled through the room. My coven, still standing, exchanged glances that radiated quiet pride. Before I could return to my seat, Superintendent Eleanor Grace leaned toward her microphone.

"Thank you, Miss Blackwell." Her voice carried the same gentle strength as before. "I've had the pleasure of meeting some of your coven members over the years, and I believe your presence in Gryphon and theirs has been a positive one. I appreciate your willingness to speak openly tonight."

I dipped my head, my chest loosening slightly at her words, though the knot of tension in the room still lingered. Not everyone here had made up their mind yet. From the second row, Reverend Thomas rose to his feet, his worn clerical collar sitting snugly beneath jowls that gave him the saggy, wise-eyed look of an old Basset hound.

"Miss Blackwell," he began, his deep voice measured like a practiced sermon, "I won't lie—I came here tonight with some reservations." He paused, letting his words settle before continuing. "The mayor told me there'd be someone from the witch community speaking, and I confess, I jumped to conclusions. But listening to you, I'm reminded of the scripture that says we will know people by their fruits. What you've shared tonight speaks of kindness, peace, and goodwill. If what you've said is true—and I've no reason to doubt you— I hope this community can set aside its prejudices and welcome you for who you are."

A soft ripple of agreement moved through the room, though it wasn't unanimous. As I took my first step away from the podium, the sound of a chair scraping across the linoleum cut through the quiet. A man in the back row stood abruptly, his wire glasses balanced precariously on his nose, the gleam of his worried forehead shining beneath thinning hair.

"That's all fine and good," he said, his voice tight with barely restrained anger. "But how do we know your coven isn't just waiting for the right moment to... to enchant this town? You say you're different from the Stygian, but how can we trust that? You're witches!"

Reverend Thomas turned to him with a calming hand raised. "Mr. Tanner, I don't believe Ms. Blackwell and her coven are casting the kind of spells you see in Hollywood films. They don't have superpowers. Isn't that correct, Miss Blackwell?"

I hesitated, standing behind the podium as the weight of the moment pressed down on me. Our confession alone wasn't enough to sway the room—to convince them we, as witches, were any different from any other faith that sent its hopes, wishes, and prayers out into the Universe, waiting for some divine or cosmic response. I could step back now, let Gryphon continue seeing us as nothing more than the quirky neighbors who grew their own herbs and burned a few extra candles, or...

My gaze swept the room, landing on the Lughaidh who had accompanied me tonight. Their expressions were hopeful, courageous. If they weren't ready to declare to the world what we could do, they were doing one hell of a job hiding it. Confidence radiated from them. Tonight, we were fearless. Ready. This was why we'd come here. To reveal who we were, what we could do. To step out of the shadows.

One by one, I caught slight nods of approval—LaDonna's long, gray waves swaying with her subtle head bob; Luke's unmistakable tip of his bearded chin; Conall's sharp, almost eager tilt; the steady gaze of Betony's hazel-and-gray eyes that could have been carved from granite; Jake's cheeky smirk; and Terry's deliberate, no-nonsense agreement. My heart swelled as I lingered briefly on each of them. Then my eyes met Mayor Tanaka's, his tailored suit offset by a mouth drawn tight with tension, though his nod was unwavering.

Now or never.

I straightened, cleared my throat again, and faced the microphone once more. "Reverend Thomas, that's not entirely true."

My words hung in the air, drawing a few nervous looks from the crowd.

Closing my eyes, I opened the spiritual gate within me and allowed the Source to flow more freely, drawing deeply until every nerve tingled with cool fire. Though my vision was physically obscured, I still perceived everything. The sweat on my skin. The smell of the lemon-scented cleaner used to polish the podium. The hum of the electricity through the wires in the room. The sounds of breath being drawn as everyone waited to see what I was about to do.

I hadn't really come up with a plan for this part; sometimes, I trusted the Source. Which chose this moment to draw my attention to just how incredibly thirsty I was.

My mind traveled to the plastic bottles of water each council member had before them on the table. Without touching them, I *knew* how the soft plastic of the bottles would bend under the slightest pressure from my fingertips. I sensed which bottles were coldest, which had been opened, and which were still sealed, the liquid cool and pristine inside. Under the podium, I sensed the sleeve of empty plastic cups waiting in their cardboard nest.

With a slow, deliberate motion, I opened my eyes and reached beneath the podium, drawing a cup with a faint brush of plastic against paperboard. The room held still, their stares dancing like static against my skin. Without a word, I raised my hand toward the nearest cold, sealed bottle.

The water stirred within, responding to my will. It shifted and swirled, as if waking from a long rest. The cap popped off with a gentle crack of plastic, dropping to the tabletop with a faint *plink* before the water within snaked outward and upward in a slender, glistening stream. The audience gasped as the water defied gravity, twisting lazily through the air like a living, crystalline ribbon. It caught the light in delicate prisms before spilling smoothly into my waiting cup.

I held it up, the faintest smile tugging at my lips. "Sometimes," I said, my voice cutting through the stunned silence, "you just have to see it to believe it." I took a much-needed sip of water.

Silence gripped the room. I became acutely aware of the cameras pointing in my direction and noticed the cup in my hand trembled slightly.

A thunderstruck voice emerged from near the reporters. "So the old stories are true."

Every head turned toward the source. Dr. Ruth Calloway, Gryphon's elderly local historian, stood with surprising vigor, her round glasses perched on the end of her nose and her favorite scarf—a tattered map of ancient England—draped around her neck. I recognized her as a regular customer; she liked to experiment with whatever seasonal coffee concoctions I brewed every year.

"The tales of witches protecting this part of Alabama from harm go back to the late eighteen hundreds," she declared, her voice trembling but resolute. "The Lughaidh coven has been here longer than most of us, I'd wager. I've spent years studying Gryphon's history, and if you bother to read the records, you'll see that it was their ancestors who warded off disasters and helped settle many land disputes. What Miss Blackwell said rings true to the town's history, whether you like it or not." She stared everyone down indignantly, as though daring anyone to argue.

I pressed my lips together to keep my jaw from dropping open. She knew about the coven?

Fairchild looked flustered, but shockingly kept his mouth shut. The balding man in the wire glasses shifted uncomfortably in his seat, clearly unsure of how to respond.

Then came the quiet, nervous voice of a woman in her fifties who clutched her purse tightly, her knuckles white. "But what if the Stygian are telling the truth too?" she asked, her voice barely above a whisper. "What if all witches are dangerous? What if we're just lucky they haven't done anything to us yet?"

Reverend Thomas turned toward her, his expression calm but firm. "Fear can cloud our judgment," he said gently. "But it is not fear that builds strong communities. It's understanding and trust. The Word tells us in 2 Timothy that 'the Spirit God gave us does not make us timid, but gives us power, love and self-discipline.'"

I could have kissed the man in relief. *Thank you, Mother Goddess, for Reverend Thomas.*

Sheriff Porter chose this moment to speak again, his tone measured. "We've had our share of trouble lately," he said, his eyes once again finding mine. "But I've been in this town long enough to know who's causing it and who ain't. I haven't seen nothing to suggest Miss Blackwell or her coven are causing trouble. If anything, they've been some of the kindest folks I've met."

The room settled into an uneasy quiet, the debate seemingly at a standstill. I looked around, gauging the mood of the council members and the crowd. This was far from over, but at least I'd planted the seed. Whether it would grow into trust or suspicion was yet to be seen.

As the meeting resumed, I caught Mayor Tanaka's eye one last time. His subtle nod told me everything I needed to know: I hadn't changed everyone's mind, but I had earned the ear of several townspeople who could make a difference. For now, that was enough.

$$\text{☽〇☾}$$

If I'd known how washed-up I'd look on camera, I might have put on lipstick.

I had to stay up and see if the footage the local news stations captured would broadcast that evening. Sure enough, there I was on the eleven o'clock news. Usually, I'm in bed way before that with some ice water, a good book, and Rex curled by my side—Conall, too, if I'm lucky—but I was too wound up after the council meeting to even think about getting any shut-eye.

When the meeting let out, the townsfolk shuffled out quietly, murmuring uncertainly, which surprised me. I half expected to be accosted like Hollywood stars on the red carpet dealing with paparazzi. I supposed they were unsure how to interact with someone who did what I'd just done. Even Miss Linnie only gave me a slight wave goodbye before she left. The look on her face was hard to decipher. Fear? Worry?

Confusion? I couldn't tell.

The reporters, however, caught me on my way out, just as I'd suspected they would. They peppered me with rapid-fire questions so insightful I was sure Mayor Tanaka had tipped them off that tonight's meeting was one not to miss. I was still so dazed from the meeting—and the sheer force of the Source within me—that my replies to their questions spilled out before I'd even had time to think. Now, as Conall and I sat curled up on the couch, the flicker of the television illuminated the tiny living room. I watched, spellbound, as the footage of my water trick splashed onto the screen, followed by the words the Universe had spoken through me playing out for all of Gryphon to hear.

The screen cut to my face, tired but resolute, my voice steady despite the whirlwind inside me.

"Not all witches are evil," I said, the words sounding surprisingly certain. "Many—most of us—spend our lives trying to make this world better, to heal what's broken, to protect what's good. We draw on the Source—the power behind all life, the essential force within the universe. That power isn't ours to abuse; it's ours to honor. And we believe that if we live in harmony with it, we can help guide the world toward a brighter future.

"I know there are witches who have strayed from that path. The Stygian... they're real, and they are dangerous. They don't draw from the Source the way we do. They twist it, corrupt it, turning something beautiful into something destructive. They want chaos, and they want fear.

"But we—the good witches, the healers, the protectors—we are fighting them. And we need you. We need this town, this community, to see us for who we really are. Not monsters or threats. Just people, like you, who want to live in peace and help this world thrive.

"The Source flows through all of us. It's the thread that connects us, no matter who we are. Even if you're not a witch, if you listen to it, to your inner guidance, and you trust in its wisdom, we can overcome anything—even the darkness the Stygian would unleash."

The camera lingered on my pallid face for a moment before cutting away. I grabbed the remote and clicked the TV off. Conall squeezed my hand, his touch familiar and comforting.

"That was beautiful, Murph," he murmured, his voice low and warm.

Leaning into his shoulder, I let the weight of the night settle. "I hope it was enough," I whispered, staring at the darkened screen.

Chapter 16

I'd known my stunt at the town council meeting would stir up some buzz around Gryphon and maybe Huntsville, or as far as Birmingham or Nashville. Hell, I'd counted on it. Figured it might hit the local morning news broadcast, spark some polite debate among local reporters on whether what I did was legit or just an elaborate party trick or video manipulation. Folks would get into conversations about it at the grocery store or during Sunday School. Maybe the shop would see a dip in traffic, or attract a fresh crowd of looky-loos from around town and the surrounding area hoping to catch me pulling another Criss Angel act when I thought no one was watching.

What I hadn't counted on was the internet.

Ho. Le. Crap.

By the time I'd had my second cup of coffee, my little water show had gone viral, spiraling out of our sleepy little town and crashing onto midday news broadcasts in Huntsville, Birmingham, and Nashville. The story had officially grown legs and was taking a jog across state lines. By mid-afternoon, it was everywhere—Facebook, TikTok, Instagram—platforms I actively tried to avoid with the exception of my measly Witch's Brew website. Turns out, avoiding tech doesn't stop it from dragging you into its clutches when you accidentally poke the beast.

And the comments? Oh, the comments. Just as bad as the dumpster fire of discourse that lit up after the Stygian mess.

"Who keeps editing this garbage? People are so gullible."

"Nice CGI bro. Try harder next time."

"Grow up, FFS."

But it wasn't all skeptics and trolls. Viral tales sprouted like weeds—worse, like bamboo. I've heard that crap grows three feet a day. Some genius spliced a grainy, low-res clip of my council meeting into footage of a supposed "poltergeist" yeeting books off shelves in a Gryphon bookstore a couple of years back. A breathless amateur YouTuber stitched it together, his voice-over dripping with conspiracy-fueled glee. "Is this the same force? Could Gryphon be America's next supernatural hotspot?"

The comments were predictably worse.

"It's swamp gas."

"In northern Alabama? Seriously?"

"My cousin's neighbor's aunt swears her porch light flickered once. Coincidence? Think again."

By that evening, I'd been tagged in Gryphon's local Facebook and Instagram groups so many times that I started wondering if I could delete my profiles without causing offense. Memes popped up faster than I could keep up. One plastered a blurry shot of me mid-water-trick with the caption: "Water Wizard of Gryphon." Another had me photoshopped as Gandalf, bargain-bin staff and all, with a tagline that read, "You shall not splash!"

The conspiracy nuts took it to a whole new level.

"This is clearly a government experiment testing tech on small towns!"

"Nope it's aliens. The ones in the ocean. Their starting to takeover!"

"It's witchcraft! Repent!"

My little hometown of Gryphon had become the internet's newest viral obsession. The swirling vortex of memes, conspiracies, and half-baked theories ranged from somewhat accurate to mildly funny to full-on terrifying. And somehow, in the middle of all this, I had to figure out how to get back to normal while remaining out of the broom closet. Assuming normal was even in the cards.

By late afternoon, Rita stopped by the shop, laptop in hand, to let me know the Worldwide Witches website had exploded. Traffic ranged from the curious ("Are witches real?") to the threatening (The bible says thou shalt not suffer a witch to live. Yall are a abomanation and deserve what's comin!!) The misspellings would've been laughable if the intentions weren't so chilling.

I kept in touch with the coven throughout the day, checking in between one odd internet revelation and the next. None of them had been dragged into the digital shit storm I had, probably because they hadn't been the ones facing the cameras. Lucky them. Or maybe not.

I was the Summate, sure—the pinnacle of the Craft's power potential—but this wasn't about me. Then again, the whole idea was to show the town that we weren't some lurking threat and that our ability to wield magic wasn't a dividing line between us and them. We were blending in, living alongside everyone else. Had been for years. And no one knew. That was the point.

I am not a person who lives for technology. I know everyone loves their phones and streaming services and whatever. And, I mean, I have a smartphone, but I'm not that person—give me a good book, and I'm entertained for hours. However, with everything that had been going on since the town council meeting, I was glued to my phone like a teenager who'd just gotten her device back after a month of being grounded from it.

My need to stay informed was currently wrestling with my desire to keep my sanity, and, spoiler alert: sanity was losing.

I was in the middle of my after-work rush—a generous term for the handful of folks trickling in for coffee and whatnot—when the news van rolled up.

Stars above. Here we go.

Doyle and Crystal, my new, ever-watchful supernatural bodyguards, had been lurking at a corner table all day, keeping an eye out for any troublemakers while Rene and I ran the shop. Doyle, with his super-vampy strength, was there to manhandle anyone who got too bold, while Crystal's portal-cutting abilities meant she could whisk me and Rene out of danger in a flash. With my wards up, it was unlikely we'd encounter too much trouble inside Blackwell Manor, which was good. The last thing we needed was a camera crew catching Doyle physically restraining someone while Crystal opened a wormhole in space like we were in a low-budget superhero flick.

And yet, the thought of the news crews finding out that Gryphon's town witch had super-powered backup was... oddly tempting. But nah, not today. Not unless they were ready to step out of that closet.

One super-person at a time is probably wisest. For now.

I didn't recognize the emblem on the side of the SUV and camera, but it didn't take long to figure out the crew wasn't local. Once the reporter and her camera operator stepped through the door, I caught sight of the logo: a station out of Chattanooga. *Great.*

A small part of me took some comfort in knowing that if her intentions were bad, the wards would have steered her away from passing the threshold. That was something.

The reporter was one of those women who probably could've done without half the makeup but still wore the layers she'd added well—thick eyeliner, a bold pinky-plum lipstick, facial contouring, the works. Her braids were immaculate—intricate, glossy, and undoubtedly expensive. Her suit was a shade of pink somewhere between bubblegum and cotton candy, like it was daring me to find it sweet. She had kind eyes, though—a warm brown that softened the overall effect—and a nose that was a smidge larger than average. Not a flaw, really. More like a quirk that made her face interesting.

Her camera operator couldn't have been more different. Short and stocky, with pale skin and a cheerful face smattered with freckles across her nose and cheeks, she looked like she'd just stepped into a birthday party where cake and balloons were waiting for her. There was an eager friendliness about her, a vibe that made you want to hand her a cupcake and ask her how her day was going.

Both of them radiated *nice*. Not the fake, calculated kind you learn to sniff out after a few years of retail work, but the for-real-no-kidding variety. I didn't know for certain if it was a front or not, but my gut told me I didn't have to put my guard all the way up just yet.

They waited until the line at the counter was gone—which won them more personality points in my book—before approaching the counter with ready smiles. The camera operator glanced at her old-fashioned wristwatch, probably calculating how long it'd take to edit any footage they shot for the late-night news.

"Miss Blackwell?" the lady in the pink suit said. "I'm Levonia Bradly, and this is my camera operator, Leah. Do you have a few minutes? I'd love to talk about the events at Gryphon's town council meeting last night."

I brushed some cruller crumbs off on my jeans and put a smile on my face. *Guess I'm the face of good witches for the time being.* "Sure. Um… one sec." I poked my head into the kitchen, where Rene was refilling the creamer dispenser. "Hey, can you watch the front for a few minutes? I've got a… thing."

This interview was going to go *great* if I continued with language skills like that.

"Sure," Rene said, hoisting the refilled thermos easily with one hand. "You OK?"

The question wasn't merely about whether I was physically alright; he wanted to know if I sensed a threat in whoever had approached me.

"I'm fine. Really. Just an interview." My voice came out a little too high-pitched to be convincing, so I tacked on, "Thanks," and exited before he could question it. I was nervous, but not because I felt threatened. Last night, the news cameras had been at the back of the room until the reporters approached me as I was leaving. Then, I'd been full of the Source and a touch high from adrenaline and the odd relief that came from knowing that the secret I'd carried for twenty-seven years was out in the open. This time I was… me. Murphy Blackwell, metaphysical store and coffeeshop owner, and town witch.

Remembering how I'd looked on the television last night, I took a moment to add some strawberry lip gloss before stepping out from behind the counter. Running my fingers through my hair and praying it was enough, I approached Levonia Bradly.

"I uh… I-I guess you have questions?" I asked, hating how awkward I sounded.

Levonia's smile was the sort that was friendly, reassuring, and confidence-boosting all at the same time. The woman had a gift.

"I do. The station heard a little about what happened at the town hall meeting—what you did with the water—and I was wondering if you could explain to our viewers about how you did that."

Arching an eyebrow in her direction. "You mean the witchcraft?"

"So, that *is* what you used?"

"It is."

Levonia tilted her head slightly, her braids catching the fluorescent lights and gleaming like spun silk. She motioned toward Leah and the camera. "Do you mind?"

"No," I said, forcing myself to sound more confident than I felt. "Do you need me to stand somewhere in particular, or…?"

"You're perfect right there," Levonia assured me with a gesture at the ceiling lights. "The light from the window looks great with the overheads. Right, Leah?"

Leah, already recording, gave a thumbs-up without looking up from her viewfinder.

Levonia turned to the camera, and with a quick inhale of breath and a subtle shift in posture, she transformed from the friendly woman who'd approached me into a television personality. "I'm here at Witch's Brew in the town of Gryphon, Alabama, with Murphy Blackwell, the woman who shocked the small town of Gryphon last night when she appeared to magically pull water several feet through the air and into a waiting cup. In less than a day, the internet has exploded with debate about whether her power is real." Turning to me, she asked, "Miss Blackwell, you said you're a witch. Is that correct?"

"Yes, I am."

"Is this something you've always been able to do, or is it

something you had to learn?"

I glanced at the microphone. *Speak up. Say what's on your heart. Don't look at the camera like a deer in the headlights. And don't say 'um.'*

"It's not like I woke up one morning and thought, You know what? I should move some water around today," I said, crossing my arms. Levonia gave me a subtle nod, which assured me I was doing fine. "It's a skill. It takes practice, discipline, and yeah, a little natural talent doesn't hurt. There are a lot of types of witches, and each type has a specific brand of abilities, and I'm… well, I'm unusual by witch standards. I'm a Summate. That means I can work with any branch of the Craft I want. And my power is exceptionally strong."

"Fascinating," Levonia said, her curiosity genuine enough to be disarming. "Do you see witchcraft as a science, a religion, or something else entirely?"

I blinked, caught off guard by the question. Most people went straight for the whole "Are you evil?" angle, or worse, started asking if I could curse their exes. "I guess it's kind of its own thing. There's structure to it, but not rules to follow. It's not something you can sum up neatly in a scripture or grimoire. Everyone has their own spirit that they lend to their practice. It's… complicated."

Leah, the camera operator, chimed in, her voice as bright as her demeanor. "Complicated, but super cool."

I snorted, guessing that bit was going to end on the proverbial editing room floor. "Depends on who you ask." I had a feeling Leah was the one who'd caught the lead on this story.

Levonia leaned forward slightly, her curiosity unfeigned. "And last night, when you used your abilities, were you trying to send a message?"

I hesitated, considering my answer carefully. "Not a

message, exactly. More like proof. Proof that we're not a threat, that we've been here all along without causing problems. My shop's been here for almost ten years, but last night was the first time I've displayed my power. But if it takes a little magic to make people believe in us, in witches? Fine."

Levonia nodded thoughtfully, then glanced at the camera. "Would you be willing to demonstrate some of that power now?"

I should have seen that coming. I knew if I did, it'd mean dealing with reporters camped out on my doorstep for weeks, but we'd already decided as a coven that hiding wasn't an option anymore.

I scanned the room for something small and manageable, but also nearby so Leah wouldn't have to travel with her camera. My eyes landed on the candle display behind me—rows of wax-filled glass jars, each labeled with its intended purpose: empowerment, good luck, protection, and so on. An idea sparked.

"Ms. Bradly, pick a number between one and twenty," I said.

Levonia's lips quirked up in a faint smile, catching on to what I was planning. "Seven."

"OK."

I pulled in a deep breath and centered myself, tapping into the beautiful, golden flow of the Source until my body felt nearly weightless. The skin at my temples buzzed slightly, and the joy it always brought filled my heart to bursting. I dialed it back a little; it wouldn't take much to do what I needed to.

Eying the display, I chose seven candles at various spots and sent a faint burst of heat energy to the wicks. Seven candles flickered to life.

The delighted smile on Levonia's face was catching.

"And if I'd said twenty?"

I took a moment, selected another thirteen—which was nearly the entire display—and with a blink of an eye and a push of Source energy, they ignited as well.

"You don't see that every day," Leah whispered, her voice reverent.

"That's incredible," Levonia said, struggling to keep her professional tone intact. "Thank you for the demonstration. I suppose those candles aren't for sale anymore, are they?"

Feeling emboldened, I waved a hand, extinguishing the flames in a synchronized sweep. A tiny pulse of Source energy pulled the melted wax upward, reshaping it. The blackened wicks straightened, char fading to fresh white thread, as if no flame had ever touched it, restoring each wick to its pristine white state. A final touch of effort refreshed the spell within each candle for its designed purpose—an invisible touch, but necessary.

"Anyone can have trick candles," I said with a smile. "Trick wicks that turn white again? That's another story."

Leah stepped forward with the camera, focusing on the white wicks below the still-dissipating smoke.

Levonia smiled, jotting something down on her notepad. "Thank you, Miss Blackwell. I think our viewers will appreciate your openness—and your demonstration."

"Yeah," I said, glancing at the camera. "I hope so. Thank you for allowing me to address folks again."

Leah packed up the camera while Levonia offered a handshake, her professional polish never slipping. "Thank you for your time, Miss Blackwell," she said, her warm smile returning. "I think this will make quite an impression."

As they walked out, I leaned against the counter, watching through the window as they loaded their gear into their sleek white news van. The quiet of the shop felt more pronounced after their departure, but my thoughts weren't so calm. Whatever impression I'd made, it was going to stir the pot even more—and I wasn't sure Gryphon, or the world, was ready for the ripples.

Chapter 17

It's hard to explain what it's like to be the Summate. I grew up knowing witches had power, but inside the Lughaidh coven, it was usually the slow-burn, sneaky kind. Not the smite-thy-enemies kind.

Take LaDonna. She's a green witch. Her garden practically worships her. The woman could toss seeds at concrete, and a healthy garden would burst through the pavement days later. Her plants sprouted earlier and lasted longer than even the best horticulturist could ever wish for. But her gift was fairly subtle—unless I juice her up. Then the woman can pull roots from the ground and use them as a protective shield in a matter of seconds. I know. I've helped her do it.

Not that LaDonna's magic isn't hardcore on its own. She's got a hell of a way with animals. Oh, and she bestowed a power upon my fiancée that makes it possible for him to turn into a dog. On purpose, before you ask. It's a handy trick when he needs to be sneaky.

Then there's Luke and Conall, the orange witches. They see the future. Sometimes in stars, sometimes in water, sometimes in a half-empty whiskey glass at three in the morning. If that's not enough, they can astral project—a gift that worked out really weird when I tried to learn. I wound up jumping into Conall's body. First when he was human. Then as a dog. Both were awkward as hell to live through, but the dog hop was worse. Imagine having a canine's sense of smell around a sour jar spell full of vinegar and dog crap.

Joey's our walking fortress. He's a Black witch—protection magic runs in his bones. Wards, shields, anti-hexes—you name it, he can build a wall against it and then some. His power doesn't just keep the bad out, either. It bolsters folks who've been knocked around spiritually, giving them the strength to find their footing again.

Miriam's a Rose witch, which makes her our resident healer in the more *stitch-you-back-together* sense. Bones, bruises, even the heartache most folks try to swallow down— she's got a gift for mending what's broken, seen and unsee.

Terry? She sees ghosts. Unless they're half-fae, like my dad. (Don't ask. It's a long, weird story.) And you already know about Jake's being a music witch and Hanna's crazy blend of glamor, love, and kitchen witchery. She can make you fall for her and feed you into oblivion at the same time.

So, yeah. I've seen some shit. And none of it—absolutely none of it—prepared me for the full-on apocalyptic circus that broke loose after Levonia's broadcast.

Good thing the Lughaidh coven also has a chaos witch.

Conall stepped inside just as Levonia and Leah climbed into their news van, his heavy-lidded brown eyes carrying a flicker of concern. And not because of the news crew.

"Another interview?" he asked, pulling me into a slightly distracted hug before kissing me hello.

"Yeah," I said. "She was actually really nice. Like, *genuinely* nice. I like her."

Conall's eyebrows drew together, and he let out a long breath through pursed lips.

My stomach flipped. "What? What's wrong?"

"Call Bet," he said, lacing his fingers through mine to keep me from freaking out too much. "You're gonna need her here tomorrow."

I didn't ask why. Conall was an orange witch—if he said I'd need Betony, then I'd need Betony. My sweet, protective, *somewhat ominous* fiancé.

"Should I ask her to come over and stay the night? So she's already here first thing?"

His gaze flicked upward, searching for that mysterious orange-witch part of his brain that got little cosmic memos from the universe.

"Yeah," he said, almost disappointed. "It's gonna hit early. Do you want me to take the morning off? I can call Dad."

We ran through logistics. Decided he'd take the first couple of hours off just in case the impending storm wasn't a "mild inconvenience," more "holy hell, what fresh chaos is this?" Once we figured out which level of weird we were dealing with, we'd go from there.

Surprisingly, I slept fine, tucked against Conall's side, my head resting on the ink of his *As Above, So Below* biceps tattoo. When morning rolled around, I'd almost forgotten about his little prophecy—until I walked into the living room and spotted Betony curled up on my couch.

She was wrapped in her favorite blanket of mine, the blue one covered in horoscope symbols, a couch pillow wedged under her head. The only sign that she'd *voluntarily* spent the night was the fact that she'd actually claimed the couch instead of lurking somewhere in a corner like a cryptid. She'd even slept in her clothes.

I padded off to brush my teeth, shower, and throw on jeans and a *Resting Witch Face* t-shirt. By the time I was back in my bedroom, grabbing socks and my Converse, I heard it. A sound I had never heard this early, especially this close to my house.

Voices.

Not just one. *Several*.

My spine locked up. Cars? Sure. Dogs barking? Miss Linnie's Yorkie had a lot to say most mornings, as did the basset hound catty-corner from my place. The occasional siren? Sure. But voices outside my window? At this hour?

That wasn't normal. The rare voice at this hour was usually a neighbor walking past on their way to Walker Hill Cemetery or Gryphon High. I held my breath to listen more closely, but there was no denying it. It was definitely voices.

I crept to the thick drapes covering my front windows, pulled one back a hair, and peeked outside.

Vehicles. News vans. Random cars parked up and down Oberon Street like some kind of media invasion. And clustered outside in the sticky morning air? A crowd.

A *big* crowd.

Shit. I let out a deep, slow sigh and dropped the curtain.

"That bad?" Conall muttered as he dry-washed his face with both hands.

"Yeah." I exhaled. I ran a hand through my hair. "You called it."

He had. And now I had to deal with it. I'm an introvert. This? This was my worst nightmare.

Betony needed to be awake soon if she was going to help me that morning. Thankfully, my panicked energy must have poked her brain for me. By the time I got to the living room, she was stirring. She sat up, blinking sleep-heavy eyes, and brushed back her white-blond hair. A pink splotch on her cheek marked where her cheek had pressed against the pillow.

"S'going on?" she asked groggily, stretching her pale arms toward the ceiling.

I crossed to the window, nestled between two built-in

bookshelves, and peeked out at Oberon Street again. "The crowd Conall predicted has arrived."

She let out an impressed breath. "Damn. They're early."

I shrugged. "He said they would be. That's why we asked you to stay over."

She swung her legs off the couch and searched for footwear. "Are you gonna talk to them before you open?"

I scoffed. "No."

Betony found her chunky boots and shoved her feet inside, still wearing mismatched footies. I have no idea how she can stand the way that feels. Sleeping in socks is odd enough, but short socks in calf-height boots? My skin itched at the thought. When she stood, the thick soles nearly put her at my height.

"Maybe you should," she said, pulling her backpack off the arm of the couch and fishing inside for her toothbrush. "Morning's when you get your best crowd, right? You really want them around here causing a scene when you're trying to muster up customers?"

"They can't come inside the shop," I informed her. "Did some Googling last night. If they try to stick around when they aren't welcome, I can call the cops and have them arrested for criminal trespassing." I flicked the curtain aside again, watching the gathering. "Not that I think they'll get that far. The wards we set up last time were pretty solid."

Betony joined me at the window, and together we studied the dozen or so vehicles clogging Oberon Street. At least they'd had the presence of mind not to steal the handful of parking spaces in front of the shop. That might've given me grounds to have them trespassed, too.

"Are there more on Beatrice?" she asked, meaning Beatrice Bend, the road that met Oberon at the intersection on the corner of my property.

I sighed. "Probably."

Behind us, Conall's bare feet padded across the wooden floor, and the bathroom door clicked shut. As Betony and I silently spied on the would-be scandal-chasers outside, the sounds of Conall's morning routine filled the space—the faucet running, the medicine cabinet opening, the familiar scrubbing of his toothbrush against his teeth. The normalcy of it eased my pulse a little.

"I'm telling you," Betony said, "I think you should talk to them before the shop opens. This could go on all day. Who knows how many times you'll have to deal with people wanting to see what you can do?"

I raked a hand through my hair and exhaled. She had a point.

"I wonder if I should, I don't know, hold a press conference? That's not weird, right?" I shook my head before she could answer. "No, it is weird. I'm not a cop, or a politician, or—hell, I'm not even someone important." My heart thudded at the thought of addressing that many people at once. Worse, the idea of having to do it again and again. For days. Maybe weeks.

"You are," she said. "They just don't know it yet."

Betony crossed the short distance between us and extended her hand, eyebrows raised in silent question. I nodded—this *was* why she was there, after all—and she placed her palm gently against my forearm. The moment she made contact, my tension eased, the swirling panic in my head smoothed out like ink in water. She siphoned off the stress inside me like it was an energy drink straight into her bloodstream—she thrived on others' messy, wild energy.

It only took a few seconds. By the time she pulled away, the tightness in my chest had loosened, and my thoughts felt less like a pinball helplessly colliding against slingshots and bumpers.

"Thank you," I murmured.

She flashed a small, satisfied smile, the kind I wished I saw more often, and her hazel eyes shone. The ring of gray had grown a little, the way it tends to when she's charged.

We headed downstairs, where I made scrambled eggs and started the coffee. Conall joined us, slicing up apples, while Betony worked on toast. The smell must've lured Rene downstairs, because he appeared in time to grab a plate. Ever the barista, he immediately started fixing everyone's coffee to order.

We sat, eating together at the island in the kitchen in the quiet morning light, and for a moment, everything felt… normal. Just breakfast with my weird, wonderful, thrown-together family before the pending pandemonium started.

As I chewed, I filled Rene in on the situation outside. He took it in stride, unfazed. "I'll run the shop with Betony while you handle them."

I checked the clock—6:45 AM. Fifteen minutes until I unlocked the doors.

I exhaled. "I'm going to talk to them now, before we open. Betony, I want you with me, in case…" I let the sentence trail off, but everyone knew what I meant. *In case I need someone to keep me from losing my cool.*

Once breakfast was done, Rene offered to clean up, while Betony and I stepped out to speak to the gaggle of people outside. Conall lingered behind, but I knew he'd be watching intently from the large window facing the street.

Stepping outside felt like walking onto a stage for a drama I hadn't signed up for. Camera lenses swung toward me. Lights went on. Someone's phone was already facing me— an influencer, probably.

I strolled across my veranda, crossed my yard, and

planted my feet at the edge of my tiny parking lot—right where the wards ended. I folded my arms. "Alright. Let's get this over with."

A man in a blue windbreaker with a smile full of what had to be veneers was the first to pounce. His mic flag boasted a station out of Louisville and the words *Your City. Your Story.* "Murphy Blackwell, people are saying you have abilities—real, supernatural abilities. Can you prove it? Show us what you can do?"

I let out a slow breath. *Here we go.*

A woman from another station who'd probably led a previous life as a pageant queen stepped in. "Are you a witch, Miss Blackwell?"

There it was. The big question.

I quirked an eyebrow, determined not to make it easy on them. "Define witch for me."

I could practically hear all the cameras zooming in, sensing a soundbite.

"I mean, you *do* own an occult shop," another reporter interjected. "And multiple witnesses claim to have seen… unexplained things happen around you."

"Yeah," I said dryly. "It's almost like people who sell books about magic sometimes believe in magic." It wasn't an answer, but it wasn't a denial, either. Hell, maybe I could run for office if Mayor Tanaka ever stepped down.

A GenZ-aged guy holding his phone aloft—another influencer, judging by his hyped-up energy—jumped in. "Come on, do something incredible! Move something with your mind. Call a spirit. Set that van on fire!" He jerked his thumb toward a news vehicle. "Give the viewers what they want!"

Betony made a noise in her throat that sounded a bit too close to a dog growling. I held up a hand. Strangely enough,

I wasn't freaking out at all. Maybe it was because everything they said and did struck me as mind-bogglingly ridiculous.

Plastering on a saccharine smile, I said, "Oh, sure! Let me grab my wand and curse y'all real quick." I widened my eyes. "Or wait, do you want the one where I turn into a cat? That one takes longer, but it's a real crowd-pleaser."

Uncertain laughter rippled through the gathered crowd. Not everyone—some of them still had that hungry look, waiting for me to slip up—but enough.

I let my expression go flat. "Listen. I run a business. I sell books, candles, and the occasional tarot deck. If you're looking for a magic show, try Vegas."

One of the influencers piped up. "Are you denying that you have powers?"

I glanced at Betony. She gave a slight, knowing smirk.

I turned back to the cameras, my smile honed as a blade. Calling up just a *hint* of Source energy and recalling a bit of tech witch instruction I'd received from Rita, I waved my hand... and everyone's electronic devices stopped working. Camera lights went out. The influencers' brows furrowed as they tried to figure out why their phones stopped recording. I hadn't ruined their equipment... but it'd be a while before any of it started working again.

"I'm saying I have a shop to open. And unless you're here to buy something, you're blocking private property."

With that, I turned on my heel and walked back inside.

Betony let the door swing shut behind us and grinned. "That was *so* much better than a press conference."

Chapter 18

Should I have "given the people what they want?" I wondered as I watched the morning's news vans peel out, only to be replaced in less than an hour by another swarm idling just outside my legal perimeter. Like vultures, but lazier. I couldn't help but think about the ones I'd talked to before the shop even opened—how they'd had their footage, only to have it zapped before capturing the actual proof they sought. No floating coffee cups or floating water. No undeniable evidence. *Oh freaking well.*

My usual early-morning rush was still rolling in decent business. Most of my regulars didn't give a damn whether I was a legit witch, a clever poser, or blissfully unaware of the latest scandal. I liked to think they were cool with the idea that I was the real deal.

Meanwhile, Lughaidh's group chat had erupted into a full-blown debate since the town hall. So far, no one else had been publicly outed for their abilities, but no one else was making water float in midair, either. Maybe it was time to change the narrative. The Stygian were out there shouting to the world that they were witches; we needed to make it just as clear that not all witches were villains. My reputation aside, I wasn't the only one in Gryphon capable of some damn impressive feats. I opened the chat and started typing.

Lughaidh Group Chat

8:03 AM

I have an idea.

8:04 AM
Rafael
Let's hear it

8:04 AM

LaDonna, this one's for you.

8:04 AM
LaDonna
I'm listening. What's the plan?

8:05 AM

You know what's wrong with the
Magnolia Memorial Tree, right?

8:05 AM

LaDonna
Sure, it's Verticillium Wilt. Poor
thing's been dying for years

8:06 AM

How hard would it be to heal it?
Like, all at once. In public.

8:07 AM
Terry
Oh, I love that idea!

8:07 AM
Jake
Can I get in on this somehow?

8:08 AM

That's a good idea. Bring your guitar.
You can play and use your music
to inspire good energy.

8:09 AM
Luke
Oh, this is going to be fun.

8:09 AM
LaDonna
Murphy, that's such a good idea! It will be such a positive event for the town. Yes!

8:10 AM
Terry
When should we do it?

I quickly scanned the weather and skimmed the town calendar. The next big event was Music in the Park at Puck's Green, the sprawling park where the Magnolia Memorial Tree had stood since it was planted in honor of those lost in the Korean War. Over the decades, that venerable tree had witnessed countless weddings, concerts, and celebrations. Now it was fading, sickly and brittle. Once word had spread about its incurable disease, the people of Gryphon were heartbroken.

LaDonna could fix that.

8:15 AM
Friday. The town is doing one of their Music in the Park events. Should be a good crowd. LaDonna, would you be OK if I stood on the sidelines for this one?

8:16 AM
LaDonna
That'd be fine. Oh, I'm so excited!

I was, too. It was the perfect moment for my high priest-ess to shine—helping to revive a beloved town symbol was practically poetic. And it was an excellent opportunity to show a positive example of the Craft.

It might not draw the same crowd—or the newscasters—that an assassination would… unless someone tipped off the press ahead of time. I glanced at the line of news vans parked along Oberon Street, a grin tugging at my mouth that proba-bly looked a little too mischievous.

Rene, who'd just served our last customer an iced caramel latte, caught the insuppressible smile on my face and mir-rored my expression.

"What happened?" he asked.

"LaDonna's gonna heal the Magnolia Memorial Tree."

"No way. That's sick!" he crowed.

I loved how Rene, a relative newcomer to Gryphon, was so enthusiastic about saving a town icon he'd only learned about this year. We exchanged a quick fist bump—his ver-sion of celebration ending in a playful, exaggerated finger ex-plosion.

That's when the Iced Caramel Latte girl—small, with a cropped, tomboyish cut that framed delicate features and large, watchful eyes—stepped hesitantly back to the counter. She had the sort of fragile beauty that made me think of elves.

Wait. Are elves real, too? Goddammit, I do not have the bandwidth to wonder if every unusual-looking person is a su-pernatural creature right now.

"Is there something wrong with your coffee?" Rene asked.

Iced-Caramel-Latte-Possible-Elf-Girl looked down at her feet and batted her long lashes. Either she was really shy, or she was flirting with Rene. Or both.

"The coffee is fine," she breathed. "I just…" Her

enormous eyes met mine, and a flood of words poured out.

"Can I interview you? I'm so sorry—I don't know how to do this. I just started my channel, and I'm trying to find amazing people to talk to, and—" She swallowed, cheeks burning, gaze skittering away. "And you're amazing."

Well. That was unexpected. Now how could I say no to that?

I rested my hands on the counter, giving her a measured look. "You sure you want me?"

She nodded rapidly.

"Fair warning," I said. "Last folks who tried didn't leave with any usable footage."

Her brows pulled together. "Because…?"

I shrugged. "Because I didn't let them."

A flicker of uncertainty crossed her face, but then she squared her shoulders. "Then maybe you'll let me. I'll have an exclusive."

Brave. I liked her.

I sighed, glancing at the clock. "Fine. Five minutes. And you're buying another coffee."

Her lips parted, caught between a relieved breath and a grin. "Deal."

I made a motion to Rene that he'd be in charge for a few minutes, and Elf Girl and I found a quiet corner of the shop to sit down. She moved light on her feet, like she barely touched the ground, her feet shod in well-loved white ballet slippers.

While she set her phone on a tiny tripod and pulled a small circular light from her backpack purse, I decided to start interviewing her first.

"Well, you know my name. What's yours?"

"Elidriel," she said softly.

If that isn't an elf name, I don't know what is.

"Elidriel?" I repeated. *Yep. Pure fantasy novel material.* She nodded, her attention still focused on adjusting her setup.

"That's beautiful," I added.

"Thank you."

"Prettier than Murphy," I said, half-teasing.

She looked up then, blinking at me with something between dismay and genuine confusion, like I'd just insulted my bloodline. "Murphy is a *beautiful* name," she said, as serious as a funeral. "It's very Irish. You're of Irish descent, right?"

Oddly specific. I squinted at her, wondering if she'd deduced that from my name alone. "Mostly," I said, suddenly reminded that I did not know where my father's side—the fae side—came from.

It really was sad how much I knew about the fae. Was there such a thing as an Irish fairy? Or did my father come from some other plane of existence? Because that would explain why his ghost didn't behave like normal ghosts.

Worry about that another time, Murphy.

Elidriel's hands were absurdly tiny compared to her phone, a high-end model known for its insane picture quality. Her small tabletop light fixture and phone tripod were quality merchandise as well, and when she finally pulled out a fuzzy microphone, I recognized it as one Jake and Lorina had been lusting after for weeks, but claimed they couldn't buy because it cost a fortune.

Elidriel wasn't just playing at this. Whatever she was—a journalist, an influencer, some hybrid of both—she was all in. I just wasn't sure how that squared with the shy, wide-eyed girl in front of me.

Satisfied with her setup, she sat up with a forceful nod that made her tiny body bob up and down in her seat.

"Ready?" she asked.

"As I'm gonna be," I replied with a smile.

She clicked a tiny remote, and the phone's camera timer flicked to life. Just like that, something shifted. The camera turned on, and so did she.

It was subtle, but undeniable. Much like Levonia, Elidriel's personality shifted ever so slightly once the camera started rolling. A brightness entered her eyes, and energy poured from her that was positively contagious. She reminded me of Rita. Could Elidriel be a tech witch like Rita? Part of me said yes, but that label didn't feel quite right.

Her voice, still soft, had an undercurrent of confidence now, a surety that hadn't been there before, as she addressed the camera. I wondered what size following she had.

"I'm in Gryphon, Alabama, home of Murphy Blackwell, the witch who has astonished the internet recently by displaying her ability to manipulate matter—first water, then fire." Elidriel's voice, soft but clear, carried a quiet authority now that the camera was rolling. "Miss Blackwell, there's been a lot of speculation about how you and other witches learn magic. Some say the Craft is passed through the bloodline, others believe it's something that can be learned. How would you describe it?"

Good question. I pondered the best way to answer. "Some people inherit talent. Some find magic in themselves that they didn't know was there. I'm a little of both, sort of. I didn't know the extent of my power until just last year."

Elidriel nodded, but I caught the flick of her fingers as she adjusted her grip on the mic. Nervous? Maybe. But she powered through. "Your abilities have sparked a huge debate online. Some say you're proof that magic is real, while others think it's all an elaborate trick. What do you say to the skeptics?"

I huffed a quiet laugh. "If someone doesn't believe in

magic, nothing I say is gonna change their mind. Computers make it easy to manipulate images, so folks can—and do—create things like that a lot of the time. Sometimes for entertainment, sometimes to straight up mislead folks. If they see it with their own eyes, though? That is a little harder to disprove."

She considered that, then shifted in her seat. "That brings me to my next question. Do you think magic comes with responsibility?"

I tilted my head. "Sometimes. If we have the power to help someone and choose not to, that's just as much a misuse of magic as casting an unjustified curse. Don't you agree?"

The corner of her mouth twitched, but she didn't back down. "Fair point," she admitted. "But some people believe magic should stay in the shadows. That revealing it to the world might be dangerous."

There it was. The real question beneath the question.

I let the silence stretch a little before I answered. "Truth has a way of slipping through the cracks, no matter how hard people try to bury it. Witchcraft has always been around. Some people believe in it. Some don't. I believe everyone has at least a small ability to tap into the Source's power. With the Stygian coven out there trying to make the world fear witches, maybe it's time for people to see we aren't all bad."

Elidriel nodded slowly, but her expression had turned guarded, thoughtful. She set the mic down gently, steepling her fingers, and for the first time, really looked at me.

"I think we might be related."

I blinked. "That's... not where I thought this was going."

Her fingers curled, tightening in her lap. "It's just a theory," she admitted. "But I have family ties to Gryphon. And my abilities—" She hesitated, then exhaled, as if bracing herself for something. "I'm not a tech witch like your friend Rita.

I'm fae."

I stared at her, waiting for the punchline, but she wasn't joking. The air between us grew positively electric. My thoughts sped ahead, chasing connections. How long had she been following my progress with the WorldWide Witches? And how did she know I was thinking she might be a tech witch? Was she—?

Yeah, a little voice in my head said, *I can read minds. I don't mean to invade, I can't stop it.*

My stomach did an uncomfortable little flip. That contagious energy of hers, that brightness in her eyes—it made sense.

She wasn't just good on camera. She was mesmerizing. Because she was fae.

I leaned back, letting the weight of that revelation settle. "Well," I said finally, "that explains a few things."

Her hands tightened around the microphone, her knuckles white. "You're not surprised?"

"Oh, I'm plenty surprised," I said. "But you're not the first supernatural person I've met who wasn't a witch. Crystal and Doyle over there? Also... not exactly human. I'll leave it at that."

She exhaled a shaky laugh, relief flickering across her face. "Then maybe you'll understand why I wanted to talk to you."

A glance at the camera slipped out before I could stop myself. "You felt the need to record your big reveal?" The edge in my voice gave away more of my misgivings than I intended.

"I'm sorry," she said quickly. "I just... who would believe me?"

I gave a casual shrug. "I do. I mean, it's possible. I am part fae. Not exactly a stretch."

"Your father's name was Ryan Turner, right?" she asked.

I stiffened. I hadn't even been thinking about him. Could she really rifle through my head like a damn filing cabinet?

"Yes," she said, wincing. "Sorry. It's not like I try. But sometimes, when I want an answer, it just... pops into my head—if it's nearby."

I exhaled slowly, wondering if I was justified in my knee-jerk urge to get defensive. Elidriel seemed like a nice enough kid, though.

"My father's name was Rory Turner," she went on. "He had a twin brother named Ryan."

Twins. That would mean...

"Identical?" I asked.

She shook her head. "Fraternal. He only lived here in the States off and on until he reached his twenties. He headed back to Ireland. Said he felt drawn there, since it's the easiest place to reach Tír na nÓg. That's where he met my mother. They married. I took their American surname, so my surname is Turner as well."

"Tir na... nÓg?" I stumbled over the unfamiliar syllables.

"The um..." her head bobbed back and forth as she sought a way to describe it. "The Otherworld. My father had a... special relationship with it. And with the um, deities there."

Deities. Her father hung out with deities. Did my father ever visit Tir na nÓg, too?

The timer on her phone kept ticking away. We were way over that promised five minutes, but neither of us seemed eager to stop.

"Was your mother fae as well?" I asked.

She nodded, observing my every expression, every move.

"So, you're full fae. Not half, like me?"

"Yes."

It was only then that I noticed her eyes—an unreal shade of emerald green. She must have hidden that feature until after her confession—it wasn't easily overlooked.

A dozen questions surged forward, the same ones that had been circling since February when I first found out my father was fae. I hadn't spoken to him since that night, not after the Lughaidh coven beat back the Stygian, and everything I thought I knew about myself was once again proven untrue. And ever since, the questions had piled up. Things I wish I'd known about him, about his time with my mother. About what it meant for me to be part fae.

But now…

For the first time, I wasn't just looking at old books, half-truths, and memories. I was likely looking at family. Someone who might actually have answers. And more questions.

I exhaled, letting that settle. "Huh."

Elidriel's mouth quirked. "Huh?"

I huffed a small laugh. "Yeah. Just—out of all the things I thought I'd learn today? Finding out I have a long-lost fae cousin wasn't on the list."

Her smile was brief, but real. "Guess that makes two of us."

The timer kept ticking. The interview was over, but the conversation? That was just getting started.

Chapter 19

I debated calling a coven gathering again to introduce them to Elidriel, but gave them at least one night off, instead. The Stygian had gone an entire day without causing global chaos and destruction (that I knew of). The reporters outside Blackwell Manor were losing steam, their enthusiasm fading with every hour I refused to leave the house. I sent Doyle out with a message for all of them to be sure to be at Music in the Park on Friday, but today was only Wednesday. Maybe some of them would leave and come back. I hoped they did.

All in all, things were looking pretty damn good. And I didn't feel like tempting fate.

So instead, I invited Terry over.

Terry, our resident indigo witch, held a weird mix of unsettling and invaluable gifts. Most people who know about witches assume indigos merely talk to ghosts—wrong. Terry doesn't just see the dead; she sees so much more. Impressions, threads of connection, the echoes of seemingly insignificant everyday items. She once steered a guy in my shop toward a dusty, random-ass tarot deck I'd had on the shelf for probably five years. Two days later, he came back raving about how it matched a deck that belonged to his grandfather, who'd made the connection when they compared decks.

"How do you do it?" I asked her once.

She shrugged. "Things tell me where they belong."

Creepy as hell sometimes. But useful.

When she first told me about growing up with her ability, I felt so awful for her that every detail of the story stuck with me. Her mother never understood why Terry refused to play with secondhand toys. It wasn't that she was picky. The toys *remembered* things. Every imprint left behind clung to them, and Terry absorbed it all. As a kid, every outing into the world outside her home overwhelmed her—she was drowning in echoes of the past. She felt every birthday thrill, every argument, every heartbreak, like layers of other people's lives playing out in her mind, like mental movies she couldn't turn off.

"I used to wish I could wear gloves all the time, like old-school Southern ladies," she'd told me once, swirling her drink. "It hurt too much to touch things with history."

LaDonna, being the powerhouse she is, caught on relatively early and hooked Terry up with another Indigo witch from an outside coven who helped her learn to control it. These days, Terry could filter the noise when she wanted to, which was the only way for her to live a normal life. If she let it in, there was no telling what she'd constantly be picking up.

Tonight, Terry didn't arrive alone. To my delight, Betony showed up with her, which felt…well, like a coincidence that wasn't really a coincidence. And when Conall stopped by after work, I started getting that gnawing sensation in my spirit. Like the universe was nudging pieces into place.

Almost as if we had a violet witch present. And no, violet and indigo are not the same, but they are close—much like in the spectrum. Violet witches are fate weavers who can sense the flow of destiny, lightly influence events, and serve as agents of change—someone whose presence subtly alters outcomes. Like indigo witches, violet witches can place their fingers on the pulse of universal energy and sense vibrations—indigo into the past, violet into the future. Violet witches don't outright manipulate fate, but they always seem to be in the right place at the right time, whether it's influencing events or learning important details.

Maybe Elidriel had an indigo-like power she didn't know about yet. Or maybe—and this was the thought that dug its claws in and refused to let go—maybe it was Rene.

After six months of living under my roof, he still hadn't told me what kind of witch he was. The kid was eighteen—had to know by now. He just wasn't saying. He was a teenage boy, after all.

I didn't want to bug him about it, though. He already struggled with authority. And I didn't want him thinking I wanted to milk any of his witch powers to my advantage. Hell, there was a better-than-decent chance his mother only had him for one reason: to be a disposable vessel for the Sovereign Darkness. Maybe that's why Rene hadn't said—he still struggled to trust adults.

The thought made my stomach turn. *What a fucking bitch.* I hated that woman with every molecule of my existence.

I shoved the thought away just as Terry and Betony walked in, ten minutes to seven, right before I locked up. The shop had been dead all day, probably because of the reporters parked on the street, so I'd already counted the register, tallied sales, and, thanks to Rene, had most of the closing work done.

Rene and Elidriel had been hanging around earlier, but I'd shooed them upstairs when their conversation kept disrupting my counting down the register. They were close in age and got along well enough, but they were also like two cats who had just met—interested, circling each other, but not sure if they should trust the situation or bolt.

Terry took one look around and smirked. "You were waiting for me to get here before anything interesting happened,
weren't you?"

I rolled my eyes as I shoved my tiny take for the day into
the safe and gave the dial a spin. "Absolutely. Wouldn't dare
summon fate without my personal mystic."

She snorted, but didn't let it go. Her gaze flicked over me,
then tilted slightly—that look she gets when she's picking up
something I can't see.

"Well?" I crossed my arms. "You're getting something,
aren't you?"

Her eyes drifted toward the ceiling, where Rene and
Elidriel had disappeared. "Yeah," she drawled. "And it's
weird. Real weird."

Betony sighed, already exasperated. "Great. Just what we
need. More weird." She cast a glance at the table where Crystal and Doyle had pretty much set up camp since they arrived,
currently deserted. "Where are the newbies?"

"Crystal took Doyle out for… a drink," I said.

Betony wrinkled her nose. "Where?"

I sank into a chair, and Terry and Betony followed suit.
Conall strolled behind the counter to grab a bottle of water.
"Some forest in Germany, apparently," I said. "Doyle likes
the hunting there."

Betony narrowed her eyes. "A forest?"

I laughed. "He doesn't drink from humans. Said he's—"
I made air quotes "—a 'crittervore.'"

Terry and Conall cracked up. Betony looked vaguely hor-
rified.

"Speaking of newbies," I said, steering the conversation
back. "There's someone upstairs you three need to meet." My
stomach fluttered at the thought of introducing Elidriel to
even a small part of the coven—especially Terry. What if she

touches something Elidriel came into contact with and I wind up finding out she's an impostor, or worse? With everything going on, there was a chance the fae girl was planning a bit of gonzo journalism to make herself famous. Yes, I had the wards, but I'd never had to protect against fae magic before.

Rather than holler up the stairs, I sent Rene a quick text. Seconds later, the rhythmic thump-thump-thump of footsteps—one heavy, one light—echoed down the back staircase, followed by bursts of laughter as he and Elidriel strode through the kitchen and into the coffee shop. They were still talking, their conversation an effortless back-and-forth that made them sound like old friends rather than two people who'd only just met. I guess they got past that circling cats phase.

The moment Betony and Elidriel locked eyes, something shifted. The air grew tight, charged with an energy so intense that I swore the floor beneath me rolled, as if the whole room had subtly adjusted itself around them. Even seated, I felt my stomach dip, the sort of weightless sensation that comes right before a fall.

Across from me, Betony had gone rigid. Her fingers curled into fists against her thighs. The baby hairs around her head lifted, fine strands floating as though pulled by static. Her jaw was clenched so tightly that the muscle in her cheek flexed, and when she finally blinked, I realized her hazel eyes had gone a cool, swirling gray, like moonstone catching the light. But she didn't appear distressed so much as *entranced*.

She wasn't afraid. She was locked in, focused, eyes fixed unblinkingly on Elidriel as if she were seeing through her into a universe beyond.

I nearly forgot why I had called the meeting. I barely caught myself before blurting out something stupid. Instead, I gripped the table and watched, my pulse a slow, deliberate beat against my ribs. Nothing bad had happened, but everything had just become extremely... Cadence would call it *extra*.

"Betony, Terry, Conall... this is Elidriel," I said finally, clearing my throat. "She's fae. And... she might be my cousin."

Elidriel's bottle-glass green eyes, which reciprocated Betony's stare, widened. She hesitated, as if weighing her words, then nodded stiffly. "It's—it's nice to meet you."

She didn't extend a hand. I suddenly realized she had never offered to shake mine, either. *That doesn't necessarily mean anything bad. Some people aren't big on physical touch. Hell, you and Betony are both that way.*

Rene narrowed his eyes. "Bet, you good?"

Betony blinked, and the gray in her eyes flickered, shifting, before her usual hazel crept back in around the edges. "Yeah," she muttered. "I'm fine. Just... disassociating a little, I guess."

Terry exchanged a look with me, and I could tell she wasn't buying that explanation any more than I was.

"Did you say cousin?" Conall asked, shifting the attention back to Elidriel as his gaze flicked between us like he was trying to spot a resemblance.

I leaned back, letting out a slow breath. "Her last name is Turner. Her father is Rory Turner, who had a fraternal twin brother named Ryan Turner. Now, I don't know how common fae men named Ryan Turner are—"

"Not common at all," Elidriel interjected. Her voice was quiet but confident. "There are so few fae left in the world. That's why I'm almost positive we're related."

"So," I said, "We have yet another non-human in town."

Terry huffed out a laugh. "Betony, I was right. This is *weird*."

Betony let out a long breath. "Weird is an understatement." She shot a glance at the table, as if she also needed something solid to ground herself. "At this point, a statistically significant portion of folks in Gryphon aren't human."

I smirked, but the truth in her words settled deep. "And I'm also pretty sure we can add Mayor Tanaka to those numbers."

Conall nearly choked on his water. "The mayor? Are you serious?"

I nodded. "He hasn't exactly confided in me. I don't know what he is. And if I told you what gave me that idea, you'd think I'd lost my mind. But it wasn't what he said so much as how he said it. You know?"

Rene and Elidriel pulled up chairs, and the rest of us adjusted, forming a loose circle around the table.

I glanced back at Betony, whose power still hummed in the air. Her eyes were a fraction lighter now, but the charge rolling off her skin hadn't dimmed. I wondered if Elidriel could see it, too.

"You look… charged," I said. "I'm thinking you need to release some of that chaos energy. And I have just the thing."

She arched a brow, wary. "What's that?"

I spread my hands. "Well, we've got an orange witch here with a gift for prediction, an indigo witch who can sense the threads tying things together, a gray witch vibrating with enough excess energy to light up Huntsville, and a Summate. Between all of us, I'd say we have a decent shot at figuring out if Elidriel and I are actually related."

"Not a bad idea," Conall said.

"And," I added, locking eyes with Betony, "maybe we ask the universe for a little guidance on what the hell to do about this whole coming-out-of-the-broom-closet situation. The Stygian have a massive lead on us, but we want to make sure we do it right, you know?"

The air had just started to settle when Rene cleared his throat.

"I can help with that first part quite a bit, I bet," he said, voice casual. "I'm a silver witch."

Silence hit the table like a dropped stone.

I should have seen that one coming. His mother was a gold witch, one with the gift of prosperity and financial success. But silver witches…

Damn.

When they call on their power, a silver witch becomes a reflection of what's hidden, a bridge between what's seen and what isn't. They are mirrors to the universe, revealing what others can't see, reflecting knowledge that exists beyond time, memory, or perception—something that makes them both feared and revered among witches. A silver witch sees into the cracks of reality itself, sometimes even catching glimpses of what might have been in other worlds. They don't read minds, but they see the truths people refuse to face—the things buried, rewritten, or lost to time. When they look at someone, they might see fragments of past lives, hidden thoughts, or emotions too buried to name. To stand before a silver witch is to stand before a mirror that doesn't lie. They see what they see, and whether they speak or stay silent— that's between them and the universe.

No wonder Ericka had wanted him to be the keeper of the Sovereign Darkness.

And now he was sitting across from me, looking completely unbothered that he had just upended everything I thought I knew about him.

I exhaled and rubbed the back of my neck.

"Well, shit," I muttered. "Guess we really are asking the universe for answers tonight."

Chapter 20

I'd never seen Rene exercise his gift before, or any other silver witch for that matter, so I'm sure my excitement showed. Silver witches aren't exactly common. Everyone else leaned in as well, eager to get started. Rene, however, paused. For a guy who usually carried himself like he owned the room, he suddenly looked... hesitant. Maybe it was the pressure of performing in front of an audience or nerves about demonstrating his powers in front of his peers. Maybe he felt a little inhibited in front of me, being the Summate. Hard to say.

He held up a finger, indicating he'd like a second to center himself. Everyone around the circle grew silent so he could find his focus.

He closed his eyes. Centered himself. And for the first time, I really looked at him. Not just as Rene, the cocky, self-assured young, male witch I'd come to know, but as a young man. Dark hair, strong features, a brow heavy enough to give his expressions some real weight. He had that whole young Jeffrey Dean Morgan thing going on. And while he was masculine, he was also totally unbothered about showing his softer side. He cared deeply for his friends and had big 'lift you and your emotional baggage' energy. No wonder Betony, who usually stuck to dating women, had made an exception for him.

As he focused, I felt a pull, a gentle coaxing as the halo of Rene's energy came in contact with my aura, which is typically indigo. (Yeah, I know, aura colors don't match the colors witches have assigned their specific talents. Don't ask me why. I don't make the rules.) He then extended his corona toward Elidriel, whose aura, I noted, was a gorgeous color of seafoam green. It suited her perfectly—beautiful and mystical, just like her.

Once he had a spiritual finger on the pulses of our energies, he opened his eyes and let out a nervous breath. He wiped his hands on his jeans hastily before reaching one hand in my direction, the other to Elidriel. I wasted no time in plopping my palm into Rene's waiting hand, but Elidriel faltered.

I tugged on a sliver of Source power, just enough to get a read on her.

"Whoa," Rene said, voice tinged with awe. "That's cool, Murphy, but next time, maybe warn a guy?"

I smirked. "My bad."

A few questioning looks flickered around the circle. "Source," I explained. Understanding passed over their faces.

Turning my attention back to Elidriel, I pushed past the surface of her hesitation. I couldn't exactly read minds like she could, but impressions? Those I could pick up fairly easily.

She wasn't afraid of hurting Rene. She was afraid of touch itself. That realization hit me like a gut punch. It was the same guarded wariness I'd seen in Betony, the kind that hinted at wounds that never quite heal. So much so that I wondered if she, like Betony, had been a victim of abuse. Poor Betony had suffered from both verbal and physical abuse from her parents in the worst ways imaginable. Had Elidriel struggled with that, too?

I met Elidriel's gaze and softened my voice. "It's okay,"

I told her. "You're safe."

Her impossibly large eyes widened even more, but something in my tone, and whatever vibes she picked up from my and Rene's heads, must have reassured her. She nodded—just a slight, reluctant dip of her chin—before finally pressing her hand into Rene's.

The moment we connected, the world shattered like a mirror struck with a hammer.

Reflections of ourselves spun in every direction, cascading through an endless funhouse of color and light. Yellows flared like electric sunbursts, blues pulsed like neon at twilight, reds and greens coiled and twisted like living ribbons threading through pools of silver. Feeling a little motion sick, I turned in place, trying to find the real Elidriel among the kaleidoscope of shifting images. She was doing the same.

And then—contact.

Our auras merged in a swirl of indigo and sea-foam green. The colors blended into something rich and deep, creating the beautiful palette of the ocean at nightfall.

It was my turn to say, "Whoa."

From across the table, I heard Elidriel murmur, "Ooh."

Rene's voice softly interfered, causing the colors in the mental landscape of mirrors to vibrate slightly. "I've got what I need," he said. "Are you ready to come out?"

I wasn't. Not really. I could have stayed in that colorful funhouse with Elidriel's sweet spirit beside me for hours watching the hues bend and flex and dance around us.

Letting out a regretful sigh, I said, "Yeah, alright. This is… this is incredible, Rene."

He sounded pleased. "I can't see what you two see, but I'm glad it was good for you." His tone took on the calm cadence of someone guiding a meditation. "Take a slow breath. Wiggle your fingers and toes. And when you're ready… open your eyes."

I followed his instructions, surfacing like a diver returning from deep waters. When I blinked back to reality, Elidriel was already watching me, her face mirroring the wonder I still felt. Even here, in the waking world, our auras shimmered together, still entangled.

Rene's voice pulled us the rest of the way back.

"You two are definitely related," he said judiciously. "But, uh… here's the thing. She's not your cousin."

"I'm not?" Elidriel's face fell.

I frowned. "Wait. But you said we're related."

Rene blew out a breath like a man bracing for impact. His gaze darted around every face at the table before settling on mine.

"She's… uh…" His throat bobbed in a swallow. "She's your sister."

Silence fell over the room. Elidriel's expression flickered through a dozen emotions—shock, confusion, something dangerously close to hope—before settling into wary skepticism.

I swallowed hard, my mind scrambling to process what Rene had just dropped on us. A sister. Not a cousin or more distant blood relation. A sister. My mother was human, which meant Rory wasn't her biological father—my father was.

I turned to Elidriel, words catching in my throat. What the hell was I supposed to say? Welcome to the family? Sorry for the late notice?

She blinked rapidly, like she was trying to shake herself out of a dream.

"…Are you sure?" she asked, voice barely above a whisper. I had a feeling she'd poked around inside Rene's head to verify he had confidence in his words.

Rene's expression was solemn. "Yeah. I'm sure."

A storm of emotions swelled in my chest—too much, too fast. But beneath the confusion, beneath the sheer impossibility of it all, something in me already knew. The Source knew.

I exhaled slowly, glancing at the way the tangled edges of our auras, still mingling like they'd always known each other, blurred with unshed tears.

Sister.

Chapter 21

I didn't much feel like going through with my plans for the evening after that. The revelation that Elidriel was my sister was almost too much for my heart and mind to bear. My emotions swung wild between wanting to climb onto the roof and holler for all of Gryphon to hear that I had family—real, blood family—again and wanting to crawl into bed, curl up in a ball, and let the shock roll over me in waves until I could make sense of it.

Oh, and then there was the small matter of figuring out how our coven was supposed to announce our presence to the world. Preferably with no one winding up dead, which was clearly the Stygian's preferred method of broadcasting their existence.

Conall's hand landed warm and solid on my arm. "We can continue this tomorrow," he said, his voice as steady as his grip, his brown eyes as soothing as a warm chocolate chip cookie. Damn, that man knows me well.

"Yeah, Murph," Betony chimed in. "We can wait until tomorrow to figure out how to counter the Stygian's next move. Or, you know… whenever."

Whenever? As if the Stygian were taking their time. Doyle had told us that their friend knew our "witch situation" was about to blow up. I thought back to the assassination on the third. The bombing on the Fourth and those poor, dead children. The massive bird attack in D.C. The poor rabbits unable to move as horses controlled by the Stygian stampeded them. And that was the list of what we knew about. The U.S. barely reported on its own messes, let alone what was happening in Mexico or Canada. We rarely heard any news from Europe, Africa, or Asia. Who knew what fresh hell the Stygian was stirring up across the globe?

How do you say Stygian in Russian? Or Swahili? Would news outlets realize the connection?

I scooted my chair forward and sat up taller, shoving down the bone-deep exhaustion wearing at my soul. "No. We're doing this tonight. For all we know, the Stygian are launching attacks every day, and we're not hearing about it. We have to take a stand, we have to let the world know that not all witches suck, and the sooner, the better. But we definitely need some guidance. Rene?"

He met my gaze, astute as always, and I could see the caution behind it. Like he was already bracing for whatever mess I was about to hand him. That silver sheen shimmered softly around his pupils, like moonlight on oil.

"We're at a fork here," I said quietly. "Conall's got eyes on what happens next—if we keep going the way we are, if no one throws a wrench in the works. I need you to look deeper. Past the surface. Past what it wants us to see."

A silence stretched, and his eyes darted back and forth a trace as he thought. Not hesitation. Calculation.

"If there's a lie wrapped around the truth, I need you to cut through it. Can you still do that? Are you too tired?"

His expression shifted a little.

"I know you're drained. We all are. But if you've got anything left—just enough to peel back the top layer—I think it could make the difference between walking into a trap, or finally out of one."

Rene's knee bounced under the table, and when he caught us all watching him, he stilled it with effort. He reached back to rub his neck, his fingers digging into the tension there.

"Yeah. I mean, I can do it."

I arched a brow. "You don't sound sure."

He dropped his hand to his lap, a determined set to his jaw that hadn't been there a moment ago. "I can do it. I'll do it."

My posture eased. "I can give you a little juice if you need it."

Relief flickered across his face. "That'd be great."

Turning to my fiancé, I gave him my full attention. "I guess I don't need to tell you where you fit in."

Conall's grin made my heart stumble in its rhythm, as it always did. "Nope. Like you said, I'll see what the future holds if we keep going down the current path."

"Perfect. Terry?"

Terry brushed her long, brown hair over her shoulder, the clever eyes behind her glasses alert as always. "Yes, ma'am?"

"This might make you uncomfortable, but I need you to explore the connections between us. See if you can pick up any echoes—anything hidden that needs to come to light."

Betony smirked. "And I'll keep y'all from losing your shit."

The laugh that rippled through us was strained.

We reached for each other's hands, forming a loose circle. All of us, except for Elidriel. She hesitated, then asked, "What about you, Murphy? Other than helping Rene? And how do you even do that?"

She doesn't know. Not really. All she's picked up is what she's seen in the interviews and what little she's picked up in my head.

"I'm a Summate," I explained. "That means... well, Rene

just let us know he's a silver witch, and you've seen a little what that means. Conall is orange, so he has the gift of prophecy. Terry's an indigo witch, Betony's a gray, she sucks up chaos. We're all a little different, right? Each witch, every color, has a specialty. The occasional one has two, but that's pretty unusual."

"Sure, that makes sense." Elidriel nodded, taking it in.

Conall gave my hand a squeeze, his thumb brushing over my knuckles in silent support. I shot him a small smile before turning back to my newfound sister.

"I have them all," I continued. "Any power a witch can have? I've got it. And a lot of it." It used to feel like bragging, but after having to explain it enough times, it finally sank in that, as the saying goes, it ain't bragging if it's true.

Elidriel's mouth parted slightly, her eyes flicking over me as though she could see the magic curled inside me, waiting to be called upon. "Oh. That's… incredible."

"Do you have magic, too?" Betony piped up, leaning forward with interest. "I've never met a fae before. I'd love to learn what y'all can do. And it is there a difference between fae and fairy?"

Elidriel nodded, twirling a tendril of her short hair between her fingers. "There is a difference, but… let me explain the magic first. Fae do have magical power. It's… very Earth-based. Or—not Earth, really. Organic? Does that make sense?"

"Sure," Betony replied. "Like, if you can touch it, breathe it… if it's part of the fabric of the universe, you can tweak it. Is that right?"

Elidriel's lips curled at the corners, a flicker of appreciation in her expression. "That's exactly right."

Was it appreciation, though? I wasn't so sure. There was a different intensity in the way she and Betony were watching each other—something more focused, more charged. It wasn't like the wary way Betony studied Doyle, who I was pretty sure she trusted about as much as a wooden nickel, or the initial tension between Elidriel and Rene. No, this was different. There was curiosity here. Interest. Maybe even attraction, simmering just beneath the surface.

"And, so—there is a difference between fae and fairy," Elidriel said, like she was starting a TikTok video explaining a task. "Fairies are one type of fae. All fairies are fae, but not all fae are fairies. Make sense?"

"Totally," Bet said.

I studied Elidriel for a beat, then gestured toward our forming circle. "Would you like to join us?"

She hesitated, something unreadable flashing across her face before she shook her head and leaned back. "Not this time," she whispered. "Maybe in the future. If that's alright?"

"Absolutely," I assured her.

I squeezed Conall and Betony's hands, feeling the familiar press of energy crackling beneath my skin, waiting to be channeled. Drawing in a steady breath, I met each of their gazes in turn.

"Alright, y'all," I murmured. "Let's get started."

$$\text{)}\bigcirc\text{(}$$

Feeling somewhat like LaDonna as I took the lead of our session, I signaled that we should start by drawing in a deep breath and closing my eyes. Through the spiritual link that flowed through our connected hands, I sensed them doing the same.

I wasted no time. This time, I dove so deeply and quickly into my power that tapping into the Source was like sinking into a current of liquid fire —a charge of pure energy so vast and bright that it made my skin hum. My soul felt buoyant, light enough to drift right off the chair. My breath hitched as a rush of love and freedom flooded my chest, expanding outward until I thought I might dissolve into the radiance itself.

The Source within me unfurled, tendrils of spiritual energy slithering through my veins, coiling in my core. I directed it outward, weaving delicate filaments of power like living vines, stretching and curling around the hands, wrists, and arms of my coven mates. The charge in the air sharpened, electric and alive. Gasps and soft murmurs of appreciation rose around the circle as the force sought each witch's unique power, strengthening their connection to it, making it richer, deeper. I could almost taste the shift—metallic like ozone before a thunderstorm, tinged with something sweeter, like cinnamon and brown sugar.

"All right, Conall," I said, quieter now. "Let's see where your future takes us."

I reached for the thread between us, that subtle pulse of magic he never tried to hide from me, and let my senses drift.

The vision settled fast—Gryphon's town square, sunswept and deceptively normal. Too many people milling around for a weekday. Booths in the park. Something festive was humming in the air, bright and busy. Probably a town event, like a holiday celebration.

I held that image steady in my mind and cast it toward the other side of the circle.

"Rene?"

His answer came low and distant. "Mmm."

"Gonna open the line to you now," I said. "You good with me taking a look while you do your thing?"

Another pause. Then, "Mmm. Sure." His voice was slightly strained, like he was speaking from a dream.

It hit me then—this was Rene's first time feeling the full

weight of Source energy flowing into him, and he was probably over there losing his mind a little. A laugh tickled the back of my throat, but I held it in. Poor guy. Terry had experienced it before. Betony and I had practically made a habit of balancing each other out with energy exchanges. And Conall? Well, he had the added benefit of me tapping into power during sex, which I did. Often. Because, honestly? Sex was already amazing, but add in Source energy and… well, damn. The bed felt ready to levitate.

Gently, I reached for Rene's aura, careful not to disrupt whatever trance state he was settling into. The moment my focus drifted across the circle, I noticed it—the color of his aura was more than uncommon. I realized then what great lengths he'd gone through to ensure I'd never had a reason to see it before then. It shone stark white, impossibly bright.

Unheard of. That's usually only found in extremely old souls or really enlightened people. What is with this kid?

I tucked that curiosity away for later. For now, I pushed deeper, slipping into the flow of his magic and bringing Conall's vision of the future with me.

And I was *blown away.*

Where Elidriel's and my combined vision had been like a kaleidoscopic funhouse of mirrors, Rene's was something else entirely—a tangled, living weave of fractured realities. Layer upon layer of possibility sprawled before me, chaotic and shifting, a hundred thousand possibilities folding and unfolding all at once.

Where Elidriel and my vision combined was a colorful funhouse of mirrors, Rene's image was of the fabric of multiple realities—a many-layered jumble of confusing and contorting scenes. Pictures of the group where we sat broke into at least a dozen varieties of goodbyes, then divided into multiple scenes again as everyone exited, and dozens of paths taken home. Conall both stayed the night and left to go home. Elidriel lingered for hours in whispered conversation, yet in another flicker of reality, she left immediately.

I followed Terry's and Conall's thoughts through a few of the fractured futures they might lead. Then Betony. Then...

Holy crap.

My mind reeled, twisting in on itself as I struggled to keep up. It was too much. The sheer volume of diverging paths made my thoughts feel tangled in an impossible knot, like playing a mental game of Twister and constantly losing track of my limbs. Every time I tried to focus on one trajectory, another looped me back, dragging me into another layer of reality.

Hold up, Murphy.

The voice was mine, but not mine—Rene's words carried through the vision.

This is weird, dude. My thoughts pulsed out in response.

Yeah, well, usually I don't have this much juice making things all glitchy. His energy pulsed, erratic but steadying.

My bad, dude. I winced.

Nah, you're good. Let's work through Conall's vision and see what's coming, K?

I felt a tug on the edges of my consciousness, and the next thing I knew, I was in a black-walled room alongside a version of Rene that looked a little younger than the Rene I thought of. I wondered if this was how he thought of himself.

The surrounding air smelled of aged wood, parchment dust, and a whisper of dried lavender. The floor beneath us creaked underfoot, polished but worn, much like the one in Witch's Brew.

"This is where it starts," Rene murmured, taking my hand and pulling me forward—

—and suddenly, we were standing in one of Gryphon's four town squares. Each of the town squares branched from Hamlet Street, two to the west and two to the east.

"Come on," he said. Trusting the guy who had way more experience than me to know what he was doing, I followed him as we jumped through the intervening space to Puck's Green. It was Music in the Park night, though whether it was this coming Friday or a distant one, I couldn't tell. The scent of trampled grass, fried food, and the lingering odor of sun-warmed asphalt told me it was a summer month. A few feet away, a toddler in a sagging diaper squealed with delight, sticky hands clapping together as he teetered after a wayward balloon. A golden retriever, tongue lolling, bounded after a thrown Frisbee, catching it mid-air to the cheers of its owner. The rhythmic slap of a hacky sack being volleyed between a group of college kids mixed with the warm, buzzing hum of cheerful conversation.

Near the bandstand, a warm-up riff hummed through the amp as a guitarist checked his tuning. The mellow, brassy tang of a trumpet followed, blending with the click of drum-sticks tapping out a lazy rhythm. The musicians—clad in easy, worn denim and faded graphic tees—moved about the makeshift dais with easy camaraderie, their relaxed smiles promising a good show.

A couple on a picnic blanket shared a bottle of wine, their laughter drifting over the evening breeze, while vendors manned pop-up booths offering everything from hand-poured candles to fresh-squeezed lemonade. Overhead, string lights hung from tree to tree, their gentle golden glow just beginning to flicker to life against the deepening twilight.

The entire square hummed with energy, with that brand of lazy, small-town contentment that came with pleasant music, warm summer nights, and familiar faces. Time raced forward, and everything surrounding us rushed by in a zoom until nearly full dark. Folks were settled in now, relaxing as the band played. Conversation was a soft drone under the cheery tunes of New Orleans-style jazz. The environment was a poster for contented, small-town charm.

Then everything changed.

It was subtle at first—a shift in the mood, like the air pressure dropping before a storm. The hum of conversation thinned, voices tapering off one by one, like someone slowly turning the volume down on a radio.

Just as I was about to convince myself that it was all in my imagination, they moved.

A woman with a baby in her lap stood so suddenly the child gave an abrupt cry, its tiny fists clutching at her sundress as she rose. A teenage boy, mid-laugh with his friend, jerked upright as if an invisible string had yanked him to his feet. A businessman in a polo shirt and half-eaten hot dog in hand did the same.

One in each pair and at least one in every small group.

The Frisbee that had been tossed so freely now landed, forgotten, in the grass. The golden retriever sniffed at it once before whining, ears flattening as it backed away.

This was no flash mob. Their eyes were empty, vacant pits reflecting the glow of the string of lights above them. Their faces slack, expressions wiped clean like a photo overexposed to light. They moved in eerie unison, stepping away from their conversations, their drinks, their laughter—

My stomach turned.

The Stygian is going to drown them.

The thought wasn't entirely mine. It rippled through the vision, through Rene's magic, through the tangled web of shifting possibilities.

Because of us, Rene's voice said in my mind. *You're here.*

Betony's here.

And you're here, I added.

Bruh. She hates all of us... even me.

Goddamn Ericka freaking Moore and her fucking Stygian asshole coven. My fury seared through the vision like wildfire, my body pulsing with the intensity of my loathing. I wanted them gone. I wanted them *erased*.

And as I wished it, the world around us blurred, warping with the force of my thought. Colors smeared, light distorted like heat waves rolling off asphalt in the dead of summer. The square wavered, edges curling like the corner of a photograph being set too close to a flame.

Then, with a snap, the vision reset. The crowd was still there, but now, so were they.

Deterrents.

At first, they were just figures at the edges of my awareness, flickers of motion in the shifting light. But as I focused, they solidified, emerging from the hazy distortion of time and possibility like shadows stepping into the sun.

Where there had been puppeted bodies marching in eerie unison toward the river, now others were blocking their path.

A woman in a sleek leather jacket stepped directly into the path of a man in a button-down, placing a firm hand on his chest and stopping his forward momentum with a press of her hand to his chest.

A ghostly pale man moved like a streak of silver and shadow, cutting between a cluster of dazed festival-goers. Energy crackled at his fingertips, tiny static sparks dancing as he stepped into their path.

A teenage girl, with blond curls bouncing against her shoulders, whispered something against the skin of a woman in a sundress. The woman blinked, shuddered, then stumbled back, her advance slowed, at least for now.

One by one, they moved in, halting the procession, diverting the entranced from their fate with quiet precision.

And while I wasn't terribly familiar with many people in my small town because of years of self-isolation, I sensed that those doing the detouring weren't from around here. They weren't ordinary citizens.

They were supers, and they were stopping the Stygian's victims from marching to their deaths. Somehow, some way... we weren't alone in this fight.

The scene shattered, broken apart like a mirror forcefully struck by a sledgehammer, each fragment reflecting a glint of silver mirrors into other possibilities before vanishing into nothingness. A violent jolt brought me back to where I sat in my chair inside my shop. The scent of freshly brewed coffee, the warmth of the overhead lights, the quiet hum of my world—everything about my surroundings was familiar. Comforting. Yet my mind clung to the spectral threads of the vision Rene had traced into our future. I struggled to remember as many details of the prediction before they faded like the remnants of a dream after waking.

The woman in the leather jacket.

The ghostly pale man.

The curly-haired teen.

Who were they? And how were we going to get them to Gryphon to save the people the Stygian planned to kill? When were they planning to pull off this insane plan?

And again—why Gryphon? The same question had been gnawing at me ever since Crystal brought it up on the Fourth. If the Stygian wanted a confrontation, why not draw us out, force us onto their turf? They were smart enough to manipulate circumstances, to pull the right strings and leave us no choice but to comply. Instead, they were bringing the fight here, to our home.

I frowned, my fingers curling against the worn armrest of my chair. Erika's last known base was in Atlanta. She knew the city, had networks of people at her beck and call around the entire freaking *globe*. She could have unleashed hell anywhere.

Why Gryphon?

Why *Gryphon*?

"Murphy, you OK?" Conall's gentle voice coaxed me from my reverie.

I fidgeted in my chair for a second as I did my best to burn the images of the supernatural people who had saved our townspeople from a demonic Pied Piper into my mind. I needed to cement the vision in my memory—the people, the details, the way the supernatural interlopers had moved to protect the town from what was coming.

"Yeah," I murmured, rubbing at my temple. "I'm okay."

His throat bobbed as he swallowed, a shadow of unease crossing his face. "The Stygian are coming. They're planning a strike on the town."

I nodded. "Did you get a sense of when? I didn't pick up that detail."

"Soon," he said, voice tight. "It's happening at Puck's Green—at least, that's what it looked like. I heard music, so probably—"

"Concert in the Park," Rene supplied, his gaze locked on Conall.

"Well, that means it could be the second Friday of any month," I said. "I saw a woman wearing a leather jacket, so maybe the weather was cooler."

Rene shook his head. "Think of all the people in shorts, though," he pointed out. "And the baby in a diaper. I'm guessing that since she had a gift, maybe something in the leather lady's body chemistry makes her feel cold all the time."

Any other time, the words *leather lady* would have opened Rene up to a joke. Instead, I frowned, unhappy that he was on to something. "Yeah, you're right. It's probably summertime, then. Which means this could come as soon as this Friday."

A heavy silence settled over us, thick with unspoken worries.

This Friday.

How the hell were we supposed to pull together a team of supernaturally gifted people in less than a week? I mean, sure, Rita could put an alert out on the WorldWide Witches forum—they were already alert to the problem. But what would we tell them? And how many would willingly step up to take on a ruthless coven willing to slaughter anyone to make a point?

The Lughaidh would fight. I knew that much. And if we would, others would, too. *There has to be more out there— people like us, people who won't stand by while the Stygian spills innocent blood.*

Still, I cringed at the way my mind kept grouping us under one label. Super-people. It sounded ridiculous, like we were some knockoff Justice League. That had to go, even in my head. We weren't superheroes. We were just…people. People who happened to have abilities we kept hidden, living among the world like a mystical underground… society. A secret society. Like the Illuminati.

Hell, were they real, too?

I scanned the room absently, my gaze catching on a book resting on a nearby shelf: *Beyond the Numinous: Consciousness, Magic, and Reality.*

Something clicked.

Numinous.

Mysterious. Divine. Otherworldly. It was perfect. We were the Numinati. Singular: Numinari. The moment the word took root in my mind, I knew it fit.

"Crystal," I breathed. "Her friend knew we'd need her help. She's here to help us find the others and bring them here—the ones we need to save Gryphon."

My mind was reeling, and Betony leaned forward to place a gentle hand on my knee. Her touch drew my chaotic thoughts into a single, steady current.

"Doyle and Crystal know more," I continued, the word solidifying in my mind. "More of us. The Numinari. I just thought of the term. We're all... numinous. Connected to something beyond the ordinary."

Betony's mouth curved into a crooked grin. "I like it. It fits."

"It does," Terry agreed, though her focus had shifted elsewhere.

My gaze followed hers to the one person in our circle who hadn't spoken yet. "Terry," I prompted. "What sort of echoes did you see?"

She pressed her lips together, flicking an uneasy glance at Rene before fidgeting in her seat.

Must be a night for uncomfortable revelations.

"Rene's mom—"

"Ericka," he said scathingly. His anger wasn't directed at Terry, but she flinched all the same.

Terry started again, this time softer. "She hasn't... given up. On you. On her plans for you. She still thinks you're her key to—"

She hesitated, hands working as if she could pull the words from the air.

Rene filled in the blanks, his voice flat. "She thinks I'm going to help her burn the world down." His jaw clenched. "I grew up hearing it constantly."

Rene had to suspect it, but hearing it out loud still shook him. His break from the Stygian wasn't as clean as he'd believed.

This time it was Rene who Betony soothed by pulling off some of his anger. In the space of a few breaths, the fire in his eyes calmed to a friendly sparkle, and he gave her an appreciative nod, which she returned. She gave his knee a friendly pat and sat back in her chair.

A light switch flipped on in my kitchen—or what I thought was a light switch. Given that this is an older house full of witches, anything is possible. Then, in the quiet of the room, I heard a gentle *whoosh* followed by the noises of physical effort.

What in the—?

Then, just as I pushed up from my chair, a voice cut through the quiet.

Newly familiar voices emerged from the kitchen. Doyle and Crystal had returned. Those of us in the circle shot one another knowing glances that danced between nervous, determined, and unsure. They were the first two of our new group—the Numinati. Elidriel had been our third.

"Anyone here?" Crystal called.

"In the coffee shop!" I hollered.

Laughing, the two of them strolled through the swinging doors to where our group sat in silent, exhausted contemplation. Doyle, pale as he was, actually looked flushed. Guess that's what a fair-skinned vampire looks like when they're full. Crystal, as always, carried herself with the confidence of someone who had already decided she belonged. She was right.

"You all look like you just came from a funeral," Crystal observed.

"We're going to need your help," I informed her.

"Well, shit," she said, a dry laugh threading through her words. "I *knew* that."

"To gather others like you," I clarified.

Crystal arched a brow, interest flickering in her expression. "Other... unusual people? With powers?"

Elidriel, who had been quiet until now, leaned forward slightly, her lips curving into a knowing smile. "Welcome to the Numinati."

Chapter 22

In a stroke of genius, or maybe just desperation, knowing the next Music in the Park was tomorrow night, I brought Hanna with me to help recruit new Numinari for our cause. Not only is my best friend drop-dead gorgeous—an undeniable draw for any heterosexual man with a pulse—but she's a red witch. Charisma rolls off her like perfume. It's all part of her magic.

Plus, she brought muffins.

Our first stop that morning was deep in the northern Georgia woods. Hanna and I slipped through the narrow tear in space Crystal rendered and emerged in a world of towering pines and sprawling Georgia oaks. The air smelled of damp earth and fresh rain. Crystal came through last, contorting herself in a way that looked way too practiced as she maneuvered through the fiery portal. When it hissed shut behind her, she tossed me her silicone mitts, and I stuffed them into my backpack.

Ahead of us, a two-story farmhouse sat in a wide clearing. The white wood siding gleamed with fresh paint, and the veranda covering the front porch was nearly as wide as the one on Blackwell Manor. Behind the house, an old red barn, its paint long faded, slouched in the shade of a few towering Georgia oaks. An ancient Ford tractor rested beneath its eaves.

"Let me knock," Crystal said, crossing the veranda with the comfort borne of familiarity and pulling open the screen door to rap on the front door. "Miles is... well, he's not the social type. Not big on talking, either. But he knows me. I bring a friend out to visit him every month."

Every month on the full moon, I'll bet.

Our first recruit, Miles Simmons, was a werewolf.

"Miles?" Crystal hollered, "It's Crystal. I've, um... I've got a couple of friends with me." She paused. "We brought muffins."

A lengthy interval ensued, and I was about to suggest that perhaps Miles was out, but eventually heavy footsteps approached the door and yanked it open. On the other side stood a man who was pale, lean, and strikingly handsome. A jagged pink scar ran from his temple to the corner of his mouth. It did nothing to lessen the impact of his good looks.

"Hey." His gravelly voice delivered that one word in a way that was authoritative, and I half expected him to turn us away.

Crystal gave him her best, most easygoing grin. "Miles, this is Murphy and Hanna. Friends of mine. We were hoping to chat with you for a few minutes."

I glanced at Hanna, expecting her usual confident charm radiating from her pores like... well, like the spell it was. Instead, she stood frozen, eyes wide, lips slightly parted like she'd forgotten how to breathe. She lifted the basket of muffins without a word, like she was presenting an offering to a particularly intimidating god.

Miles flicked a glance between Crystal's hopeful expression, Hanna's mute awe, and the proffered basket. Then, with a tilt of his head, he motioned us inside.

I followed, suddenly invisible for the first time in days, and absolutely fine with that.

Hanna set the basket reverently on a sturdy wooden table, stepping back as if afraid she'd disturb the moment. That's when it hit me: my best friend—the woman who treated men like a box of assorted chocolates, meant to be sampled—was utterly, completely, *instantly* twitterpated. Miles had taken her breath away.

Huh. I'll be damned.

Miles pulled back the tea towel covering the muffins, plucked one out, and sniffed. A slow, lopsided smile lifted the unscarred side of his mouth.

"Cranberry orange," he murmured, nodding his approval. "Nice."

He led us to a cozy living room, the furniture a mix of deep greens and warm browns. Once we had settled in, he turned to Crystal, giving her his full attention.

"Well," he said between bites, "Michael's not with you, and none of you smell wolfy, so I'm guessing this is a new variety of disaster?" His husky voice spoke in a calm, measured way, which made his delivery feel thoughtful and intimate. I could almost smell the hormones coming from Hanna at the sound of it.

Crystal huffed. "Does it have to be a disaster for me to visit?"

Miles lifted an eyebrow—the one without the scar.

Crystal rolled her eyes. "Okay, okay. You're right. There's kind of a... a..."

"Disaster?" This time, the smile reached his entire mouth.

She shot him a glare and slumped deeper into the couch. "Murphy, help me out here."

I leaned forward, and Miles turned his gaze on me for the first time. The shift in his focus was almost physical—I nearly flinched under the weight of it.

I cleared my throat, forcing a casual tone. "I feel like

we've got you at a bit of a disadvantage here. We know what you are, but you know nothing about us." I glanced at Hanna, who was still gazing at Miles like he might start glowing at any second. "Hanna and I are witches."

Miles didn't so much as blink. "What types?"

That stopped me short. Most people outside of the witching world didn't ask that—didn't even know to ask that. The question alone told me he wasn't entirely in the dark about the Numinari—or whatever he called them.

I studied him a second longer before answering. "Hanna's red and brown, both." His eyes flicked briefly to my best friend, but if her mix of magic meant anything to him, he didn't show it.

"And you?"

I hesitated. I was getting a bit tired of this part and wondered how much of that showed on my face.

"Are you familiar with what a Summate is?"

He paused, considered the word for a moment, then shook his head. "No."

I nodded, pressing my palms together as I gathered my words. Miles took another bite of muffin, watching me as he chewed, waiting for an explanation.

"The short version?" I said finally. "I'm every type of witch."

His chewing slowed. His dark eyes held mine, considering, calculating. Then nothing.

I'd seen people react to my magic in all kinds of ways—curiosity, fascination, even outright fear. Miles didn't react at all. Which I found oddly liberating. I decided that despite his gruff manner, I liked the guy.

He swallowed and gave me a long, unreadable look. "I'm guessing that's the crux of the problem?"

"Yes and no," Hanna said, finally rediscovering her

voice. "The bigger problem is the Stygian coven."

"The ones on the news?" he asked. He popped the last of his muffin into his mouth and dusted crumbs off his hands with his jeans.

"Yes," I said. "They've been causing trouble, and they're planning something worse. We were hoping you'd be willing to help."

Miles studied us, his posture stiff, a subtle scowl pulling at his mouth. He wanted to say no—I could see it in the tightening of his jaw, the stiffness in his posture, the way his fingers curled slightly against his knee.

Then his eyes found Hanna's limpid brown ones, her rapt attention, her soft expression. And everything in him softened, too.

"What do you need me to do?"

)O(

Miles agreed to come to Gryphon to help us, but he'd have to wait until the next day because of work. I got it. Hell, I was grateful he was coming at all.

We discussed how he was going to get there (Crystal would bring him through one of her magical doorways) and what time (after work, but before Music in the Park). That done, there wasn't much left but to move on to our next potential recruit.

Hanna's gaze drifted to the basket of muffins as we stepped toward the door, her fingers twitching slightly, as if debating whether she could subtly reclaim a few before we left. I knew what she was thinking—she should've set some aside for Miles instead of offering the whole thing. Miles, however, misread her hesitation.

"I'll bring you your basket tomorrow," he said.

Is it possible to speak with a smolder? Because that was the only way to describe his voice.

Hanna's lips parted, but no words came. A moment later, she stammered, "Oh—OK." Her voice cracked on the last syllable. Maybe it was just me, but I could've sworn her knees buckled a little, too.

Oh, these two were going to be *fun* to watch.

Had Conall and I ever been like that? Doubtful. He'd always been handsome—objectively, frustratingly so—but back when chaos witch was still the label I wore, dating was off the table. No way was anyone getting dragged into my brand of hell. Didn't mean I couldn't appreciate just how damn good he looked, though.

Miles saw us out, and as soon as the door shut behind us, I caught the firm slide of the deadbolt lock clicking into place. The sound settled strangely in my gut. We were deep in the Georgia woods, with no visible road—not even the distant hum of passing cars to remind me the outside world existed—but he'd wasted no time to lock the distant world out. And while I found it deeply entertaining that my friend had fallen so spectacularly into infatuation, I wasn't entirely sure how comfortable I was with her attraction to a man so withdrawn. I mean sure, Miles had pretty cool vibes, and he'd agreed to help us go into battle, but he clearly distrusted people.

That was a problem for another time.

"Where to now, Crystal?" I asked.

"Savannah, Georgia," she said with an exaggerated drawl.

"Georgia again?" Hanna asked. "What is it with Georgia?"

"Hell, what is it with Gryphon?" I asked. "We're no better."

"Worse," Hanna groaned. "Maybe the whole Southeast is

fucked."

"You'll like this guy," Crystal said, readying her finger and pretending she hadn't heard us. "If we can get Bully on board, he'll be great for the cause."

Hanna turned to me and mouthed, *Bully?*

I shrugged and kneeled to pull the silicone gloves from my backpack.

☽○☾

We emerged from the new fissure in space into an alley just wide enough for a single car. A strip of weeds grew ankle high in the center of the dusty lane, their stalks brittle from the heat. The sweet, woodsy scent of Miles' land was gone, replaced by the layered fragrance of an old Southern city—summer azaleas laced with old, sunbaked brick, the faint metallic tang of iron, and the smell of vehicle exhaust. The distant breath of salt drifted through the air, a reminder that the Savannah River—and the ocean beyond it—wasn't far.

"Come on," Crystal said, motioning us forward as she slipped around a cluster of timeworn brick buildings.

I saw why she'd chosen the alley. The moment we stepped into the street, we were in the thick of it—a thriving, historic part of town. Gryphon wasn't a young place—its founders incorporated it in the 1880s—but Savannah was something else entirely. I'd bet it had Gryphon beat by at least a hundred and fifty years, maybe more. And this neighborhood? This was old Savannah, one of the earliest settlements, where history pressed in from all sides.

Spanish moss swayed in lazy drapes from the sprawling limbs of ancient oaks. Magnolia trees stood nearby, their waxy leaves glossy in the afternoon sun. The scent of bourbon and beer wafted from a bar down the street, mingling with the city's heavy, damp warmth.

By the time we reached the front of the building, my shirt was sticking to my back. This town was way more humid than home.

Crystal led us to a recessed entryway in a three-story brick townhouse. The doorway sat back from the street, a pocket of shade carved into the building's façade, its iron lantern unlit in the dim afternoon glow. We stepped into the alcove, grateful for the brief respite from the sun, and Crystal rapped her knuckles sharply against the door.

This time, we didn't have to wait long. The door swung open, revealing a man built like a wrecking ball.

"You're wearing glasses," she said by way of hello.

"*Crystal Novak*," he rumbled, his voice deep enough to roll through my chest. "It is *good* to see you." His deep brown eyes flicked over us, lingering on how we had huddled together in the shade of the small alcove. One thick brow lifted in silent question.

"Friends of Vivian and Michael?"

Crystal snorted. "Not yet. These two are... more like you than they are like them. Murphy, Hanna, meet Bully Bosworth. Bully, these are my two new friends, Murphy and Hanna."

Hands were shaken, greetings exchanged, Bully and Crystal shared a powerful hug, and we stepped into a deep cave of a home, rich with the scent of patchouli and something faintly herbal.

As my eyes adjusted, I took in the space. The décor was a riot of contradictions—bright, garish blankets draped over furniture that looked squashy enough to swallow a person whole. A velvet painting of three yellow elephants frolicking in a river took up a sizeable portion of one wall, positioned next to an aggressively tall houseplant. The place balanced the line between ostentatious and cozy with reckless abandon.

I liked Bully immediately.

Our host motioned to the chairs around his living space and offered us sweet tea. We agreed, and within minutes we were all sipping tall glasses of iced heaven with a hint of mint added for extra coolness. It was glorious.

"So what brings you to the Bosworth abode today, little one?" Bully asked.

Crystal rolled her eyes at the comment about her height and replied. "We have… another situation. Not as bad as the Little Rock thing, I don't think, but… we could use more folks like us. Murphy, what did you call us?"

"Numinari," I said. "It comes from the word numinous."

"Imma need an explanation for that one," the big man replied.

"Mysterious. Unique. Some might even say divine," I offered with a modest shrug.

He settled back in his seat and let out a hearty chuckle. His dreads danced as he laughed. "Oh, I like that," he said. "Nu-mi-na-ri. I *like* it. Tell me more about what's going on."

While Miles seemed like a straight-to-the-point kind of guy, Bully struck me as someone who needed to know the story. So, I gave Bully the Cliff's Notes version of my past, keeping it straight and fast, but even skimming the highlights made it feel long. I shared how Betony's folks had killed my parents, along with Hanna's and Conall's. How for most of my life, I'd thought I was a chaos witch, only to learn Betony was the actual source of all that wild, unpredictable power— I was just reflecting it.

Then I moved on to Erika, who'd rolled into Gryphon with her perfect smile and smooth lies, playing the role of a witch from Atlanta. How she'd nearly wormed her way into our coven, acting like she just wanted to belong when, in reality, she'd come to kill me. To use Betony's chaos to crack the world wide open, all while her son played host to the worst damn nightmare Earth had ever seen.

I laid out the Stygian's recent attacks and wrapped up with Conall and Rene's vision for Gryphon that would strike on a Friday, but that we were unsure which one. That it could be as soon as the next day.

Bully let out a deep, booming laugh. "Damn, girl. You been through it, huh?"

Tired of talking, all I could muster was, "A bit." I finished off my sweet tea with a long swig.

Bully excused himself to grab the pitcher in order to refill our glasses. The moment he stepped out, Crystal leaned in and whispered, "Bully is a witch, too, I think. I don't know what kind."

From the kitchen, Bully bellowed back, "Thaumaturgist."

Crystal shot me a bewildered look and hollered, "What's the difference?"

"Spelling," he called, then let out another deep, belly-shaking laugh. I couldn't help but laugh along.

Bully returned carrying a heavy glass pitcher of sweet tea, the ice clinking against the sides, mint leaves swirling in the golden liquid. He topped off our glasses, his massive hands somehow delicate with the fragile vessels, then settled back onto the couch with a groan of relief. His presence filled the space, not just because he was big, but because of the way he sat, the weight of him settling like a man who knew exactly who he was.

He let his dark eyes drift over the three of us, studying, thinking, before finally asking, "What you need me to do?"

"Can you help us find people? Like you did for Michael and Vivian?"

He licked his lips, thinking, then nodded. "Doyle still got

that list? Back in the day, he had a database—helped me track down a lotta folks last time. I got some locator spells, but that list would make things easier."

"He's back in Gryphon," I said.

"DB will help, I'm sure," Crystal added, sitting up straight, like she was ready to run out the door and find him herself.

Bully's eyes lit up. "Dorian? Your torch-tongue friend? How's he doing?"

Torch tongue?

I listened as the two of them traded names like currency. Benny Cavanaugh—controls animals. Ivor—harnesses electricity. Dorian—breathes fire. The list went on, and I quickly lost track.

Hanna shook her head. "It's like y'all know an entire supernatural army."

Crystal and Bully exchanged knowing grins. "We kind of do," she said with a smirk.

I tapped my fingers against my knee. "What about Doyle's friend who sent you to help us?" I asked. "Jerusha?"

Bully's brows lifted, his expression unreadable. "Jerusha?"

"Vivian," Crystal said, as if the name alone was an explanation.

"That's right," Bully said, the memory clearly coming back to him. "She was born Jerusha. Is that what she's going by now?"

"Most of the time," Crystal said.

Part of me was dying to know more about the person who had pointed Doyle and Crystal in my direction, the two who were clearly going to be wildly influential in my near future, and likely the future of several others, but I didn't want us to get sidetracked.

"If we can get Doyle back here with his list," I pressed on, "and Crystal can help you travel to where these people are—"

Bully cut me off with a wave of his enormous hands. "Don't need Crystal's help. I got a gift."

He lifted his hands, and his fingertips glowed like tiny LED bulbs. Where Crystal's magic was a bright golden beam, his was a cool, smooth blue.

"You—you're an aerocleaver too?" I asked.

With a flick of his wrist, the glow disappeared. "Nah. I got my own mojo."

"He can shoot his power from his fingertips and doesn't need to draw a door," Crystal explained. "It's pretty freaking awesome. And doesn't need silicone gloves."

"I thought you said you were a witch," Hanna said.

"Thaumaturgist," Bully smiled in correction.

"I'm gonna need an explanation for that one," I retorted playfully.

"It means I can see through the layers of spatial reality and pull two spots together for easy travel."

I crossed my arms over my chest and contemplated the idea. "Possibly a special type of silver witch," I guessed.

"Nah, see… Y'all used to that European magic. My traditions? My people's magic? It comes straight from Africa."

"Oh, that's cool." And it was. "I'd love to talk to you about that sometime—I don't know anything about African magical traditions. Bet it's fascinating."

Bully leaned back, looking thoughtful. "Maybe we can chat tomorrow night. Y'know, while we wait for this wack-ass coven to make a move."

I exhaled, the weight of the upcoming events pressing. At least we had a plan now—get Doyle, get the list, and use Crystal and Bully to round people up.

Bully leaned forward, resting his elbows on his knees. "Y'all staying here tonight? Or you running off to stir up trouble?"

Crystal smirked. "Why not both?"

Bully barked out a laugh, shaking his head. "Y'all wild." He drained his tea and set the glass down with finality. "Alright, then. Tomorrow night. We'll be ready."

I nodded, my stomach tight with anticipation. Tomorrow sounded so damned *soon*. Ready or not, Gryphon was about to become ground zero.

Chapter 23

Conall and I stood in my backyard. I'd wrapped up my recruiting trips Thursday afternoon, and now it was Doyle and Crystal's turn. They were working off the list Bully had mentioned, trying to track down Numinari around the world and pull them into the fight. Hopefully, they found enough folks to help us beat the Stygian's plans—whatever they wound up being.

Maybe it was my imagination, but the evening air in Gryphon seemed to carry the weight of impending change, along with the coming storm, thick with the scent of damp earth from a few new plants LaDonna had brought for me, and the burning wood and herbs from the nearby fire pit. I stood with Conall under the sprawling oak in the backyard, the gnarled branches above us reaching toward the cloudy sky. The flickering light of the fire cast shifting shadows across his face, deepening the lines of frustration that mirrored my own.

"Alright," I said, folding my arms. "One more time. Close your eyes, breathe deep, and focus."

Conall sighed, but he did as I asked. His dark brown hair, tousled by the evening breeze, fell over his forehead as he pinched the bridge of his nose. I pressed my fingertips to his wrist, letting the steady hum of Source energy pass through me and into him, a controlled current meant to refine the connection, but not overwhelm him to the point he struggled to stay grounded. I'd tried to ride along with his first few attempts, but either I was overwhelming his ability to See, or... well, I found it hard to believe there was nothing for us to find. Hence this solo mission.

"Anything?" I asked after a long pause.

His brow furrowed. "I see the park, the crowd... I feel the heat, the anticipation. It's happening. It's real." His voice carried the breathless wonder of someone who had Seen.

"But no idea when?" I pressed.

His eyes snapped open, his frustration evident. "That's the part that won't come into focus. I feel it—it's close. But the time is too slippery. It's like trying to hold water in my hands."

So neither of us got a clear view of what time frame we were looking at. I clenched my jaw, barely resisting the urge to pace. If only we knew what band was playing. The website for Music in the Park remained frustratingly vague when it came to naming its featured bands. If I had that detail, I could check which band looked like the one I'd seen in the vision and narrow down the date. But all it advertised was "a delightful mix of family-friendly entertainment from rock'n' roll to jazz and everything in between." In other words, nothing remotely helpful.

"Why do you think you can't see? Is it because too many decisions still haven't been made? If it's going to be tomorrow, you'd think it'd be really obvious by now. Or is it something bigger—something forcing us down this path, no matter what we do?"

Conall exhaled, shoving his hands in his pockets. "If the universe is messing with us, I wish it would just send a damn memo instead."

I huffed a dry laugh, but the unease in my gut didn't

lessen. We needed that date. Without it, we were throwing everything we had at a moving target and just hoping for the best. And if we were wrong—if we brought a bunch of Numinari to small-town Alabama for a quiet night with nothing to show for it—would they even come back next month? Probably not.

I didn't want to dwell on that. Maybe Doyle wouldn't make it through his whole list, and we'd have a few names left over if we needed reinforcements later. Next month. Or the one after.

Ugh.

Inside the house, the energy was frantic but focused. Hanna, Betony, and Bully had their hands full pulling Numinari from all over the planet, each call and message a carefully placed domino in a formation we hoped wouldn't collapse. Meanwhile, Rita, Terry, and LaDonna were working their own magic, rallying the WorldWide Witches to join us in Gryphon. Although I'd been messaging with Elidriel regularly since we'd uncovered our unexpected bond, I didn't feel right asking her to help—much less asking her to see if there were any fae willing to lend a hand. It was too early in our relationship to ask such an enormous favor.

It was a logistical nightmare, but the pieces were falling into place. People were coordinating time off, local folks were opening their homes, and everyone was chipping in to help purchase last-minute plane tickets and reserve rooms in nearby Douglasville. Rita even set up a crowdfunding page for those who wanted to help but couldn't make the journey themselves because of the late notice, lack of sufficient finances, or what have you. The generosity pouring in was humbling—witches, psychics, and seers sending what they could to fund the fight they wouldn't be present for.

And still, I couldn't shake the weight pressing on my

chest.

We were asking for blind faith. Asking people to step into something without fully understanding the danger they might face. Worse, we weren't even sure if this Friday was the Friday, or if we'd have to start all over again in another month. Maybe the one after that.

Maybe longer.

I hated it. I hated not knowing.

And I hated that no matter how much power I pushed into Conall, the answer remained out of reach.

☽○☾

It was getting late. And I was exhausted. But my high priestess had yet another job for me.

August Webb, a rock'n'roller with a smirk that could sell sin and a side hustle that involved more copper tubing and Mason jars than I cared to ask about, was LaDonna's new neighbor and another indigo witch like Terry. He and his significant other, Ida, had recently inherited a respectable-sized plot of land from his uncle, complete with a towering Victorian house that should have been charming. *Should* have been.

But some houses don't just sit pretty. Some houses have opinions. And this one? It had recently had a whole lot to say.

August and Ida's property bordered LaDonna and Luke's on the north side of town, where Gryphon met the Appalachian foothills—a neighborhood of stone-etched street signs, year-round wreaths on the doors, and garage-kept cars worth more than the houses farther south. The more upscale part of town, if that could be said about a tiny village like Gryphon. But from what I'd heard, there was nothing nice about what August and Ida had been dealing with.

"They've had some recent damage to their home," La-Donna said, her voice measured, her face unreadable. Which was a damn red flag if I'd ever seen one. LaDonna didn't do unreadable—not unless she had a reason. And that reason was now becoming my problem.

I shifted my weight, already not liking where this was headed. I wanted to stay and help coordinate the relief effort. But if what August and Ida said was true, their house could hold several folks coming to town who needed a place to crash while they were here. And we were running out of spaces and funds pretty quickly.

"And you want me to...?"

LaDonna tilted her head, her dark eyes assessing. "See what you sense needs to be done when you get there."

Aw, hell. That was a loaded answer if I'd ever heard one.

August and Ida flanked LaDonna on the left. To her right stood Dylan Marsh, a water witch in town from New Orleans, Louisiana, who'd arrived today to help us with our Stygian problem.

Water witches came in shades of aqua or turquoise—because of course they did. Mystical forces had a way of making the obvious feel profound sometimes. The distinction shouldn't have mattered, but in my head, it did.

Turquoise was Ericka's color. The Stygian leader wore that bright, electric blue-green like a personal banner, a neon sign flashing danger. In my mind, it was impossible to separate it from her.

And now here was Dylan, an aqua witch, casually swirling the ice in his glass using his finger, but not touching the liquid, the water shifting under his influence in slow, deliberate loops. A couple at a neighboring table watched in utter disbelief as if waiting for him to reveal the secret.

I let it go—out of the broom closet, remember?

Logically, I knew I needed to get over my association with the color aqua. Dylan wasn't Ericka. The color wasn't cursed. But try telling that to my gut.

I glanced past LaDonna to where Jake and Lorina stood. Jake adjusted the strap of his guitar case, his affable grin not quite reaching his eyes. Lorina, meanwhile, looked down-right uneasy, shifting her weight like she wasn't sure if she wanted to be here or bolt.

"We're going too," Jake said. "Music might help settle things. And we figured if the house doesn't want to cooper-ate, maybe we can sweet-talk it."

Lorina snorted. "Or piss it off."

Jake's grin widened. "Either way, it'll be interesting."

Understatement of the damn year. From what vibes La-Donna was giving off, this house was going to be a chal-lenge—I just couldn't tell what type yet.

Miriam stood behind the register with Hanna, ready to take care of the shop in my absence for the last two hours of the day. I didn't think they'd have to deal with too much trou-ble. Only one lone reporter lingered at the edge of my prop-erty tonight—an older guy in a Honda Accord who'd driven in from Lexington and was too polite to be pushy but too stubborn to leave without a story. Plus, it was going to be a slow night—it was raining torrents out there.

I sighed. Ida's bright gray eyes met mine, reminding me of the lovely shade of gray that ringed Betony's eyes when the power inside her surged.

"OK," I grumbled.

Jake and Lorina raced through the rain to join me in my Toyota, and Ida and August rode with LaDonna and Dylan in LaDonna's Mercedes back to the property neighboring that of my foster family.

My sour mood turned around after only a few minutes in

the car with Jake and Lorina. The banter between the two of them could earn them a fortune if they ever found someone willing to follow them around and record their antics.

Lorina drew in a sigh, and her nose wrinkled in disgust. "Oh my God, Jake," she groaned dramatically, tossing her head back against the seat. "Why do you always smell like a mix of pine trees and bad decisions?"

"First of all," Jake said, pointing at her with exaggerated offense, "that's my signature scent, thank you very much. Second, at least I don't smell like—" He leaned in, sniffing the air near her. "—eucalyptus and heartbreak."

"Excuse you, I smell like elegance and a hint of rosemary," she shot back. "You wouldn't know because your body wash is literally labeled For Men Who Don't Read Directions. Hell, you probably use it to wash your long-ass hair, too."

"You wound me," he clutched his chest, mock-pained. "I'll have you know, this body wash was hand-selected because the lady at the store said it was 'earthy and musky with a touch of mystery.'"

Lorina snorted. "Yeah, because she worked on commission, and you look like you'd impulse buy anything with a guitar on the label."

I bit back a laugh as Jake opened his mouth to argue, index finger raised like he had a point to make, but nothing came out. He just grumbled something under his breath and crossed his arms.

"Anyway," Lorina said, flipping her curly bobbed hair, "tell the truth. You picked it up because some dude on TikTok said it makes women obsessed."

Jake gasped. "That is slander."

"You *literally* showed me the video."

Jake slumped in his seat. "OK, well. Did it work?"

Lorina rolled her eyes. "Yeah. I obsessively want to throw you out of this moving vehicle."

Jake laughed, shaking his head. "You're actually the worst."

"And yet, here you are. Unable to escape my gravitational pull."

Jake slouched back in the seat again, tree-trunk-sized legs sprawled out like he was claiming the whole car. "You know, if I had a dollar for every time you roasted me, I'd have—"

"Negative forty-seven dollars," Lorina cut in. "Because you'd blow it all on guitar strings and those weird energy drinks that smell like battery acid and give you gut rot."

"OK, first of all," Jake said, holding up a finger again. "I'm an artist. Strings and caffeine are vital expenses. Second, at least I don't make people cry for fun."

"That happened *one* time," Lorina said. "And she had it coming."

"You told a girl her vibrato sounded like a dying goat."

"And? It low-key did."

Jake turned to me with exaggerated devastation. "See what I deal with?"

I did. And it was adorable.

The driveway to August and Ida's grand Victorian home was barely large enough to accommodate our vehicles—overgrown plants encroached on the path like bushy sentinels. I wondered why they hadn't trimmed them back until I recognized the thick bramble of thorny blackberry bushes. A natural barrier. Both a witch's ward and a physical deterrent. The fruit was growing in full and heavy, practically dripping off the vines, and I had a feeling LaDonna had a hand in that.

I was a little concerned about my car getting stuck in the muddy driveway. That concern vanished, replaced by a new line of thinking by the time my back tires rolled onto the property. I knew why LaDonna wanted me here. There was a residue of energy lingering in the air that hinted at the potential for danger, much like the heavy smoke and lingering embers after a forest fire. As if there was a shattered entity of something massive and evil that had once stood its ground on the earth rolling beneath my tires. And though it had fractured, scattered, bled into the soil, I knew that with the right catalyst, it could come back together again.

Holy shit.

"You feel that?" I asked Jake and Lorina, wondering if it was evident to them as well.

"The vibe here is way off," Jake said, rubbing his arms like the temperature had dropped.

Lorina wrinkled her nose. "Forget pine trees and bad decisions. This place smells like neglect and despair."

The wrongness of the place was nearly suffocating. No one in their right mind would want to live here. Why were we even wasting our time on this—

Then the Victorian house came into view.

Oh. That's why.

A once-stunning, three-story architectural masterpiece stood now smothered in Virginia creeper and trumpet flower vines. What had likely started as a touch of elegance had long since developed a relentless grip on the house, tendrils winding tightly around the siding and creeping over the wraparound porch. The azalea bushes had grown wild, nearly swallowing the lower windows, and the faded trim was stripped raw in places and peeling in jagged flakes in others. Time had been cruel to this house. Or maybe something else had. Now, in the unforgiving daylight, the house stood exposed, not just to the sun but to time itself, its former beauty faded beneath years of neglect.

This is where they want to house people from out of town?

I suddenly knew what my role was in this story. From the exterior, the wear appeared mostly cosmetic; the bones of the house had weathered the time well. But judging from the overwhelming atmospheric sense of neglect and despair (Lorina had pinned the vibe well), a supernatural force was at play here. Or had been. I got the impression that the worst of what had once dominated this space had dissipated, but that the entity behind the force once latched onto this property was lingering in stray traces that longed to re-anchor themselves. It wanted to take root again and grow.

And it wasn't the sort of roots LaDonna could kill off.

I parked beside LaDonna, and the seven of us got out of the cars; I stood with one hand on the driver's side door, half in the misty rain, half wanting to get back in and drive the hell out of there. LaDonna watched me with intrigue as I stood, my finger on the pulse of the Source, measuring the energy pooling outside the home. It vibrated with a wrongness, like the echo of a thousand screaming ghosts trapped just beyond the veil.

I turned slowly toward LaDonna and the others.

"What the fuck happened here?" I asked with a quaking voice.

I hadn't meant for it to come out so accusatory, but it did. Ida flinched. August didn't. He just watched me, weighing my reaction like it confirmed something for him. Finally, he turned to LaDonna with a laugh and a knowing nod.

"You said she was good," he said. "Wish we'd known her before we ever stepped inside. We might've been a little more careful."

"You've been *inside*?" I asked, incredulous. The idea of walking into the epicenter of all this energy made my skin crawl.

"It is beautiful," Ida said, tilting her head as if she could still see the house as it once was. "Or... it was. Could be. It needs help, though."

I scoffed. "I'll say."

I allowed them to lead me through the front door, my skin in goosebumps the entire way—and not from the chilly evening rain—my stomach rebelling against the traces of negative forces that hovered all around, longing to find a home again.

They opened the front door, and my eyes nearly bugged from my skull. The floors... I can't even imagine what must have done that sort of damage to the floors. The way that planks around the house lay curled in ways that reminded me of ribbon turned into curlicues by a blade. What on earth could cause that?

"Don't turn on your third eye," LaDonna cautioned.

Ever have anyone tell you not to picture a purple dinosaur? You pictured a purple dinosaur, didn't you?

Well, I'm no better. My third eye flickered to life for just a moment, but it was enough. Fuzzy, dancing residue of what appeared to be the same stuff in Rene's silver witch visions floated throughout the house. Fractals upon fractals of reflective surfaces drifting through space. But they were more than mirrors. They felt like echoes of portals to other worlds.

"Whoa," I breathed.

"Told you not to," LaDonna chuckled.

"Yeah, well, you know I've never been great at following directions," I joked, taking a timid step into the house almost as if I expected it to swallow me whole.

"Welcome to the Wenke House," August said grandly.

Ida beckoned for Dylan to follow her. Together, they wandered off toward a massive carved fireplace, moving cautiously over the buckled floorboards, Ida pointing out the various items of the home's artistic merit. And despite everything, the house had charm. The builder must have spent a fortune on woodwork. It adorned the fireplaces, the mantle, the banister... pretty much anywhere there was wood—and there was a *lot* of wood—it had been turned into a work of art, each piece painstakingly carved by hand.

And every piece of it hummed with power.

My brow furrowed as, through the Source, I perceived lines of energy emitting steady lines of power from various spaces of the house—especially those hand-carved items. Aware that it might overwhelm me, I opened my third eye again, and my breath hitched.

The paranormal equivalent of what appeared to be blindingly gold laser tripwires connected those specially made sections of the house together. They stretched across the space, linking fireplaces to staircases, staircases to door frames, an entire intricate web of contained energy. The house wasn't just holding magic. It was channeling it. A flash of lightning outside only made the dazzling strings of power more brilliant.

"Whoa," I said again.

Mindful of the torn-up floorboards, I approached what was probably once the sitting room or parlor.

"This is incredible," I murmured, stepping into what had probably been a sitting room.

"What?" August asked, all humor gone. "What is it?"

I turned to face him. "Your house is channeling a *massive* amount of energy."

"Still?" he asked, eyebrows raised.

My mouth snapped shut. I hadn't realized it'd been hanging open. "You knew?"

He gave a half-shrug with a well-muscled shoulder. "I mean, yeah. The guy who built this place built it to hold on to energy."

"Well, it's working," I said.

August frowned.

"That's bad, I gather?" I asked.

"The guy—Wenke—he was twisted. Tried to start a cult using this house. Trapped ghosts here. Turned this place into a supernatural Grand Central Station."

Which explained the ghostly echoes I'd heard outside and the residual portals inside.

"We got rid of him," August explained. "But the stuff he put into the house is still here, apparently."

A beat of silence passed before he asked, "Can you fix it?"

Arms crossed, I considered. Despite the horrible past that presented a potential for disaster, the Wenke house had tremendous possibilities.

"I'll do you one better." Turning back toward the pulsing lines of energy, I let the weight of the power, the pull of old magic, wash over me. Despite Wenke's intentions, the power itself held no malice, no benevolence. It was just raw power, waiting to be shaped.

"I'll change it." My gaze didn't waver. "I'll make sure this energy works for good."

August studied me for a moment, then nodded.

The house groaned, a slow, settling sound, as if it had overheard me and wasn't sure how it felt about my promise.

Yeah, well. Too bad.

This was happening.

Chapter 24

"I'm going to need some quiet," I said as I let in more of the Source, which lingered like a barely audible whisper at the edges of my perception. It pressed against me now, then grew within, until my skin hummed with it, my nerves on fire with an electric whisper. The surrounding colors deepened, shifting from muted dusty hues into something richer and truer—ochre, carmine, indigo, the colors of memory. I saw the intensity of the hue they once embodied. I breathed in the heavy, musty air, the ghost of furniture polish clinging to the aged wood, the salt of human sweat. The patter of rain on the windows sounded like nature's softest drumbeat.

"Should we leave?" August asked.

I shook my head, my eyes already closed, hands rising instinctively as I reached outward, past the physical, past the seen. The house answered as I knew it would. It was alive in a way most places weren't, a structure less built than woven, only partly made of the physical structure, the rest composed of a web spun from the tattered edges of people's souls as they entered and exited. Not all at once, not even enough for them to notice—just slivers, paper-thin fragments, caught and cocooned, wound deep into its bones.

A rush of moving air told me August was motioning to Ida, his breath parting the stillness as he told her to halt the tour with Dylan, to give me quiet. It hardly mattered. I was already slipping into the current, already opening the flood-gates to the Source. And once I did that, nothing—no voice, no movement, no force of the waking world—could sever the connection.

Slowly, I envisioned the connection between my spirit and the Source expanding, the radiant power pouring over me like a luminous waterfall, one I allowed to enter and consume me entirely until it was impossible to tell where it ended and I began. The power surged, unyielding, pouring over me like a river of light. It seeped into me, a rhythm both foreign and familiar, something I could never fully command but had long since learned to trust. I let it thread through me, and from there I showed it how we needed it to extend into the warped floorboards, the cracked walls, the iron nails rusting in dark, unseen places. I followed the house's blueprint, not only of wood and stone, but of memory—of every moment it had held its people together. Some, even after they died.

A streak of aquamarine joined my blazing prismatic force—Dylan's touch, his influence whispering through the moisture in the air, pulling from the rain outside, coaxing the swollen boards to soften and realign. The wood sighed as it settled, yielding beneath our joined will, finding where those who dwelt here might love them, could trust them to hold them up, to support them. Where they could be a piece of a home full of love and light, a crucial component of this glorious dwelling place.

Still, the house's bones were only part of the work. The rest ran into the fabric of its making, into the home's soul, if it had one. It had been designed for something darker, to feed, to steal, to ensnare. Undoing that intent would mean I had to reshape its very nature, to shift the centuries-old hunger into something gentler and generous.

I sent feelers through the foundation of the home, to the

specially designed boards and walls within and without, sensing the points in them that had been built with a darker purpose. With a gentle caress, I reached for the heart of the house, for the spell stitched between the beams and bricks and molded into the decorative facets, and I willed it to change. To give instead of take. To strengthen rather than deplete.

It was a lot. The architect had put a great deal of thought into designing the home. Way more than I could understand and undo in a few minutes' worth of work. I had to trust that the power within me understood my intentions and knew a way to turn a nightmarish plan into a blessing for everyone who entered. To let it be a place of sanctuary, not sacrifice. Let it be a home that offered its power only when asked, only when needed.

The shift was subtle, like the hush of snowfall, like the deep exhale of a long-held breath. With slight alterations to the physical form of its design, the house exhaled. It accepted.

It would be beautiful now. Magic, when wielded with care, always was. And for a moment, I felt something very close to envy.

This house was going to be magnificent.

Lessening my grip on the Source was difficult. It resisted, reluctant to leave me, to pull back into the air like mist retreating from dawn. I let it go by degrees, each exhale lightening my limbs, softening the edges of the power thrumming beneath my skin.

The air around me seemed to cool as I did so, and I realized Dylan was using his power as a water witch to control the moisture in the air and bring down the temperature in the house.

Handy.

"Music," I murmured, half a request, half an invocation.

And, as I suspected, Jake and Lorina were at the ready.

The first quiet strum of a guitar spiraled into the air, light and golden, weaving through the stillness like fireflies at dusk. My heart, which already felt ready to burst, swelled until it could have filled my entire chest.

And then Lorina sang.

The tune was a familiar one—not one of their originals, but one from a popular band they covered a lot—and I knew the haunting melody as well as they did. I refrained from singing, though. To do so would have taken away from the stunning perfection that was Lorina's voice. It was too pure, too perfect in the moment, sending a shiver through me that had nothing to do with Dylan's cooling magic.

And in the mostly empty space of the house, her stunning soprano filled each room and chased away any lingering shadows that might have hidden in the furthest reaches of the house until none remained. The beautiful Victorian was no longer the Wenke house.

It was now fully August and Ida's home.

When the song ended, the quiet that settled over us was one of spiritual bliss, a contentment that none of us wanted to let go.

"LaDonna, you didn't tell me you had a sirenborn in your crew," Dylan said, his voice reverent. "That was... something else."

Lorina made a face like he'd just accused her of a crime. "Sirenborn?" she repeated, drawing the word out like it tasted bad. "Dude, I just have a good voice."

"No," Dylan said, shaking his head. "No, my dear, you are definitely sirenborn. Once you've heard the pull of a siren, you never forget it. There's something... other in it. Something that doesn't let go."

Lorina folded her arms tight over her chest, staring at the

floor like it had personally betrayed her. "No. No way. I'm just—"

"A freak of nature who can belt any note in the soprano range like she's got a Broadway demon in her pocket?" Jake cut in. "Been telling you for years, man. You're not normal."

"I *am* normal," she snapped, whipping around to glare at him. "I'm not inhuman, okay? I'm me. That's all."

Then she turned on her heel and stalked out of the room, shoulders squared, her entire exit practically screaming, *Not inhuman. Don't even think about it.*

Jake watched her go, then sighed. "Yeah. That totally screams 'regular-ass person.'"

He strummed a few lazy chords on his guitar, glancing at Dylan. "So, sirenborn, huh? That a 'we should be worried' kind of thing, or more of a 'damn, that's cool' kind of deal?"

Chapter 25

"Bully, if I hear about another sort of superhuman or shake another magical being's hand, my brain may explode," I said, dragging a palm that was quickly growing sweaty down my face. "I'm losing track of all the names and faces and abilities, and…. Every mythical creature in literature can't be real, can they?"

It was Friday, about half an hour before Music in the Park was set to kick off, and I was a sweaty, nervous mess. Betony had tried to drain the frantic energy from me six times before I told her to let it go. No amount of magical chill was going to fix my nerves tonight unless I walked around immersed in the Source the entire evening. Which, to be honest, was sounding better every minute, even if it did leave my brain so heady I could hardly think.

We were going through with the plan—LaDonna would heal the Magnolia Memorial Tree tonight. The goal was to time it right, just as the crowd started to swell, but well before the music kicked off. A little show of goodwill from the neighborhood witches to get the night started on the right note.

"You'd be surprised," Bully responded, his voice carrying easily over the sounds of the crowded park. "Hell, some folks coming tonight are djinn. That one surprised me."

"Djinn?" I asked. "I've heard the word, but I'm not familiar with what they are."

"Djinn are… unusual. They're not angels or demons, but their power runs right up there with the divine. Some good, some bad, most just *be*. Think of 'em like fire—keeps you warm, cooks your food, but touch it wrong, and it'll burn you down to nothing."

"So, we can trust these ones?"

Bully rocked his head back and forth, not quite committing. "We can work with 'em. Trust? That's a stretch. They're in this for themselves. Djinn aren't about doing favors. Everything's a bargain, even if they make it sound free."

I shot him a look. "What were they promised to get them to help us tonight?"

Bully chuckled. "Lucky for us, this bunch loves a good fight. And they hate the Stygian."

"Really? Any idea why?"

"No clue," he said easily, scanning the park with practiced calm. "But I ain't about to turn down an ally tonight."

I noticed the coven moving, one by one, to the Magnolia Memorial Tree. Bully and I joined them, weaving our way through the clusters of people. Puck's Green was sprawling. For a town this size, the park was almost too big—a donated stretch of land built up for the town at a time when someone thought Gryphon was going to be a much bigger deal than it ever turned out to be.

I panned the crowd looking for something specific from the vision that would tell me tonight was going to be the night, but many of the details had grown too fuzzy. Hell, I hadn't had a chance to meet all the people who'd shown up to help yet, so I didn't know if the curly-haired teen or the woman in the leather jacket were among our group. I did meet the ghostly pale man, though. His name was Ivor Blitz, but his nickname was Lightning. He was rail thin, jittery, and had perpetually anxious eyes. I guess maybe that was a side effect of what made him Numinari—the man channeled electricity.

"You were going to tell me about your magic a little," I reminded Bully.

Bully let out a breath, the kind that said he'd been waiting for me to ask. "My magic ain't like Crystal's, though it gets you to the same place. What she does, that's cutting through the veil, reaching through the fabric of space. What I do? It's old. Real old. Back home, they call it the Serpent's Path—a road that bends where it shouldn't. Some say the first travelers learned it from Nyame, the sky god, after Anansi earned the right to carry stories and wisdom down to Earth. Others say it's the work of Eshu, the trickster—he walks between worlds and speaks every tongue ever spoken."

He tapped his chest. "Me? I open the door. I connect two places, pull the path tight, like drawing a line between 'em. Folks back home say the world ain't just what you see—it's got layers, folds, shortcuts if you know where to look. That's what I tap into. I don't break through a veil—I just show people a road they weren't meant to see."

"That's really cool. What else makes your magic different from ours? Do you know many witches like me?"

"It's not something you're born with, like Numinari powers. And it ain't pulled from chaos or built from rituals. What I do—it's older than all that. It's tradition. It's knowledge passed down. It's about understanding how the world fits together, and knowing how to move through it without disturbing the balance."

He glanced at me. "Witches like you—you work with energy. You pull it, shape it, bend it. What I do? It's more like walking a road that's already there, one most folks can't even see. My people knew that, long before the world got chopped up and named. They knew the land remembers. The sky teaches. And if you listen close enough, you'll hear which way to go."

His gaze settled on the magnolia tree ahead. "It ain't about power—it's about respect. Working with what's already there. That's why I don't force nothing. Don't push through barriers. Don't twist reality. I open the way that was always meant to be walked."

I met his soulful brown eyes, struck by the simplicity of it, how much it lined up with what I did, even if the logic was a little different.

"You know what, Bully?" I said, nudging his arm. "Your power and mine—I believe it's all part of the same thing. We even think about it in a similar way."

Before he could respond, LaDonna stepped up to the Magnolia, setting her hands lightly against the rough bark. The sickly tree was struggling, its branches sparse, the once-waxy green leaves now drooping and brown along the edges. A few yellowing leaves clung stubbornly to the lower limbs, a sign it was trying, even as the wilt stole its life from the inside. At its base, the soil was dry and cracked despite the recent rains, and dark streaks climbed the trunk like old scars.

A few people nearby cast curious glances at LaDonna, but most dismissed her as a tree-hugging hippie talking to plants. Her beatnik wardrobe probably helped.

I nudged Bully again, grinning. "This is gonna be good."

LaDonna closed her eyes and pressed both palms flat against the rough bark of the Magnolia. A ripple of energy shivered through the air, subtle at first—like the noticeable hush before a storm. I thought I was the only one who perceived it, then I saw Bully sucking in a deep breath as if he'd caught a whiff of something delicious on the air. Then the ground around the tree darkened, as if drawing up a liquid richer than water from deep in the soil.

At first, nothing happened. A skeptical murmur moved

through the crowd, wondering if the magic trick was over. But then a single curled leaf near the bottom of the tree unfurled, its brittle brown edges flushing back to deep, waxy green. Another followed. Then another.

The transformation spread like ink in water, but instead of shadowy plumes, magic climbed the branches in shimmering waves, chasing the sickness as it rose. Leaves plumped, their veins surging with new life, shifting from sickly yellow to the deep, glossy emerald they were meant to be. The dark streaks climbing the trunk faded, as though they were being pulled inward and broken down until they vanished.

The branches, once heavy with wilt, straightened, stretching toward the sky with slow, deliberate grace.

A rich, floral scent wafted through the air—not just the perfume of the magnolia blossoms, but an older, richer fountain from deep in the earth that had been awakened.

Then came the bloom.

The tight, closed buds along the branches swelled, their thick white petals peeling open like they'd been waiting for this moment to awaken. One by one, magnolias unfurled, heavy and fragrant, their scent rolling through the park in warm, honeyed waves.

The crowd gasped. Some clapped. A few just stood frozen, staring in awe.

LaDonna exhaled, her shoulders slumping slightly, but her hands stayed pressed against the bark like she was listening, making sure the tree roots had taken hold of the gift she'd given. Her lips moved even now, as if whispering comfort to the tree, that it was safe, that the illness was vanquished. Hell, that was probably exactly what she was saying.

And then, just for a second, the Magnolia pulsed. Not physically, but in a way I felt in my spirit, a resonant heartbeat of magic settling into the earth. Like it was saying thank you.

LaDonna beamed.

"That was fucking cool," Bully breathed.

"That's LaDonna," I said proudly. My foster mother, the high priestess of the Lughaidh coven, and the most amazing woman I'd ever known.

"Band's here," Bully noted.

My head swiveled, and I let out a soft, nervous sound. The instruments being pulled from their cases were the same as I'd seen in Rene's vision. The band members and their clothes, too.

This was going to be the night the Stygian struck Gryphon.

Chapter 26

We hadn't trained for this. There was no battle plan. No neat little flowchart for what to do when everything went to hell—just a handful of us setting up a loose perimeter along Feste Way, the road closest to the river. The rest was instinct, an unspoken understanding that if tonight was the night the Stygian finally made their move, we'd be scattered throughout the park, ready to intervene the moment the coven's mind-controlled followers started marching toward their so-called destination.

More like Final Destination.

The bottom of the Tennessee River.

I know, I know. Alabama's landlocked. No foreboding, crashing ocean waves ready to pull folks under, and while we have cliffs, they're not exactly the dramatic kind people hurl themselves off of in a trance during a pinnacle scene in a movie. But we've got our fair share of water, and the Tennessee River is nothing to mess with. On average, that thing is four to six football fields across. She snakes six hundred and fifty-two miles from the Appalachian Mountains near Knoxville, past Chattanooga, then takes a lazy dip into Alabama, then arcs south of Huntsville before curling back north toward Paducah, Kentucky, where it meets the Ohio River. Along the way, it feeds into a couple of big lakes thanks to the Tennessee Valley Authority's reservoir dams.

Gryphon is pretty damn close to one of those reservoirs. In other words? Not a friendly little creek with a pedestrian bridge. It's wide. It's deep. And near us, it's a monster, especially after a torrential rainstorm like the ones we've been having lately. The Stygian couldn't have found a more effective way to cull the herd than by talking a crowd of mind-controlled people into walking straight into that black water.

I yanked my phone from my pocket and typed out the only two words our group chat needed to see:

It's tonight.

That was the signal for Bully and Crystal to start porting people into a warehouse over on Industry Avenue—the one August had told us about. It's an old, abandoned storage facility, which made it the perfect place for our Numinari to use their portal powers without gawkers. Just a block and a half from the park, it was close enough to get people where they needed to be but out of sight of civilians who might ask too many questions.

"Catch you on the flip side," Bully said before taking off south toward Horatio Street, his pace brisk, all business.

I lifted a hand in a half-hearted wave but didn't trust my voice to work past the knot of nerves in my throat.

Now came the hard part—figuring out where in the hell to stand to be positioned best.

Ten acres doesn't seem that big until you're lost in the middle of a crowd, scanning the sea of faces, trying to spot your friends. I shifted onto my toes, trying to pick out familiar faces, my fingers running over my knuckles in an unconscious rhythm I couldn't seem to break. Nerves. Habit. Probably both.

About two hundred of the people swirling through the park were Numinari—late-night arrivals from Thursday, more filtering in throughout Friday. I only knew a few of them, and none of their names came to mind. But that didn't matter. They were here, and that was enough. I loved them for their bravery.

I saw Conall by the fountain at the center of the park. Although he was a good distance away, I knew his posture and hair and that he'd chosen to wear a purple T-shirt and some athletic shorts. The man next to him had to be his father—same frame, same quiet intensity. They were by the vendor tables, pretending to browse while they talked, their focus half on each other and half on the crowd. Watching. Waiting. Yet still making it look casual, like this was just another Friday night and not the start of something big.

LaDonna was still by the tree, as was Luke, who'd joined her after she was done ridding the Magnolia of its illness. He was hugging her proudly, undoubtedly sharing words of admiration about her success with the tree.

Miriam was a few yards away—her flowing pink shirt and light blond hair were unmistakable.

Terry… ah, over by one of the food trucks, along with Hanna and Joey. Probably a good idea to have a few of us over there. The food trucks always drew a sizeable crowd. Besides the usual lemonade and hot dogs, tonight's fare included two town favorites, El Fuego Rojo and Fork and Dagger. The thought of the bourbon-glazed short-rib sliders from the latter made my mouth water, and my stomach reminded me, not-so-politely, that I hadn't eaten.

On the opposite side of the park, I could make out a towering, husky guy with long hair and an acoustic guitar standing next to a thin young woman with dark, curly, bobbed hair. Jake and Lorina. Good. Unless Lorina's folks caught her here hanging out with Jake the Witch. Then probably not so good. The last thing we needed tonight was a screaming match between the ultra-religious and the magically inclined. Cadence hadn't come with us. Since she didn't have magical powers, she was minding the shop tonight, along with a couple Numinari to guard her.

Betony was back at the warehouse with Crystal, Rene, and Bully, helping to point folks in the right direction.

Hanna's dad, Rafael, stood fairly close to me, but not close enough to make conversation possible. He lifted his phone just enough for me to catch the glow of the screen—my message, already read. He met my gaze and gave a subtle nod. He was ready.

I'm not sure if I was ready or jumpy. Any time someone stood, my head snapped in their direction, my neck moving like it was on a damn swivel. I was watching for that telltale stiffness from my memory—the unnatural, puppet-like control the Stygian had used in Rene's vision. Which, in retrospect, was kind of dumb. The band was still tuning their instruments; the crowd hadn't even hit critical mass yet, and the sun was still up. Too early for the horror show.

Which was good—because not all of our Numinari volunteers had made it yet, either.

I wanted to pace, but that seemed like a great way to look openly unstable. And to be fair, I was unstable—at least at that moment. Probably not the best look for someone people were supposed to trust when the Stygian made their move. So, instead, I settled for cracking my knuckles again. No dice. They weren't ready. My nervous habit was officially failing me.

My phone buzzed in my pocket. I pulled it out. It was a message from Conall.

Try to relax. Everything will be fine. And this is your daily reminder that you are the Summate and capable of hurling cars through the air.

I snorted. Technically true. And useful, too, considering

I'd saved his ass earlier this year by stopping his Camaro from rolling off a ledge and turning him into a cartoon pancake. One of many times the Stygian had tried—and failed—to kill me. Thank the goddess.

I started to type back but stopped, thumb hovering over the screen. My stomach was tight, my breath was too short, and my nerves were wound so tight I could have snapped a steel cable.

But sure. Everything was fine.

I lifted my head and spotted Conall leaning against the fountain, arms crossed, smirking like he had all the time in the world. When he caught my eye, he gave a wave. I returned it halfheartedly.

This was stupid. Except for the one enormous battle last February when we knocked them out, we were always playing defense. The Stygian called the shots, and we reacted, scrambling to stay one step ahead. Every. Freaking. Time. They struck, and we dodged. They pushed, we fell back on our asses. They tightened the noose, and we clawed for slack. It was like trying to outrun the tide with a broken leg—only a matter of time before the water swallowed us whole.

And that was the game, wasn't it? They didn't have to beat us, just wear us down. Mentally, spiritually, physically. Keep us tired. Keep us on edge. Keep us waiting for the next punch instead of throwing our own.

But how the hell were we supposed to win against something this massive? The Stygian weren't just in my backyard; they were a global force. A hydra with a thousand heads, regenerating faster than we could cut them down. You don't just take out an opponent like that. You don't *vanquish* them. Hell, I wasn't even sure we could survive them.

Then it hit me.

I thought about my house burning. About how Rita and

her mother had shown up just as the last embers cooled, dropping the WorldWide Witches cyber coven into my lap. How the girl I thought was just a teenage misfit loitering in my shop turned out to be the daughter of the very people who murdered my mother—and a chaos witch, of all things. How after beating the Stygian, I'd ended up fostering the favored child of the Stygian high priestess.

Then, a stranger knew to send an aerocleaver my way. A woman with a vampire friend tied to Numinari from all over the world. One of them had a power like mine, pulling distant places together like they were neighbors.

That wasn't just dumb luck, and it sure as shit wasn't random. Something way bigger than me had a hand in all of this. The Source had been pushing, shoving me, and the whole town, into place this entire time. And maybe I'd been resisting harder than I wanted to admit.

Life was a chessboard I hadn't even realized I was standing on, and I was already in play. Whether I liked it or not, whether I felt ready or not, I had a role to step into. And if the Source had been maneuvering me into place all this time, I had to believe it had a reason. A plan.

Which meant I needed to learn what that plan was. Starting now.

I wasn't a tactician or a hero. Hell, half the time I barely felt like an adult. But I was the Summate, and no amount of doubt or denial was going to change that. This wasn't going to be easy. But I had to trust that the Source knew me better than I knew myself, and that with LaDonna's help, and the love of my coven, I could learn to be the leader it needed me to be.

No small feat for a woman who'd spent years as an agoraphobic.

I exhaled, steadying myself, and scanned the park for

what felt like the millionth time. The Numinari would come in from the Falstaff Road side of the park, opposite Beatrice Bend, where the food trucks and bandstand were located. That meant they'd have a clear route in. That was good. I had no idea what the incoming tide of folks were like, but if high-voltage Ivor Blitz and the woman wearing a leather coat in ninety-degree weather were any indication, they'd struggle to blend in here in Gryphon.

Since I had a minute and I was dying to do anything to distract myself from the upcoming intervention, I did an image search for *djinn* on my phone. Most of the pictures were of warrior-like beings in various colors—the most popular being blue—with smoke instead of legs.

Please, for the love of everything holy, let them show up with legs.

Were any of these people we'd recruited going to freak people out? What if we accidentally let our presence be known before the Stygian struck?

Maybe that wouldn't be bad; it'd give us a chance to introduce the town to the Numinari in a setting where folks were likely to accept. But then we'd have to figure out what the Stygian were planning next. Chances were, they'd regroup and strike again.

And again.

I caught myself clenching my jaw and forced myself to loosen it. *You've already gone over this. Multiple times. Now, it's time to think like a leader. Get to the bottom of things.*

How the hell were we supposed to make them stop? What was it going to take to get them to leave us the fuck alone?

Part of the reason for the Stygian's relentlessness was probably connected to Erika's warped attachment to her son. But that was only part of it. She hated me. She wanted Betony's chaos power. If Ericak was out of the picture, would the Stygian even care about us anymore? Or was this fight bigger than just her? Maybe if we just took Ericka Moore out as the leader… or just took her out, period…

Part of my spirit curdled at the idea of causing someone's death. The other part of me thought of it as self-defense. Defending the world, even.

Would Ericka be here tonight? If so, what was she facing? Vampires. Witches. Werewolves. Djinn. What else? Hell, *I* didn't even know who the good guys were tonight—and wouldn't until they stopped folks from being steered to their death like possessed cattle.

Though it looked odd, my attention was riveted to the opposite part of the park from where the action was taking place. I was on the lookout for more of us. Unlike the day Crystal and Doyle showed up at my door, I'm usually not automatically aware if someone has supernatural gifts. If I turned on my Source power, I'd see their auras, maybe get a sense of their strength, but that wouldn't tell me what team they were playing for. Because here's the thing: some people do really messed-up shit for what they think are good reasons. And some people do good things for all the wrong ones—like the djinn coming here to fight with us because they love a good scrap.

Morals, magic, the world itself—it's a tricky thing. Life doesn't come in neat little boxes of good and evil. It's a mess. A tangled, complicated, frustrating mess.

But enough philosophy. I needed to find Diaper Baby.

Keeping an eye out for a baby clad only in a diaper—the only person from the vision I recalled with some clarity, probably because the kid had been so close to me—I strolled casually among the throng. It shouldn't have been hard. How many nearly naked toddlers could there be in a crowd this size? And yet, it took longer than I expected to spot him.

Puck's Green is an oversized park, given Gryphon's small population, and there were a surprising number of people out tonight. Possibly because the rain had brought in slightly cooler weather. The sun had done a decent job drying out the grassy field during the day. It was a perfect evening for the park, which meant a ton of people had arrived. Not so perfect for someone trying to find a diaper-clad toddler. I struggled with simultaneously watching my footing, watching for in-coming Numinari, and finding Diaper Baby.

When I did, nestled between the two people I assumed were his parents, I wondered how I hadn't seen him sooner. Scanning the park, I triangulated where I'd stood with Rene in the vision. There was the golden retriever. The hacky sack kids, though they hadn't broken out their hacky sacks yet, and probably wouldn't for several minutes. Ok. I was in a good place. Ground zero for whatever nightmare was about to un-fold. I checked my watch.

The music wasn't set to start for another ten minutes. Sun-set, I knew from checking earlier, wasn't until around 8:30, and things in the vision had gone south around twilight. I had two and a half hours plus to kill before the shit went down, if things went according to the vision.

Which was probably good. It'd take time for our addi-tional team members to teleport—or whatever you call it—to the warehouse and make their way to the park.

I sighed. I sat. I waited.

And, not gonna lie, there was a not-so-insignificant part of me that wanted to head back to the house, cover my head with a pillow, and curl up with Rex and let him purr me to sleep.

Chapter 27

Funny thing about sitting alone in a park in a friendly town like Gryphon—you wind up making friends whether you like it or not.

By eight o'clock, I'd learned more about Diaper Baby than I ever expected. His name was Lance. His parents, Connor and Lacey Pratt, were Auburn grads who worked from home—cybersecurity for him, marketing for her. Lance was ten months old, an early walker, and in possession of a devastatingly effective bye-bye wave that he deployed on literally everyone who glanced his way. He was also the sole grandchild of a pair of doting grandparents who lived all the way up in Duluth, Minnesota.

I also learned that Connor had a deep love of craft beer. Every time he reached into their picnic basket, a can materialized in my direction like a friendly but persistent summoning spell. I declined every time. He took it in stride, cracking open his own with the practiced ease of a man who considered craft beer less of a drink and more of a personal calling.

So, I sat there, pretending to enjoy the band, nodding along like I was just another townie soaking in the evening. I kept the conversation light, the kind of pleasant, neighborly exchange Southerners had perfected over generations—the unspoken code that said, Yes, we are having a lovely moment together, but no, I will not be inviting you over for fried chicken and sweet tea. All the while, the weight of what was coming pricked at the back of my brain.

Because in just a few minutes, Lacey would stand. She would dump Connor onto the ground, her body no longer hers to control. And I would watch the will of the Stygian snap her up like a marionette on taut strings.

Lacey was the woman in the sundress from my vision. The one who dropped her baby. The baby who now had a name and a precious bye-bye wave.

Nights like this, I regretted how much time I'd spent cloistered away, avoiding the town so Betony's chaos energy wouldn't ricochet through me and cause constant disasters. I barely remembered my old classmates, not that I'd recognize them now. I'd dropped out in my sophomore year and finished school at home because, as it turns out, a hormonal teenager reflecting chaos energy is NOT a good thing for public education.

There were wonderful memories, though. Like the time I got mad at the creepy, misogynistic P.E. teacher and made the showerheads in the girls' locker room explode while he was "inspecting" them as class returned.

For the record, no one was hurt. Much. And the pervy bastard learned to stay out of the locker room after that.

But my point is, I didn't really know many folks from town. Which meant I had no way of distinguishing who might be Numinari and who was just there for a beer and some live music.

As the evening turned into night and the sun dipped lower, it cast everything into a dusky, watercolor palette, transforming faces into nothing more than shifting silhouettes. I tried to focus on the scene around me and my breath, the current state of peace—the calm before the storm. The ground underneath my thin towel clung to the last heat of the day as the cicadas droned their twilight song as if trying to harmonize with the band. The fairy lights in the tree branches flickered on, and the scene took on the evening summer pigments I recalled from the vision; the towering oaks formed a backdrop for the blues band, their leaves a shifting mosaic of dark green and gold. The sun, hidden beyond the tree line, set the sky ablaze in stunning copper, rose, and deep indigo hues.

Fireflies flickered lazily through the park, their glow pulsing in the dimming light, creating a summer game any country kid knows well: catch the lightning bug. Children's laughter carried through the air like the scent of night-blooming jasmine, and my heart swelled with love for this town.

The band switched tunes, and my breath stalled. This was the one I recalled from the vision—their song about a "girl they knew name-a Becky Sue." This was when the Stygian would strike. If things had held steady from the vision, anyway.

I took out my phone and pulled up the group text, noting for the first time that at the top of the chat were the words: Channel * 563 members.

Five hundred and sixty-three members? Holy shit. Did we actually get them all here on time?

I quickly punched in a text to the group: *Brace yourselves. It'll happen any second now.*

Then, without hesitation, I texted my friend Officer Kenny Hendricks: *I can't tell you how I know, but I'm letting you know now that something really bad is about to go down in Puck's Green. Not sure if you're on duty, but send everyone you can.*

I hit send and prayed I was right and didn't just cry wolf. I didn't have to worry about the local law enforcement taking me seriously. After years of living like a chaos witch and being at the center of repeated problems in town, the police tended to take me at my word.

My gaze flicked across the park, scanning the crowd. No one looked suspicious. No one was muttering incantations or drawing sigils in the dirt. Where the hell were these fuckers? Probably hiding in the trees.

The music carried through the air, deceptively easygoing.

There's a girl that I knew, name-a Becky Sue,
Wore vintage boots, had a faded tattoo.

I wanted to stand and brace for action, but at the same time, I didn't want to draw unnecessary attention to my presence. If the Stygian noticed me there, there was a chance they'd back away from their plan.

Sipped black coffee with a bourbon bite,
Spoke in poems 'bout her Mr. Right.

With nothing else to do but wait, I positioned myself to be able to see both the band and Lacey, who was now playing the role of Lance's jungle gym. Their laughter nearly drowned out the music.

Oh, Becky Sue, where'd you roam?
You played my heart like an old jazz tone.

The two of them were enchanted with one another, their smiles mirror images, one baby, one adult. Then, the light went out of Lacey's eyes, and everything in her posture slumped. Her head lifted slowly as she rose to her feet, unaware that her precious child had slipped from her slack arms.

City lights or a mountain view,
Ain't no place that could capture you.

I threw myself backward, catching the baby—barely—before he hit the ground. He let out a startled cry, but nothing compared to the shriek he would have made if he'd landed wrong.

Lacey didn't even look at him. Didn't acknowledge that her son had just fallen.

She was already moving, her steps mechanical, her body jerking like something unseen wrapped its hand around her spine, pulling her forward.

People were noticing now as random friends and family stood and made their way west, toward the river. Conversations shifted to murmurs of concern, then confusion.

Lacey took half a dozen steps before I was able to stand. After shoving Lance at his father, I jumped to my feet and pursued the wife and mother, who was, at the moment, on a one-way trip to the Tennessee River.

Conversation around me grew as queries turned into concern, then into alarm. I heard several cries of "Where are you going?" "What is he doing?" and "What's wrong?"

I headed Lacey off, stood directly before her, and placed my hands on her shoulders.

This was the part I hadn't a clue about. How enthralled were these people? Was it a slight hypnosis? Or were they hell-bent on reaching their objective? How hard of a fight were we in for?

"Lacey? Hey! Snap out of it." I shook her by the shoulders, but the glazed look in her eyes never faltered. The fight in her wasn't terribly strong, but she wasn't giving in, either—not even a blink. Whatever guidance they'd given their thralls was deeply instilled.

So much for this being simple.

"Lacey!" I tried meeting her eyes, but that was pointless. She might as well have been blind. Her body resisted me, pushing forward with increasing force, and I sensed the longer I held her, the harder she'd work to fight me.

Connor caught up, Lance tucked into his elbow like a football, his expression stricken. "What's going on?"

"They're under a thrall," I explained, at which point Connor noticed it wasn't just his wife heading toward the river.

His face twisted in horror as he tracked the slow-moving wave of people, their steps eerily synchronized, eyes blank as they shuffled toward the rushing water.

"What the hell?"

"Lacey!" I shook her hard, but she only let out a soft, pitiful noise, like a child denied something they didn't understand.

Holding them would not be enough to prevent them from fulfilling their spellbound obligation. Based on the speed with which Lacey's agitation was growing, it was only a matter of time before she started causing a ruckus. So, what were our options? Maybe the spell was timed, but I doubted we could hold them too much longer without hurting folks. Was death the only release from their captivity?

No. No, the Stygian wouldn't make it that easy. That merciful. They were too cruel, too intent on making a statement. And they knew there'd be cameras. Nowadays, there are *always* cameras. People loved getting their clicks, and using an unbelievable event like this was guaranteed clickbait. This wasn't just a mass execution; it was a spectacle, just like the Stygian planned. They'd woven a spell that would carry these people to their deaths—and then let them wake up just in time to know they were drowning. I was sure of it.

But how did they plan to wake them at the pivotal moment?

Water.

Release from the spell would be triggered by contact with water! As soon as these people jumped from the bridge into the rushing river, they'd come to their senses, only to realize they were yards from shore and in the middle of the rain-swollen river.

It *had* to be water. I knew it in my soul. Its rightness reverberated with that Source energy in me, and I was certain

I'd found the answer to our problem. The question now was, would a splash be sufficient to wake them? Or did they need to be drenched, soaked through to the skin, to shake free of the Stygian's grasp?

Lacey's resistance turned vicious. Her hands, curved like claws, raked at my arms, her manicured nails too thick to break the skin but sharp enough to leave burning welts. The others—dozens, maybe hundreds—were starting to fight back, too. Low, frustrated groans rumbled from their throats, a sound too damn close to a zombie movie for comfort.

"Connor! Trade me!"

Connor, still slack-jawed with shock, snapped to attention. "Huh?"

"Take your wife! Hold her back, and whatever you do, don't let her go! Give me Lance. I need to get something from your basket. And I might need to send a text."

"Oh. Uh, OK."

Bless him and his slightly too many craft beers. If he'd been thinking straight, he might have questioned why, in the middle of a full-scale supernatural crisis, I needed to rummage through their picnic basket and fire off a text while holding on to his kid. But he wasn't thinking straight, so he awkwardly passed me the baby and took Lacey's arms, dodging her clawing hands like an amateur boxer in a bar fight.

I dashed as fast as I safely could with a baby in my arms to Connor and Lacey's picnic basket, then propped Lance on my knee as I rummaged through the contents for a water bottle. I knew they'd had one earlier—I'd watched Lacey use part of it to mix a bottle of formula for the baby.

Water... water... Could beer work? Is there enough water in beer to do the trick? Damn it, Connor. You packed enough for an entire tailgate party.

Seconds ticked by, and with every moment, those captive

to the Stygian's spell grew more agitated, their effort more forced. I could hear the sounds of struggle, the occasional loud cry of pain as the bespelled landed blows on the people trying to hold them back. The spell was getting stronger. Or maybe the people under its grip were just getting desperate.

It took several moments of frustrated digging, but at the bottom of the basket, buried beneath at least a dozen cans and a plastic bag full of empties, my fingers wrapped around a smooth, cold plastic cylinder.

"Aha!" I yanked the water bottle free, triumphant.

"Ha!" Lance echoed with a gummy smile, completely unaware of the crisis at hand.

I pressed a quick kiss to his forehead. "Let's go try to save your mommy."

"Ma-e," Lance babbled.

"Yeah. Exactly."

Baby in one hand, bottle in the other, I rushed back to Lance's struggling parents. Yeah, there were a couple of people en route I could have tested my theory on, but I'd gotten attached to the little family.

Back at Lacey's side, Connor fought to keep her in place. Lacey was thrashing with nearly superhuman strength.

"Connor, hold her as still as you can, OK?"

Connor shot me a wild-eyed *Are you serious?* look.

Yeah, I know. Easier said than done. The woman was fighting like a cat in a sack.

"I'll try."

I cracked open the bottle and, doing my best to keep Lance away from Lacey's flailing arms, squirted the cold water in Lacey's face. She burbled frustratedly, sputtered—

—and woke from the clutches of the Stygian spell.

Her body snapped rigid in Connor's grip, then sagged like someone had cut the strings holding her upright. Her breath came in ragged gulps. Her lashes fluttered, and her eyes took in her surroundings for the first time in the last several minutes.

"Wh—" She coughed, blinking furiously, her hands lifting to swipe at the water dripping down her face. "What—what just happened?"

"You were under a spell," I told her. "You were walking toward the river."

Lacey's lips parted, but no sound came out. She turned her head, taking in the chaos around her—people still struggling, clawing toward the water like sleepwalkers drawn to a cliff. A couple of patrol cars had arrived at the edge of the park, their lights spinning in confusion as officers stepped out, trying to make sense of the madness. Horror flickered across her face, turning it stark and pale in the faint overhead lights. Connor, finally convinced she was back to normal, dropped his arms from her shoulders.

"Oh my God," Lacey breathed.

"You're OK now," I said, shifting Lance against my hip, not ready yet to hand him to his mother. "We need to wake the others."

Still shaking, Lacey nodded, but the shock hadn't worn off yet. I could see it in the dazed way she swallowed, and her limbs trembled with aftershocks. She'd been moments from plunging into that river, leaving her husband without a wife, her baby without a mother. If I'd figured it out too much later, she wouldn't be staring at me with wide, shell-shocked eyes.

Well, it worked. That was great. Fantastic. Amazing, even. But now I had a bigger problem. How the hell was I going to tell *ten acres* of panicked, screaming people that the only way to save their loved ones was to douse them in water?

Wait… Dylan. The water witch. And the fountain. Damn,

I'd barely had a chance to watch the man work his magic before tonight. If I'd met him sooner, maybe I could've learned something, trained, prepared to help him. Instead, I was about to be stuck taking a crash course in water witchery smack in the middle of a catastrophe.

I threw my head back and bellowed, lungs straining.

"Dylan!"

Lance flinched at the sound, his tiny face scrunching up as he peered at me with great disappointment, as if I had betrayed some sacred trust by being so incredibly loud. But he didn't cry, thank the Goddess.

Connor reached for his son. "I'll take him."

I somberly handed Connor his child and turned in a circle, squinting in the dark, searching for Dylan in the narrow puddles of light under the sidewalk lamps.

"Dylan Marsh! Can you hear me?" My throat burned, but I didn't care. Every second counted. "It's Murphy! I need your help!"

A few people nearby whipped around at my shouting. One man, some grizzled-looking guy in a faded Alabama cap, shot me a glare. "For fuck's sake, shut up!"

I ignored him. They were scared. I got it. But I didn't have time to baby their nerves, and I wasn't about to lower my voice to make anyone more comfortable.

I cupped my hands around my mouth and tried again. "DYLAN!"

I scanned the writhing crowd in case he'd heard me and was running in my direction, but the park was a blur of motion—people struggling against their spellbound loved ones, children crying, hands reaching, desperate voices shouting names into the chaos.

I didn't have time to search the whole damn park.

"Murphy!" a familiar voice called out.

I turned to see Officer Kenny Hendricks trotting toward me, eyes wide and alert. "Can I help? Who are we looking for?"

"Dylan Marsh," I said, breathless. "Uh, mid-thirties. Tall. White. Wavy brown hair. Blue eyes. I think he's wearing a green t-shirt and jeans."

Kenny gave a sharp nod and pressed the button on his shoulder mic. "All units, be on the lookout for a white male in his thirties, Dylan Marsh—green t-shirt, brown hair, blue eyes. May be trying to help, not hurt. Repeat: not hostile." He glanced back at me as he moved off. "We'll find him."

I gave him an appreciative nod, but found myself cursing as I wrenched my phone from my back pocket and punched out a message to the group with shaking fingers. Hopefully, some of the Numinari caught the text and could show people how to release the thralls, if nothing else.

Splash them. Face if possible. Water breaks the spell. Dylan, can you use the fountain to hit a bunch of people quick?

I hit send, sucked in a breath, and braced myself. Now I just had to hope Dylan was able to check his damn phone. And fast.

Chapter 28

I reckon the time between hitting *send* and seeing Dylan's reply wasn't as long as it felt, because it felt like forever. The seconds stretched, pulling time—and my nerves—apart as I watched the people around me clutching their loved ones, hollering names, pleading, shaking shoulders that remained limp and unresponsive. I got a bunch of pings telling me the Numinari had seen my message and were doing what they could. But no response from Dylan—the one person who could use water most efficiently.

Maybe he hadn't seen the message yet. Maybe he had, and he was thinking. Either way, I wasn't about to stand there empty-handed and waiting.

First, I reached out, sending feelers along the park's perimeter and beyond, searching for the telltale, stumbling gait of someone under the Stygian's control—someone who might have slipped past our patrol. But no one had. Our barriers held. Good. That was one thing that went right.

I inhaled deeply, filling my lungs with summer heat and the scent of sweat and dust. But in my mind, I wasn't just breathing air—I was drawing in every ounce of power I could reach, every scrap of energy humming nearby. The connection was always there, like a deep well waiting for a steady hand. I let it flood me, spill into my limbs, until my skin tingled and my fingertips itched from holding so much force inside. I felt like I could lift the sky.

Then I shaped it, willed it into something useful. Orbs of light gathered in my hands, bustling and whizzing like fireflies caught in a mason jar. And with a whisper and a flick of my fingers, I sent the orbs drifting outward, willing them to find the people who needed them most. The orbs carried a little extra strength to everyone with a grip on their loved one. I hoped it was enough to get them by until Dylan was able to—

My phone buzzed in my back pocket for the millionth time. I pulled it out and finally saw a message from Dylan:

Let's turn the tide!

The man had dad jokes. In the middle of a crisis. I was both subtly amused and slightly disturbed.

Keeping my connection with the Source, I opened my third eye to use that power as well—a talent Conall had been working on with me, but one that was still… odd? Amazing? Hard to describe. Combining the two skills allowed me to see, at least at some level, the unified field that connected all things. It was like staring into the threads that wove the universe itself together. The force is a shimmering lattice of energy, networks of light and shadow weaving through everything, binding existence together in an intricate, ever-shifting web. Colors I couldn't name bled into one another, pulsing with a rhythm that felt like a universal heartbeat, a deep, resonant hum reverberating in my bones. It was an overwhelming experience—my senses got completely flooded at first, until I resisted the urge to filter through the chaos and allowed my mind to just… be. To feel what I saw instead of trying to box everything into categories. To allow my spirit to understand without my mind needing to put everything into words. The words could come later. Now, it was time to watch Dylan's magic and learn.

That's when I saw Dylan.

More accurately, I saw the energy that was Dylan—the shape of his power bending and moving around him, drawn toward the old cast-iron fountain in the center of the park. Water sloshed and trembled in the basin, responding to his call, rising in smooth ribbons that curled around his arms like living things. He lifted his hands, and the water lifted with them, suspended in midair like an offering.

Then, with a quick flick of his wrist, he sent it flying. And the water obeyed like a well-trained dog.

To the normal eye, it might've looked like nothing more than water arcing in the dark. But to me, through the lens of the Source, it was something else entirely.

It was light.

Not a glow reflected from the streetlamps or the hazy beams of moonlight. This was something purer, something antediluvian, primitive, and universal. Threads of energy spun through the droplets, refracting light in the air like sparks struck from flint. Each bead of water pulsed with power, illuminating the night in shimmering ribbons as Dylan worked.

The first jet of water shot forward, hitting a teenage boy square in his face. His mother gasped as he shuddered and blinked rapidly, like he'd just woken from a nightmare. Another stream struck a man bucking in his wife's grip, his face twisted in something between rage and despair. The water soaked down the front of his shirt, and for a moment, he froze, his wild struggle faltering. His breath hitched, and his whole body seemed to deflate as clarity returned to his eyes.

Dylan moved like a conductor leading an orchestra, his hands shaping the water, guiding it. Each motion sent another wave arcing through the air, seeking out those still caught in the spell. The park stretched for acres, the chaos rippling outward in all directions, but Dylan didn't hesitate or falter.

Water lifted and split, darting like silver fish in the dark, diving toward the lost. I watched as the light within it found them, clinging to their skin like dew, sinking in and working past the barrier of whatever had taken hold of their minds. A girl no older than twelve collapsed in her father's arms. A woman with wild, tangled hair gasped as if breaking the surface after being underwater too long.

One by one, Dylan worked, pulling water from the fountain, sending it streaking through the air to find those caught in the spell. He twisted his fingers, and the water rose as if it were eager to be used. He pulled water from the ones already freed, drawing it back into the current, weaving it into the life-giving stream that surged through the night, seeking the next lost soul. Each splash and dousing brought them back gasping, shaking, and confused, but awake.

Some collapsed, quivering and sobbing. Others stood frozen, blinking like newborns seeing the world for the first time. As they awoke, the realization spread—people were catching on to the cure. Everywhere, desperate hands poured water over their loved ones from plastic bottles, travel mugs, whatever they could find. One poor guy ended up drenched in the icy runoff from the bottom of a massive cooler, gasping as the shock jolted him back to himself.

For the record, beer worked, too, I noticed.

And still, Dylan worked. And I followed, watching and listening, unraveling the secret of how water and magic wove together, how he called to the spirit within one of the Earth's oldest and most powerful forces. He didn't command it; he courted it, coaxed it, loved it. With the Source as my power and my open third eye as my map, I saw how his soul sang for water in all its forms, how the elements within it answered him like a long-lost lover. It was contagious, that love. Or maybe the water had always been waiting for me to hear. Either way, I felt that love sinking into me, pooling in my marrow, and before I knew it, I was helping Dylan wield water in life-saving sprays.

Nearing the end of his efforts, Dylan encountered a guy—early forties, red-faced, the kind of loudmouth who had likely spent the past several minutes barking orders at people struggling to resuscitate their loved ones instead of lending a hand. "This is all a globalist hoax," he'd hollered earlier, arms crossed, smirking as others fought to keep their loved ones from throwing themselves into the river. "Y'all are falling for it—deep state mind control, mark my words. They want us scared. They want us weak. And now you're telling me it's magic? That's what they want you to think!"

Dylan turned his hand ever so slightly.

A thick column of water surged from the fountain, arcing high into the air before coming down hard, right on top of the guy's head.

He sputtered, choked, wiped his face, and whirled around, wild-eyed. "What the hell?"

Dylan didn't even look in his direction.

I bit the inside of my cheek, fighting a grin. Maybe it wasn't the most mature use of magic. But damn, it was satisfying.

I'm bad at telling time—especially when wielding magic—but I'd wager the whole episode was over in maybe half an hour.

The moment I let my third eye close and loosened my grip on the Source, exhaustion slammed into me like a runaway truck. My body was instantly limp, physically exhausted, and spiritually drained. I sagged where I stood, my limbs heavy, my mind a sluggish mess of static. Every nerve felt raw, every muscle useless. If this was how the people we'd just saved felt, I didn't envy them.

The park was too quiet now, eerie in the way disaster zones always are after the smoke settles. Without my third eye lighting up the park with its neon lattice of universal connections, I finally noticed the bright white lights piercing the darkness. Way too bright.

Fucking *cameras*. Oh, yeah… We had alerted the media there for LaDonna's healing of the tree. Instead of leaving when the magic was over, they'd stuck around. And they'd seen everything. They'd captured the Stygian's next big trick, another sickening display designed to terrify the world and prove that witches were exactly what they wanted everyone to believe—dangerous, chaotic, evil. And they hadn't just done it anywhere. They'd done it here. In my town. In Betony's town. In Rene's town.

But they hadn't planned on losing.

No doubt their lackeys were already texting up a storm, sending frantic messages about how their little horror show had gone off script. And tonight, they'd get to watch every major news outlet broadcast their failure. That was a small, satisfying victory.

The last bit of fight in me fizzled out. I let my legs give up, falling hard enough to make my teeth click together. The backs of my legs itched where my denim cut-offs met damp earth. Somewhere in the haze of my wrecked brain, I watched an ant crawl across my scuffed-up Converse like that was the most interesting thing in the world.

We'd beaten them this time. And going forward, we would *not* play defense. That game was over.

"Mama Murph!"

My gut twisted. I knew that voice. I'd heard it before, too many times. That was a Betony-who'd-been-crying voice. The kind that made my heart seize in my chest.

Shit, what went wrong? Did we not save everyone? I should have checked! Just because everyone was inside the park doesn't mean we saved them all...

My heart galloped. My body was spent, but panic shoved it into motion anyway.

"Mama Murph!"

"Over here!" My hands fumbled for my phone, fingers sluggish with exhaustion, but I still managed to flick on the flashlight, casting a shaky beam through the dark.

Betony barreled toward me like a bull, her breath ragged, her body shaking with the force of her sobs. Behind her, Jake and Lorina weren't far behind, wearing thunderstruck expressions.

Jake's left eye was swelling shut, his nose a bloody mess. Lorina didn't look better—her hair was a mess, one sleeve ripped, and a trail of blood on her chin. Looked like they'd wrestled down a thrall and barely come out on top. Some part of me ached for them, wanted to reach out, make sure they were okay—But it wasn't the injuries that set my teeth on edge. It was Betony.

Betony's panic cut through everything else.

She wasn't just crying—she was coming apart. She ran like she didn't even know what her legs were doing, her hands clenched tight at her sides like she was struggling to hold herself together. When she came fully into view, her face was splotchy and red from crying, her eyes nearly as swollen as Jake's growing black eye.

When she spoke again, her voice was broken, thick, terrified.

"Rene," she gasped, barely able to speak. "Mama Murph, they got Rene!"

Chapter 29

I didn't need to ask who Betony meant by "they." The Stygian had captured Rene. Spearheaded by Ericka, no doubt, who still had designs for her son. Still trying to drag him into her twisted little nightmare.

Had this whole debacle in the park been nothing but a smokescreen to find and kidnap him? No. Even if we were the ones who'd asked the media to be there, they were the ones who wanted the world to watch as they toyed with life and death, wanted to prove that they could slaughter whoever they set their mind to on a whim.

And she wanted every witch breathing to know they had done it right before the Summate.

Well, fuck them. Fuck them all the way to the River Styx they named themselves after and back again. They thought they could take Rene from me? From my home town? From under the Summate's nose?

Fuck. Her.

I flung my hands to the sky, and power roared up to meet me.

The Source hit hard, a rush of searing, electric heat ripping down my spine like I'd thrown my damn fingers into ten waiting light sockets. Righteous anger burned through me, sharpening my focus. Normally, I had to fight the surge of power down, wrestle it into the necessary channels before it knocked me on my ass. This time, the magic wasn't over-whelming—it was obedient. It surged forward, eager, like a storm waiting to be unleashed. But this time? This time, it came eagerly.

It wanted this fight.

Rene's trail was already calling to me, his energy bright even against the chaos. Six months of living under my roof had imprinted his presence on me, giving me more than a lit-tle familiarity with his energetic fingerprint.

I shoved through the crowd, barely registering Betony, Jake, and Lorina keeping pace behind me. The air was thick with movement—shuffling feet, hushed murmurs, and the occasional wail as people came to grips with what had hap-pened to them. Streetlights flickered weakly against the press of bodies, their glow swallowed by the deeper, unnatural darkness still clinging to the edges of the park like mist. The Numinari pulsed around me like neon afterimages, raw and chaotic, their energy signatures slashing through the night in erratic bursts of light and heat. Some flared like open flames, wild and uncontrolled, while others crackled and faded like dying embers.

It was overwhelming. But I didn't need to sort through all of them. I just needed to find *him*.

Rene's energy was different. Steady, unique, something I could pick out in a cosmic cataclysm of energy. It didn't claw at the edges of my senses or burn like the others. It wasn't an inferno or a wildfire raging out of control. It was quieter. In-tentional. A low, warm candle flame, steady in the wind. Even now, after he was gone, his presence lingered, a hum beneath the clamor. I recognized it like a normal person might recall a loved one's favorite cologne.

And then I found it.

The last traces of his energy clung to the air and settled

into the damp grass at the base of a gnarled tree, like he'd only just been there, like I could reach out and touch him. I crouched, pressing my palm to the ground, letting the snowy-cool currents remnants of his presence trickle up through my senses.

He had been here. Standing. Holding his ground.

But then, the cool presence shattered. The thread of Rene's energy didn't trail off naturally. It broke. Jagged. A violent, unnatural severing like a frozen lake fracturing under the force of a plummeting stone. My stomach clenched at the sudden emptiness where he should have been.

The voices around me blurred into background noise. The wind shifted, stirring the branches above me, but I didn't move. My fingers wove through the grass at my fingertips. My pulse was steady, slow, controlled.

I have his trail, and I am not losing him.

With a burst of furious earth energy, honed from years of watching LaDonna weave her green witch magic, I shoved magical feelers racing along the pavement, tunneling like wildfire through dry brush, seeking every crack, every inter-section, every winding back road. The city unfolded in my mind like a map drawn in molten light, tracing veins of energy over cracked asphalt, snaking through intersections, and pounding down alleys.

Like the glimpse of a cat sneaking around a corner, I caught it. Rene's signature, moving way too fast as it hurtled down the nearby streets. I followed the path like a bloodhound with a scent, tracking it until I was on the heels of a black GMC Savana, careening down Benedick Boulevard toward the nearest highway.

Rage spiked inside me.

Not today, bitch.

I needed to be careful. At these speeds, a reckless move

could send them skidding into another car or cause the whole van to roll over. I needed precision. But they *would* be stopped.

Heat.

Tremendous heat. In four separate locations. All at once.

The rubber sagged, losing structure instantly, collapsing into bubbling, tar-black pools that spread across the asphalt like candle wax. The van lurched, its frame jerking violently as the metal rims carved shrieking gouges into the pavement. Sparks flared in the darkness, glowing embers kicking up against the undercarriage like fireflies caught in a twister.

Momentum carried the vehicle forward a few more feet before the weight finally betrayed the driver. It groaned, shuddered, and came to a hard, jarring stop, rocking slightly on ruined wheels.

I pulled on the memory of Hanna's glamor spell, the feel of it curling around my skin like mist. The words formed on my tongue before I even fully recalled them.

Hanekudah mi'panai timash,
Lo yishar mimena reshima ba'olam.
Tikach oti ha'ruach ha'ktana,
V'tashlik otah b'chalon shama.

I didn't need the words any more than I needed Hanna's ointment to work the invisibility glamor. But they steadied the raging power flooding inside me. Kept it from eating me alive. And gave my power a focus.

The connection between Rene and me was built on six months of shared space, of meals at the same table, of quiet conversations in the kitchen after midnight. I reached for it, reached for him, and let my magic slip through the gap like a whisper in the dark.

Rene.

It was clear Rene had been fighting his captors from the

moment they stuffed him into the van, thrashing, twisting, refusing to make it easy. A hand had been in his hair, forcing his head down, another yanking at his arms as someone cursed and fought to cinch the zip ties tight around his wrists.

"Hold him down, dammit!" one of them snarled.

"I am holding him!" The second witch grunted as Rene wrenched an arm free, jerking sideways with enough force to slam him into the opposite seat.

"Then hold him harder!"

Rene kicked out, his heel connecting with a shin—hard. The witch gripping his arms swore and nearly lost hold of him.

"Kid's like a fucking rabid dog!" Kicked Shin exclaimed.

The other man wheezed, clearly out of breath from fighting, but didn't let go. "Stupid little—just sit still, damn you!"

He didn't. Rene bucked sideways, slamming his shoulder into another, sending them sprawling against the opposite seat. His breath came fast. He was young and strong, but they were stronger, and there were two of them.

I saw the moment I was waiting for—a split second where Rene was out of their grasp. Clenching my fist, I sent the magic curling around him like a cloak, weaving him into the shadows, slipping him from their sight. He wasn't gone physically, but to them? He might as well have dropped straight into the ether.

"Where the hell—"

"He's gone! Where'd he—shit!"

Hands scrambled for something that wasn't there. Rene, seen only by me, danced out of reach with feline grace. One of them let out a sharp breath, turning in frantic circles in the confined space.

"Ericka's gonna kill us," the first muttered.

"Not if we kill him first—"

They barely had time to finish the thought before Rene pivoted and drove his elbow backward into a gut, knocking the wind out of the witch behind him. The man staggered, choking on a curse, but Rene didn't wait for him to recover. He lunged for the nearest door, fumbling for the handle. It stuck. Locked.

I felt his panic spike, and I *pushed*. A sliver of magic lanced forward, burrowing into the lock, urging the worn mechanics to give.

He threw his weight against the door. Once. Twice. The metal groaned, but held. Ericka must have added a spell or two of her own to the latch.

Come on, I thought, pouring more of myself into the effort.

Rene reared back and slammed into the door with everything he had, shoulder first. Something inside the locking mechanism gave with a dull pop.

Another hit—this time, a pointed kick just beneath the handle—and the door jolted free, swinging wide with a violent lurch.

The night air rushed in as he stumbled forward, boots hitting asphalt.

And then—he ran.

"The fuck?!"

"I thought you said he was gone! How—"

The voices behind him rose in a confused, frantic roar. Someone cast a desperate spell—an arrow of directed air—in Rene's direction, missing by inches.

Didn't matter. He was already moving, already gone, feet pounding against the pavement as Rene tore down the street like hell itself was after him. Which, honestly, wasn't far off.

I didn't know where the other Stygian coven members

were, but I saw no need to give the ones in the van a chance to recover and chase their quarry. With a wave of my hand, I used a spell I'd learned to use on myself on nights when my mind would not stop spinning.

Sleep.

The driver slumped forward. The men dropped like stones. The van was silent.

I let out a long, slow breath, releasing most of the power I clung to, but kept Rene invisible. No telling where the rest of those bastards were hiding.

Chapter 30

When I pulled my focus away from Rene and back to the world around me, I realized I'd drawn a crowd. Crystal, Doyle, Lorina, and half the Lughaidh coven had gathered around, their eyes fixed on me like I held the winning lotto numbers. Pretty much everyone but Miriam was there, but she was probably still making the rounds, patching up the folks who'd taken the worst of that compulsion spell.

"He's safe," I said, "for now."

A few of them let out shaky breaths, and their tense faces eased somewhat.

"He could still use some backup, though. Just in case there are more of those bastards lurking. Uh, Joey, Doyle—go cover him. He's hauling ass up Benedick Boulevard. Just, um… listen for the footsteps. He's kind of invisible right now."

Nervous laughter rippled through the group surrounding me, and Joey and Doyle sprinted south on Benedick in search of Rene's rapid footsteps.

"There they are!"

That *voice*. That syrupy, saccharine-sweet, overdone Georgia drawl that set my teeth on edge had somehow managed to add an edge of accusation and venom to her performative kindness.

"Those are the witches who cast the spell on everyone!"

Oh, fuck. She's really going to try to pin this on us.

Have I mentioned that Ericka is a heinous thundercunt?

I forced a calm expression, though fury simmered just under the surface, and turned to face Ericka. Standing beside her was Virginia Yarborough—of course. How lovely that Betony's mother had joined us.

And the newscasters, of course. Because why not?

And Pastor Carrigan, too. *Perfect.*

I wasn't sure which church Pastor Carrigan led, but I knew it was either the large First Baptist Church or the even larger First Methodist Church across the street. I was pretty sure it was the Methodist one. The one with the radio sermons and the billboard telling folks which sins were currently trending.

The reporters had undoubtedly trailed Ericka to where I stood casting the spell to retrieve her son from the kidnappers. They stood just outside the chaos, their cameras rolling, the harsh glare of their floodlights cutting through the night. They weren't interfering—just watching, waiting, their lenses hungry for scandal. Their lights created shadows that stretched unnaturally across the street and sidewalk behind me, giving the scene a surreal, stage-lit feel.

I wanted to kill her. I was aching to strike her down, to get some sort of retribution for everything she'd put so many people through.

But, you know, cameras. And witnesses. Not a good time.

I sighed. "Ericka, why would you even say that? You know we live here. Why would we try to hurt our own friends and neighbors?" *More importantly, why aren't you brave enough to admit you're the high priestess of the Stygian, you discount drama queen with a god complex?*

"Because they don't accept you!" she shot back, her voice ringing through the makeshift stage of streetlights and camera flashes. "And why would they? You know what the Bible says about witches?"

Oh, I did. I ran a metaphysical shop in small-town Alabama. I'd heard it plenty of times. Not to mention that La-Donna made sure I was familiar with many of the world's major religions growing up. But I also didn't think the Bible was a history book—or that picking and choosing verses made for a solid argument. Unfortunately, I had to tread carefully unless I wanted to piss off a crowd of already-riled-up Christian Southerners.

"Do you know what the Bible says about bearing false witness against your neighbor?" I retorted.

"We're not lyin'!" Virginia bellowed, her voice raw with a faked righteous fury that could have earned her an Academy Award. "Y'all are some demon-worshipping heathens!"

I clenched my teeth so hard my jaw ached. Part of me wanted to ask her to pick a lane—were we demon-worshipers or witches? But pointing out the distinction would only prove I knew the difference, and in this crowd, that was as good as confessing to one side or the other. And neither was acceptable to most of them..

"Why are you here, Ericka?" I asked, pitching my voice into the exasperated tone of a mother asking why her kid had blown their whole allowance on Amazon impulse buys.

"I'm here because I'm on a mission to stop the Stygian!" Ericka declared, puffing up like she was about to smite someone. She was nowhere near the actor Virginia was, and I wondered who on earth would buy her bullshit. But I also knew some folks heard whatever they wanted to hear.

"And you're the leader!" Virginia added, backing up Ericka's accusation with a pointed finger. "You could have destroyed the town tonight, but *we* stopped you!"

Betony stepped forward now, her pale face flushed in the

glow of the streetlights and camera glare. "You're seriously walking around like you don't belong behind bars? Like you didn't just slip out of county lockup? OK. The *audacity* of some people."

Pastor Carrigan's brow twitched, and for a brief second, uncertainty flickered across his face. He glanced at Virginia, something unreadable in his expression, before turning his attention back to me.

And that's when I saw it. His eyes... he wasn't all there. They had him under compulsion.

"Ms. Moore and Ms. Yarborough warned me there would be a horrible event here tonight brought on by dark forces," Pastor Carrigan said solemnly. "And they were right."

"Yeah," I said, deadpan. "Because they caused it. She's the head of the Stygian." I motioned with my head toward Ericka. "Its high priestess, in fact."

"Impossible. These two have been with me all night," he countered.

I barely resisted the urge to roll my eyes. "The Stygian are more than just two people," I said. "These two didn't have to be physically present for the spell to work."

I had a feeling Ericka and Virginia had been taking part in the mind control spell the whole damn time, probably whispering their incantations while the good pastor stood right there, compelled not to see a damn thing. But explaining that to him? Yeah. That'd be a waste of breath. He thought they'd been with him all night and didn't remember them taking part in anything hokey, so as far as he was concerned, they were blameless.

One reporter stepped forward, microphone at the ready. "Are you saying there are *other* witches in town who would do something like this?"

"None that live here in Gryphon," I replied evenly. "But

these two? Yeah. They absolutely would."

Ericka and Virginia both started squawking, their voices overlapping in a tangled mess of outrage and sanctimony. But it didn't matter—whatever they were saying was swallowed up by the hungry cacophony of reporters, each one jostling to get their mic in position, shouting over one another in pursuit of the perfect soundbite.

"She didn't do it," a voice from the crowd shouted. The tone was vaguely familiar. "Murphy didn't do it."

Connor.

Holding baby Lance in his arms with Lacey at his side, he pushed his family through to the front of the crowd and shouted, "Murphy was the one who figured out how to save everyone. My wife Lacey was the first one cured of the…" He faltered, struggling to put a name to what had happened.

"Compulsion spell," I offered. "The Stygian had people in what's called a thrall."

"*See!*" Virginia exclaimed. "How would she know what it is if she didn't cause it?"

"That's ridiculous," Lacey insisted. "Murphy saved me!"

A few murmurs rippled through the crowd, but Virginia's accusation, regardless of how well acted, didn't hold as much weight when actual witnesses were contradicting her. The tide of suspicion was shifting.

And then, as if the Goddess herself had impeccable timing (which of course she does), Dylan Marsh strode onto the scene.

"Dylan was the real hero," I said, motioning for him to step forward. He joined me and we faced off, the two of us against Virginia and Ericka with the camera crews there to record the whole confrontation. Only where I had my coven, Lorina, and a few Numinari at my back, they had Pastor Corrigan and… well, the rest of the town.

I placed a hand on Dylan's back and spoke clear and loud to ensure the microphones caught my next words. "It was Dylan who broke the spell by sending water to splash everyone awake." I didn't bother getting into the details of how I knew about the attack beforehand or how I'd pieced together the solution. That'd come out if it needed to—preferably when I wasn't standing in the middle of a verbal firing squad.

"So he *is* a witch!" Ericka crowed, eyes flashing with the same delight a cat gets when it traps a mouse.

"Yes," I said flatly. "As am I. But we are not the enemy here. We are not part of the Stygian."

Dylan stood with his hands behind his back like a soldier at ease, and I noted he was manipulating his hands as he casually shifted his weight from one leg to the other. The humidity around us thickened, carrying the scent of damp earth and something charged, like ozone before a lightning strike. He was summoning water again. But why?

Determined to keep the focus on either me or Virginia and Ericka's nonsense rather than whatever Dylan was planning, I pressed on. "I have been a member of this community my entire life. I love Gryphon. And I would never put the people who live here in danger. In fact, I'd die to defend it."

Dylan had summoned up a snowball-sized globe of water from the atmosphere as easily as whistling. With the air of a man engaging in a well-rehearsed vaudeville trick, he flicked his wrist behind his back. The sphere of water jumped from his hand, arched over his back, then his shoulder—

And splashed Pastor Carrigan smack in the face.

The good pastor reeled back, sputtering, his usually slicked-back gray hair now plastered to his forehead. He sputtered, blinked, and shook his head to dislodge the water from his head.

"What—what in the—?"

He swiped at his dripping face, took in his surroundings, then stared at the crowd, flabbergasted and confused.

"How'd I get here?"

Ericka and Virginia surged forward, spewing reassurances that oozed false concern as they attempted to strong-arm Pastor Carrigan off-camera. But Pastor Carrigan, who'd unexpectedly found himself in the middle of the park flanked by two overly concerned strangers, wasn't about to be led off just anywhere.

A new voice joined the conversation.

"Pastor Carrigan, are you alright?"

It took only a breath, a flicker of movement in the periphery, for me to realize who it belonged to. A small, involuntary gasp from Lorina confirmed it.

Her mother.

She moved like a figure from an old oil painting—tall, severe, draped in a dark fabric that caught the light in hard angles. I saw now where Lorina got her delicate build. Her mother's hair, black as a raven's wing, slipped over her shoulder as she reached for Pastor Carrigan with a hand both delicate and unyielding. Behind her bustled a sturdy, hard-shelled turtle of a man with no neck to speak of, and a beard that looked somewhat out of place on his lantern jaw.

The moment Carrigan found his footing, Lorina's mother turned. I noticed she still had a name tag on—the sort you see on bank employees or realtors. It read *Kathleen* in black letters on a bright gold tag.

Lorina had already ducked behind Jake, trying to disappear into the crowd, and tiny Cadence stepped into the space where her tall friend had stood just moments before. But mothers have a sixth sense about these things— even the non-witchy ones.

Kathleen's gaze sharpened. "Lorina?"

Lorina pulled further into Jake's substantial shadow, shrinking as though she could slip between the folds of reality itself. "Mom—"

Her mother's lips pressed together, forming the thin, bloodless line of a woman balancing rage and disappointment, each one fighting for purchase.

"What are you doing here?" Her voice cut through the crowd noise like a knife, and Lorina flinched.

Lorina swallowed. "I was just—"

"Just what?" Kathleen stepped closer, her presence vast despite her willowy frame. "You know what Pastor Carrigan has said about these people. What *I* have said." Her gaze flickered to me, Dylan, the coven, then the gathered Numinari, pausing just long enough to register her distaste before snapping back to her daughter. "And yet here you are, standing with *them*."

"I'm not *with* them," Lorina tried, but even she didn't sound convinced.

Kathleen's expression hardened. "You expect me to believe that? You're hiding behind Jake, for God's sake."

Jake cleared his throat. "Uh. Not hiding—"

The look she shot him could have soured milk in its jug.

Lorina squared her shoulders, but I could see the tremor in her fingers where she clenched them at her sides. "Mom, it's not what you think."

"Oh?" Her mother tilted her head slightly, the movement eerily birdlike. "Because what I think is that my daughter— who was raised in the church, who knows right from wrong— has thrown in with witches, standing against her own people."

Lorina flinched, but to her credit, she didn't back down. "I'm not standing against anyone. I'm just—" She hesitated, voice lower now. "I just wanted to understand."

The words landed like a stone dropped into a deep well.

Kathleen's expression flickered, just for a moment, something moving behind her eyes—grief? Regret? And then it was gone, replaced with something colder. She exhaled slowly, voice nearly a whisper.

"You sound just like your father."

It was not a statement. It was a sentence.

Lorina's entire body went rigid, and it was then that I realized that the burly man escorting the dear pastor away was not Lorina's biological father.

The cameras still rolled, their red lights glinting like tiny, mechanical eyes. The world was watching. Why? Were they waiting for something witchy to come from this family drama?

I lifted a hand. All of the floodlights cut out simultaneously, plunging the crowd into abrupt, disorienting darkness. A chorus of startled curses and confused murmurs rippled through the newscasters and onlookers.

Kathleen stiffened, her gaze snapping to me. For the first time, doubt flickered across her face before reality hit her. This wasn't smoke and mirrors. This wasn't a trick. I wasn't a fraud. I had *genuine power*, and now she knew it.

And it scared her shitless.

"Nobody else needs to see y'all airing your family business," I said, my voice cold as iron.

For a long, awful second, no one spoke. The murmurs of the crowd swirled around us, Lorina and her mother standing at the center of it all, locked in a silent battle, tension trembling between them.

Finally, Kathleen straightened, brushing an unseen offense from the front of her dress with clipped, precise motions. "Lorina Beth, you are coming home."

Lorina's jaw clenched and her slender hands balled into fists at her sides. "No."

That single word hung between them like a storm cloud.

Kathleen inhaled sharply, and I swear I saw her nostrils flare. "Excuse me?"

"I *said* no." Lorina's voice trembled, but the steel beneath it and the unwavering way she met her mother's eye was undeniable. "I'm not a child. I make my own choices."

Kathleen's eyes flashed. "Then make the right one."

Silence.

Lorina swallowed hard, glancing at me, then Jake, then back at her mother. She was at a crossroads, and we all knew it.

Kathleen exhaled through her nose as her patience evaporated. "If you walk away with them, don't bother coming home."

Cicadas droned in the trees, their relentless hum filling the silence left in the wake of Kathleen's words. Somewhere in the distance, a dog barked agitatedly. A few blocks away, a car backfired. The world moved on, indifferent to the splintering that was happening before us.

Lorina hesitated. Then she lifted her chin, straightened her spine, and stepped out from behind Jake and Cadence to stand beside me.

Her mother sucked in a breath and her eyes widened in disbelief. A decision locked into place behind them.

She turned without another word and walked away.

Lorina didn't move, didn't so much as breathe, as her mother's retreating figure melted into the crowd. Her jaw still held its stubborn set, but her large brown eyes shone heavy with unshed tears.

Jake took her hand. She accepted it without a word. Cadence took Lorina's other hand, and tears broke from Lorina's eyes, streaming down her cheeks.

Dylan leaned in and murmured, "So... is this the part

where I should splash some holy water on her, or...?"

Lorina let out a shaky, half-choked laugh that shook the heavy tears from her eyes. "Water won't fix the spell she's under."

The moment was broken. But the damage?

That would linger.

Chapter 31

Virginia and Ericka had taken the opportunity to slip away while Lorina and her mother were engaged in their verbal volley. The cowards. Without Pastor Carrigan to prop up their supposed "good Christian standing"—and with Connor and Lacey lending credibility to the idea that I hadn't just bewitched the entire town—maybe they were afraid no one would believe them over me.

The reporters were not giving up, though.

They'd solved the temporary issue with the lights and now crowded closer, their cameras and microphones stretching toward Dylan and me like a field of metal stalks, each voice rife with insatiable curiosity. The sultry air vibrated with the rapid-fire barrage of questions.

"Why do you think the women with Pastor Carrigan are part of the Stygian coven?"

"How long has Dylan had power over water?"

"Do you intend to confront the Stygian about recent events?"

"Does your coven have a name?"

I lifted a hand, palm out, a gesture meant to halt the onslaught. "Hold on, hold on," I said, waiting for the noise to settle. When they realized I was serious, the questions died down.

A flicker of motion caught my attention—someone

breaking away from my coven and moving toward me.

Conall.

He leaned in, breath warm against my ear, voice pitched low enough that only I could hear. "It's not over yet."

I turned, blinking against a sudden glare—someone had swung a camera light directly into my face, burning my vision with a white-hot halo. My mouth formed a dumb-sounding, "Huh?"

Conall's gaze was dark with knowing. "It's not over."

Of course not. Because why would it be?

Maybe Ericka and her lot weren't the cowards I thought. Maybe they'd run off to execute Plan B. Panic coiled tight in my gut, an instinctive, animal reaction. Was the crowd in danger? I wondered if I needed to clear the park, but I knew that if I handled the situation wrong, I'd create a stampede.

I shot Conall a look of thanks—I'd take cryptic warnings over no warnings any day—and turned back to the gathered press. The influencer, who had demanded I "give the people what they want" just a few days ago, lurked in the mass of bodies, phone in hand. No sign of Elidriel. I wondered where she was and deeply hoped she was safe.

Y'all, the show's over for tonight," I said, sounding sure enough to sell it, even if I had a bad feeling the curtain hadn't really dropped. "If you're with the news, I'll talk to Mayor Tanaka about setting up another town hall meeting. Get in touch with them if you want to be there. We can answer your questions then. But I think we've all had enough excitement for the night. Go home."

The reporters exchanged glances, reluctant but resigned. One by one, cameras powered down, voices quieted. The crowd who'd shown up for the concert—the bulk of them non-magical, I confirmed with a quick magical pulse—began to drift toward the sidewalk.

Then came the first note of distress. A ripple of confused murmurs.

Here we go. Mother Goddess, what'd they do now?

The chorus of alarm came from the very edge of the park. By the time I reached the nearest cluster of folks who were, strangely, toeing the line where the grass met the sidewalk as if standing in an odd side-by-side queue, the murmurs had swelled into a discordant chorus.

Once I stood nearer the ruckus, the air pressed strangely against my skin, heavier than the evening humidity could account for. A vibration ran through me, a sensation not unlike the lingering tone of a plucked harp string. Beneath my ribs, my pulse thrummed in quiet sympathy, as if something fundamental in the atmosphere had shifted, tuning the world around me to a frequency just outside my perception.

People reached forward, baffled by their inability to move beyond the park's perimeter.

"What is this?"

"What's happening?"

"I don't *see* anything."

Someone grabbed a fist-sized rock and chucked it toward the road, only to have it bounce off a glassy barrier that wavered slightly from the contact.

Using the waves as a focal point, I reached for the Source and followed its contours upward with my senses, tracing the unseen wall past the treetops, where it arched like a glass dome over the far side of Puck's Green. I exhaled, listening— not just with my ears, but with the part of me attuned to magic. Beneath the quiet panic, the worried murmurs, the rustle of wind through the trees, something else stirred. A whisper beneath sound itself.

This was no ordinary warding. It was denser, reverberating. Not merely woven from air, but from the very vibrations

that carried sound. A standing wave. A locked frequency. The
space around us had been tuned like a string on an instrument,
the harmonics calibrated just so, sealing us in with an un-
breakable hum too deep for the ear to detect.

The Stygian had trapped us inside the park, undoubtedly
hoping the panicked crowd would turn on us.

A flicker of red lights signaled the news crews scrambling
back into position. I barely needed to glance over my shoulder to know what they were doing—adjusting cameras, flipping on mics, leaning into the moment with the hunger of
scavengers sensing fresh carrion. I shook my head. A Don
Henley song drifted unbidden through my mind—they didn't
care if it was good news or bad, only that it was news.

A woman to my right ran from the group and vomited into
a nearby bush, likely a side effect of the pulsing barrier.

LaDonna and Luke arrived, slipping into place beside Conall and me, their gazes sweeping over the invisible barri-
cade. Around us, people pressed their hands, shoulders, even
their foreheads against the unseen wall, recoiling as if they
expected the empty air to yield—and yet it did not.

"Any idea what it's made of?? Conall asked.

"Not exactly," I said, watching another person stagger
back from the wall. "But it's not just air—it's tuned. Like
we're inside a vibrating bubble. Standing this close feels like
my inner ear's gone haywire."

LaDonna pressed a hand to her stomach, frowning.
"Yeah. I feel it too. Like I'm just a half-step out of sync with
myself."

A disorienting pulsation. A frequency. And if it was a frequency, that meant it could be disrupted.

"Hey, witch!"

The voice shot through the uneasy murmurs like a
cracked whip, blunt and full of accusation. I turned toward

the source, heart thudding with the heavy rhythm of exhaustion and preemptive rage.

The man was broad-shouldered and thick around the middle, his face ruddy from either the summer heat or the sheer force of his temper. His thinning hair clung to his scalp in damp patches, and sweat shone at his temples. His eyes, small and set too close together, narrowed on me like I was a cockroach skittering across his dinner plate. He jabbed a thick finger in my direction.

"What's this all about? Are you pulling something?"

A low rumble of agreement rippled through the crowd. Another voice, this one female. "It's always witches lately! Everything was just fine before you lot started stirring up trouble."

A wiry man with a military buzz cut and a jaw that looked like it had spent its life clenched added, "It ain't natural. Y'all aren't natural."

Well. Fantastic.

I sucked in a breath, biting down on the snarl bubbling up from my already frayed nerves. My very soul longed to unleash on the jerk that *I was not the enemy.*

But then the crowd shifted.

The newcomers moved through the gathered people like a graceful mist rolling off the water at dawn. They were breathtakingly beautiful, but not in the way that made you think of polished perfection. No, their beauty had an edge to it, something primeval and untamed, like the sea before a storm. Their skin bore the hues of the ocean's landscape—from the pale gold of wind-swept dunes to the dark, earthen richness of volcanic shores. In the dim light, some of them shimmered, a fleeting iridescence catching the eye before vanishing like a trick of the moon.

Sirenborn. At least a dozen of them.

Their eyes held the most power—jewel-toned and glassy, as if capturing light in a way human eyes never could. They were the color of sea glass, of emerald tides, of deep amber caught in sunlit foam. They watched the crowd with unreadable expressions, equal parts detached and amused, as if they had seen a thousand such accusations before and had never once cared.

At their center, the one who led them was tall and curvy, draped in gauzy layers of teal and indigo, colors that made me think of the ocean at night where it met the starry horizon. When she moved, it was fluid, effortless, a step away from dancing. She strode to the edge of the park, folks wordlessly clearing a path for her and her followers. Raising a hand, she tested the wall, shook her wavy tresses, and turned back to the crowd.

She lifted her chin, her voice calm, yet carrying the weight of authority.

"This isn't her doing, or ours. It is dark magic. But we can get you out. If you let us."

The crowd hesitated, their fear momentarily at war with their distrust. I didn't know what to think of them either, other than I was one hundred percent certain they'd come to help the town tonight. And that made them friends.

I sidled up to the leader, but kept my voice loud enough to let the crowd know we weren't conspiring.

"What's your plan?" I asked.

The siren leader's lips curled in a half-smile. "We break the frequency."

Oh. That sounds simple enough. Except not at all.

One man who had been griping—a guy with a beer gut and a farmer's tan—snorted. "Break the what now?"

"The barrier isn't physical," she said, which explained why I found myself rubbing my temples as the lingering pressure of it hummed in my skull, as if I could knead away the sensation. "It's sound. A standing wave holding everything in place. Like an invisible tuning fork, vibrating at just the right frequency to keep us trapped."

A few of the sirens exchanged knowing looks, their jewel-toned eyes flickering with something unreadable—understanding, perhaps even recognition. I had the unsettling feeling that this wasn't the first time they'd encountered something like this.

The leader nodded toward her sisters, then turned back to me. "If we introduce a counter-frequency, we can disrupt the resonance and shatter it."

I rolled my shoulders, trying to shake off the creeping sense that this was going to hurt. "Right. Cool. Just one question—how exactly do you plan to do that?"

She smiled, and in that moment, I was certain of two things:

One: I was about to hear something that would make my eardrums beg for mercy. And two: whatever they were about to do wasn't merely about sound. It was power, deep and tidal, like the hush before a wave breaks or the breathless pause when the sea pulls back to strike.

They started singing.

The first note was so soft it barely existed, more felt than heard—a vibration that settled into my bones before it reached my ears. Then another voice joined, threading through the first in a seamless, haunting harmony. Another followed, and another, each one layering into an intricate weave of sound, neither song nor speech, but something more.

It wasn't just music, it was force. Pressure. Sonority. A ripple through the air itself, like fingers brushing the strings of an unseen instrument, plucking at something fundamental within the air of the atmosphere itself.

The very air shuddered, and the barrier reacted.

A shimmer flickered across the unseen wall, bending and distorting the space around it like the surface of a pond disturbed by a single drop of water. The crowd gasped as the barrier groaned under the strain of the sirens' song. The sound wasn't loud, yet it filled every inch of space, pressing against my skin, tightening around my ribs like a phantom tide.

And then—another voice. One I knew incredibly well.

Lorina.

She stood just beyond the sirens, hands pressed to her throat, her eyes wide with something between fear and wonder, as if she hadn't quite convinced herself that the sound rising from her lips was hers. But it was.

Her voice slipped effortlessly into the harmony, finding its place within the shifting chords like she had been singing with them all her life. Because, of course, she had. Whether or not she had known it, the gift had always been there waiting.

In the dim light, her skin—pale pearl and soft as moonlit sand—gleamed with something new. A shimmer barely perceptible but undeniable, as though the truth of what she was had finally surfaced, no longer content to remain hidden beneath the skin.

She blinked at me, startled and a little scared. "Murphy…?"

I met her gaze, steady. "Keep going," I murmured, my voice barely above the wind. "You've got this."

And she did. In that moment, she embraced what she had always been.

She was sirenborn.

And with her voice joining the others, the barrier began to break.

Chapter 32

As the sirens' song intensified, the air vibrated as if the sonorousness of their voices was rearranging the very molecules around us. The once-invisible barrier flickered in and out of sight, no longer a seamless, imperceptible force but a shifting distortion, warping like a heat mirage rolling over pavement. A low hum pulsed through the area, deep enough to rattle my teeth, a sound that wasn't just heard but felt—an undercurrent of pressure threading through every fiber of my being.

Then, a fracture.

All at once, the red lights of the news cameras flickered erratically. Screens flared with bursts of static before cutting to black. Somewhere behind me, a cameraman swore.

"Lost signal!"

"Someone check the feed!"

The sirens' melody swelled, threading through the fabric of the barrier, unraveling the magic that held it in place. The disruption pulsed outward in waves, rattling the reporters' equipment, sending sharp feedback bursts through their earpieces. One of them yelped, ripping the comms from her ear as a piercing screech I heard from several feet away screamed through her mic.

The voices of the sirens wove together, layer upon layer of sound pressing into the atmosphere, pushing and pulling, working steadily at the harmonic structure of the barrier. Fractures spiderwebbed outward in luminous strands, the unseen force buckling under the weight of their song.

Then came the final, sharp note. Pure as a fresh snowflake. A razor-edged frequency that cut through the unnatural reverberation like a blade.

And the barrier shattered. The air rippled—a surreal, liquid-like shimmer in the now-empty space where the wall had stood.

The sensation of pressure vanished instantly, leaving an almost dizzying lightness in its wake. My breath hitched as the tightness in my chest disappeared, the strange, off-kilter pull that had been throwing off my balance dissipating like fog in sunlight. The moment stretched, hanging weightless in the air. It felt like resuming my balance on land after being on a boat for hours.

A breeze stirred my hair, and I only then realized how unearthly still the air had been. Then, the world roared back to life.

People stumbled forward, no longer held in place by the unseen force. A collective gasp rippled through the crowd as the spell collapsed, the lingering hum of trapped energy fading into silence. Some fell to their knees in exhausted relief, while others turned to the sirens with a mix of awe and wariness. Their voices rose in hushed, frantic conversation, disbelief and adrenaline battling for dominance.

But the news crews? They were livid.

"What the hell was that?" A reporter slapped the side of her camera as if she could bully it back into working. The monitor remained dark, the screen flickering with waves of static.

"Everything went down at the same time," another muttered, yanking off a now-useless headset. "Mics, cameras, live feed—we lost the whole damn thing."

A journalist near the front shook his camera, his expression swinging between hope and frustration. "Please tell me someone got something," he groaned. His assistant checked the playback, frowning as he scrolled through nothing but a black screen.

A long pause. Then the assistant swore under his breath.

"No audio. No video. It's just… blank."

One newscaster with a head full of graying hair and an orangey fake tan panned the crowd of his peers anxiously. "Did anyone get any of it? My station will gladly pay to use whatever you captured."

No one spoke. No one had anything useful.

The realization settled over them like a lead weight. They had just witnessed something undeniable that could change everything, and they had no proof.

I wanted to laugh, but instead, I exhaled slowly, rolling my shoulders and trying to shake off the eerie phantom hum that still thrilled my bones. The sirens stood motionless, their expressions unreadable, watching the frustration play out with an air of detached amusement. Their leader turned to me, the faintest smirk curling at the corner of her lips.

"We don't like to be recorded," she murmured with a wrinkle of her nose that was both adorable and snarky.

I huffed out a quiet laugh, still catching my breath. "Me, either."

The cameras stayed dead. The feeds remained silent. And thankfully, the truth of what had happened here tonight would stay exactly where it belonged: with the people who had lived it.

The siren leader took a step forward, her eyes, the color of cognac diamonds, sweeping over the crowd—until she stopped, staring at Lorina.

I felt my young friend shift beside me, wary under the sudden weight of attention. The siren tilted her head slightly, curiosity flickering across her face. "I didn't know you existed."

Lorina blinked. "Uh. Rude?"

The siren's lips quirked, but her eyes stayed sharp, studying Lorina like she was a puzzle piece that should fit, but didn't.

Lorina folded her arms, chin lifting, but I saw the tension in her shoulders, the ingrained caution creeping into her voice. "What's that supposed to mean? Like... in general? Or like personally? Because I'm pretty sure I exist." She rolled her lovely brown eyes skyward. "Current existential crisis notwithstanding."

The siren let out a slight hum, eyes narrowing slightly. "You are of the water," she said. "But you don't hear it, do you?"

Lorina hesitated. "I mean... I hear water. I drink it. I shower. Big fan of hydration." She waved a hand. "But I'm guessing that's not what you mean."

The siren's gaze softened, something like realization dawning. "Your family never told you."

Lorina tensed, glancing at me, then back at the siren. "Told me what? That I was raised in a cult that recently decided anything not fully human is one bad day away from kicking off the apocalypse? Because yeah, they told me that once they heard about the Stygian starting shit and realized that witches might be, you know, real."

The sirens behind their leader exchanged knowing glances, something unspoken passing between them.

Lorina exhaled sharply, her nervous energy shifting closer to defiant curiosity. "OK, so let's say for a second you aren't about to murder me and wear my skin like a wetsuit—

"

The siren leader gave a single, sharp laugh, shaking her head. "We don't do that."

"Not helping," Lorina muttered. Then, more seriously, "Who are you? Like, really? I always thought sirens were a myth. And if you are real, why haven't I heard of you? I mean, social media exists."

The siren's expression darkened slightly, but not with anger—more like old pain resurfacing. "Because those who know our names rarely live to speak them," she said, voice quiet but carrying weight. "Many of us were born in the sea, but some… were made by it. Women were cast into the water by fearful men. They called us curses, bad omens, unnatural. They feared we would bring ruin."

Lorina's breath hitched slightly. "Women thrown overboard," she murmured.

The siren leader nodded. "Not all of them drowned."

"My great-grandmother… I was told she was lost at sea," Lorina breathed.

A silence stretched between them, something unspoken settling in the space between question and understanding.

Lorina bit her lip, then exhaled. "Okay. That's… objectively badass. Also terrifying. But mostly badass."

The siren leader's smirk returned. "You'll understand more, in time."

Lorina crossed her arms. "Yeah, see, that's exactly the kind of cryptic crap that makes people not trust you. And it's not exactly like my human family's been forthcoming."

I pinched the bridge of my nose. "Lorina."

She threw up her hands. "What?! I think I deserve some straight answers!"

The siren leader only smiled. "Soon."

Lorina groaned. "Oh my *God*, I hate this."

I sighed. "Welcome to my life."

The crowd buzzed louder than the cicadas in the trees, the air electric with disbelief, relief, and something close to reverence. Silent now, the sirens stood apart but within arm's reach of one another, their expressions unreadable as they watched the aftermath of their intervention. Nearby, reporters fumed over lost footage and broken equipment—I could already hear them scheming how to spin the story without proof. Not my problem.

A woman I vaguely recognized from Gryphon—a familiar face from town, the kind who probably knew everyone's business but did it with a smile and a plate of fresh chocolate chip cookies—stepped forward. She looked like a person who still hand-wrote thank-you notes and used the word "bless" unironically.

She adjusted her purse strap over one shoulder, tilting her head at the siren leader. "Now, I hope I don't sound ignorant, but I gotta ask—what exactly are y'all?"

The siren leader's gaze flickered over her, unreadable as ever. "We are sirens and sirenborn."

The woman hummed thoughtfully, not at all cowed by the otherworldly presence before her. "I see. And, uh, should we be expectin' more... folks like you?" Her attention switched between me and the siren leader. "Witches and... sirens?"

The murmurs around us picked up again.

"Yeah," a man in the crowd piped up. "If sirens and witches are real, what else is out there?"

I exhaled, my fingers flexing at my sides. I knew where this was going, and I knew exactly how difficult the idea was. The world had a hard enough time with witches—hell, in Gryphon, there were plenty who undoubtedly muttered about how unnatural we were.

But many of us knew it was time to step forward. We'd

taken one step already. Tonight, we'd take another.

Before I could answer, movement caught my eye. Doyle. And right behind him, Rene and Joey.

How did Rene become visible without me doing the—oh, yeah. Silver witch.

I didn't tense, but I sure as hell made sure I was standing between them and the sweet woman who probably made homemade bundt cakes for PTA bake sales. As much as I liked Doyle, as much as I believed he wasn't a threat... there was no easy way to explain to a crowd of anxious, confused humans, Oh hey, by the way, one of them is a vampire who drinks blood to stay alive.

Doyle caught on to my actions and had the good sense to stay quiet, leaning against a lamppost like he happened to be here. Rene watched the exchange with his usual dry amusement. Joey looked like he wanted to say something, his eyes darting back and forth between Doyle and me, but Doyle's firm hand on his arm kept him still.

And then Miles stepped forward.

Hanna's maybe-sorta-crush. The quiet, broad-shouldered man who always seemed just a little too intense and aware of his surroundings.

"I'm a werewolf," he said simply.

Silence slammed into the crowd like a hammer.

Someone sucked in a breath. The woman in front of me pursed her lips like she was trying to decide if that was better or worse than the sirens.

Then Dorian Bradley—DB, who I remembered meeting earlier because of his amazing, lanky, bronze good looks and boyish charm—grinned and strode forward. "And I breathe fire."

He exhaled a controlled plume of flame, bright against the evening air. It licked toward the sky, harmless but impossible to ignore. Gasps rippled through the gathered people, some stumbling back in instinctive fear, others pressing forward with wide-eyed wonder.

I must have been shaking my head faintly because DB shrugged, his grin widening. I noticed how his eyes were the same golden bronze as his skin.

"C'mon, Murphy," he chided with a wiggle of his eyebrows. "If we're doing this, we might as well have some fun."

And then, as if the night hadn't been weird enough, Mayor Tanaka stepped forward.

The mayor of Gryphon, the same man who had presided over every town hall meeting, every Fourth of July parade, every painstakingly polite argument over zoning laws, stood in front of the stunned crowd, adjusted his cufflinks, and sighed.

"Well," he said, his voice carrying the same patience he used when people got riled up about parking permits, "since we're sharing, I suppose I should tell you—I'm a kitsune. It's an old word for what I am—a fox spirit with a long memory and the ability to take on more than one form."

And then his eyes—usually dark, warm, and brown, nothing out of the ordinary—flashed gold. Not a reflection. Not a trick of the light. Gold.

The woman in front of me let out a slow breath, rubbing her hands over her skirt. "Well. That's somethin'."

From somewhere behind me, Joey muttered, "Holy shit."

I sighed. "Yep."

I didn't think the world was ready for vampires. But apparently, it was getting everything else.

Chapter 33

The rest of the night was a blur of frantic questions and nervous laughter, the air thick with restless energy that comes when reality tilts on its axis. In the flickering glow of street-lamps, the folks in the park—and the Numinari who'd swooped in to save their asses—ended up having an impromptu Q&A that stretched long past a reasonable hour.

Mayor Tanaka taught the town a little about what a kitsune was, for which I was grateful—I'd never heard of them, either.

"Kitsune are fox spirits," he explained, voice carrying steady authority. "In Japanese folklore, they're known for their intelligence, their shapeshifting, and their long lifespans. Some are messengers of the kami Inari, acting as protectors and guides. Others are cunning tricksters. But all of them exist just out of sight—guardians, mischief-makers, and watchers of the veil between worlds." He glanced at the Numinari standing nearby. "Until now."

That quieted a few folks down. People liked the idea of a supernatural protector—especially if that person was the town mayor.

One by one, more Numinari stepped forward to show the public their talents or explain what they were. Ivor, the nervous, pale man, demonstrated his ability to harness electricity, the flickering arcs casting long, ghostly reflections in the wide-eyed stares of those around him. Nuhadir and Rahiq, twin djinn who moved with the flawless ease of professional dancers, introduced themselves with low, powerful voices. Rahiq smiled the whole time as if he found the situation amusing. Crystal revealed her portal-opening gift, and Elidriel emerged from the crowd to casually drop that she was fae. That last bit went over surprisingly well—more than a few people looked downright delighted at the idea.

At some point, someone blurted out the inevitable: "Wait… are vampires real too?"

Yeah. That was a fun moment.

I admitted they were, because what was the point of lying at that stage? Panic ensued. Not full-blown run-for-the-hills chaos, but enough gasping and whispering to make me rake my hands through my hair and mutter a few choice words. I got everyone's attention with a few broad sweeps of my arms and reminded them that nothing had actually changed, and they weren't in any more danger today than they'd ever been. Vampires existed yesterday, last week, last year. They just hadn't known about them. And, like humans, there were good ones and bad ones.

Some people took that well. Others… not so much.

Doyle stepped forward and introduced himself. Plenty of folks found him downright charming. Naturally, I checked to see if he was using a glamor to pull that off.

He wasn't. Well. Not much.

Meanwhile, Conall stuck close, throwing in answers for the crowd when he had them and generally being the rock-solid, dependable guy he always was. It helped. Having him at my side always did. The looks of pride he shot my way several times as I handled the crowd were a great mood booster, too.

By two in the morning, I was running on fumes, and most

of the crowd had headed home. Only a small crowd, dying for answers to their myriad questions about the supernatural, lingered. My legs ached, my brain felt like it had been wrung out and left to dry, and I still had a shop to open in a few hours.

"I swear, if I don't get at least four hours of sleep, I might actually die," I muttered, scrubbing a hand down my face.

"Don't be so dramatic," Betony said, stretching like this was just another night. "You can go home. We've got this."

I glanced at the ragtag group—half teenagers, half Numinari I'd only met yesterday—and hesitated. But between Jake's magic-laced guitar, Betony's knack for neutralizing chaos, and a few responsible adults lurking nearby, I figured the town wouldn't burn down while I stepped away. Probably.

If the town burns down, I will need more than luck.

☽○☾

Opening the shop went the same as usual on Saturday morning, except for the part where I was dragging ass from sheer exhaustion. I woke up, got dressed, turned on the lights, started the coffee, verified the till, and updated the chalkboard with the daily specials, leaving a blank spot for whatever sweet concoction Hanna brought later.

At seven a.m., I unlocked the front door and waved at the Kentucky reporter in his Accord, who had all but set up camp outside. He waved back, flashing a set of teeth so white and straight they had to be veneers. Matched his hair. I wondered if he'd been lurking in the park last night with the rest of the media swarm. Probably. But I didn't remember seeing him. Maybe he'd actually gone to bed at a reasonable hour. Lucky bastard. I wondered how long it'd be before news reporters came rolling in wanting to hear more about last night.

By nine, I started noticing an odd number of cars parking along Oberon Street and Beatrice Bend, only half of which were news vehicles. By nine-fifteen, folks were milling around outside their cars, chatting in little clusters while more people trickled in. Reporters were putting their microphones in the faces of regular folks, clearly interviewing them. But why?

I didn't like where this was going. I called Officer Hendricks because, let's be real, I'd had enough surprises for one week. It was likely he couldn't do anything, but I figured if anyone in town was willing to protect me other than Conall—who was at work—it was Kenny.

At nine-thirty on the dot, the crowd started pulling cardboard placards from their trunks, handwritten messages taped to wooden stakes. And just like that, they started marching. The newscasters were all over it.

I stood there, momentarily speechless, watching as they stomped a narrow path up and down the sidewalk in front of Blackwell Manor, pacing their grievances into the pavement.

After a few seconds, I turned to Rene. His face mirrored exactly how I felt—stupefied. And way too alert for someone who was probably running on two hours of sleep.

"You have *got* to be kidding me," I scoffed.

Rene shook his head. "Can't fix stupid."

Intrigued despite myself, I moved to the big front window to get a better look at their signs.

Witchcraft Destroys Souls!
God's Light vs. The Devil's Lies!
Witchcraft = Sin
Magic = Mind Control
Stop the Occult Agenda!

Real creative bunch.

Then came the chanting. It started simple—" *No witches here! No witches here!*"—then rolled into "*God above, no dark love!*" And by the time Officer Kenny Hendricks pulled up, they'd settled into a rhythmic chorus of "*No spells! No lies! We won't be hypnotized!*"

OK. That last one had a little catchiness to it.

Kenny's patrol car had them shifting uncomfortably for a second, and they stopped chanting. But when he strolled past without so much as a glance in their direction, they relaxed and got back to their holy ruckus.

Kenny stepped into the shop and sidled up to the counter. Neither of us said anything. Kenny shook his head and tapped his fingers on the worn wooden surface.

"I wish I could tell 'em to get lost, Murph, but they got a permit," he said. "Picked it up first thing this morning. A buddy of mine works security at City Hall. Told me they got some kind of special condition. Something about 'exceptions exist for spontaneous events responding to current affairs.'" He made air quotes around the phrase, his tone thick with irritation.

I sighed and slid onto the tall chair behind the counter. "Technically, they're not hurting anything," I had to admit with a limp shrug.

"They're idiots, but they're not hurting anything," Rene agreed reluctantly.

Kenny huffed a laugh and leaned in a little. "Get this— Mayor Tanaka came out of his office while they were still there, and my buddy said the second he looked at them, they froze up. Then he gave 'em a flick of those gold eyes, and they bolted like their asses were on fire."

A snort escaped before I could stop it, and just like that, the three of us were chuckling.

"You sure are taking this supernatural stuff in stride," I

said, giving Kenny a side-eye.

His expression sobered. "You remember Madam Ubora's Sights and Sounds over on Industry Avenue?"

"Sure," I said. "Purple building. Had that sign with the hand and an eye in the center. Always smelled like cinnamon and sage inside."

Kenny nodded. "Madam Ubora was my auntie. She was from Haiti. Practiced magic."

I raised a brow. "Blood auntie?"

He shook his head. "Honorary. But my momma and her were like sisters."

"She always seemed like a sweet lady," I said. "My mom and I used to go to her shop sometimes. Mom loved her book selection."

Kenny's lips twitched into a genuine smile. Something warm, yet a little sad. "She loved to read. She was real happy when you set up shop a few years back."

"Why's that?" I asked.

His gaze dipped, and for a second, I saw something heavy in his expression. Grief. "She caught cancer," he said, voice lower now. "Didn't tell many people, but she knew she wasn't gonna be around much longer. It gave her some peace, knowing there'd still be a place here for folks to get what they needed after she was gone."

My hand flew to my mouth. "I didn't know," I stammered. "I just thought the shop closed and—"

Kenny waved a hand, cutting me off with that effortless Southern grace that somehow made you feel forgiven before you even finished apologizing. "It's alright, it's alright. Like I said, your timing was perfect. It made Auntie Marcy—her name was Marceline, but I called her Marcy—happy to know someone was picking up in this little part of north Alabama where she left off."

A lump rose in my throat so fast I barely had time to swallow it down. My eyes burned hotter than I liked, and my voice nearly gave out when I managed a choked, "I'm glad to know that."

Kenny gave me a wry grin. "I guess that's part of why I always had a soft spot for ya," he admitted. "Even when you was a walking disaster. Whatever happened to the accident-prone Murph I used to know?"

Blinking back the tears, I matched his crooked smile. Without looking, I reached out with Source power, lifting my massive coffee cup from the counter behind me and floating it straight into my waiting hand.

"I got better," I said with a wink.

Chapter 34

The Lughaidh group chat buzzed nonstop throughout the day, messages flying back and forth as everyone tried to process the fallout from the night before. With the Big Reveal—the moment the Numinari stepped forward and announced their existence to the town—there were bound to be repercussions. Gryphon was still reeling, and so was the coven. Naturally, they had questions, concerns, and no small amount of curiosity about what came next.

Lughaidh Group Chat

8:03 AM

Anyone else wake up to a headache and a whole lot of "What the hell just happened?" or is that just me?

8:07 AM
LaDonna

You're not alone, hon. My phone has been going off all morning with people asking if what they saw was real.

8:09 AM
Luke

As Betony likes to say, can confirm. Her phone has been driving us nuts

8:45 AM
Betony
I think the real takeaway here is that
last night was wild and I personally
am thriving

8:52 AM
On two hours of sleep? You
and Rene are nuts.

9:05 AM
Terry
Speak for yourself, Bet. My brain still
hurts. And I didn't stay nearly as
late as y'all did.

9:15 AM
Rita
Yeah, you might wanna hydrate, buddy.
Last night was trending in at least three
different circles. The conspiracy forums
are already calling it "The Gryphon
Incident."

9:20 AM
Speaking of incidents, there are
Protestors outside my shop. They've
been out there all morning waving
signs and yelling about the devil. The
newscasters are thrilled, as you can
imagine.

9:27 AM
Conall
You need me to come down there?

9:38 AM
Nah, they're just yelling and waving

signs. Haven't tried anything bad
yet. I'll let you know if it gets worse.

9:52 AM
Joey

Be careful People get brave in
groups. And stupid.

10:01 AM
LaDonna

Murphy, you be careful. If they're still
out there later, I'll swing by with some
lavender lemonade. Something about
old Southern women offering drinks
throws people off balance. And the
lavender might be my special variety ;)

10:16 AM
Betony

Can confirm. My meemaw used to disarm
entire church groups with her homemade
sweet tea

10:20 AM
Terry

So, big question—what happens now?

10:28 AM
Luke

Not everyone who showed up last night is
leaving town

10:38 AM
Oh?

10:45 AM
Luke

Side note, Dad's crew is over at

August and Ida's place right now
hooking up some air conditioning.
The Numinari staying there should
be more comfortable soon.

10:52 AM
Rita
Man, they barely got here and they're
already getting Southern hospitality

11:01 AM
That's just how we roll.
But wait—who's staying?

11:22 AM
Luke
Not sure yet. Dylan, Doyle, and
Crystal for sure. Some of them are
still figuring it out, but I'm getting
the sense that a lot of them aren't
eager to leave just yet

11:28 AM
Joey
I'll dig around and see if there's
any official movement. If they're
sticking around, we need to know
why.

11:48 AM
LaDonna
That's something we should all
discuss in person.

11:51 AM
Agreed. My place, later today?

12:26 AM

Betony
Oh hell yeah, secret meeting vibes

12:36 AM
Terry
It's literally not a secret, Bet.

12:45AM
Betony
Let me have this

11:53 AM
Rita
Time?

11:58 AM
Let's plan to meet right after I
lock up the shop.

12:27 PM
Conall
I'll come by right after work

12:48 AM
LaDonna
Luke and I will bring food. Y'all
need to eat something that isn't
eating profits from Murphy's shop.

1:28 PM
Joey
I'll bring the beer

1:36 PM
Betony
I'll bring… chaos

1:45 PM
Terry

That is both the most and least
helpful thing you could say, Bet.

Alright, see y'all later. Try not to
cause any extra problems before
then. ;)

By the time the sun dipped low, the rest of the coven had
checked in on the chat, confirming they'd be there that night.
August sent a few cryptic texts, casually mentioning he'd be
bringing some visiting Numinari to talk to the coven—if I
didn't mind. And then Bully reached out. No clue who gave
him my number or if he just figured it out somehow, but he
wanted to stop by with a few others as well.

What the hell. Might as well make it a party.

I shot Joey a message, telling him to grab plenty of beer
on his way over—and maybe a couple of bottles of red and
white wine, just in case, promising that the coven would all
chip in to help pay. Then I asked Terry, the coven treasurer
(yes, we have a treasurer), to make sure Joey didn't pay out
of pocket.

Conall showed up after work, true to his word, with a bottle of my favorite bourbon in hand. That meant one of two
things: either he thought I deserved a reward, or tonight was
going to suck. Based on his expression, I guessed it was the
latter.

Fucking great.

"That good, huh?" I muttered, setting the bottle on the
counter and reaching for a glass.

Conall shrugged, the universal sign for *I know something
you don't, and you're not gonna like it*. "Let's just say you
might want to be a little... relaxed before company shows
up."

That was never a good sign. I dropped some ice into the glass, poured in lemonade, and topped it off with a generous splash of bourbon. Stirred it with an iced tea spoon like it was just another summer drink instead of the prelude to bad news.

The first sip hit like a lazy July afternoon—cool, tart lemonade easing in before the bourbon coiled around it. It was warm and rich, with just enough bite to remind me that one sip too many would have me making questionable decisions. It went down too easy. That's what made it dangerous.

"Go slow," Conall warned, his tone light but edged with concern.

"I know," I replied, leaning in next to him as I took another sip. "Do you have any idea why folks want to stay in Gryphon? Any insights?"

He ran a hand through his hair, his warm brown eyes crinkling at the edges. "I haven't seen any signs of a disaster looming just yet, but I haven't looked too far into it. I came right here after work."

"Do you want to check a little farther before folks show up?"

He grinned, and damn if that easy warmth in his eyes wasn't more soothing than the bourbon. "Let's let this one play out. If they're sticking around because of some looming catastrophe, Luke and I can put our heads together and see what shakes loose."

I set the glass down, my fingers absently tracing the condensation droplets sliding over its surface. "It's just odd," I grumbled, more to myself than to him. "LaDonna's supposed to be the high priestess around here, and I'm the Summate. You'd think someone would give us a damn heads-up about what's going on."

"Unless it's the kind of news they think is better delivered in person," Conall offered.

I lifted my glass and took another drink.

"That's what I'm afraid of."

Chapter 35

Every chair I owned—every single one, including the wobbly kitchen stool and the footrest from my living room—had been dragged downstairs and set up in the two rooms on the north side of my house. The tables were stacked in the front shop room, displays pushed back against the walls, and Conall had dug out my emergency stash of folding chairs from the back storage. Then Conall, Jake, and Luke went across the street to see if Miss Linnie had anything we could borrow and returned with armfuls of folding chairs. By the time everything was set up, it looked like we were hosting a massive magical AA meeting.

It wasn't enough. Blackwell Manor was packed to the point that the smell of warm, summer-baked bodies mingled with the usual aroma of coffee and baked goods. The lack of elbow room was triggering a low-key claustrophobia. If it wasn't for Jake strumming a calming tune in the corner he often occupied on Friday nights and the occasional quick grip on the forearm from Betony, I probably would have chewed my fingernails down to the quick. Lorina sat to one side of Jake, humming something inaudible under the drone of the crowd. I was pleased to see Cadence, Jake's long-time girl-friend, at his side again. She bobbed back and forth in slow time with the melody, her frizzy blond curls swaying as she moved.

For half a second, I was tempted to crack open my third eye and take a peek at all the magic humming through the rooms to get a better sense of who and what I was dealing with. But the logical part of me knew that was a terrible idea. Like staring straight into the sun. Besides, Rex had a knack for pointing out his favorites, and my little black familiar's favorites were always going to be mine. I watched him take in each person as they entered, his bright green eyes scanning the guests with the kind of regal disdain only a twenty-year-old black cat could muster. Occasionally, he deigned to let someone stroke his back before strutting off to another corner of the room.

He was an asshole—but he was my asshole.

Once everyone was as settled as they were gonna get, La-Donna and I stepped up to the front—well, technically, the back of my shop, depending on how you looked at it. I motioned to Betony and Rene to draw the blinds, and they did after politely shooing away a couple of latecomers crowding the windows.

I let out a slow breath, scanning the room, my eyes landing last on Conall, who stood at the wall to my right. He caught my gaze and gave me the barest nod—nothing flashy, just a slight motion to remind me of his love and support. It helped. So did Rex returning to my side and winding around my legs.

Forty, maybe fifty people, crammed into two rooms downstairs. Some were even spilling onto the back porch and into the yard, murmuring to each other like they were waiting for a sermon, a show, or maybe a good old-fashioned disaster. I hoped against hope it wasn't the latter.

My foster mother and I had a nonverbal exchange made entirely of head tilts, eyebrow choreography, and subtle hand gestures that went something like this: I cocked my head at the crowd to signify the floor was hers. She raised her brows, dipped her chin, and gave me that look that said, *They'll listen better to you. You're the Summate.* I gave a reluctant flick of the eyebrows, a tiny shrug, and a micro-frown to say, *Yeah, fine, but it's dumb,* because she *was* the local high priestess, after all. She offered a demure smile and motioned for me to go ahead.

I nodded unenthusiastically and stepped forward. Well, half a step. Like I said, it was a crowded room.

"Hey, y'all," I said to get everyone's attention. The conversation dimmed but didn't quite die. My voice doesn't carry well.

"Hey—listen up," I said louder.

Still, a few voices lingered. LaDonna let loose a deafening two-fingered whistle that could've stopped a freight train. Silence fell.

I stuck a finger in my ear and pantomimed dramatic ear pain. That got a laugh.

"Everyone, if you haven't already met her, this is LaDonna, the high priestess of the Lughaidh coven here in Gryphon, Alabama." A few heads nodded, some registering the info, and others were clearly already familiar.

"I'm Murphy Blackwell. Her, um, daughter. And… the Summate."

Even now, both claims felt a little weird to say out loud. Sometimes it was easier to call LaDonna my mother than explain the whole "foster" thing. And declaring I was the Summate still felt like I was bragging. Like, who am I to be the one the Universe blessed with every skill a witch could want?

Not for the first time, I wondered how many witches would trade their gift if they could. Or did the Universe know how to pair magic with personality? I was nearly thirty and had never asked, but resolved to consider it at another time.

Murmurs spread across the room as folks who didn't know me whispered to those who did. Someone near me said, "She's so young."

Well yeah. What'd they expect? A wizened old wizard with a long, gray beard?

"Hey, y'all," I repeated louder, cutting the chatter. "I just want to thank everyone who made the trip here. Y'all left your homes to help people you didn't even know, and that means the world to me. I think I can speak for all of Gryphon when I say we're grateful. You're heroes, every one of you."

The Lughaidh coven led a round of applause. It rippled through the room and fizzled just as quickly.

"Now, I've heard some of y'all aren't in a rush to leave. And while we've got some damn good orange witches who can peek into the future, I thought maybe it was smarter to just ask you directly. Not that you aren't welcome, but… why are y'all still hanging around?"

I tossed that out with a bit of humor, and it earned a few chuckles. There was a brief pause, then someone stood.

A lean Black woman rose, regal and self-assured. Late middle-aged, with gray-streaked locs tied into a patterned headwrap and deep-set eyes. She wore a dark green robe with gold embroidery and held a wooden staff adorned with bones and bundles of dried herbs in one hand.

"Miss Blackwell, my name is Soraya Batiste. It is an honor to make your acquaintance," she said. Her voice was smoky and smooth—reminded me a little of LaDonna—but with a Lowcountry Southern drawl that was much more genteel than that found in Alabama. I didn't need to be told she was an ancestral witch. Spirit communication radiated from her like perfume.

"I believe," she went on, "that many of us are here to ensure the continued safety of you, your coven, and the town of

Gryphon."

I opened my mouth to argue—then shut it. She had a point.

I'm the Summate, dammit. I should be able to handle this, shouldn't I? But who was I kidding? I couldn't beat the Stygian alone. I might have every sort of ability a witch could hope for, and maybe I had an abundance, but I was only one witch.

I glanced at Conall again. He hadn't moved, but his eyes were locked on me. An ever-steady presence. My presence.

"There's more," a man said, standing. He was well over six feet tall and broad-shouldered, a soft yet strong sort of handsome with a teddy bear vibe that made me think he probably gave great hugs. Dark hair, salt-and-pepper beard, and wire-rimmed glasses atop a prominent nose. His t-shirt said, "Roll for snacks."

I liked this guy immediately.

He turned red under the attention and gave a sheepish little wave. "Uh—hi. I'm Benny Cavanaugh. From North Carolina. Yeah, um… Regarding Gryphon. And the Stygian. There's… lore."

Lore?

A few chuckles rippled through the crowd.

He scratched the back of his neck. "I mean… Gryphon isn't just another town on a map. It sits on a geomantic fault line—"

"Geomantic?" Miriam asked.

Benny nodded. "It means the land itself holds power—like, the shape of it, what's under it, how it's been used. Like a ley line… but stronger. A convergence point built on part of the Earth's natural energy grid, where underground cave systems and the power of the Tennessee River all interact. These layers feed each other, and after several millennia, they can grow unstable. Dangerous. The magical potential here in Gryphon is off the charts. But it's more than that.

There's a vast resonance chamber buried in there. The Stygian don't just want to hurt people—they want to use the power in that chamber to fracture this place wide open. And, I imagine the rest of the world, too."

Now *that* got everyone's attention.

)O(

Luke cleared his throat. His voice sounded louder than it should've in the quiet of the shop.

"You're talking about the Bluebelow."

I was leaning against the back wall, but I perked up at the mention of the mythical local spot. "You mean the Hollow Cave you told me about?"

He shook his head. "Used to be called that, only Hallow was spelled—with an A, meaning sacred. Old-timers thought it was blessed."

I snorted, and my forehead wrinkled so hard that I probably looked like a Shar-pei puppy. "A blessed cave?"

Luke shrugged. "Somewhere along the way, folks started calling it the Bluebelow. No one really knows when it changed or why. Might've been the glow down there. Some folks say that certain spots have a faint blue shimmer. Or maybe it's just because the deeper you go, the weirder it gets."

"So, rebranding with a side of urban legend."

A few murmurs rolled through the room like dry leaves skipping across pavement. The scent of old coffee, lavender blackberry cleaning spray, and wood smoke from the fireplace should have been relaxing in its familiarity. Bully leaned back in his chair, arms folded, eyes on Luke.

Benny, whose shoulders had lowered now that he was getting used to being the center of attention, added, "Sacred's not a big enough word for it."

Luke shot him an intense look from under his brows, but he didn't argue. Just nodded. "My great-granddad used to say the cave listened. Not like an echo that reverberates—like it *heard* you. That it understood what you meant, not just what you said."

"That's because it's not just a cave," Benny said. "Like I said, it's a natural resonance chamber—one of the rare places on Earth where sound doesn't just bounce; it generates magic. Kind of like the power found at Stonehenge when a drum is used in a specific spot. Every intention, every emotion... it layers in the vibrations. Builds. Amplifies. What's more, magic doesn't just work better in there—it *evolves*. You don't just cast spells in the Bluebelow. You shape outcomes. Twist possibilities. Push the boundaries of what's supposed to be possible. You speak inside that cave, and you're not casting a spell—you're rewriting rules about how the world works."

A stool scraped quietly across the wood floor. People were leaning in now, some sitting on the floor near the fireplace, others wedged into corners and window seats, their earlier conversations long forgotten. I saw more than one person mouthing the word Bluebelow.

Conall shifted from where he stood near the wall. "So, if someone goes in and says the wrong thing..."

"They don't get a do-over," Benny said. "The cave doesn't bounce your words back. It records them and builds on them."

"I've heard it's tied to the river, too," Luke added. "The Tennessee runs close enough that it seeps in and picks up traces of that magic and carries it downstream."

I blinked, surprised to learn this about our local river. "It does?"

"Yeah," Luke said, glancing toward the front window like he could see the river through the darkness. "The way I've heard it is, the current brushes up against the edge of the cave's field. Picks up traces of that power like silt. Every flood, every surge... the river carries a little more of that magic with it."

He paused, his thumb grazing the edge of his thick leather belt like he was trying to remember something exactly right.

"My great-granddad used to talk about the cave like it was sacred ground. Said it was too easy to bring something with you that didn't belong and cause echoes that made the butterfly effect look like a drop in the bucket. Too easy to leave changed.

"He never took me there. Never let me go, either. Always said it was better left alone unless the land called you to it."

He gave a soft, humorless laugh. "Folks used to whisper about it when I was a kid—called it cursed, or holy, or both, depending on who you asked. You know how Appalachian Mountain stories go. Then, over the years, people just... stopped talking about it. Like the silence around it grew thicker the less folks mentioned it."

Benny picked up the narrative again. "And when the water rises, or the stars line up just right? That river acts like a damn amplifier. Cranks the cave's reach up to eleven."

A shiver crept down my spine as a rustle passed through the room—not loud, just the quiet shift of several bodies reacting to a hundred puzzle pieces clicking into place and everyone realizing the picture they'd been building spelled out *disaster*.

I cleared my throat. "So what happened in the past? Someone tried to use it?"

Benny gave a short nod. "I've heard that there was a

group of witches—way before the Stygian—who didn't just *find* the cave, they… engineered it. Like, they found the raw potential down there and did something to amplify it. Rerouted energy. Layered spells. Whispered intentions into the stone until the place started listening."

Luke frowned. "You're saying they made the cave what it is?"

Benny shrugged. "Far as anyone knows. They were powerful—and a little unhinged, from the sound of it. Thought if they got everything just right—timing, phrasing, alignment—they could change how magic works. Maybe more than that."

Luke's voice dropped. "But it didn't work out."

"Not the way they planned," Benny said. "Something went sideways. Real fast. They managed to get the resonance part right, but the ritual got cut off. Some say they died or that they vanished—or worse. Like maybe the cave swallowed 'em. But whatever they started? It didn't stop. The echoes of it… they're still in there. Sleeping. And growing."

My stomach turned. "And now the Stygian want to finish what they started."

Luke nodded once. "That's why they took Rene. Why they were after Betony. They're trying to reassemble whatever was started down there—pulling together the right voices, bloodlines, and spellwork. They think they can wake it up."

I didn't like the way he said *wake it up*. And deep down, I had a sinking feeling that whatever "it" was, it hadn't been sleeping peacefully.

Which explains why they were trying to summon the Sovereign Darkness here, too. Sure, there were ley lines all over the globe, but Gryphon was a town with an unstable—what had Benny called it?—a geomantic fault line sitting on a resonance chamber where an evil spell lay incomplete.

Everything was tied to that cave. And Gryphon.

Conall's brow furrowed, and he glanced at me, concern shadowing his expression. "If they do, what happens? And how do they know where the last spell left off?"

Elidriel stepped forward from near the window. Her voice was soft and eerily still, her eyes magnificent green gems. "They used fae to uncover the history of the cave. Ones who've worked with its magic since before there were many humans on this land." She paused. "They tortured them."

"So they have the intel they need to finish the spell?" I asked. "You knew about this?"

Her voice was barely a whisper now. "I believe they do. It was just a story before. About a horrible group of witches who came after our people. Not..." Her eyes dropped to the floor. "I didn't know."

Luke's jaw flexed, his eyes scanning the room. "That means they've got everything they need to change the world. Not just Gryphon. Not just Alabama. Everything."

Benny added, "The very water passing through the cave would carry their magic. It would spread with every storm, every raindrop, every ounce that evaporates and falls somewhere else. If they break the fault line, water could pour through the cave like never before. Reality might fracture. Or reset. And whoever speaks the final words would be the one holding the pen."

"Wouldn't that kill them?" I asked. "All that water? If the fault cracks and lets in the river?"

"Not if they have a good enough water witch," Dylan said. "Or several decent ones."

Damn.

Somewhere to my left, I heard someone's breath hitch. The faint tick of the wall clock filled the quiet like a countdown. My pulse thudded in my ears, steady and sharp, like I

was already bracing for impact.
     I didn't say anything.
     No one did.

Chapter 36

I shifted my weight from one leg to the other, arms crossed tight over my chest. Conall stood nearby, close enough to anchor me, far enough not to hover.

"So why the hell did they screw around at the Park yesterday?" I asked. "Why not head straight to the cave, toss off their little death spell or chaos bullshit or whatever, and be done with it?"

A beat of silence followed—until a voice from the back cut through.

"It wasn't just about harming Gryphon," Betony said.

Heads turned like a school of fish, tracking the speaker. Betony flinched under the attention, her pale cheeks coloring beneath a curtain of bleach-blond hair. But she didn't stop.

"They still want to use Rene somehow," she went on, voice steadier now. "That's why they tried to take him. They had to draw him out into the open and have him distracted so they could strike."

A low murmur ran through the room, and someone blurted, "Someone was taken?"

"Attempted to," Rene called out, raising a hand. "I'm fine. Thanks to Murphy."

A few heads swiveled back toward me. Great. Now I was the one who'd kept the town's golden boy from getting hex-napped. I wasn't sure if I was supposed to bow, curtsy, or salute.

"Why would they want Rene?" Luke shifted beside me. "I know Ericka tried to use him before, but… he left. He defected. Surely she has witches around who are more willing. I mean, yeah, he's her son, but—

"He's a silver witch," I said.

Luke's eyebrows rose. "That would make sense. They probably want to use his power to make sure the spell hits the cave just right and opens the right future. Or maybe to replay a piece of the last spell they're still missing."

"But how?" Bully asked, puzzled. "I don't see Rene offering up his services."

"I suspect they were gonna sacrifice him," I said, disgust tightening my chest. "Body, soul, everything. Let the dark power ride him like a damn Cadillac if it meant blowing a hole through reality."

Benny and Bully let out matching exhales through tight lips. In any other situation, I'd have laughed. Now it just made the room feel heavier.

I gave Rene a sheepish look. "Sorry."

He waved it off, though his brow furrowed.

"It *is* a ritual," Benny said. "But like spells, rituals can shift depending on how they're worded. The right phrase, right tone… it can steer the whole thing in a new direction. If they had a way to know exactly what to say to get exactly what they want…"

"Which is why they tortured the fae," LaDonna murmured. "They needed the right words for the ritual to work."

Everyone in that room knew exactly what the Stygian was aiming for. Ultimate power.

"Well, they didn't get him," I said, lifting my chin. "So they'll have to find some other way to tune their creepy-ass ceremony."

Which they might have. Silver witches are rare, but not impossible to find. And the past few days had made one thing clear: if someone had the right magical gift, moving a person across the globe wasn't hard at all.

"When you think they'll strike?" Luke asked Benny.

Benny scratched the back of his neck. "Depends. Any major star stuff happening soon? That's usually their style, right?—line it up with the heavens."

"No," came a voice from the center of the room.

Everyone turned. The speaker stood still and serene, a wiry man in flowing blue-and-white robes, long white hair pulled back in a ribbon that looked like it might be silk. Round glasses caught the overhead light just so, like the glint of a blade. He looked like he'd wandered out of some forgotten legend—and by the way he held his spine, you knew: this man was not wrinkled-old. He was ancient-old.

"I am Master Liang Ren," he said. "I read stars. I feel when power shift. This month, sky is quiet."

"That's good," LaDonna said. "Thank you, Master Liang"

He nodded once, a kind of nod that felt like a closed book: not dismissive, but complete.

I made a mental note to find him later if the chance ever came. The man radiated knowledge and well-tuned power—two things I lacked. If I was ever going to be a decent Summate, I'd need to learn from someone like him.

Assuming, of course, I lived through this mess.

"What else can they use?" Betony asked.

Conall shifted beside me. "There's no sabbats until next month. What about deity days?"

I considered those for a moment, but another possibility seemed more likely. "Weather. If the river swells, it would increase the power."

"Any big storms coming up soon?" LaDonna asked.

Terry was already pulling her phone from her jacket pocket, thumbs working fast. She was our resident weather hawk—and for good reason. Living in Alabama makes most folks appreciate and respect the power of one of Mother Nature's most destructive forces.

Her brows pulled together, hard. "That's... not good," she murmured.

I didn't like that tone. Not from Terry. "What?" I asked, my voice a whisper shy of panic.

"It's a news bulletin. Something weird." She looked up, eyes wide behind her glasses. "Y'all need to hear this."

Thanks to Rene, Witch's Brew had Bluetooth speakers mounted high on the shelves—hidden between plants and jars of incense sticks. Terry had synced her phone dozens of times to play music while she worked the counter, and now she tapped her screen to send the audio to every corner of the shop.

The voice of Todd Majors, our local weather guy—the one with the calm delivery and the sad eyes—piped through the speakers, sounding tighter than usual.

"Uh—this is Todd Majors coming to you live with a... well, an unexpected update. Our meteorology team has been tracking a developing pattern over northeast Alabama, and... I—I'm just gonna be straight with y'all. We've never seen anything like this.

"What looked like a minor pressure front around noon has rapidly expanded. It's pulling in moisture and wind from multiple vectors. Not in a spiral, not in a wedge—just... converging. All of it. It's not moving like a cold front, or a warm front, or—hell, it's not moving right at all. The models keep changing every time we run them. They can't keep up."

I shot a look at LaDonna. "Weather witches," I breathed.

She nodded, stone-faced. Weather witches weren't as rare as Summates or chaos witches, but working in concert, they could have a massive impact on the atmosphere.

Todd Majors continued. "At this rate, we're looking at the potential for severe atmospheric instability in the next twenty-four to forty-eight hours. I mean serious—I'm talking flash floods, high-velocity winds, supercell formation, maybe even tornadic chains. But I need to be clear: we don't know. The pattern's erratic. Wild. Frankly, it shouldn't even be possible.

"We're advising everyone in the affected area to keep close watch. Get your emergency kits ready. Keep your phones charged. Stay alert. If this thing develops, you may need to shelter quickly. Don't wait for the sky to turn green. And please keep checking in. We'll update as we can, but right now… we're in uncharted territory."

The speakers fell silent as Terry adjusted the sound, and no one spoke. Even the air felt still, like the world was holding its breath.

Conall's hand found the small of my back. Solid. Warm. Reminding me I wasn't alone in this, not really.

The stars might've been quiet, like Master Liang said, but down here?

Down here, a storm was about to roar.

☽○☾

"Y'all, I suspect we're dealing with a slew of weather witches," I announced to the still-stunned crowd, everyone processing the storm warning Terry had just blasted through the speakers. "Now, I know not all of y'all are from the South, but we are *very* familiar with the damage a tornado can do around here. And if you feel the need to find a storm shelter and protect yourselves, I promise—no one here's gonna think less of you for it. Not everyone in this room is immortal."

I tried to keep it light, aiming for gallows humor over grim reality, but my voice was too taut around the edges. My hope was that it landed as encouragement for the squishy mortals among us—better to bow out early than die for the sake of peer pressure.

No one moved.

Not one soul panned the room, not a single person seemed unsure whether to stay or go. Just fifty-ish brave-ass weirdos, all still, all staring forward, ready to take on whatever the Stygian threw at them. Willing to throw down for Gryphon, even knowing what that might cost them.

OK, then. I was impressed.

I didn't know if I'd have had that level of intestinal fortitude before this whole Summate thing landed in my lap. The idea of facing off with the Stygian again terrified me. Last time, we'd needed ancestral magic and the ghost of my dead fae father to pull it off. This time?

This time, I didn't even know what sort of magical menagerie we had packed into this town. So many people had come to help us steer folks clear of the river, I'd long since lost track of them all. Lines were being drawn, and decisions needed to be made; knowing people's gifts would be super helpful.

"Anyone here a weather witch? Aside from you, Paul," I called, trading a look with Conall's dad before turning to the crowd. I zeroed in on Ivor Blitz—our very own gaunt-cheeked, sun-deprived, lightning-slinging little gremlin.

Ivor's face split in a crooked grin that somehow worked despite his teeth being in open rebellion against standard dental geometry.

"Sorry," he said, snapping a few sparks from his

fingertips for flair. "Just electric. I can charge your car or fry a microwave, but I can't harness actual lightning or anything."

"That could still come in handy," Conall said.

I nodded, then pulled in close with Conall, Luke, and LaDonna for a quick sidebar. "Has anyone been tracking who's in town and what their gifts are? I don't even know how many witches we have, let alone anyone who might knock a tornado off course."

"Rita," Conall said, with the smallest upturn of his lips and a glance to Gryphon's favorite tech witch.

Of course.

I huffed a little laugh and joined Conall in sending Rita a soft, affectionate smile. "Knowing her, she probably built an app in the last two days just to track everyone's magical vitals."

"You're not far off," Rita called, raising her phone like a digital torch. "I just modded the WorldWide Witches app— W3. Patched in a few Numinari-specific upgrades with help from a couple of exhausted code-witches. It's got magical specifications, affinity flags, proximity pings... basically, if someone goes globe-trotting or vanishes off the grid, we'll know."

"That's... freaking amazing," I said, grinning at her. "Seriously. What would we do without you?"

She gave a theatrical shrug, all casual genius. "Figured if the world was ending, we should at least be able to group text about it. We added almost all the folks who arrived in Gryphon recently, and a lot of the WorldWide Witches have signed up, too."

Around the room, phones were already out, screens lighting up like fireflies. Conall pulled his from his back pocket and tapped through to the app. He snorted with loud amusement.

"Love the app description," he murmured. "'W3: Numinari Overlay. Don't worry, it won't brick your phone. Probably.'"

I leaned in over his shoulder, peeking at the interface. The
app had loaded quickly—sleek, minimalist, with a soft glow
around the edges of a black app screen displaying a local
map. Little glowing dots blinked across town—green, silver,
orange, blue. Each dot was tagged with a name, a photo, and
a brief profile, including gift type, magical class, and affilia-
tion. The symbols next to them flickered like digital sigils—
one for telepaths, another for healers, and a spiral pattern I
didn't recognize for elementalists, and a wide variety of others. A massive pile of dots converged on the corner of Oberon
and Tatania. Someone had labeled Ivor "Lightning" Blintz as
Class: Electric / Mood: Crackly.

Conall scrolled, and I watched a list populate under the
map. Names. Covens. Powers. Known affinities. Risk levels.

One witch had a note beside her name that read *Chaos-
aligned. Likes knives.* I made a mental note to avoid her before coffee.

"Damn," I whispered. "It's a magical damn superhero
registry."

Conall gave a low chuckle. "It's like a witchy FitBit
crossed with an FBI database."

"She's a modern-day Ada Lovelace," I said, "only with
better hair."

He smiled at that, and I let the moment hang between us
for half a second before reality surged back in.

Outside, a storm was building, and we had a town to save.

Chapter 37

I opened the back door leading into the shop's rear and waved everyone inside with broad sweeps of my arm. The eaves overhanging the back of my house were generous, but the weather was turning bad quickly. Even as I ushered the last of them through to the dining room and kitchen, the rain took on a bent that wasn't natural—especially not for July. The pace was blunt and oddly rhythmic.

The air pressure crashed down, thick and sudden, and I braced for the wind to carry the tornado siren's cry straight through the storm.

"Y'all make yourselves at home," I said, motioning to the shop area, which was being reassembled back into a coffee shop by the Numinari crowd. "As much as you can, anyway. Rene? Betony?"

My two unofficially adopted kids perked up. Betony rose on tiptoe to see over the shuffle of bodies and chair legs.

"See if anyone wants coffee. Or anything, really. Might be a long night."

As I approached the kitchen, I spotted Hanna and Miriam slipping behind the counter to join the teens. Witch's Brew had never been this full. I wondered how long the wine and beer Joey brought would hold out.

Jake arched an eyebrow in my direction, and I mouthed, "Keep playing." He gave me a subtle, knowing, close-lipped smile, his droopy blue eyes crinkling at the corners. *Keep the crowd calm* was my unspoken request. Jake understood the assignment.

Benny, Dylan, and Soraya joined Bully and me, along with a handful of my coven family, in my kitchen, where we continued war planning around the butcher block island in the center.

Dylan paced a rut into the floor in front of the stove. Terry's phone kept pinging with alerts from her weather app—little chimes raising tension in a room full of already fraying nerves. I was about to tell them to go burn off their energy somewhere else when Conall pressed a warm, steady hand over mine. That look in his eyes—dark, unruffled—quieted me more than I'd admit out loud right then. Betony's gift could leech chaos from a room, but Conall? He anchored *me*.

"The storm isn't a distraction," Conall said. "There's a purpose to the strength of it. There has to be."

LaDonna nodded. "Agreed. They're likely planning to use it to trigger destruction—wind, flooding, tornado. They want to cover something worse."

Soraya turned her cavernous eyes to Luke and Benny. "You said they were likely here for the... Bluebelow, you called it?"

Luke nodded. "It's likely. Very likely."

She tilted her chin, giving him a motherly look so withering I didn't know how he wasn't physically backing away from it.

"But you're not positive," she said.

"No, ma'am."

Luke was a good Southern man, but he didn't call just anyone ma'am. That was the power of Soraya's gaze.

"It's the only thing that makes sense," Benny insisted, pressing a meaty hand to the butcher block as he leaned forward intently.

Soraya's gaze swung toward him. Benny's mouth snapped shut, and he leaned back.

"I think," she said, low but firm, "before we spend more time on a path, however *likely*, we'd best make sure we're on the *right* one."

"She's got a point," I said. "It'd be just like the Stygian to make us look one way"—I wiggled my right hand— "while they pulled their real trick over here." I gestured with my left.

"It's not likely," Benny muttered.

"Do you have an orange witch among you?" Soraya asked.

"Two," Luke said, nodding between himself and Conall.

"Excellent," she replied. "If the two of you can confirm the Stygian will be found in the Bluebelow tonight if all continues its course, then that's where we go."

I still didn't know who this woman was, but I liked her. No posturing. No bullshit. Just wisdom and action. Pretty much how I imagined LaDonna would be in a couple of decades.

Conall touched my arm. "Can I use your mirror?"

I was already moving. "Be right back."

I dashed upstairs to my private spell room—what I called my Room of Power—where the scrying mirror waited, its black surface oval and dark as a moonless lake, surrounded by an ornate frame and handle. By the time I returned, Conall had cleared a space on the kitchen counter. I handed it over without ceremony. He nodded his thanks and began.

Luke moved slower, more deliberately. He passed through the swinging doors and crossed to the low shelf tucked beneath the front counter, where I kept a well-loved sample tarot deck in its box meant for guests to flip through, but mostly forgotten, except by him.

The Tarot of Marseille. My foster father's favorite. Most folks I showed admired the art. Luke drew three cards with the reverence of a man handling sacred tools.

No one spoke. No one wanted to disturb the ritual about to take place. The only sound was the quiet rattle of the storm beyond the glass, the faint harmony of Jake's playing mingled with Lorina's muted vocals, and soft conversations in the next room. Even that seemed to dim.

Luke flipped the first card. Then, the second. He paused, studying both.

It was Conall who finally broke the silence.

"They'll be in the cave."

Luke turned over the last card, slow and sure.

"Confirmed." He tapped the face of it once. "La Maison Dieu. The Tower."

A few of us made the usual sounds—the wince, the hiss through teeth. The rest waited for an explanation.

Luke looked up, his expression grave.

"Sudden upheaval. Collapse of old foundations. Destruction, yes, but also revelation. The Tower alone doesn't point to the cave. But I pulled La Lune and L'Hermite along with it."

"How do you get the cave from those?" Benny asked.

Luke held the deck steady in one hand and gestured to the spread with the other. "The Moon card shows a dark circle between two pillars. You tell me what that looks like. And the Moon rules dreams, the subconscious, illusion, hidden fears… That's cave territory if I've ever seen it."

"And the Hermit?"

Luke's gaze lingered on the third card. "The Hermit is the archetype of solitude. A cave-dweller by nature. He retreats from the world to seek inner truth. Carries a lantern to light the dark. You don't have to look far to see what that means."

The storm growled low against the windows. Then, from somewhere in the distance, tornado sirens wailed.

☽ ◯ ☾

Terry had been glued to her favorite weather app like some kind of digital tarot deck, scrying symbols not in star charts but in Doppler loops. Every few minutes, she'd mutter something under her breath—half prayer, half profanity—but she didn't speak this time. She just sucked in a sharp, audible breath, the kind that snapped heads around like a whipcrack.

"What's up, Ter?" I asked.

She didn't answer. Her hand trembled slightly as she turned the phone toward us. Her eyes were wide and unblinking, caught in that stunned limbo between disbelief and dread. Like her brain had just hit a wall it couldn't reason past.

My first thought was that we all needed to find shelter quickly. Thankfully, city hall wasn't far off, and it opened its basement to anyone who didn't have a shelter. I'd used it many times. Finding immediate shelter wasn't the concern, though.

I'd seen a lifetime's worth of storm maps. Alabama weather was nothing if not theatrical—bright swaths of green, yellow, orange, and blood-red bleeding across the screen, the classic palette of incoming chaos. But nestled inside the mess was something too precise, too symmetrical. A perfect spiral had formed, two mirrored halves—one pale, one dark—curled around each other in an eerie waltz. The center of the storm sat between them like the spine of a coin, narrow and unmoving. It was unmistakable.

A yin-yang made of wind and destruction passing north and east of us.

She tapped the center of the spiral with one finger.

"That's not just rotation," she said, voice low. "That's a twister. A big one."

She didn't have to say the rest. I'd lived in Alabama long enough to know what it meant when the storm curved like that. But mother goddess, I'd never seen one so massive.

My stomach clenched. That shape wasn't meteorological—it was symbolic. It looked planned. And the second I saw it, the question struck like lightning: What the hell did the Stygian want with a tornado?

I scanned the terrain in my mind's eye—the cave nestled in the foothills, the Tennessee River tracing its lazy path nearby like a silver thread. We already knew they were heading to the Bluebelow, but a tornado wouldn't do much to a cave system unless they meant to collapse the entrance. That felt counterintuitive. They wanted access to whatever lay within. No, this wasn't about destruction—it was about leverage.

It had to be the river, but how? Luke's voice surfaced in my memory, heavy and grim: "It seeps in. Picks up traces of that magic."

But even the wildest twister couldn't drag a river sideways and pour it into the cave like a bucket. This wasn't Sharknado: Occult Edition. Still… what if it wasn't about dragging the water? What if it was about raising it?

The idea slammed into me like a crowbar to the ribs. I snatched my phone and pulled up a map of TVA infrastructure, fingers fumbling to type on my tiny screen. There it was—one of the larger reservoirs, an old one—smack in the middle of the tornado's projected path.

"Could it damage a reservoir?" I asked, tossing the question to the group.

"Not usually," Luke said. "Those bad boys are built to survive Armageddon, more or less."

My heart almost lifted in relief. Then Conall spoke.

"What about a magically weakened one?"

"Fuuuuuck," Benny said. He shot an apologetic glance at Soraya. "Sorry."

Soraya didn't even blink. Her gaze stayed fixed on my screen, storm light reflecting in her irises like distant lightning. Dylan's attention shifted toward me, expression calm, jaw set.

"You want me to divert it."

Not a question.

"Yes," I said. "If they're trying to flood the cave, we have to stop the water before it even thinks about getting there."

Terry's phone chimed, a single mechanical ding that cracked through the room like bone. She stared at the screen, eyes wide.

"The tornado's almost on top of the reservoir. Minutes. Maybe less."

"There's no time to get him there," Soraya said, and her voice held the sort of finality that ended arguments before they started.

I turned to Bully. He met my eyes without flinching. No swagger, no theatrics—just that quiet readiness that lived in his spirit. Something in me eased.

"You up for it?"

He nodded once and uncrossed his arms, brushing them gently with his palms. I suspected that was part of his ritual— a gesture of significance to him.

"Get him somewhere safe, but close enough he can work. North end of the TVA dam. Then check Rita's app. He's gonna need some help." I turned to Dylan. "Can you sense things? Like when water's shifting underground?"

He offered a quick nod.

"Well… stop it from doing that, if you can. We need to

divert as much water from the cave as possible. That's how the Stygian are hoping to transport that ritual they're doing—if I'm understanding it right."

From opposite corners of the room, Benny and Luke gave subtle nods.

Dylan ran a hand through his curls and exhaled slowly. "I got you."

Bully stepped forward, rolling his sleeves with unhurried precision. His hands began to glow—a soft, pulsing blue, elemental and ancient. Light shimmered from his fingertips as he moved them through the air, casting ripples like heat waves that distorted the surrounding space. The room shifted, bent. He was reaching beyond it.

"Hold on to your hair, boy," he muttered, stretching a hand toward Dylan. "This ride don't come with seatbelts."

Dylan didn't flinch. He clasped Bully's hand, and in the next instant, they vanished.

The air snapped shut behind them like a door slammed hard by the wind, echoing oddly through my kitchen space.

We moved out of the kitchen, past the swinging doors, into the quiet cathedral of Witch's Brew. Usually, the shop felt like a sanctuary. The familiar creak of the old floorboards under my Converse usually brought comfort. Tonight, it just felt... fragile.

The lights out here burned low, casting syrupy shadows across the shelves of apothecary jars and charm baskets. Every scent clung too tightly—lavender, peppermint, and a sour note of anxious perspiration. The Numinari were waiting.

DB, our torch-tongue, broke the silence. He sauntered over like he was stepping onto a stage, conjuring a slender flame from between his lips that he caught in his palm. He angled it toward Cadence, who stood with one hip cocked near the tea display, watching him like she already knew the punchline.

"Y'all ever seen a flame flirt?" DB asked, grinning like a fox, his golden eyes flickering in the light of the flame.

The fire in his hand shimmered prettily, spiraling like it had a sense of humor. Cadence arched a brow, unimpressed.

"She's cute," she said. "Bet she burns out quick."

Jake chuckled, pride in his girlfriend sparkling in his eyes. "Oof. Fatality."

I didn't smile. I didn't move. Something in the room had shifted.

From the far side of the shop, Ivor let out a long breath, thick with static. Sparks snapped off his fingers in quick, ir-ritable bursts, raising his wispy white hair in the static-filled air until it floated like fog catching fire.

"Parlor tricks," he muttered with an eye roll toward DB's failed flirtation.

Behind the apothecary counter, Rita was rearranging spell jars. "Parlor tricks are so last season," she chirped with an adorable nose wrinkle in Ivor's direction.

My eyes landed on Miriam, who'd settled into the arm-chair by the reading nook. She was massaging oil into her palms—lemongrass, maybe. Something cleansing. Her wand lay across her knees, limewood polished to a glow. She watched the room like a mother watches a pot—measured, but ready to snatch it off the heat.

Then I saw my sister.

Elidriel sat curled in the arched front window like a ques-tion mark made of moonlight. She wasn't watching anything. She was listening—to the night, the wind, something none of us could hear.

Then, the light surrounding her... shifted. Warped. Like the air itself didn't know how to encompass her anymore.

That's when I felt LaDonna's breath stutter beside me.

"They've started," she whispered.

My gut twisted.

LaDonna's magic ran deep—Green witch, Earth-tied. She could feel spells strike the land like tremors through roots, even from miles away. If she felt something now, it wasn't just theory. It was happening.

I looked past Elidriel, out into the black, depthless sky. The stars shimmered like crystal chips scattered across silk, too still for comfort.

I reached for the Source, trying to tune in to whatever Elidriel had caught on the wind. But the moment I touched it, my ears filled with sound—if you could call it that. An overwhelming resonance, like a cathedral of tuning forks vibrating at once. Too many notes, all wrong together. It wasn't just noise—it was intention. Something was being called forth.

The ritual had started. Maybe not fully, but the spell was in motion. And the cave—the Bluebelow—knew it. How long would the rite last?

That's when Elidriel moved.

She stiffened, every part of her still, but vibrating, like a harp string pulled too tight. Her bright eyes went glassy. Not unfocused, exactly, but also not hers. Something else was looking through them. Some*one* else.

She slid from the windowsill in one smooth motion and dropped to her knees like gravity had claimed her all at once. One hand spread flat on the old wooden floor, silver rings clicking softly as she caught herself. She wasn't trembling anymore but looked like a vessel barely holding something in. I was reminded, oddly, of one of my mother's old Southernisms: they look like ten pounds of sugar in a five-pound sack.

Intrusive thoughts have the oddest timing.

Then, a low, strange hum started. Not in the air, but beneath us. Below the floorboards. Below the foundation. Stone under stone under wood. It passed through the bones of the shop, through wood, nail, and stone.

I could feel it rise—slow and steady, like heat off a memory. Something buried, but not dead.

"Listen," Elidriel breathed.

And we did. Everyone froze as if entranced.

"The cave dreams," she said. "It remembers what bled it open."

She wasn't just sensing it—she was linked to it. Whatever the Bluebelow was—whatever had been buried there—it knew her. It remembered the blood it had been bound to. Fae blood.

"They didn't mean to create the resonance," she continued, the sound layered now—hers voice joined with another, older and grieving. "Only to seal something dark beneath it. But they used my kind to do it."

"Anchored their spell in us," she said. "Left us buried in the stone, like teeth."

Like teeth? I envisioned fossilized teeth embedded in centuries-old rock so primeval the two had fused into one. I knew it wasn't far off.

From what Elidriel had pronounced, our fae ancestors were not participants in the ritual. They'd been living batteries sacrificed to fuel the Bluebelow.

"How do you know this?" I asked her, voice barely audible.

She lifted her gaze. Eyes like moonlight caught in glass. Not entirely here. Not entirely gone, but she didn't answer. She showed us.

The lights in Witch's Brew dimmed—not flickered. Dimmed like the entire room had taken a breath, pulling in the ambient light and holding it deep in its chest.

From the floor came a pulse. Not a thud. Not a jolt. A ripple of memory rising from the earth through the bones of the house. It was magic you don't see, but you feel in your blood. In your soul.

Something old remembered her, remembered *us*. The witches who'd used my sister's ancestors to trap power inside the cave so strong that it had the strength to undo the world as we knew it.

A draft stirred the room, though none of the windows were open. The flame in DB's palm flickered, guttered, and died, after which the air held still, too.

Elidriel didn't speak again—not at first. She stayed kneeling, palm flat against the floor, silver rings catching the dim light like frozen raindrops. Her head tilted slightly, as if hearing something rise from far below—a voice folded in time.

And then she stood. Slowly. Fluidly. As though the earth itself had given her back to us. She stepped toward me, barefoot on the old pine floor, her movements soundless, her presence suddenly too large for the diminutive shape that held her.

Her blond hair caught the light like threads of moonlight, and when she looked at me, it wasn't just Elidriel anymore—it was something older, something sacred and dangerous and *summoned*. Her eyes, which had been a beautiful bottle-green, now held the green of lush, ancient forest floors, of primitive ferns in mystical valleys. It was the memory of everything she'd ever been. Every fae who'd bled into the seal. Her gaze locked with mine—calm, ancient, and unwavering.

I blinked, suddenly aware I'd been staring—entranced. It felt like waking from a dream I hadn't known I'd fallen into.

"It's time to go," she said.

Chapter 38

The question was—where exactly were we going?

We needed a plan, but a quick one. We had fifty-ish Numinari waiting for a chance to help, but I didn't want to bring absolutely everyone with us. Not only did I have no idea how large the cave was, I had horrible visions of bullets ricocheting off stone walls and piercing folks through vital organs. Just because the Stygian had magic on their side didn't mean they were above using firepower. That meant we needed an A team—the ones going into the Bluebelow to face the Stygian—and a B team, who'd stay behind in Gryphon to hold the line, monitor the rising water, and step in if all hell broke loose.

Because, let's face it—hell was very likely breaking loose. Possibly literally.

Benny spread a map across the butcher block island like something hallowed. The paper looked old—creased at the corners, soft from years of being folded and refolded, probably stored under a stack of dog-eared field guides. A thick line of the Tennessee River curved like a spine through the center, with topographic lines fanning out across the hills. And just below the oldest watermark, someone had scribbled in charcoal pencil: Bluebelow?

"I thought this might help," Benny said, not quite meeting my eyes. "Found it in one of my dad's old hunting stashes.

He grew up near the North Carolina–Georgia border, but he liked to hunt all over the Southeast so he could track ley lines whenever he came across one. I guess he thought there was something down here in Gryphon. He didn't know what, but he marked this spot and circled it. Twice."

Rita gave a soft whistle. "That map's got some history."

Benny gave a slight shrug, his voice dropping. "Didn't even know it was in there. One of the barn owls—Junebug—started hooting like mad and wouldn't shut up until I opened the storage trunk. She perched on the damn thing like she was guarding a treasure. Once I lifted the lid, she flew off like her job was done."

He looked up then, sheepish but proud.

"It called to me," he said. "Or her. Maybe both of us."

"What's your gift, Benny?" LaDonna asked.

He offered a sheepish grin. "Green witch."

"I thought so," she replied, and the two of them exchanged a quiet, knowing look.

The map on the counter had become more than a topographical sketch. Between Elidriel's quick enchantments, blessed with her newfound ancestral insight, and Rene's silver gift that allowed him glimpses of the suppressed or forgotten, it now pulsed faintly, veins of light tracing the caverns below Gryphon, like those beneath the skin.

We stood in a loose circle around it. Everyone was quiet now. No jokes, no flippant commentary—the kind of hush you get before a storm breaks.

I rested my hand on the edge of the map, fingers grazing the glowing lines.

"Not everyone's going in," I said, and though I didn't raise my voice, every head turned. "It's not safe. And I've got a sneaky feeling it's not a place that welcomes strangers. The Stygian might have to pull some stunts to be let in themselves."

I let my words sink in a second before I added, "We don't have time for a long debate. The cave isn't going to wait, and the Stygian won't give us a second chance. So here's how we're doing it. A small team goes in. Everyone else stays top-side, keeping things in town from unraveling."

From the back of the room, a quiet voice cut through the stillness.

"I'll go."

He hadn't spoken before—not since arriving. Eli Mercer. I'd seen him standing alone under the porch overhang earlier that evening, watching the sky like it spoke to him. Now, he stepped forward. Not tentative, bold, or confrontational. He seemed like an easygoing guy. A blue-collar worker with a serene expression.

He looked to be in his late thirties, maybe a little older. Dressed in quiet shades of gray and brown, a palette that dis-appeared into woods or dusk. Everything about him was neu-tral—the set of his shoulders, the shape of his voice, the way his hands hung loosely at his sides.

"Caves are… acoustic nightmares," he said. "My gift can help."

Rene tilted his head. "What gift do you have, Eli?"

And then the world stopped making noise. It didn't get quiet. Sounds didn't muffle. In less than a breath, all sound vanished. I couldn't hear the scrape of shoes on wood, the creak of the building, or even the whoosh of my exhale. I opened my mouth to speak and didn't hear my own inhale. Nothing.

Then, just as fast, it lifted. The hum of the ceiling fans returned. A floorboard groaned near the door. Outside, a windchime jangled in the stormy wind.

Eli hadn't moved other than a slow blink of his eyes. No

Salty

hand gestures. No flare of magic. Just that same stillness, like the silence hadn't come from him, but *through* him.

"It's easier to show folks," he said with a modest shrug.

I gave him one to match. "I'm convinced. You're in, Eli."

Rene stepped forward without hesitation, light flickering in his brown eyes, the silver having retreated to a subtle ring.

"I should go. If the cave's hidden—or if the magic inside masks traps or... other layers—you might need me to see through it." He paused. "Also, I've got a pretty serious bone to pick with one of them." His smile turned sharp. "So. Yeah. I'm in."

Soraya stepped beside him, spine straight, expression stoic.

"If this is ancestral," she said, glancing toward Elidriel, "you'll need someone to speak to the blood memory. I know how to appeal to such things—how to speak to those who've gone before."

LaDonna caught my eye. I didn't need to ask her. She gave me that faint, knowing smile and said, "This old earth's been whispering for days. I plan on hearing what it has to say."

"Ivor?" I said, turning toward him. I didn't know why he needed to go—just that he did. The Source inside me was pushing, insistent. I couldn't explain why this funny-looking little man mattered. But he did.

He grunted, already strapping a leather bandolier across his chest, his fingers crackling with residual static. "Sure. I like caves."

"Ivor," Rita called from behind the counter, a smile tugging at her voice even though she didn't look up. "You don't strike me as the cave-exploring type."

"Exactly," he said distractedly, and kept going.

I really hoped the little guy made it out OK. I could tell

from the tender look on Rita's face as she watched him prepare to go spelunking that he'd grown on her quickly. I didn't understand half of their exchanges, but they did, and that's what mattered.

Then I glanced at Miriam. Her hands were already rubbing oil across her palms—something clean and citrus-sharp to cut through whatever rot might cling to us when we came back up. She gave a small nod. "I won't get in the way. And there's no way I'm going in." She shuddered violently. "But if someone comes out bleeding or broken, you'll want me near."

My gaze slid toward Jake, expecting hesitation.

He just stepped forward and set his guitar case down with care. "Thought you'd never ask," he said, flashing a grin.

Behind him, Lorina stiffened. Her arms crossed.

"Nope," she said. "Uh-uh. If he's going, I'm going. We both gotta help our friend Rene get some… justice or whatever."

"Lorina," I started.

She planted her feet. "Jake's music—it syncs with mine. You said it yourself. This cave magic is all about frequency. Sound. Voice. That means me."

Jake gave me a sideways look that said *Don't even bother arguing*, and for a second, I thought about telling her no. But the truth was… she was right. She wasn't just some kid who'd stumbled into this. She was officially Numinari—one of us. And if her voice helped counteract whatever the Stygian planned, we'd need her now more than ever.

I gave her a nod. "Alright. You're in."

She exhaled, relief loosening her tight shoulders.

"Crystal, you're our ticket to the cave's entrance. And you'll come inside with us in case we need a quick getaway, but I want you staying back, away from the action, OK?"

The petite aerocleaver gave me a quick salute. Her eyes sparkled like someone who'd been waiting to be useful.

"Doyle?"

He lifted his chin, the barest smirk pulling at his mouth like he'd already been planning his entrance. His bright blue eyes narrowed, gleaming with anticipation.

"You're muscle. And speed. We might need both."

"I'm in," he said, voice low and clipped.

"Me as well," a vaguely familiar voice said. Miles, the werewolf, advanced to join the group. I'd almost forgotten he was part of the contingent still in town.

"Fair enough," I said.

I stepped back from the table, letting the map glow.

"Joey, you're the outside line Protection detail. Keep the perimeter. Rafael?"

Hanna's eyes grew large as I called her father, our coven's white witch, to the front. White witches had the power to cleanse—tainted water, spoiled energy, even the lingering aftertaste of dark magic. If anything bled out of the Bluebelow, we'd need that kind of purity fast.

"You're outside with Joey and Miriam. If the cave starts reacting above ground or the water grows tainted, we'll need you to purify it as fast as possible. Any other white witches willing to be close to the fight can join you."

Rafael nodded. "We'll be ready."

Terry stepped forward, rubbing her hands together like she was restless to work. "I need to be in the A team," she said, glancing at me with a familiar spark. "If this cave's got ghosts—and let's be real, it absolutely does—you're gonna want me inside." Her voice dropped. "And if anything whispers from the walls, I'll be the first to hear it."

Hanna gave a tight smile. She knew her strengths were with people, not stone. "If anyone comes back shaken, I'll handle it."

DB stepped forward, one long finger raised like he was calling dibs. "If you run out of light or need something set on fire, I'm your guy."

I studied him for a beat. That swagger was half bluff, half burn, the kind that came with youth and just enough power to be dangerous. I weighed the risk, felt the tug of hesitation— and then the Source nudged me with the answer.

I gave a slow nod. "All right. You're in."

Then I turned back to the others who weren't going. I glanced toward Betony and caught her eye before she could volunteer.

"Betony," I said gently, "you're staying in Gryphon."

She blinked, clearly surprised. "What?"

"It's not a punishment," I added quickly. "It's because you're too powerful. Too important."

That made her scoff a little. "You're literally walking into a cave full of ritual magic to confront a doomsday cult, and *I'm* too powerful to bring?"

"Exactly," I said and stepped in closer, voice lowered so only a few nearby could hear. "If the Stygian got their hands on you, they could use the power in the cave to tap into your chaos magic. Feed off it. Twist it into something explosive. I can't take that risk. You know how volatile chaos magic is when it's not contained—and in that cave, nothing's going to be contained."

She frowned, lips pressed tight.

"And besides," I added, "if it all goes sideways, we'll need someone strong enough to mop up the chaos here in Gryphon. To pull it back in. You're the only one who can do that."

Betony's eyes darkened, but she nodded, her jaw tense.

"I hate this," she muttered.

"I know. Me too."

We exchanged a long look—then she gave me the tiniest nod and stepped back, arms crossed, brimming with frustrated acceptance. I turned to move on, but something itched behind my eyes. A pressure in my chest, subtle but steady. The Source.

Damn it. What did I miss?

I hesitated, then sighed and headed for the back door, aware of a room full of eyes following my path. Rain pattered softly against the kitchen windows. I stepped out barefoot onto the porch, wood slick and cool underfoot, and found the Mason jar where I'd left it beside the cracked flowerpot, half-covered in fallen flower leaves and glistening with rain.

Inside, the bright pink paint curled like oil on water. Angry, bitter stuff, steeped in spite. I hadn't known what to do with it when I'd spelled it off the fence marked with hateful words. Still didn't. But the Source whispered one word, clear as thunder, in my mind.

Betony.

By the time I stepped back inside, the jar was slick in my hand, cold as a river in winter.

Betony glanced up when I approached.

"I have something for you," I said, and held it out.

Her brow furrowed, but she took the jar without hesitation. The dried paint shifted inside like it heard her name, some of it catching in parts of still-gummy dregs.

"I pulled that off the fence," I said. "Didn't know why I kept it. Didn't know what it was for. But the Source says it's yours."

Betony turned it over slowly, watching the chips and gummy residue shift inside. Her magic stirred in response—just a tremor. Barely there. But I felt it. She picked up on the chaos that had driven the "artists" to vandalize the sanctity of my backyard.

She looked up, something unreadable in her expression. "What am I supposed to do with vandalism in a jar?"

"No idea," I admitted. "But if it matters, you'll know. When it's time."

Betony tucked the jar into the crook of her arm and gave a low, humorless chuckle. "Great. A mystery rain-slick hex-bomb. Just what I always wanted."

I gave her a crooked smile. "Call it an insurance policy. Or a breadcrumb. Or… hell, I don't know. Just… don't throw it away."

"I won't." Her tone was quiet now. Serious. "It feels like it's waiting."

"Yeah," I said. "So are we." Raising my head and my voice to include the rest of those present, I continued. "The rest of you."

The room perked up.

"I need you to do what you came here to do. Keep Gryphon safe. Patrol the streets. Watch the riverbanks, the back roads, and people's movements. If the Stygian's plan goes sideways—or if they dig up whatever they're down there to find—there's a good chance they'll try to sow chaos up here, too."

Several heads nodded. Wands shifted in hands. Feet braced a little firmer on the floor.

"Any water witches and white witches who decide to stay back," I continued, "get close to the river. Keep your ear on it. If the magic starts leaking into the current—"

"We'll purify it," someone said. I didn't see who. And I didn't say the rest of my thought out loud: *As long as it doesn't kill you first.*

As the crowd began to murmur and shift, I caught sight of Rita still standing behind the counter, her hands clenched into subtle fists at her sides.

"Rita," I called out, cutting through the movement. She looked up immediately.

"I need you to use the time we're gone to contact the WorldWide Witch coven."

Her brows lifted a hair, disappearing under her colorful bangs.

"Ask for anything they're willing to give—distance-based protections, ancestral spells, deity magic, whatever support they can send."

Rita quickly nodded, pulling her phone from her back pocket. "I'll reach out to every satellite hub I can. If they've got anything in their toolkit to slow the Stygian down—or keep us alive—we'll use it."

"I knew I could count on you."

She smiled faintly, the kind of smile that had steel under it.

This was it. The ones meant to walk into the belly of the land were chosen. Thank the goddess no one had put up a fuss. "Grab what you need," I said. "If the Stygian have already started, we need to move—now."

The room dissolved into motion, but a hush threaded through it deeper than silence. Like the air itself was bracing.

And somewhere nearby, the Bluebelow waited.

Chapter 39

As the Lughaidh finalized their preparations, Terry and I looked over her phone to watch the latest on the storm, which was *not* getting better. The weatherman looked like he was about ten seconds from weeping on air. His tie was crooked, mouth twitching as the radar spun behind him like a primitive video game—red, green, gray, all in that dreaded yin-yang telltale tornado shape.

When the words we'd been bracing for crawled across the bottom of the screen, Terry angled her phone toward me like it was evidence of a crime. "Dam's gone. It hit the reservoir."

Water roared, thick with debris, churning dark through the trees. Emergency lights at the sides of the reservoir spun helplessly over the wreckage, painting red across the ruin. The newsroom gasped, but none of it surprised me. I prayed Dylan and Bully had picked high ground—and that Dylan was strong enough to bend that wild surge before it swallowed everything in its path.

"We've got confirmation," the weatherman said, voice cracking. "The Lower Gryphon Reservoir has been breached. I repeat—the dam has broken."

His voice cracked on the word breached, and that was all I needed. I finished lacing up my boots, and my body moved before I finished the thought.

"It's time. Let's go."

Chairs scraped. Bags swung. Lorina knocked into a table hard enough to bruise, but didn't utter her characteristic curse—she was locked in.

I did a headcount without looking like I was doing a headcount.

Miles, Jake, Rene, Terry. Hanna was already rolling her sleeves. Miriam was pocketing salves. Betony, standing with B team, had that quiet steel in her spine that meant she was already preparing to suck any chaos out of the air, should she need to.

I turned toward Crystal, who waited patiently to cut a hole in space and carry us to the next battle. Too much was in motion. Too many threads pulling taut.

Too much could go wrong. And we were running out of time.

"Alright, Crystal," I said, my heart hammering in my chest like an out-of-control freight train. "Let's go."

$$\text{)O(}$$

Stepping through the portal felt like being wrung through layers of reality. One moment, I stood in the cool, coffee bean-scented air of my coffeeshop—now thick and uncomfortable with too many bodies and too much tension—and the next, I crossed the white-hot edge of the rift and landed in the pounding, humid downpour outside the cave.

The air hit like a weighted blanket soaked through. Rain slammed down in sheets, loud enough to drown thought, filling the world with its percussive sound. The soft drone of fans and murmured conversation behind us vanished instantly, replaced by thunder's distant growl and the slap of fat raindrops in the forest. It was a lot to absorb all at once, like every sense had been dialed to eleven, and I forced myself to take deep pulls of the heavy air to encourage my body to center itself.

The cave mouth yawned ahead, wide and dark. No, not just dark. Predatory, like the gaping maw of a shark. I didn't doubt that a few steps in, we'd find stalactites hanging like teeth, waiting to bite.

Let it go, Murph. If you start anthropomorphizing the damn cave, you're already losing.

Against my better judgment, I waved everyone through the mouth of the cave, more out of necessity than confidence. We needed shelter, and this was the one available. One by one, the others emerged from the portal's light and joined us under the stone lip. Still, I couldn't shake the feeling that the Bluebelow saw us coming.

Conall was the last through, materializing at my side just as I finished my mental pep talk and centering breaths. The portal behind him flickered and sealed with a snap of ozone and silence, the fading center glow reminding me of the edges of burned paper.

"You good?" he asked, voice pitched low. Like we'd already entered sacred ground.

I nodded wordlessly, not trusting myself to speak just yet for fear that my hesitation might shine through.

He touched my side, a palm's width of steady warmth. "Let me know if I can help, okay? Other than trying to fast-forward my premonition skills, that is."

I huffed a quiet breath, the closest thing I had to a laugh just then. I ran a hand through my rain-soaked hair, straightened my spine, and nodded. "I will."

He gave me a pat, then turned to sling his pack over one shoulder. He moved with an ease I envied—shoulders set, steps sure. Like whatever happened next, he'd already made peace with it.

And me? I wanted to find a dark corner, curl up, and wait for someone to tell me it was over. But I was the one who had to lead us in. That's what a Summate does, right? We carry the flame. Or we walk into the fire first and hope we can drag everyone back out.

Part of me itched to charge in alone, drag every drop of Summate magic up through my bones, and light the place up like a bomb strike. But that kind of reckless thinking was a fast track to a sealed tomb and a world without a Summate—assuming I was the only one. Real guns were off the table, too. I kept picturing bullets pinging off slick stone, ricocheting into someone's skull. Truth be told, I was still learning the shape of my power. Letting it loose inside the Bluebelow might be worse than bullets—louder, wilder, and a hell of a lot harder to control. The plan, if you could call it that, was to amplify the power of those who understood the extent of their gifts.

Forcing a stoic expression onto my weary face, I faced the party of brave souls who offered to join me in this mission—Rene, Jake, Terry, Lorina, DB, Ivor, Eli, LaDonna, Miles, Doyle, and Elidriel. Flashlights were pulled from backpacks and clicked on one by one, beams sweeping over wet stone and uneven ground. Ivor had a squat battery-powered lantern instead—practical and bright, its glow pooling in a wide circle on the cave floor. Which was pretty brilliant, honestly. A lantern could be set on the ground and still radiate light fairly well—better than a flashlight. At the moment, the light sources cast soft shadows, making the contours of the cave dance like something alive.

I had a strange feeling this might not be Ivor's first underground battle. I made a note to ask him later, if we survived the night.

Joey and Rafael were already at work casting protection

and pulling negative energy from the atmosphere. Miriam and Hanna put their heads together over Miriam's magical first aid kit—a weathered leather satchel that smelled of lavender, ironwort, and singed rosemary. Inside were beeswax-wrapped poultices for shock and spell burn, vials of red clover tincture to cool magical fevers, thread soaked in comfrey and ash for stitching enchanted wounds, and a roll of burn balm thick with calendula, plantain, and old green magic. A finger-length wand of lime wood, etched with generations of healing sigils, rested in a pocket. Hanna pulled out a bundle of dried elderflower and crumbled it into a small cauldron, her fingers moving with calm precision.

Miriam's eyes met mine briefly. No words passed between us, but the message was clear as day: they'd be ready if it went bad down there.

The air shifted as we reached the first bend in the stone wall. I glanced back once at the faint halo of daylight still clinging to the mouth of the cave, which was down to a sliver. I gave the gang staying behind a somber nod. No speeches. A wordless, heartfelt thank you. Then, I turned toward the throat of the cave and led the way in.

The deeper we moved, the more the storm faded behind us. The slap of fat rain pellets dulled. Thunder softened. The storm noise dropped away, swallowed by stone. Our footsteps echoed in soft crunches and dry scuffs, torchlight flickering over pocked limestone. The walls pressed close, damp and cold. Though the path beneath us stayed dry, the scent of minerals lingered—dusty, metallic, earthy as wet pennies left to rust.

The silence thickened. Not dead silence, but something close—a hush laced with magic, as if the cave itself had begun to drink us in—our breath, our heat, our spark. The passage, which had initially been large enough to allow a pickup truck to drive in easily, narrowed quickly. It smelled of dust, minerals, and long-forgotten water, like the inside of a tomb left undisturbed too long. There were no markings, no shimmer of magic, no signs that this cave was anything special. Just rock and shadow.

A slow doubt unfurled in my chest.

There are thousands of caves in these mountains. What if this isn't the Bluebelow?

The Appalachians are full of caves. It would be laughably easy to pick the wrong one and not realize it until something important failed to show up. Like the villainous coven performing some world-ending ritual.

I didn't want to say it out loud. But I was thinking it. Hard.

The light from our flashlights caught on jagged walls and outcroppings that looked like massive dinosaur ribs. Then, the passage narrowed until we passed through a tight bend that forced us to go single file while clutching our belongings close. At one point, Jake knocked his shoulder against the wall, banged his guitar case next, and muttered a curse.

"This place gives me hives," Terry said. "Like the cave senses that we're here, and it doesn't like it."

"Comforting," I muttered quietly, so the others wouldn't hear the edge creeping into my voice.

Still no signs of the Stygian. No whispers, no distant chanting or sudden *whoosh* as a spell flew past. No gurgle of the Tennessee River underfoot. Just the rhythm of our steps, our labored breathing, and the occasional scrape of someone adjusting their gear. Eli was right, though. The rock walls were an acoustic nightmare.

Then, without warning, the passage ended. Stone rose before us like the back of a beast—jagged, unyielding. It appeared that the earth had swallowed whatever path had once continued here. Unless someone had brought a pickaxe—and the will to tempt whatever lay buried—we weren't going any farther.

I stopped with a hand on my hip and exhaled slowly through my nose. "Well, that's just… perfect."

Terry caught up behind me, peered around my shoulder, flicked her flashlight back and forth, then up and down, and grunted. "Well, damn. This is some real Indiana Jones bullsh—"

"Wait." I squinted, flashlight angled just past where Terry's scan had left off.

There—off to the left. Easy to miss. A narrow crevice, nearly swallowed by shadow and stone, was tucked behind the jutting overlap of the rock wall. I shifted toward it, ducked slightly, and stepped through. My beam caught something manmade, or at least deliberately shaped.

Stairs. Worn stone, spiraling down. But unmistakable.

My stomach tightened—not with dread this time, but certainty. This *had* to be it. It had to.

I stepped closer, and that's when I saw off to the right, just above eye level, a carving in the stone so faint it could've passed for a trick of shadow. The letters weren't English. They belonged to something much older. Weathered by time but not erased, the script curled like vine work and flowed like smoke, etched just deeply enough into the rock to be laced with green-blue threads—like oxidized copper or lichen turned to glass. When my flashlight caught it, the color didn't just reflect the beam. It bent it, scattered it, and turned the light into a shimmer of broken moonlight across the wall.

Elidriel moved beside me without a word, raising her small fingers to trace the lines, her short fingertips caressing the stone as if she held the rock dear to her heart. Her eyes shimmered with emotion, as if she were listening to something inside the stone.

"It says," she murmured, voice low and sure, "Do not descend unless the song of the stone still knows your name."

The words slipped down the stairwell like breath through a reed pipe, echoing back in soft layers, a quiet chorus rising from the dark.

A hush settled over the group. Even Lorina didn't wisecrack.

I looked at the steps again. No doubt left now.

"We're in the right place."

It had to be.

Pointing my flashlight at the wall less than an arm's length away from me, I took the first cautious steps, one hand against the wall, flashlight in the other, and dying for a handrail. The walls were slick with moisture. Narrow and steep, the path downward was wide enough for one body at a time. The others followed in silence, their breath hushed, footsteps careful. The walls pressed in so near that if I extended my elbows, they'd brush against the rock on either side. Every inch forward felt like I was willfully stepping into a trap where the walls were too tight, the air too thick, as though the mountain itself wanted to swallow me whole. I flashed back to my earlier thought about a shark's mouth full of stalactite teeth. A few times, the passage was so narrow the wet stone scraped my shoulders. My mind went to Jake, the gentle giant, and how he must be walking sideways just to fit. I prayed he wasn't claustrophobic.

Each step downward echoed with faint, gritty scrapes, and the deeper we went, the thicker the darkness became. Not just absence-of-light dark. This darkness felt alive, pressing in on the edges of the flashlight beams like it wanted to absorb every tiny, battery-powered ray.

Finally, the cave opened before us, the narrow stairway spilling into a long, shallow chamber. I halted at the threshold, my eyes drawn to the strange light pulsing from the cave walls. Not firelight or reflection, but a soft glow, a faint shimmer that swelled and dimmed, curling across the stone like frost traced in blue-green fire. I stepped closer, drawn in despite myself, and reached toward the wall, only then realizing what I'd taken for some mineral sheen reflecting our lights was moss. The moss, delicate as lace, clung to the walls and glowed, its light subtle but insistent. In the center of the room, a basin of still, black water caught the glow, reflecting it back like some ancient mirror. The water was dark and unmoving, yet the tendrils of moss within it swayed lazily, moving with a grace that defied the stillness of the water itself.

Bioluminescent, blue-green, sentient life. Hidden in a magical cave. In a place so deep, where no light should ever reach. In a cave so old it felt like it had forgotten the sun.

Bluebelow.

I stopped short. My breath caught. And behind me, I heard the others draw in their breath as they rounded the last turn. No one spoke for a moment, mesmerized by the sight.

"What in Sam Hill…" LaDonna murmured, her voice soft, almost reverent.

The moss grew in delicate patterns, twisting and curling across the walls in ribbons. It pulsed beneath the water's surface, shimmering and undulating in slow motion, as if responding to some rhythm too distant for us to hear. The light moved with its own purpose, undisturbed by our presence, as if it had always been there, waiting for someone to find it.

I couldn't help but wonder how anything survived down here. There was no sun. No wind. No life, as far as I could tell. Just stone, water, and the timeless weight of old magic. And yet, here it was—this vibrant, glowing life, blooming in the deepest shadows, stubborn and defiant.

I had to respect that.

Elidriel moved past me, her gaze wide and luminous, eyes reflecting the greenish light that shimmered along the stone. She crouched near the water's edge, not touching it, but close enough that the glow rose brighter, casting gentle waves across her face. Her head tilted, listening not to sound but to something quieter, stranger. The moss responded. Its light pulsed softly in recognition. It didn't remember us—it couldn't—but it knew something in us. I felt it too, low and certain, a welcome that went deeper than sight. Whatever lived in those glowing strands had found a match in us that excited it.

It was sentient. This wasn't a plant we could march through in our haste to reach the Stygian and stop their ritual. We had to earn its trust.

"It's watching us," Elidriel murmured, her voice barely above a whisper. "No—not watching. Listening."

The moss near her hand shimmered brighter, responding to her words.

Jake leaned forward, his face creased with wariness. "Is that safe?"

Elidriel didn't answer immediately. She tilted her head as if listening to a voice we couldn't hear, and then spoke slowly, as though pulling the name from somewhere deep inside her. "It's whisperweed," she said. "Born of fae magic and moss. It fed on the sealing of the Bluebelow, and was born of the spell that was cast."

Rene frowned. "It's alive?"

"More than alive," Elidriel replied, her voice distant, lost deep within a recollection. "It knows things. It's… both animal and plant, sort of. Does that make sense?"

Eli stepped forward, rubber boots sloshing in shin-deep water, and we watched to see how the plant responded.

The whisperweed shifted, parting at first like the Red Sea for Moses. When Eli paused, the whisperweed slowly, curiously, like sea grass turning toward the current, returned.

Its blue-green glow deepened, and the tendrils closest to Eli rose. I was weirdly reminded of a curious dog sniffing a stranger. A hush fell that wasn't Eli's doing.

"It likes you," I noted.

Eli looked ahead, voice quiet as dusk. "Nothing about me to like. It just knows I'll listen."

LaDonna moved closer, her boots sending small ripples through the water. One of the glowing fronds rose toward her, brushing against her ankle like a curious child. She blinked, and then her eyes widened in something like disbelief.

"…Oh my stars," LaDonna breathed, her voice hushed with awe. "She's talking to me."

"Talking?" I asked, stepping closer, my curiosity piqued.

LaDonna's gaze stayed fixed on the moss, her voice low but full of a strange excitement. "Kind of… more like… showing me things. Not words. Feelings. Smells. Colors." She grinned. "Sass."

"Sass?" Rene asked, his voice deadpan but with the edge of a smile tugging at his lips.

LaDonna grinned sideways, her eyes bright. "Girl's got strong opinions."

I glanced at Elidriel, who was now stirring the onyx surface of the water with a finger, watching with amusement as the plant played keep-away with her finger.

"Elidriel," I asked quietly, "Is it safe? Can we… walk through the water if the moss is in there? I'd hate to, you know, hurt it."

Elidriel didn't answer right away. Her dripping fingers hovered just above the glowing strands of moss, a quiet connection passing between them. A tendril of moss reached from the glassy, rippling surface of the water and wound itself around a wet digit. My sister's face lit up, and she giggled with delight.

"It's safe," she said, sliding her arm into the center of the floating bouquet—the luminous plant-not-plant—and letting it curl around her like an otter at play. "It's... glad we're here. Well, glad *I'm* here. And that you're with me." Elidriel turned to me with a knowing look. "It will trust the others because we do."

My shoulders loosened. "OK."

"Touch it," she coaxed me.

I paused, but then figured we had to acquaint ourselves with the guardian of the cave if we wanted to make our way through. I stretched a hand toward a small, shy-looking mass of whisperweed. And then... I felt it.

The fae in me.

It didn't come on like fire or thunder. It was softer than that. A plangency in my chest, like an old bell being struck far beneath the surface. A thrum beneath my skin, in the bones of my fingers where the moss touched. It wasn't just reacting—it was reaching. Stirring something in me that had lain quiet my entire life. It was as if something deep within the stone, the roots, and the glow had reached back and recognized me.

My vision sharpened slightly. The moss brightened beneath my hand, not blinding, but attentive. I could feel it sensing me the way Elidriel had described—evaluating, absorbing, accepting. Not because of anything I'd done. But because of what I *was*.

Half-fae.

The whisperweed was calling to that part of me. And it wasn't just recognition—it was ignition. Something ancient uncurled in my blood, slow and sure as sunrise. Not power exactly, but awareness. Connection.

With Summate magic, I'd always known I was channeling something vast—the pulse of the universe flowing through me, elemental and alive. I could feel it enter and leave, bright and penetrating, like a current through copper. I shaped it and directed it, but it was never mine. I was the vessel. The thread pulled taut.

This was deeper. Older. I remembered what Elidriel had said days ago—how our magic was earth-based or organic, not precisely like the elements but rooted in the living weave of the world. At the time, I'd nodded as if I understood, and I had, on a surface level. But now…

Now I *knew*.

This wasn't something you cast or conjured. Fae magic was something you entered—something vast and breathing that didn't wait to be commanded. You didn't use it. You joined it. And in doing so, you stopped being separate.

It wasn't a force you shaped with will or wand. It was a tide that carried you, a pulse you sank into until your heartbeat matched its rhythm. There was no edge between body and world, no line between thought and power. You weren't touching the magic. You *were* the magic.

Fae magic was unity—undifferentiated, eternal. To wield it was to dissolve into it, to forget the borders of your skin and remember what it meant to be woven into the fabric of creation. Every element—earth, air, fire, water, spirit— wound through every other. A living tapestry without seams.

There was no *you* in fae magic. Only the weave. Only the whole. And the aching, beautiful truth that you had always been a part of it.

"Murphy," Elidriel said softly at my side. "You felt it, didn't you?"

I nodded, still caught in the glow, overcome with the raw

emotion of realizing how universal all things are.

"Yeah. I did."

She gave me a look, part proud, part worried. Then her focus shifted, her gaze going a little distant.

The whisperweed pulsed again near LaDonna's boots, sending a ripple through the water. "She's sharing more now," LaDonna frowned. "She tried to hold them back."

"The Stygian?" Rene asked, stepping forward.

LaDonna nodded. "They came through here. Forced their way in. Hurt her."

Her hand brushed the glowing strands near her boot, soothing them like a frightened animal. The moss responded, curling slightly under her touch and glowing brighter, almost pearlescent.

"She tried to block them—entangle them, keep them from finding what they were after. She fought to confuse them. Delay them. But it wasn't enough."

"Damn," Jake muttered, his eyes scanning the chamber like he could see ghosts of the conflict still drifting in the stone. "And they still made it deeper."

"They did." LaDonna's tone grew heavier and quieter with the weight of what the whisperweed had shown her. "They're not far now. And she's scared they're going to break the seal. That they'll unearth something that was never meant to come back."

A ripple passed through the moss as if to confirm her words—subtle but unmistakable. The glow dimmed near the far wall. A warning.

The cave wasn't just alive.

It was afraid.

Chapter 40

We slipped into the cave like ghosts, moving in single file, ever watchful. Eli led with Doyle now, his field of silence cloaking us in that vast psychic vacuum as we sloshed silently through the water. Conall strode on his heels, trailed closely by Rene and DB. I trekked in the center with La-Donna, Elidriel, and Terry, trying not to watch how the walls pulsed with the rising and falling glow of whisperweed. The nonstop motion, paired with the bobbing flashlight beams in the otherwise black cave, was making me oddly motion sick.

Soraya, Lorina, and Jake marched behind me and Crystal. Miles brought up the rear.

I kept glancing back at them—what I could see of them, anyway. Was Soraya wearing down? She looked old, but spry. Looks could be deceiving, though.

Jake and Lorina shot each other the occasional supportive look that said they were scared, but willing to be brave together. Those kids were my heart outside my body, and here they were, walking on a warpath. My heart twisted in my chest, guilt hitting me hard. These kids were risking everything to face the Stygian. At my request. If they didn't make it out alive tonight...

Stop thinking like that. Just fucking stop.

I pulled my gaze back to the front and forced my breathing steady. This wasn't the time to be soft. Not the time to spiral.

The air shifted.

Not in temperature or smell, but in that strange, visceral sensation that happens when something wrong enters the room. The Bluebelow responded first when the whisperweed flinched. That's the only way I can think to describe it. Only seconds earlier, the path shimmered in watery blues and pearlescent light. The next, it faded to a bruised, uncertain gray before dimming and vanishing as if cloaked. It reminded me of those feather-duster creatures in the ocean that slip into their tubes at the first hint of danger.

Without the glowing distraction, it was easier to see what lay ahead. They were just shadows at first, looming behind Doyle and Eli—too far for detail, but too wrong to ignore. The flashlight beams barely grazed the edge.

The Stygian remained oblivious, for now. We were so close it was a lucky thing they hadn't spotted us.

The altar sat at the end of a carved sub-chamber, slightly removed from the main tunnel. We held position maybe seventy meters back. Far enough that the Stygian circle, absorbed in their ritual, missed our presence, but close enough to feel the hum of the spell bleeding through the flattened boulder they were using as an altar. And though I didn't hear a thing—no chant, no footfall, not even the scrape of a boot over stone—something in my bones leaned back, like my body knew better than to stand tall.

Their ritual shimmered with shadow and a strange black that looked like rippling oil spilling upward. The air around them warped, like heat rising off frost instead of fire. Their magic spun in sickly arcs around the altar, dragging symbols from the heavy stone. Markings shimmered on the altar's surface in the dark—blood-red and twitching. Protective wards flipped inside out. Sacrificial geometry drawn in what could only be blood.

The stone pulsed like the heartbeat of a dragon. Whatever they were summoning… it wanted out. Badly.

Then one of them shifted slightly, a mere head turning, and black-violet color sprang to life on the stone. Not black like night, not even shadow-black. This was bruise-colored and wet, a glamor clinging to the altar's surface like a rotten shell. A façade. But beneath it, the shape continued to throb.

It occurred to me then: the pulse was breaking through Eli's spell, the one that had encased us in silence.

He kept the ambient sounds, remember? To make things feel natural. Not suspicious.

I tried to reassure myself with that thought, but this was more than that. I couldn't hear the Stygian chanting, didn't know the sound of their ritual—but the pulse, that heartbeat, had found its way to us.

That was when I saw *her.* Erica, high priestess of the Stygian. Renee's birth mother. But it wasn't her. It had her spiky blond hair and insanely bright blue eyes that I distinguished even from this distance. But she was just… *wrong.*

My stomach curled in on itself, my newfound fae blood pulling taut like wire. That thing, the entity they pulled from the depths, was wearing Ericka like a sleeve—but she wasn't the source. Just scaffolding. A frame built around something uninvited.

I caught a flicker of blood-rust red in the folds of her robe. Not dyed. Stained. Deep and iron-heavy, like the runoff from ancient wounds—the kind that never healed because they were never meant to. It clung to them like dried blood, crusted and permanent. That came from sacrifice. Old. Willing or not.

Smoke-gray ringed the figures—wisps dragging low like ash that had forgotten how to fall. That was illusion magic, curling in the margins. A veil meant to trick the eye and lull the mind. But underneath it, ember-orange pulsed. Not bright or warming. Like the memory of fire. A warning that something might still be burning, and it might burn you next.

Then came the green—iridescent and wrong. A beetle-shell gleam caught in a shaft of unnatural light. It shifted every time I tried to name it, like my brain refused to process the shape beneath. That was glamor again, but this time laced with chaos. The kind nature uses to bait predators and poison the bold.

But the worst was the void blue.

One of the Stygian lifted a hand like a conductor in slow motion. With a tilt of the shoulder and a measured sweep of fingers, the color opened in the hollow of its chest like a well. Like a mouth that never closed. It wasn't blue so much as an absence. Not the presence of darkness, but the place where light had never been. A color from before color. A wound in the spectrum.

And then, just when I thought I couldn't stand another second of watching, I saw it—threaded between the lines, caught in the cracks of the altar like a light that refused to die:

Gold.

Not the gaudy kind or the soft warmth of coin or candle-light. Not the sort of gold Ericka undoubtedly thought of when telling anyone who asked what variety of witch she was. This was fae-gold. Liquid and luminous, gilded thread spun straight from sunlight. It danced when the others faltered. It held when the rest unraveled.

The blood my ancestors gave.

It shimmered not from them, but despite them, rising from the seams of the stone, from the old carvings the Stygian couldn't fully unmake. It clung to the altar like a memory. Like defiance.

Like hope.

All of this registered in a handful of heartbeats. Then I blinked, shook my head, and made myself move. It was time to put our plan in motion. We'd already spent far too long getting there.

The Stygian hadn't seen me. Not yet. But the fae in my blood had seen them, and it didn't like what it knew. This ritual was coming to a head, and we needed to stop it. Like, now.

And then Crystal fell.

She made no sound, of course. I only knew because a blank space appeared in the corner of my eye where her body should've been. Like the universe had skipped a frame and left her behind.

I spun, my heart kicking hard into my throat.

She was on the ground, curled tight around herself. One arm pressed tight over her side where blood bloomed in pulsing crimson. One hand scrabbled against stone, fingers dragging through dust and grit where a hole she'd started to carve had sputtered out—just a smear of vanishing light in the air. A torn seam in space, unfinished. Her wrists were ruined. Snapped. Hanging in a way that made me cringe.

She'd known something was coming and had tried to cut us an exit. She'd tried to save us.

She'd failed.

Miles had already shifted halfway—veins bulging, bones stretching, lengthening and snapping into new angles, teeth slicing longer—but his growl vanished into the stillness. His mouth was wide in a roar, but the silence swallowed it whole, making it look like a silent horror film reel.

Jake shouted something—probably her name—but we couldn't hear it. His wide eyes conveyed his panic, his hand stretched toward Crystal like he could drag her back by will alone. Lorina clung to his free arm, her mouth frozen in a silent scream that even her sirenborn gift could not penetrate. Her gaze flicked to me, wild and pleading.

My body moved before my mind caught up.

No. No no no no no—

We shattered. Formation undone. Ants from a kicked nest. Some surged forward away from the attacker, possibly to regroup and strike once the danger was assessed. Others fell back in search of the thing that had struck her. Arms waving, eyes wide, everyone shouting without sound—flashlights slicing through the dark like frantic sky trackers, sweeping wild across stone and shadow. Everyone was shouting. No one could be heard. It was like trying to scream underwater.

We'd trusted the silence to cloak us, but now it clung too tight and had turned on us. Now the silence was too thick. A gift turned trap. A quiet turned into a chokehold. It hugged us like a bag pulled over the head. A noose drawn tight.

I reached Crystal just as something peeled itself out of the shadows. At first, I thought it was a man, tall and thin, but then it stepped forward—or maybe it didn't step so much as ripple—and I realized it didn't have a face. No mouth. No eyes. Just a suggestion of a head where a head should be. It was built of smoke and stitched together with something darker, and where its fingers should've been, there was only blackness, seeping like oil from a cracked engine. It had mustered enough of a substantial hand to grip her ankle to drag her back into the deeper dark.

Then Miles hit it.

No warning. No sound. Just the sudden blur of teeth and claw and motion, as Miles slammed into the thing with a force that would have cracked bone, if the thing had any. Miles' hands weren't hands anymore, not really. They were talons. His mouth split wider than any human's should've, and he ripped the shadow-thing open, scattering it like ash caught in a wind that didn't belong to this world.

It didn't scream. It couldn't. It just vanished.

Had it been part of the cave? One of the Stygian? Were there more of them behind us waiting?

Crystal's eyes locked on mine—wet with pain, sharp with understanding—and I felt the truth settle before we could speak it. I followed her gaze to her fingers bent wrong, trembling with the effort not to curl inward. Her hands were broken. Useless. She knew it. He knew it.

The aerocleaver was out of commission. The tear she'd planned to use for us to escape whatever had attacked her was unfinished. Whatever power she'd called on had slipped through her now broken fingers.

There would be no door. No clean cut through space. Our chance at a quick escape was as shattered as her hands.

Miles dropped beside her, his chest heaving with heavy breaths, half-shifted and shaking with the power it took to evolve. His hands hovered over her, uncertain—ready to lift her and carry her out. DB stood at his side, prepared to assist. But Crystal shook her head, barely. A flick of her eyes. The faintest movement of her poor, broken wrists.

Still, she met their eyes with unyielding steel and gave them the smallest nod. Not a plea, not surrender—permission. A command.

Stay. Fight.

Miles hesitated. Just for a breath as he held her gaze and made sure she meant it. Then he rose. He and DB joined the others.

I didn't. I stayed frozen, just for a moment, staring at her—at those shattered hands, the blood flowing from her, that fierce light still burning behind her eyes—and I asked myself the question no one wanted to voice.

What if we didn't come back?

What if the Stygian tore through us, leaving nothing but blood on the altar and echoes in the stone? What if that thing inside Ericka broke free—and Crystal, alone in the dark with her broken hands and fading flashlight, was the last one standing?

She wouldn't be able to defend herself. She didn't look able to run. She could barely sit upright. If another creature like the one that had already crushed her came crawling out of the dark again—who would be there to save her?

I imagined her fumbling through the Bluebelow with nothing but a dying light and pain-soaked breath, bleeding with every step as she dragged herself through shadows that called her by name. I imagined her screaming. I imagined no one hearing.

And I thought—for the barest second—about pulling Doyle or Miles back, sending one of them to guide her to the cave mouth. But we didn't have that kind of luxury. Not anymore. We needed every soldier we had, every spell, every hand that could still lift a blade or cast a ward. This wasn't just Lughaidh versus the Stygian.

This was the Numinari trying to save the world from chaos.

And knowing all that, I couldn't bring her with us. Not into that ritual space. Not into the teeth of it.

Crystal couldn't fight. She couldn't cast. She couldn't even fall back without someone to catch her. Ultimately, her one contribution to the fight—her ability to help us evacuate—had been ripped from her, leaving her a frail, damaged human.

It was a brutal equation, but the answer was clear. If she stayed here, she might survive. If we failed, maybe someone would find her. The B team would eventually realize we weren't coming back out. Maybe Crystal would be the one to tell the world what happened in the Bluebelow.

Or maybe she'd die quietly with the echo of our failure trembling through the stone.

I fought to keep from flinching at the thought and forced an expression on my face that showed I, too, had accepted her request to be left where she was.

But she had made the call before I could. She knew what this moment required.

Still, I couldn't walk away without doing something—leaving somebody to watch over her. Even if that somebody was a sentient plant.

I took a few steps to my right, reached toward the cavern wall, and laid my fingers against the darkened whisperweed. Even now, it felt quiet beneath my hand—sleeping, hiding, or waiting. Maybe all three.

Recalling how I'd felt when the first understanding of how fae magic hit me, I didn't try to cast or focus on a spell.

I just… let go. Let that fae part of me—the part I usually kept buried under instinct and fear and sarcasm—rise and overwhelm me. It felt like stepping into cold water while holding my breath, then having the breath rush out and realizing I could breathe underwater.

Everything went wide and strange.

The cave pulsed against my ribs. My thoughts blurred. I felt everything—the lichen on the stone, the wet tension of moss roots gripping rock, the gentle breath of spores.

And it didn't stop there.

The whisperweed stretched its roots farther than I'd ever imagined, threading through the stone like a netting. I felt them dip into quiet pools beneath the surface, drink from underground streams no map had ever touched. I sensed the rhythm of the cave's heartbeat powered by magic and the pulse of whatever power lay within. Slow, steady, vast. The air we breathed had been filtered through stone so old it remembered when this mountain was still raw and weeping.

And I knew things.

I knew half of the water surging through the cave now was runoff from the broken reservoir Dylan was trying to hold back. I could taste the iron in it, the chemicals meant to purify it, the panic clinging to its edges like static. I could feel the pressure building in the tunnels not from above, but below—where old channels had cracked and redirected and multiplied under the weight of eons of water rushing through and breaking it down one microscopic bit at a time.

I knew which caverns had collapsed generations ago, which were hollowed out by tree roots that had long since died, and which walls could be broken with the right vibration.

I could feel the altar stone ahead—the one the Stygian had corrupted—and the massive amount of energy it had been imbued with to keep the power beneath it trapped for hundreds of years. I felt the gold light inside it shimmer and recoil, trying to hold its shape as the ritual wrapped around it like a snare. The same gold that lived in me. I didn't have to see it to know it was still fighting, rising from the seams in that black rock like a final act of defiance.

For one endless moment, I was everything. I was the dark and the water and the air inside all of us. I was the whisperweed hiding from the Stygian. I was the blood crusted on the stone. I was the memory of every witch who'd ever died trying to keep this place sealed.

It was beautiful. It was unbearable.

Make me one with everything, I thought, and almost laughed, because of course that damn hot dog joke about the Buddhist would come back now, of all times—even as my chest ached from holding too much.

At that moment, I knew the whisperweed noticed me in return.

Not in words. There were no words here, not the way La-Donna heard them, but a shift in focus, a soft awareness coiling through the roots like breath through alveoli, saturating the bloodstream. It reached back, hesitant but not afraid. Curious.

I shaped the thought as gently as I could.

Hey, I whispered, or maybe just thought; at the moment, everything was everything, and it was hard to tell where my thoughts became images or feelings. *Stay dark for now. But if things go bad for us… please light up. Show whoever needs to know where she is so they can carry her out.*

The presence didn't answer in sound. But it rippled. A nod made of breath and stone and moss. The faintest echo of consent. Then it slipped away, retreating to relative safety.

The weight of everything receded. I was just Murphy again, knees pressed into the cave floor, up to my ass in water, breath shaky, skin damp with sweat.

But I knew the whisperweed had heard me. It would remember. That would have to be enough.

And somewhere ahead—beyond the shimmer of heatless flame and the ritual's twisted light—the Stygian chanted. Still unaware, held captive by the ritual they trusted to bend the world to their will.

But not for long.

Chapter 41

Now we stood by the light of our flashlights ankle-deep in cold cave water, the Stygian lining the far end of the cave writhing like shadows come loose from their anchors. We were wrapped in thick, oppressive silence, but despite that, we were lucky the beams of our flashlights hadn't given away our presence. Eli's gift was held tight around us, muting every footstep and every breath, but it did nothing to reduce the shafts of light we carried.

If they heard us, if they saw us, we wouldn't get a second chance.

Their voices rose—not loud, but each syllable somehow laced with violence. Each word of the ritual forced their dark magic into the stone like a nail into a coffin. One of them hissed something guttural and frantic. No translation needed. They were reaching the ritual's apex.

I raised a hand to Ivor, who stood behind me like a race-horse waiting for the gate to rise.

He caught my signal, grinned like a lunatic, and gave me a salute that would've been ridiculous if I wasn't emotionally hanging on by a thread.

"Do it," I mouthed, pointing at the Stygian.

He nodded, turned toward the ritualists, and bent at the waist like he was limbering up for a keg stand, which surprised me. I don't know what I expected. Maybe a war cry. A

wave of his hands and jagged bolts of electricity shooting
from his fingertips. Maybe a spark shower and us all getting
fried like trout.

"Cover your eyes," he said, his lips moving exaggeratedly
so I understood. Then he pantomimed the action he wanted
us to take.

And maybe I should've. But I didn't. If I was going to get
the shit shocked out of me, I wanted to see it coming.

Ivor leaned down, fingers brushing the water's surface—
and just like that, something changed. The mischief drained
from his face, leaving behind a gravity that made him look
less like a cartoon sidekick and more like a serial killer. A
surge of power snapped out of him, wild and bright and bless-
edly directional. It shot across the water, arcing with serpen-
tine grace, then splintered into blasts that struck the Stygian
dead-on as they reached the crescendo of their ritual. They
didn't even have time to scream properly. Just a sharp, collective gasp, and then they collapsed, one by one. Limbs locking, muscles seizing, magic shorted out like a broken circuit.

A hum bloomed in my jawbone, like metal striking bone.
My fillings buzzed their protest, but the current had veered
cleanly Stygian-ward.

With the Stygian down, Eli released the spell of silence,
and sound rushed back in. The soft lap of water returned,
along with a faint sigh of wind through the tunnel. I heard the
small, raw sounds of my people behind me—breath dragged
in, chests loosening, bodies moving.

"Guess Ivor can aim," I muttered. "Note to self: never un-
derestimate Sparky."

"I heard that," he called, proud and smug and absolutely
not sorry. His happy-go-lucky expression had returned, thank
the stars. That last face scared the boots off me.

From behind me, LaDonna stepped forward—one palm

lifted, the other trailing fingertips through the whisperweed, which responded the instant her fingers touched it. The moss rose in slow, luminescent tendrils, reaching for her like it knew who we were fighting and was ready to help.

She didn't say a word. Just thought, and the Bluebelow listened.

The whisperweed unfurled toward the fallen Stygian with quiet purpose, curling around wrists, ankles, and mouths, binding them tight. Those who still twitched were caught mid-motion. The restraint wasn't cruel. It was clean. Elegant. As if the cave had grown tired of rot being whispered into its bones.

"Go," LaDonna said, her eyes locked on mine. "See what you can learn about the ritual. I've got this."

I nodded, the water around my legs shifting with each slow step toward the altar, stepping over knocked-out Stygian as I went. Conall followed close behind.

The nearer we got, the more my stomach roiled. The silence at the altar was absolute, and the atmosphere on the dais felt like walking into a room mid-spell and realizing the prayer wasn't to a friendly deity, but to something deeper, older, and horribly darker. My ears rang as I approached, and my skin felt slick and hot as if oil hovered above the altar like humidity. Colors swirled in the air—threads of spellwork still unraveling, unfinished, twitching like nerves with nowhere left to fire. I didn't move them. I was afraid I'd chase it somewhere worse.

The altar had sunk into the floor, black and glass-smooth, as if carved from obsidian. Its surface glistened beneath the drifting lights, slick with ritual ointments. Glyphs lined its edge—old fae markings clashing against the newer human script. The two weren't woven together. They were at war, forced into an unnatural, argumentative marriage. The

writing looked bent, like it had been dragged through someone else's nightmare and barely stitched back together.

Terrified of what I might encounter, I lit the Summate
flame inside me, heightening my senses.

That's when I noticed it. The dais rose with each slow
breath of the cave, then sank again. A shallow rhythm pulsed
beneath my feet, steady and *alive*. The water around my legs
responded in kind, rippling in time.

The altar was breathing.

Not a metaphor. Not poetic flourish.

Breathing.

And the heartbeat—gods. It wasn't just sound. It emitted
a low, wet *lub-dub* that echoed like a drum made from moving chambers of pure magic. The motion wasn't confined to
the stone; it thumped in my chest, in my bones, in the blood
behind my eyes.

That's when I noticed the walls weren't echoing the
sounds our movement made as every other tunnel in the Bluebelow had—they were absorbing it. Every other tunnel had
bounced our steps back at us like sonar. Not here. Upon the
altar, the quiet reached deep into the walls, the floor, the
bones of the cave itself. Folding every footstep, every whisper, every sound in its vicinity into its mantle. Layered like
sediment. Built on top of itself so that any sound in its presence was pulled into a magical vortex.

And that's when things really clicked. The altar wasn't
just a focus point. It was a seal.

Yes, the ancients who carved this place had created a
magnificent resonance chamber laced with fae magic and
tuned with terrifying precision. But not to amplify. To suppress. To sedate.

To cage.

Something vast and terrible had been locked beneath my

feet. Not a beast, or a god, or anything made of flesh or form, but of sound and of will. A being born of pure vibration. A consciousness woven entirely from frequency, pattern, and tone. Magic that had grown aware of itself. Bound by the perfect spell, a unique harmony that kept the sentient resonance within the cave.

The Bluebelow was its prison, and the altar was perfectly tuned silence, engineered to keep the thing that loomed beneath my feet dreaming.

And the Stygian, with their crooked chords and stolen spells, had been rewriting the song. Loosening the locks. Undermining the chord structure that held it still and humming its name back into the world.

It was listening now. The hair on my arms rose in fear. It felt us. Every step, every tremble in the water, every breath in our lungs. Through the threads of their ritual, it was already reaching, stretching toward an ultimate crack in the chorus that held it bound.

If it got out… if we accidentally triggered the wrong notes and ended the Stygian's ritual… no spell would matter. Humanity wouldn't lose its mind overnight—but it would forget how to have one. The power of the resonance would warp our current reality, bending cognition until we lost the thread of thought entirely—empty vessels with no sense of self.

The Stygian weren't just breaking a seal. They were trying to *unmake* thinking. To end the age of reason. To erase the very concept of comprehension. To turn us back into our reptile-brained selves. Talk about fucking chaos.

My knees nearly buckled. How had Ericka sold her coven on this madness? Promised to free the world from mental slavery? Pitched it as some kind of primal truth the world desperately needed?

Ultimately, it didn't matter how she'd done it. She had.

And now we had to undo it.

Jake stood still, his body alert, but not afraid. His head tilted slightly, as if catching a song others couldn't hear. His fingers moved as if already plucking a tune on his guitar in his mind—not nervously, but like they already knew the shape of the counterpoint and were ready to play. A discord. A note played loud enough, long enough, to fracture the bones of the song.

Lorina had gone silent too, though her lips trembled faintly, mouthing a melody that hadn't been born yet, but lived deep in her sirenborn blood.

They didn't need instruction, because the Bluebelow had already chosen them.

☽ O ☾

Jake pulled his guitar from the black case and scanned the cave like he might magically find a dry patch where none had existed five seconds ago. No luck. He sighed, leaned the case upright against the least-soaked stretch of cave wall like a soggy tombstone, and slung the strap over his shoulder. His hand drifted to the tuning pegs, then stopped—fingers hovering like he'd just remembered where we were and understood the potential implications of hitting the wrong note. Adjusting anything down here felt like playing Jenga with fault lines. Literally.

He paused. Tilted his head. *Listened.* After a beat, he plucked a single string.

The altar recoiled. The Bluebelow shuddered like a throat gagging on a word it refused to swallow.

I didn't have time to ask if he'd felt it too, because Soraya moved forward, stepping into the shallows like she already knew what was waiting in the dark. Her voice was soft, but it carried weight. "Wait," she said, and my breath caught. "Something's here."

She crouched low, fingers gliding across the slick stone floor as if she could read the cave's surface like Braille. The whisperweed drew back from her—I sensed not in fear, but in reverence. It moved like it recognized her, or maybe the staff she always carried. Her hand paused, then closed around something hidden beneath a thin veil of silt.

When she lifted it, my breath went cold. A length of bone surfaced in her palm—long, smooth, gleaming faintly with cave water. Not animal. My gut recognized the curve of it before my mind caught up. Human rib bone, it seemed.

A hush swept through us.

Soraya met my gaze, her eyes sharp with understanding. "They used bodies in the first spell," she said. "These aren't casualties. They volunteered. They gave themselves to the Bluebelow to keep it sealed. To cage what's buried underneath."

The chill in my chest tightened like a fist. Rene inhaled beside me, and I caught the flicker of silver in his eyes grow as his magic lit up in response. "She's right," he said. "Their essence is woven into the spell. Blood, breath, bone—it's all part of the structure. That's why a mere spell won't free the creature underneath. Why it needs a ritual that induces the perfect sounds."

Terry's hand twitched at her side, then rose slowly, almost against her will. She pointed toward the edges of the altar, toward the darkest places between the stalactites and whisperweed. "They're still here," she said, and the tone in her voice made my skin prickle.

I turned to her. "Ghosts?"

"No," she said. "More like… witnesses."

Shapes emerged, neither solid nor imagined. Not moving,

but watching. Faint, spectral, but not ghosts in the traditional sense. Echoes, maybe. Imprints of the ones who gave themselves to the first sealing.

Elidriel stepped into the ripple of their presence, her voice low and laced with that eerie clarity I suspect only the fae can summon.

"Their names are unknown, lost to time, and they can't speak. But... I hear them."

She knelt, placing one hand flat on the water's surface. The whisperweed responded immediately, flaring bright and blue-green beneath her touch. Shadows danced across the cave walls as if the light were breathing with us. Her eyes went distant. Her mouth opened—but what came out wasn't language.

It was a melody. Strange, haunting, and carved from somewhere far older than anything human. It resonated through the Bluebelow like a tuning fork struck at the center of the world. Not like Lorina's music. Definitely not human. But not entirely fae, either. Something braided between blood and memory, sorrow and purpose.

Soraya's staff flared in response, the carved top glowing like embered bone. A presence rose from within the wood, half-formed and eerie, not unlike the spectral fae lingering at the altar's edge. But this one had a face—or the suggestion of one—etched in spirals and sigils that shimmered where eyes should have been. It hovered above her hand, weightless and watchful, then drifted toward the bone she held in her other hand, extending a single gesture that sliced clean through the space between us.

"You carry a spirit with you inside the staff?" I asked, surprised by the rasp in my voice.

"My mother," she said, barely louder than breath. "She can ask them whatever you need. If they're willing to speak."

I turned just enough to catch Conall's expression. He looked like he wanted to step in front of me, throw an arm across my shoulders, and pull me back from whatever line I was about to cross, but he didn't move. He swallowed hard, eyes never leaving mine, and gave me a nod.

I licked my lips, unsure if the dampness clinging to my skin was sweat or cave water, and prayed my voice would hold.

"What…" I started, then steadied myself. "What do we need to do to reverse the ritual?"

Soraya nodded once, then extracted four small bones from a pouch at her waist. The Summate part of me tuned into Soraya's power and instinctively knew they were human finger bones. She tucked her staff under the crook of her elbow, uttered a single-word incantation, turned her palm, and let the bones fall into the other hand. They clicked against her skin with a sound too precise to be chance. They arranged themselves instantly: a perfectly symmetrical X—four bones touching at the center like they'd been drawn by a compass. Soraya inhaled, sharp and sudden. When she spoke again, her voice had gone thin with awe.

"Four keys. Four frequencies. Four bloodlines."

I felt the shift in my chest before I understood it—a tightening behind the ribs, sharp as a harp string drawn too taut. I looked at the faces surrounding me, each lit by the wavering blue-green light of whisperweed and holding more than fear. Recognition. Purpose. Maybe even a little grief for those who'd died before us.

"Elidriel," I said. "Fae."

"Rene," Conall murmured, turning toward him. "Silver witch."

"Lorina," Terry added, nodding toward the girl, whose lips had begun to shape a melody I couldn't hear yet.

"Sirenblood."

I swallowed. My throat felt tight, too thick to speak easily. But I did anyway.

"And me. Both fae and human. The Summate."

The weight of it wasn't sudden. It sank in slowly, like the river water Dylan couldn't hold back gradually filling the cave. Undeniable, cold, and final. This wasn't some prophecy waking up through us. This was damage—deliberate, surgical—and we were the ones left to stitch the wound before it festered wide open.

The seal hadn't just been forged long ago—it had been tuned. Held in delicate, deliberate harmony by bloodlines that now echoed through us. The Stygian had cracked the chord. We weren't here to finish a song.

We were here to rewrite it.

Four voices. Four powers. Four frequencies ready to counter the wrong note before it took root.

And, gods willing, we'd be loud enough to lock it down for good.

Chapter 42

We were seconds from starting the counterspell when I felt it—not a sound, but a profound silence. The Bluebelow trembled beneath us, disturbed yet again.

I turned, hand raised to cast a protective spell, instincts screaming—but I didn't see them. Not at first.

LaDonna did.

She was three steps away from where Elidriel stood with us on the altar, hands raised, lips just beginning to part. She might've been about to speak. Might've been trying to warn us.

Then the shadows broke.

Two of them—Stygian—peeled out of the dark like black ink dropped in clear water, cloaked in magic so thick it masked their presence until they were *already there*. No sound, no shimmer, just sudden violence erupting from nothing. One lunged for Elidriel, blade flashing from the folds of his robe. He was too fast. Too close. I couldn't lash out with an attack spell for fear of hitting Elidriel.

LaDonna moved without hesitation. No shield, no spell. Just her. She stepped between, arms wide, taking the blade meant for someone else.

There was no scream. Just the dull sound of impact, then the thud of her knees hitting stone as her body collapsed into itself. It didn't feel real—not at first. One moment, she was standing. The next, she was down like a marionette with its strings cut.

Elidriel screamed.

I was already moving, boots skidding through water, my hand stretched and ready to heal—but it didn't matter. La-Donna was bleeding profusely, her lifeblood rapidly soaking into the whisperweed as the plant curled around her like a creature trying to hold her soul in place.

Doyle was on the first attacker before I could even blink, his body a blur of rage and fangs. He hit the Stygian like a wrecking ball, slamming him into the cave wall with a sound that cracked bone. There was a grunt, then a sickening snap, and the man's body slid down the rock like meat that no longer remembered how to stand. The Stygian's body spasmed, then stilled.

DB stepped into the fray with a grin that should've been a warning. The second attacker turned just in time to catch the full brunt of him—fire lashing from DB's open mouth in a torrent of orange-gold flame. The heat hit like a furnace cracking wide. The Stygian screamed, staggering back as his clothes caught, his silhouette twisting in the steam rising from the water surrounding his calves. DB advanced with fire still pouring from his throat like a dragon, golden eyes gleaming like lit coals. The man collapsed into the shallows, smoke writhing from his body, and didn't rise.

They were dead. The threat was neutralized. But none of it mattered.

I dropped to my knees beside LaDonna. My hands hit the water hard, sliding across the slick stone and into her blood, thick and warm and too much. Far, far too much. The moss beneath her pulsed in panic, glowing brighter with each beat of her fading heart, curling up her sides like it was trying to hold her together. My hands were already soaked in red fluid, fingers sliding across her chest, trying to find the wound, trying to undo what couldn't be undone. Blood slicked my skin, warm and thick, and the smell of it—too metallic, too real—dragged me straight back into the worst moment of my life when my birth mother was struck by a Stygian knife.

"LaDonna…" I breathed, barely aware of my own voice. It rasped out of me like wind through a broken flute. "No, no—please…"

It smelled like copper and water. It sounded like nothing. The worst moments always do.

Her eyes fluttered open—just barely—but they found me. Her beautiful forest-green eyes locked onto mine. Not panicked. Not afraid. Just calm, knowing.

"Look at you," she whispered, voice a thin ribbon fraying at the edges. "Still burning with that fire… just like your mother did."

The words punched straight through me. I shook my head, tears threatening but refusing to fall.

"Don't. Don't do that. Don't talk like that. We can fix it—my magic. There's got to be a way. I fixed Conall…"

Her smile barely moved her mouth, but it was there. Sad, and sweet, and solid. "You were never meant to fix everything, baby. It's alright. I knew this road might end here."

Her blood-slick hand found mine. I held it like an anchor, a promise, a prayer.

"Please," I said again, the word slipping from my lips like a child's last hope. "Please, not you, too."

She didn't answer right away. Just looked past me, into the depths of the Bluebelow. I don't know what she saw—maybe nothing. Maybe everything.

"Your roots run deep," she whispered. "Always remember that. Even scorched earth can grow again."

And then her eyes closed, her muscles went soft, and she went utterly still.

The moment didn't shatter me with sound—it caved me in from the inside, quiet and merciless. It cracked along the same fault line that first split open when I was ten, standing beside my mother during a ritual gone wrong, watching her shocked eyes lock onto mine as a knife protruded from the back of her neck, and she mouthed the word *run*. That day, I had nothing—no power, no voice, and no way to stop it. But this time was worse. This time, I had everything. Every color. Every gift. All the power a witch could hold. And still, it hadn't been enough.

All the magic in the world hadn't been enough.

The moss hummed around her body, curling up her sides like it was meant to shield her from death. It pulsed low, a lullaby written in grief, and for a long, breathless minute, I just sat there, holding her cooling hand.

The others didn't stand back—they came closer. Conall crouched beside me, his hand resting gently on my back, saying nothing but holding me steady like he always did when the world tilted sideways. Rene knelt on LaDonna's other side, head bowed, his silver-lit eyes shuttered tight like he was shielding her memory from the storm gathering within him. Soraya murmured a prayer I didn't recognize under her breath. Miles stood over us like a sentinel, jaw clenched, body half-shaking with the rage he hadn't burned through yet. Terry stood, hands folded, tears pouring silently into the water at her feet. Even DB looked too solemn for words.

The Bluebelow had gone still, holy, sacred in its silence. As if it recognized what had just been lost. What I had become.

A child once abandoned to death. A woman now, carved by it.

"Murphy," Elidriel said softly, her voice like wind through leaves, "I'm so sorry—but we can't wait much longer. The Stygian cracked the seal's foundation. If we don't close it soon…"

I clenched my jaw so hard it hurt. I wanted to scream. To collapse. To burn this cave down to stone and ash for daring to take another mother from me.

It wasn't fair. *It wasn't fucking fair.*

I needed time. A breath. One goddamn moment to fall apart.

But I wouldn't get it. The seal was calling, tugging at the magic in my blood, the spellwork coiling in my bones, demanding I rise. The music was there. The Summate power in me sensed it buried beneath the grief, muffled under all the weight I hadn't asked to carry. It felt like trying to sing through mud. Like dragging melody out of a raw, open wound.

And still… it was mine.

LaDonna's blood was literally on my hands. Her voice still echoed in my head. Her roots ran through me. And if I couldn't grieve the way I wanted, I'd grieve the only way I could.

With power.

With rage.

With magic so potent, it could split stone and shake gods.

So, no gods wouldn't help me. *I* would help me. And the silence I longed to clutch to my soul?

I was about to set it on fucking fire.

Chapter 43

I stood.

Not all at once—there was no strength left for that—but I rose, bone by bone, breath by breath, like a zombie clawing its way out of the earth. My knees wobbled. My spine screamed. My hand slipped in LaDonna's blood mixed with water as I pushed upright, but I didn't fall. Her body slipped into the water, buoyed by whisperweed that cradled her reverently.

The air tasted like blood and the mineral tinge of the cave passage, thick with copper and ozone and a grief so raw it should've burned. My hands dripped with LaDonna's life, and something inside me broke open—not with a whimper, but with a howl.

The Source answered.

It didn't come gently. My Summate magic roared to the surface, not summoned but triggered, ignited by sorrow so hot it was incandescent. Every color surged at once, flaring like stars in a dying sky. Red. Green. Blue. White. Indigo. Yellow. Silver. Rose. Brown. Black. Orange. Hell, colors I'd never experienced rose within me like wisdom I'd always known but had forgotten.

All of it.

A scream caught in my throat—but I didn't let it loose. I forged it into focus.

Magic arced over my skin like lightning sparking from bone. The water hissed around my boots, whisperweed parting in reverence. The Bluebelow felt me now. Not just as a witch. As a *force*.

"I am Murphy Blackwell," I said, voice jagged with fury and grief, "Summate of the Lughaidh coven. Born of every color. Fed by fire, forged in blood."

Power pulsed outward in rings—red heat, silver shimmer, black weight.

The seal was cracked. The ritual had been marred, and the creature below was on the verge of escape if we didn't fix its prison soon. The Stygian had fought to overcome us again. But we were still here.

My hand reached back, fingers spread wide. Rene took it without hesitation, his power shimmering across my skin, cool and steady, a lens sharpening my fury into purpose.

Lorina's right hand found mine, her power humming with pitch-perfect resonance.

Jake took a step forward, and I *pushed* an extra boost of power into him and through him, tuning his guitar without plucking a string. His fingers slid across the strings that now radiated with magical sound—rich, deliberate, complex. The first note rang out like a massive bell struck in a church tower as his blue magic gift poured from his hands, spiraling around the circle like a ribbon of sound. His magic didn't just accompany the spell. It scaffolded it, each strum a stabilizing beam for what we were about to build.

I turned to Elidriel, who stood now like an avenging spirit—hair wild, face streaked with tears, blood, and whisperweed. Her lips trembled, but her eyes blazed with ancient fire. She hadn't known LaDonna the way I had. But she knew what had been lost.

Her voice hardened, trembling with grief she couldn't

name but still felt.

"We finish this. In her honor."

"We finish it," she said. "In her name."

I stepped to the altar's edge, into the seam of LaDonna's blood and the old ward lines carved centuries before I ever breathed. The lines lit up beneath my boots—slow, unsure, like they needed convincing. Like even the magic wasn't sure if I could carry this.

So, I made it sure.

"I am Murphy Blackwell," I said aloud, my voice low, guttural. "Summate witch. Daughter of Ryan Oisin Turner and Nora Elizabeth Blackwell. Blood of the fae, fire of the South, power of the Bluebelow. This is my line. My land. My people."

Elidriel's voice came next, fractured, yet sure. "I give the blood that remembers," she said, her voice not hers alone but ancestral. Timeless. She raised a hand slick with LaDonna's blood, and the moss responded with a high, luminous keen.

"I call the voice that binds," Lorina said, and sang a frequency so pure it made the Bluebelow shudder. Her voice, when it came, wasn't words. It was legacy—a call born of sea-deep blood and old songs buried beneath salt and silence. The sound rose from her not merely as magic, but as inheritance. A siren's gift, awakened. The note curled through the chamber like a ribbon of silver light, hitting octaves no human throat should reach, echoing off the wet stone in harmonics that made the very walls vibrate.

It wasn't beautiful. It was commanding. It bent the Bluebelow's resonance to our will and twisted the frequencies of the Stygian's corruption into something cleaner. It gave structure to the spell—gave it spine.

The altar shook as the stream below surged upward in a thin spiral, rising to arc over my palm like liquid glass. Cool.

Clear. Alive.

"I call the silence that shields," Rene intoned, and the air dropped around us like velvet. The guardian spirits hovering nearby stepped closer, prepared to resume their task.

And me?

I gave it everything else.

"I give the fire that answers," I said, and the ground lit beneath us, Summate magic spilling from my pores like sunlight cracking through storm clouds.

I didn't need a sigil, or salt, or an athame. I *was* the circle.

Jake shifted to a minor chord—melancholy, meaningful, beautiful. His magic caught the frequencies of each voice and amplified them. He layered music magic over Lorina's frequency in shimmering blues. Her siren tones still rang through the chamber, harmonizing with the instruments and spells like tides drawn to the moon.

And then I felt the others.

Miles, his voice a gravel-deep hum beside us. Soraya's prayer wound around Jake's chords like ivy. Terry's trembling alto cracked through her tears—raw, real, deeply human.

Even Ivor added to the spell. He didn't sing—but gods, did he sing. Lightning arced from his fingertips in bursts of neon and flame, bolts of technicolor voltage that lit the chamber like a storm painted in madness and meaning.

And then DB stepped forward, fire curling from his mouth. His magic danced through the air like a dragon on the wing—coiling, sweeping, bold. It twined with Ivor's lightning, not clashing but courting, like two forces that had been waiting their whole lives to find each other in the storm.

The Summate power thrumming through me recognized it, absorbed it, and tuned it. Each strike, each flare, moved in sync with the colors pulsing beneath my skin. Red. Indigo.

Yellow. Blue. Dancing with my grief, my fury, my will. Electricity and flame became harmony. The storm within me became structure.

And the Bluebelow howled.

It felt us—the unity, the magic, the sacrifice, and remembered its purpose. The ancient task, long slumbering beneath stone and water, stirred awake. The seal's keeper had returned.

"By blood and root, by stone and storm, we seal the wound and remember the price!"

From the corner of my eye, I saw DB step in behind Elidriel. He didn't break the chain. He dipped his head low, almost like he was preparing to whisper to Elidriel.

Then he opened his mouth, and fire ignited the altar.

Not wild. Not angry. Focused, like a well-honed blade, it jetted from between his lips in a tight stream, white-gold and clean. The sigils the Stygian had carved across the altar bubbled on contact, blackening, then flaking away like old ash. I could smell them burning—oily and wrong—until his fire seared through even that.

Elidriel didn't flinch. She just lifted her chin and stared into the heart of it, her power laced with his like they'd done this dance in another life.

The altar detonated with light.

Not just white, but every hue at once—flaring through the water like stained glass liquefied. The whisperweed swelled, glowing in spirals, singing in a silent language older than spells. The cracked seal beneath us shuddered and then began to pull itself together.

Stone groaned. The edges glowed. Magic sang.

And LaDonna's body, held aloft in a cradle of whisperweed, began to sink—not drowned, but carried. The Bluebelow was taking her not in grief, but in honor, her sacrifice etched into its roots like spells in a grimoire.

I dropped to one knee, spent but unbroken.

Jake played a final, gentle chord, and only silence remained. Not the kind that kills. The kind that heals.

The beast below was imprisoned once more.

Chapter 44

The echo of the ritual still hummed in my bones as we left the altar behind.

All of the Stygian dead were unfamiliar. Two bodies were notably absent: Ericka Moore and Betony's mother, Virginia Yarborough. Faint scuff marks led away from the site, shallow and deliberate, like someone had tried not to leave a trail but failed. Where the tracks met the nearest tunnel, the whisperweed had turned a sickly gray, recoiling from whatever cloaking spell they'd woven.

They'd escaped by casting magic strong enough to survive Ivor's blast and still wrangled a cloaking spell to slink off and fight another day.

But that was tomorrow's problem.

The whisperweed parted like it knew we were done. The seal held. LaDonna was gone. And the Bluebelow had quieted, its pulse fading into the stone like the last chord of a funeral dirge.

No one spoke.

Our footsteps sloshed through shallow water and over slick stone, the only sound a slow, rhythmic pace that felt too loud in the aftermath. My body ached not just from magic but from grief, weight, and loss. My arms hung heavy, my mouth too dry to speak. Thoughts scattered, weightless and wild, like ash in the wind.

Conall was at my side within moments of that first step. He didn't speak. He didn't ask if I was OK. He didn't need to.

When my foot slipped on a moss-slick incline, his arm came around my waist, quiet and firm enough to steady me. When a boulder forced a steep climb, he offered a hand—not outstretched in demand, but open, waiting. When I didn't take it, he climbed first, then turned, planted himself, and lifted me up with silent strength.

He was just there. Like bedrock. Like breath.

I didn't thank him. He wouldn't have wanted that. Instead, I leaned on him. Not obviously, but much like a tree leans toward the sunlight it needs to survive.

Jake carried his guitar like it was a shield. Lorina walked with her arms wrapped tightly around herself, her voice spent, but her eyes still reflecting the frequencies she'd unleashed. Rene kept glancing back—not paranoid, just protective. Like he didn't quite believe the worst was behind us. Who could blame him? He, of all of us, knew the depths of the Stygian's strength and depravity.

Miles took the rear, Doyle trekking a few steps ahead with Crystal clutched protectively to his chest. Miles' wolf-heavy rage was still simmering beneath the surface. Doyle was oddly satisfied in a way I hoped I never understood. Soraya whispered prayers in a language I didn't know, maybe to soothe herself. Maybe to soothe us all.

The farther we walked, the heavier it became. Like the Bluebelow didn't want to let us go. Or maybe it was my imagination—the depression I felt weighed me down like Sisyphus' boulder.

But eventually, after a narrow pass and a breathless climb through the crooked stairway near the surface, we saw it:

Light.

Not sunlight, not yet. Just a pale wash of gray filtering through the mouth of the cave, dawn crawling its way down into the earth.

Soon, we stumbled into the daylight, and Doyle set his friend gently onto the ground. Miriam knelt beside Crystal, hands glowing with healing light, lips pressed in fierce concentration. Hanna was on the other side, whispering words I couldn't hear into Crystal's ear while her hands moved—one gripping their shoulder, the other pressed to their chest like she was holding something in.

Rafael stood nearby, white sparks of magic flickering nervously at his fingertips, pacing tight circles like a man who didn't know what else to do. Joey hovered behind him, bruised, bloodied, but upright—his expression equal parts guilt and fury.

When Rafael saw us, relief crashed over his face like a storm tide.

"We are lucky we survived," he said, his voice hoarse. "They had a breach team—cloaked, fast. Strong. Nearly took us down before any of us could even sound a warning."

"They were good," Joey said, grim. "Real good. And we were barely enough."

I nodded, but the words didn't land the way they should have.

Miriam's hands surrounded Crystal's broken ones, light blooming around her palms.

"She's not out of the woods," she said, not looking up. "But she's still here. And I'm not letting her go until her power is restored."

Crystal might lose her power? The idea was heartbreaking. I knew how she took pride in her ability and how she helped hundreds travel to where they needed to be as soon as the need arose.

I took a slow step closer. My voice rasped out, barely audible.

"Do you need a hand?"

Miriam shook her head, firm and focused, her power unwavering. "I've got it," she said. "Save yours."

And I believed her. Miriam was steady as bedrock and just as strong—had been since day one. But I knew how much it cost to use that much power.

So, I reached out—not with hands, but with a thread of Summate magic, feather-soft and invisible. Just a little pulse. A quiet breath of strength wrapped in golden light, tucked into the space between her heart and her healing.

Miriam didn't flinch. Didn't pause. But her shoulders eased ever so slightly, like a burden had lifted—not taken, just shared.

I was glad she hadn't needed me. And I was happy I'd helped anyway.

At least I can help save someone *today.*

I watched Crystal and Miriam for a long moment. Then, I looked back toward the cave. The breath of it still touched my spine like a cold whisper.

LaDonna was gone. The seal was restored. But nothing was the same.

Conall's hand grazed mine. I laced my fingers through his.

And that was all it took. The steadfastness of his presence when I needed him gave me permission to let go.

The tears came without warning—hot and silent at first, then spilling over in heavy, unrelenting waves. Not delicate. Not dignified. But profoundly real. Salt on my lips. Heat on my cheeks. Grief ripping free from the place I'd buried it to survive.

I didn't make a sound. Didn't sob. Didn't wail. I just

wept, standing at the mouth of the Bluebelow while dawn crept over the stones like it had the right to be beautiful.

Conall stepped in closer, pulling me in, wrapping me up, his body near enough to anchor but letting me break in my own way. He watched the treeline, giving me the silence I needed to fall apart.

And I did.

Not forever. Not loudly.

But completely.

☽○☾

We'd made it out of the Bluebelow soaked to the bone and scraped bloody. Aboveground, the sky was bruised, and so were we. Telling Luke was the hardest part—there's no easy way to say your wife basically died saving the world, even if outside Gryphon, most people will never know her name. He didn't cry, not in front of us. Just nodded once, like a man who'd already felt the breaking before we opened our mouths.

We contacted the authorities and told them there'd been an accident in the caves. It wasn't the whole story, but it was enough to keep them out of the places that needed to stay sealed. After that, we got a couple hours of sleep—deep, dreamless, and nothing close to enough. But it was something. And for the first time in days, the air in Gryphon felt… quiet. Not peaceful. Just quiet.

Later, we gathered long enough to stitch together what happened topside while we were chasing the Stygian in the Bluebelow. Rita hauled her laptop to my porch, cords to goddess-knew-what spilling out like roots, her fingers flicking across keys as fast as her mouth was chattering. The screen glowed against her glasses, casting her face in flickering light. Luke had brought out sweet tea, which nobody touched.

Enter Bully, mid-stream.

"Right, so I pop Dylan outta the kitchen, and next thing I know, we're standing ankle-deep in a flood with fish flopping past our feet like they was trying to find Jesus."

Dylan lifted a hand. "He didn't pop me. He yanked me by the hand like a misbehaving toddler. Nearly dropped me in a culvert."

"Still got you there, didn't I?" Bully smirked, teeth flashing.

"You sure did," Dylan muttered, but he was grinning. "It was bad, Murph. The reservoir wall was cracked halfway through. Looked like somebody'd taken a truck full of dynamite to it and meant it. Water was hemorrhaging out of the thing."

Betony was sitting cross-legged beside the porch steps, blond braid tucked over her shoulder, fingernails still stained from cave dirt and whisperweed. "The Stygian must have planned to use the water to help carry the spell they cast from the Bluebelow."

"Or like a warning," Bully said. "Big ol' finger pointed at the town, saying *this is what happens when other witches get in our way.*"

That landed heavy. Miriam glanced up from where she was rubbing balm on DB's wrist from where he'd burned himself, her expression unreadable.

"So," I said, "let me guess. Bully started recruiting water witches like he was forming a supernatural plumber's union."

"Damn right I did," Bully said, puffing up. "I pinged Rita, and she flipped on that little app she built, the—"

"The W3 App," Rita chirped from the porch stairs without looking up. "Cross-referenced all witches with a known affinity for water or flow spells, filtered out anyone over eighty or under sixteen, and grouped by strength range." She tore her eyes from her screen and gave us a proud grin. "It was so helpful. It's going to be mind-blowing once we have more witches in the app."

"Felt like I was working with the damn Navy," Dylan added, nodding. "We had sixteen water witches show up in under fifteen minutes. One from New York. Two from Michigan, one from Oregon... dang, I forget the rest. I do remember one said she was from an old trailer park in New Mexico and hadn't done magic since Carter was president."

"Lucille," Betony said, her eyes bright. "When it was all over, she just strolled back into town like it was nothing. That's when I met her. Said she hadn't pulled off a full-scale redirect since the flash floods in '87—whatever that means. But it was like muscle memory for her, right, Dylan? She kept calling me 'baby duck.'"

"She *was* amazing," Dylan echoed.

They were all grinning now—tired, punch-drunk from surviving and lack of sleep—but grinning.

"And then the townspeople got mad," Bully said, voice cooling like a blast of air conditioning after a hot summer afternoon.

Betony sighed. "That part was less fun."

"Let me," Rita said, finally looking up. "So, while Dylan and Co. were out playing waterbenders, some folks decided to take the damaged dam as divine commentary. Middle of the night, they stormed *LaDonna's* greenhouse."

My stomach clenched.

"Pitchforks," Rita said, her fingers taking a break from typing for a moment. "*Literal* pitchforks. And those high-beam LED headlamps, so it looked like a mob of anglerfish heading for her garden beds."

"You're messing with me," I said, sitting up straighter.

"Her greenhouse? *Pitchforks?*"

"They'd heard she was a witch—obviously, her tree-healing work was not appreciated by everyone in town—and decided that the massive tornado and ensuing broken dam was a sign of God's punishment. Biblical wrath. They were yelling about 'unnatural growth' and 'green devilry' like it was Salem in the sixteen nineties."

I didn't say anything. Couldn't. Just sat there, jaw clenched, hands curled into fists.

"They never even *met* her," Betony said softly. "But they wanted someone to blame. And her name was easy. We knew something might go down. So we prepped. Not just the app. We laid a circle."

"With what?" I asked, half-expecting blood and salt.

"With paint," Betony said, showing me her pink-streaked fingertips. "A sigil circle. It runs under the flowerbeds near the entrance. You can't see it unless you're looking."

"Or if you're hateful," Rita added. "Then it lights up like neon."

Betony nodded. "I used that pink paint you gave me, Murphy. Pulled the chaos out of it and locked in some serious bad-vibes detection—like, keyed it to malice. Basically, if somebody rolled up on us with hate in their heart, the paint marked them back."

Conall raised an eyebrow. "Like those dye packs at the bank?"

"Exactly," she said, and she looked almost proud for a second. "They're gonna be scrubbing pink outta their hairlines 'til next moon cycle. Consequences, babe."

Rafael chuckled. "That's why Darla Stevens was scrubbing her face behind the Baptist church this morning."

"Broke the perimeter," Betony said calmly. "Paint don't lie."

"And then Paul showed up," Bully said, eyes shining.

Conall's father had been sitting quietly near the back of the circle, sipping from a chipped thermos like this was any old town meeting. He raised an eyebrow but said nothing.

Rita pointed a triumphant finger. "Paul rolls up in his truck with one spotlight mounted on the cab and yellow sigils flaring like sunlight. You should've seen it, Murphy. He parted the mob like Moses parting the Red Sea. I almost clapped."

"It was better than Moses," Betony said. "There were fire-flies."

"Real ones?" I asked. "Paul, I thought you were a weather witch."

Paul shrugged, reticent as usual.

"Was humid," he said. "Fireflies like that. They won't flash unless the air's right—warm, damp. I nudged the breeze, stirred the moisture just a bit. Didn't mean to call so many of 'em in, but... they followed."

"Like a bug parade," Betony said, eyes still wide.

"They aligned to his spell," Dylan said. "They danced around his hands like they were drawn to the light. People stopped and listened."

Paul cleared his throat. "Did what needed doing. Folks forget themselves when they get scared."

I gave him a nod, quiet and respectful. "Thank you."

He shrugged like it was nothing, but Conall reached over and squeezed his arm. Paul looked like he might cry, but didn't. Of course.

"And then Mayor Tanaka showed up," Rita said, like she still wasn't over it.

Dylan let out a soft laugh. "In slacks and a Henley, like it was a city council meeting, not a showdown."

"Mayor Tanaka?" I asked.

"Dude showed up chill as hell, hands in his pockets like he was just there to vibe," Betony said. "Had half the down-town crew with him—Clara from the diner, Vernon from the print shop, even Missy from the Baptist nursery still in her pajamas."

"He didn't say much," Rita said. "Didn't have to. Just looked around at the mob, then said—'If you came here to-night thinking fear makes you righteous, turn around. Gryphon doesn't do witch hunts.'"

Betony's smile was tight. "Then he added, 'Not on my watch.' And just stood there, like he was daring them to try."

"And they backed down?" I asked.

Rita nodded. "Like water down a drain. One guy muttered something about 'unnatural things,' and Tanaka looked at him with that gold flash thing he does with his eyes. That was enough."

"He's a kitsune, right?" Bully said.

"Old fox spirit," Betony said. "Total legend. Didn't shift, didn't swear—just hit 'em with that soul-check stare. Straight-up *un*bothered."

"They brought stuff," Dylan added. "Town folks, I mean. Blankets. One woman brought a tray of peanut butter sand-wiches cut into triangles. I don't know what they expected, exactly, but they wanted to be helpful, I guess."

"I cried," Betony said. "I mean, not much. But... Even though we didn't need that stuff, it was actually kind of epic."

"The energy shifted hard," Rita said. "People went from pitchforks to potluck vibes in, like, five minutes. It was beau-tiful."

My heart warmed at the thought. Maybe the pink-stained assholes might re-think their stance with most of the town and the mayor behind us.

Rita held up her phone, the screen showing glowing dots

on a map. "W3's still active. I'm gonna share what happened with the WorldWide Witches. Covens are begging for coordination like this. We could use it for more than just disaster response."

"Like a magical 911," Dylan said.

"Or an Amber Alert, if any of us go missing," Betony added.

"Y'all," I said, holding up a hand. "Can someone write all this down? Because I know I'm gonna get asked about stuff when the town council finds out there's an app tracking witches with GPS."

Everyone laughed, even Paul.

"You should've seen it," Betony said, eyes shining just a little. "We didn't just hold the line, Murph. We pushed it out. Made space. And now? The whole town's standing in it with us—like they finally get it. They *get* it."

Chapter 45

LaDonna's house had always reminded me of a treehouse built for grown-ups, and one of my favorite parts was the tall, wide, gray wooden deck cradled among branches, hugged on all sides by whispering woods. It perched there like it had grown out of the ground instead of being built, the kind of place where magic didn't have to be invited—it just showed up and stayed for dinner. Sort of like the coven often did.

Tonight, it felt empty. Hollow.

The porch lights were on—one of those yellow, flickering bulbs that LaDonna always said kept moths and ghosts away. But the house knew she was gone. The wind moved differently through the screen doors. The boards didn't creak quite the same underfoot.

We didn't say much as we gathered.

Terry sat in the old rocking chair by the swing, legs tucked up under her, a worn quilt draped over her lap despite the warm evening. She had one of LaDonna's old teacups in her hands, but it wasn't tea inside. The smell of bourbon cut clean through the damp air. The same bottle Conall had brought me before… well. When everything started going sideways.

Jake sat on the porch steps, guitar in his lap, fingers picking soft, wandering notes. Nothing recognizable. Just something to fill the silence. Something to keep the night from caving in and to ease our hearts a little.

Soraya lit a fat beeswax candle and placed it on the table beside the old rocking chair. She didn't say a word while she did it. Just lit the flame and let it burn.

A chorus of cicadas pulsed from the trees around us—steady, hypnotic, like the earth was holding vigil. Fireflies blinked lazily in the darkness beyond the rail, rising and falling like drifting sparks. The porch still held heat, thick and humid, heavy with the scent of pine and honeysuckle. That kind of deep-summer warmth that clings to your skin and won't let go.

I sat in the wicker chair closest to the door, the one with the blanket LaDonna crocheted for me two winters ago. She'd worked on it while we played cards and argued about the right way to make cornbread. The blanket still smelled like rosemary, cinnamon, and something greener—maybe mint or moss. Maybe her.

Conall didn't sit. He leaned against one of the porch columns letting out sighs every few minutes. He'd been doing a lot of that lately.

When we got here, he'd handed me a small tumbler of that bourbon topped with lemonade—no fanfare, no explanation. Just passed it to me like someone offering kindling to a dying fire. I'd held it for a long time before I took a sip. It burned, but in a good way.

The bedroom door creaked once earlier, and I knew it was Luke. Just inside. Just out of sight.

I'd been the one who told him when we first got back—looked him straight in the eyes when I said the words, even though every part of me wanted to fold. I explained her brave sacrifice, my throat so tight I thought I might choke on every word. Luke embraced me, nodded once, moved down the hall to his bedroom, and closed the door behind him.

That moment hadn't needed witnesses. It was his grief. His goodbye. I gave it to him.

He hadn't come out much since. But he'd turned the porch light on.

We sat like that for a long time, absent of spellwork or circles or plans. Just appreciating one another's presence.

Miles showed up last, barefoot and still slightly damp, like he'd been walking in the river again as he was out doing his wolfy nocturnal activities. He didn't say anything when he eased onto the steps next to Jake. Just nodded and sat.

Lorina sat cross-legged on the porch floor, her fingers curled around a cup she never drank from. Rene stood behind her, arms crossed, his dark eyes now permanently ringed with silver, it seemed, scanning the woods like they still held danger. Or maybe like they didn't. Maybe he didn't know what to do with stillness yet.

Terry finally spoke, voice dry and rough-edged. "I kept thinking I'd walk in, and she'd be in the kitchen. Rolling out dough. Chopping up herbs. Yelling at me to take my shoes off at the door."

No one answered. She didn't expect us to.

Jake's fingers found a minor chord and held it there, letting it ring.

I took another sip. The bourbon made it easier to breathe. Made it easier to feel without cracking wide open.

"She died like a green witch would want," I said finally, surprising myself. "Protecting someone. Holding the line. And in the end, she joined the plants she loved. She's an eternal protector now."

Conall didn't speak. But I felt him shift slightly closer, his warmth a quiet tether.

"She used to say grief was like broth," I said, my voice

low. "You don't toss it out or cover it up—you let it simmer. Give it time. Let it break down all the hard bits. Eventually… it feeds you. Keeps you going."

No one laughed. But I saw a few smiles flicker, thin and painful and real.

The candle flame guttered in the wind, then righted itself.

"She would've liked this," Conall said, barely louder than the breeze. "Us. Together. Here."

A cicada chirred loudly, then fell silent.

The screen door creaked again. Just once. No one turned to look. But the porch light didn't flicker. The door opened wider, and Luke stepped out.

He didn't say anything as he joined us—just walked onto the porch like he had a weight in his chest too heavy to carry inside alone. His eyes were red-rimmed, hollowed out at the edges. His jaw tight. That grief-worn look of someone who hadn't cried in front of anyone but had sure as hell done it alone.

He glanced at each of us—Jake's bowed head, Terry's teacup, Miles leaning back into the shadows. His gaze paused on the beeswax candle, then drifted to the empty chair across from mine. LaDonna's chair.

He didn't sit in it. He stood beside it.

Conall, still leaning against the porch column, wordlessly reached into his pocket and pulled out a flask. He held it out.

Luke didn't hesitate. He took it, unscrewed the cap, and tipped back just enough to warm his throat.

Then he looked at me. He didn't speak. He didn't need to. That look held everything. Memory. Pain. Pride. A knowing carved from decades of love and shared magic. A look that said, *She was mine. She was yours. And now she's all of ours.*

He passed the flask back, nodded once, and then lowered himself into the chair beside LaDonna's empty one.

The rockers creaked together—one with weight, one without.

No one interrupted the silence that followed. Not even the cicadas.

We just sat.

Surrounded by fireflies and candlelight and the thick, humming ache of summer. The porch light still burned, casting a faint glow. Around us, the woods breathed slow and deep. The house no longer felt quite so vacant. We were grieving. But not alone.

Epilogue

The sun hung low and gold behind the treetops, casting long shadows across the cracked driveway of the place I'd grown up thinking of as the old Harlan house. It had sat empty for years—gray brick, thick windows, stubborn shutters—but it didn't feel forgotten anymore. Not today.

The wind rustled the sweetgum trees just enough to remind us it was technically fall, though the air was still warm and thick with the scent of pine and dry grass. A few early leaves skittered across the porch as if they were too restless to stay put.

Betony stood beside me at the edge of the lawn, arms crossed, her gray-ringed eyes taking in everyone waiting for events to kick off. Her hair was pinned back with copper leaves, catching the sun in flashes. She looked calm. Composed.

But I knew better. I could feel the storm of gratitude and ache beneath her skin, and when she shifted her weight closer to me, I gently nudged my shoulder into hers.

"Still think you weren't needed here?" I asked, voice low.

Betony let out a breath like a laugh that hadn't quite found its footing. "You know," she said, "for a long time, I thought I was just taking up space. Like I was a stray LaDonna took in because she couldn't bear to see anything abandoned."

She paused, eyes scanning the people gathered.

"But when everything went sideways… I felt it. Something inside me clicked into place. Like I'd been shaped for that moment, whether I realized it or not."

"You were," I said. "And you didn't take up space. You saved people. Like she did."

Mayor Tanaka stepped up to the sagging porch with Luke beside him. The mayor wore a long-sleeved shirt rolled at the cuffs, his tie tucked into the front of a well-worn vest, and he still had a dirt smudge on his collar from helping clear brush earlier that morning. Luke, quieter than usual, had a hand resting on the porch rail. He looked at home there, not in the house itself, but in what it meant now.

"In a town like Gryphon," Mayor Tanaka said to the crowd, "when we lose someone like LaDonna Whelen, the question isn't how we move forward. It's who we become because of her."

He paused, and the wind stirred again—just enough to make the candle flames in the Mason jars on the porch flicker. Just enough to rustle the leaves in the hedgerow where honeysuckle had started to grow wild.

"This house," he continued, "will be the LaDonna Whelen Memorial Home—a place for young Numinari who've been cast out, overlooked, or left behind. A home for the gifted. For the unwanted. For the powerful who had no one to tell them they mattered."

From the corner of my eye, I saw Betony's chin tremble, and my eyes grew hot with tears.

Luke stepped forward, quiet and larger than life, and rested his hand on a porch column.

"LaDonna loved this town," he said, voice gravel-deep. "But more than that, she loved its people. Not the shiny ones. Not the easy ones. The broken ones. The angry ones. The ones who didn't know what to do with their magic or their grief."

Or both, I thought, sniffing hard and hoping no one noticed.

His voice caught just a little, but he didn't waver.

"This is her legacy. And we're gonna tend it."

Mayor Tanaka handed Luke an enormous pair of scissors, and Luke cut the dark green ribbon strewn between the porch columns.

Officer Kenny Hendricks gave a solemn nod from where he stood near the garden, his patrol hat tucked under one arm. "Town feels different without her," he said. "This... helps."

Terry stepped forward with a small pot of rosemary and placed it on the porch, just to the right of the door. "For memory," she said. "And for roots."

Miles stayed in the back, watching the treeline, but he gave a brief bow of his head. Soraya lit a bundle of mugwort and let the smoke curl toward the steps. "For welcome," she said. "And protection."

Miriam knelt and pressed her fingers to the threshold, her hand faintly glowing with the soft gold of healing light. "May every pain that crosses this doorway be met with care and recovery," she whispered.

Jake strummed a soft chord and murmured, "For peace."

Joey stood behind him, arms folded, but his magic shimmered faintly in the space around the porch—subtle, ward-like. Protection laid quiet and solid, like a guardian dog at the gate.

Conall stepped up next and simply placed his calloused hand on the wooden doorframe. "For strength," he said. "And for safekeeping."

With her usual quiet elegance, Hanna tucked a small heart-shaped charm—red witch work, threaded with emotion—into a corner window frame. "For love," she said. "Not the easy kind. The enduring kind."

Paul Berry added a polished stone to the edge of the porch, yellow trails of magic flickering across its surface. "For calm during the storms," he offered, looking at his son with quiet pride.

Rafael stood with his arms crossed, eyes glinting, saying nothing—but his presence radiated approval, steady as the earth itself.

Crystal was there too, her fully healed hand in Doyle's.

Holding a sprig of whisperweed braided into a strand of hair, Lorina added, "For harmony."

Even Rita showed up in a blazer over her usual tank top, pink and blue hair swept into a high bun, arms full of folders she probably didn't need for the ceremony. "She helped build something real here," she said. "Now it's our turn."

And Ivor—grumbling about bugs and old wood—wheeled in a generator small enough to fit on the porch. "Got you a backup," he muttered, rubbing at his beard. "If the grid fails, this won't." *Leave it to Sparky to think about power.* Which, given the number of storms that hit Alabama, wasn't such a bad idea.

Finally, I stepped up beside Luke and laid my palm flat on the porch post. The wood was warm from the sun, but I felt more than that—the thrum of new beginnings, the ache of the ones who wouldn't be here to see them.

"For home," I said. My voice didn't rise, but the magic did—gathering low and steady in my chest, then flowing through my palm and into the wood. "For every kid who needs one."

Betony joined me, voice firm and bright. "And for every witch who's forgotten they deserve one."

The porch post shimmered faintly under my hand, like dew catching moonlight, then settled—magic tucked permanently into the grain. Shelter, warmth, steadiness. A magical home that would stand when human hearts faltered. LaDonna had always said a house could heal. I just gave this one a little help making that happen.

Beside me, Luke reached out and touched the post where my hand had been. His thumb brushed the spot once, slow.

"She'd like that," he said. Then cleared his throat. "She'd say you finally learned how to anchor something without burning it down."

I smiled, but it wobbled.

"She taught me."

Mayor Tanaka stepped forward, holding a small bronze plaque. He handed it to Luke, who genuflected before fixing it to the front step with careful hands.

It read:

The LaDonna Whelen Memorial Home
Where all roots are welcome, and no light is wasted.

And just like that, the house wasn't hollow anymore: It had a name. A purpose.

And it was ready to grow something new.

Coming soon from Iris Kain:

Bitter: Gryphon has changed—but so has Murphy Blackwell. With LaDonna gone, grief has become her constant companion. The town she fought to protect is swelling with magic and strangers, and witches across the globe now look to her as something she never wanted to be: their leader. At the same time, her newfound sister Elidriel is pushing her to confront their father's legacy, and the ancient thresholds of Tír na nÓg are calling. But Gryphon's enemies haven't vanished—the Stygian may have scattered, but the ones who murdered her mothers are still out there. And a furious Murphy won't stop until they are gone for good.

Support

Indie Authors

Buy
Read
Review

www.ingramcontent.com/pod-product-compliance
Lightning Source LLC
Chambersburg PA
CBHW021227190726
48289CB00005B/1204